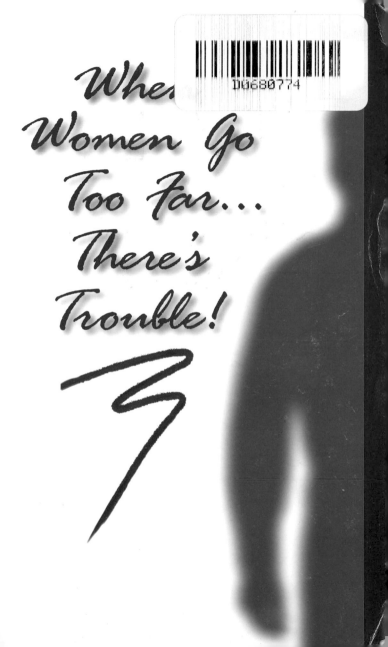

When
Women Go
Too Far...
There's
Trouble!

"Get down!"

Tallie got down all right—landing hard. She was vaguely aware of Keith shouting, then screams ricocheting through the coffeehouse . . . and what sounded amazingly like gunshots.

"Is anyone hurt?" Keith shouted. "Tallie, are you okay?"

She pushed to her feet and patted vital areas, relatively sure a bullet couldn't have penetrated her chunky sweater. "I'm okay." With her heart still pumping, she watched him call for backup.

Near the counter, she spotted Keith's Michigan State ball cap on the floor, badly soiled, and on impulse, she bent to retrieve it. She had never laundered a piece of clothing for any man she'd known . . . but then again, a man had never before saved her life.

It seemed like an even trade.

Within a few minutes of meeting Keith Wages, she had been shot at and was contemplating household chores in his honor.

This couldn't be good.

By Stephanie Bond

WHOLE LOTTA TROUBLE
PARTY CRASHERS
KILL THE COMPETITION
I THINK I LOVE YOU
GOT YOUR NUMBER
OUR HUSBAND

STEPHANIE
BOND

Whole Lotta Trouble

AVON BOOKS
An Imprint of HarperCollinsPublishers

AVON BOOKS
An Imprint of HarperCollins*Publishers*
10 East 53rd Street
New York, New York 10022-5299

Acknowledgments

Many thanks to my agent Kimberly Whalen for brain-storming the idea for *Whole Lotta Trouble* with me. Thanks, too, to my editor Lyssa Keusch and to her assistant May Chen, both of whom went above and beyond the call of duty to get this book where it needed to be when it needed to be there. My appreciation to all the people behind the scenes at HarperCollins who touch my manuscripts on their way to becoming finished books. And finally, thanks to the readers for allowing me to be a part of this fascinating industry that I simply had to write about in *Whole Lotta Trouble*.

Chapter 1

Dear Mr. Blankenship,

My name is Richard Wannamaker. After retiring from the IRS, I decided to write a story about my roller-coaster life as a cost accountant. Enclosed please find my 500-page autobiography, a volume I have fondly entitled Journal Entry—*get it?*

        Tallie winced. She got it, and about twenty others like it on her desk every week. Reams of paper containing stories utterly inappropriate for the mystery and romance fiction lines for which she acquired. It wasn't that she didn't admire the man for creating the tome, but if he'd researched Parkbench Publishing at all, he would have known they weren't looking for autobiographies. And that she wasn't a Mr., but a Miss. *Miss*—as in unmarried and unlikely to be in the near future. If only Richard Wannamaker had been on her mother's Christmas card mailing list, he'd have been privy to that tidbit, courtesy of her mother's annual *Blankenship Bul-*

letin, complete with pictures, favorite family recipes, and news. This year's headline:

YES, OUR BEAUTIFUL, SUCCESSFUL DAUGHTER IS STILL SINGLE!

It was almost February and she was still recovering from that one.

Tallie sighed and forced her attention back to the cover letter in her hand.

My brother-in-law is a tax attorney and will be handling the contract negotiation—

A rap sounded at her office door and Tallie glanced up to see her assistant, Norah, stick her fair head inside. "Is this a bad time?"

"No—please save me."

Norah gestured to the mound of curled manuscripts on Tallie's desk. "Wading through the slush I flagged?"

Tallie nodded and rubbed her eyes. "And a few you didn't. Ron tripped over one of my floor stacks the other day, so I thought I'd better do some housecleaning. What's up?"

Norah looked apologetic. "Ron wants you in his office. He seems . . . agitated."

Tallie's stomach convulsed. Executive Editor Ron Springer was always a handful for the editorial staff to deal with, but lately he'd been wound as tightly as his name implied, snapping at the least provocation. Tallie had secretly wondered if the health of the company was in jeopardy, or if Ron himself was experiencing personal problems, but she wasn't about to put her middle-of-the-road job on the line by asking. She had rent to pay, and a three-meals-a-day habit to support.

"Tell him I'll be right there."

Norah disappeared and Tallie pulled a mirror from her desk drawer, quickly checked her lipstick and her teeth, then smoothed a couple of dark strands back into her chin-length bob. Her hand stopped suddenly, and she yanked the mirror closer in disbelief.

Her first gray hair. She almost choked on the irony. While she was home during the holidays, her mother had accused her of letting her childbearing years slide by, and right on cue, here was an outward sign that her innards were aging. She knew that at thirty-four, she had no reason to complain, but it was still a blow . . . and it would remain her best-kept secret lest she give her mother another headline for the holiday news-letter.

OUR SPINSTER DAUGHTER IS GOING GRAY!

She replaced the mirror and slammed the desk drawer. Hoping that Ron wasn't about to deliver news to add more silver to her head, Tallie grabbed a pad of pa-per and a pen, then walked in the direction of her boss's office.

The bullpen was its usual beehive of activity, key-boards clicking and printers whirring, voices raised to be heard over cubicle walls. Although grateful for her ten-foot-by-ten-foot office with an actual door, she missed the camaraderie that she'd shared with her coworkers when they'd all been interns and assistants, still in awe of the publishing process and of the movers and shakers in the industry. All of the women she'd started with nine years ago had moved on to positions at other publishing houses or had left the industry altogether. She, on the other hand, had found a home at Parkbench and had managed to grow a stable of prolific and modestly successful writers. No *New York Times* best sellers yet, but she had high hopes for two books coming out in the spring.

The department walls were lined with framed covers of some of the company's best-selling authors—Dewey Diamond, Grace Sharp, Linda Addison. It still gave Tallie a thrill to see the faces and signatures of writers she'd grown up reading.

Parkbench had made its mark in the 1950s with film noir spin-offs, then they'd developed successful mystery series in the 1960s and '70s. In the '80s, the company had cashed in on the romance genre boom and continued to grow their line of thrillers. In the last twenty-plus years, Parkbench had become known as a boutique publisher, one of the few privately owned houses left after the merging madness of the '90s. They were small, but mighty, with a reputation for being author-friendly. Some of their writers had been around for longer than Tallie had been alive.

Kara Hatteras, aka Scary Kara—editor in the health and nutrition books section and Tallie's nemesis—came out of her office and arranged her Botox-puffy face into a smug expression. "Hello, Tallie."

Tallie was forced to stop, since the Nordic giant towered over her and was standing with her legs wide enough for a child to walk through. "Hi, Kara."

"Have you heard that my book *The Soup to Nuts Diet* is going to be featured on CNN?"

Tallie bit the inside of her cheek; Kara never gave credit to her authors and bragged endlessly about "her" accomplishments. "Um, no, I hadn't heard. That will be great coverage for the company."

Kara lifted her finger and wagged it precisely. "No. That will be great coverage for *me*." She dipped her chin. "I heard through the grapevine that our department is going to be reorganized. This little media coup might be just the thing for Ron to finally make me an associate senior editor."

Ahead of Tallie, she might as well have said. Tallie managed a tight smile at the woman whose surgically enhanced lifestyle was the antithesis of the books she edited. "Good for you, Kara."

Kara made a rueful noise. "Don't worry, Tallie—even though you haven't hit any home runs, I'm sure Ron appreciates the little things you do around here."

Tallie gritted her teeth. But Kara's condescension aside, Tallie hadn't heard any rumors about a reorganization—because she was going to be reorganized out onto the street? Was that why Ron had been acting so edgy lately, because he was going to have to fire someone?

Her?

"Oh, Tallie," Kara said, leaning down. "Is that a gray hair?"

Tallie froze. "No."

"I think it is."

"No, it isn't. I have to be going. Ron wants to see me." She hadn't meant to say that.

Kara looked sympathetic. "Good luck."

Tallie pushed past her and, with heart tripping overtime, headed toward the hallway where Ron's corner office was located. His assistant Lil was coming out of his door, and she gave Tallie a warning look when they passed.

Tallie's stomach churned as she walked into his office.

Ron glanced up from his desk, where he was frantically scribbling in the margins of a memo, and frowned. "Close the door, Tallie."

She did, truly worried now. Ron's handsome face was flushed, and his normally perfectly knotted tie was pulled to one side.

"Sit," he ordered.

She sat in one of two sleek Eames chairs that faced his desk. Ron collected chairs—he claimed they would be worth more than his stock portfolio when he retired. She herself would be sitting pretty if "some assembly required" furniture became collectible.

While Ron finished his note-making, she glanced around his office, never failing to be impressed by his accumulation of industry awards and the achievement of his stable of world-class authors—Britt Manning, Gaylord Cooper, Stella Roundtree. According to her sources, Ron could have left Parkbench and taken a more prestigious position at least a half dozen times, but his dedication to his authors was legendary.

Tallie adored him, and she'd wasted her first two years at Parkbench lusting after him from afar until one of her bullpen buddies, Felicia Redmon, had informed her that Ron Springer was gay.

"He is not," Tallie had said, devastated. "He's in the Army Reserves, for heaven's sake."

Felicia had scoffed. "Haven't you heard of 'don't ask, don't tell'? Oh, let me guess—there are no gay men in Circleville, Ohio?"

Tallie, sensitive about her rural upbringing, had lifted her chin. "The man who owned the two car washes in town was gay . . . allegedly."

"Well," Felicia had said gently, "let's just say that if Ron ever visited Circleville, he'd get his car washed."

"But Ron doesn't have a car," Tallie had said.

She cringed now when she remembered the conversation—her naiveté had been the butt of more than one joke among her friends.

But that was years ago—before the accent reduction class and before getting mugged—twice. Now she spoke with shortened *i*s and carried a personal alarm that sounded at twenty decibels above the threshold of pain. And she could generally tell if a man was gay.

When she had heard Ron declare that *Beaches* was the best movie ever made, she had conceded that he was, indeed, gay. The problem was, before Felicia had informed her of his sexual orientation, Tallie had confided her crush on Ron to, of all people, her mother, who had gotten it into her head that Tallie and her "handsome boss" would someday wind up together. Tallie had elected not to divulge to her mother the extent of the impossibility of her and Ron's "winding up together," because it would have simply generated more drama. Besides, what was the harm in giving her mother a little hope that she would someday find a nice guy, fall in love, get married, have twins, quit her job, and move back to Circleville to live in a house on the same street as her parents.

But if Ron canned her, she'd have to come clean with her mother, which might prompt a special mid-year edition of the *Blankenship Bulletin*.

Ron sighed noisily, then looked up and seemed startled to see her sitting there. His gaze was unfocused, his expression slack. Panic blipped momentarily in Tallie's chest.

"You wanted to see me, Ron?" she prompted.

"Oh . . . right." He ran his hand through his immaculate blond hair, leaving it standing at all angles. He tossed down his pen. "Um . . . Tallie, how long have you been working here?"

Oh, God, here it comes. "Nine years."

"Nine years," he repeated, looking thoughtful. "In that time, I think we've become friends, haven't we?"

She knew next to nothing about his personal life, but she nodded congenially.

"Good, because I have a favor to ask."

Her chin bobbed nervously. "Anything."

He sighed, then leaned back in his chair. "Gaylord Cooper will be here Thursday to deliver his last book on his current contract."

Tallie nodded. Gaylord was the darling of their publishing house—two hardcovers on the NYT best-seller list last year, both at number one. Ron had found the man's work in the slush pile fifteen years ago, and the rest was publishing history. The one drawback of working with Gaylord, though, was his . . . idiosyncrasies. The man mistrusted everyone, especially the government, and refused to use computers or telephones. He typed his intricate thrillers on an ancient Underwood typewriter and conducted all business face-to-face, including hand-delivering his finished manuscripts.

Ron shifted in his chair. "I'm going to be away from the office for a few weeks, beginning tomorrow. Since I won't be here, I was thinking I'd have you take over the editing of this manuscript."

Tallie felt her eyes go wide, but she schooled her

face into a composed expression. "I-I'd be happy to, Ron, but—"

"But?"

"But how will Mr. Cooper feel about working with me?"

"I'll give his agent a call and let him smooth the way. Do you know Jerry Key?"

Her stomach crimped. "I know of him." And what she knew wasn't favorable.

Ron sighed. "Yeah, Jerry has a reputation, but you can handle him."

She tried to smile. "If you say so."

"And I won't lie to you—Gaylord himself is one crusty customer. But once he realizes how much you respect his work, he'll come around. Just don't change a word of his manuscript, and he'll be fine."

She started to laugh, but Ron's expression grew grave.

"Seriously, Tallie, I can't stress enough how important it is that Gaylord remain pacified. He'll be negotiating a new contract after this book, and I know those bastards over at Bloodworth will be trying to lure him away. I've assured Saundra that you'll be able to pull this off."

Saundra Pellum, publisher of Parkbench, emerged from her corner office on the floor above them only to reprimand, chew out, and fire. No pressure. Tallie wet her lips. "I understand, Ron. Do you have something going on with the Reserves?" Ron put in his time one weekend a month, but considering the state of the world, it was entirely possible that he was being called up.

"Um . . . not this time," he said shortly.

"Oh. When do you expect to return?"

A pinched look came over his face, and he cleared his throat. "I don't know, but I'll be checking in periodically to answer any questions you might have." He stood abruptly, signaling the end to their conversation.

Tallie pushed to her feet, her head swirling with questions about Ron's sudden leave, but so honored by his trust in her that she wasn't going to pry.

"I'll make sure that Lil notifies you when Gaylord arrives," Ron said. "Depending on his frame of mind, he might want to have lunch. If so, take him to Spegalli's, because they receive consistent good marks on their health department inspections."

"Right. Anything else?"

He lifted his gaze, and something flashed through his dark eyes—alarm? "Watch your back, Tallie."

Her jaw loosened in confusion. She was on the verge of asking for specifics when his phone rang. He snatched up the receiver. "Ron Springer." She turned to vamoose, and as she was closing the door, Ron said in a lowered voice, "I told you to never call me here—don't you think I'm in enough trouble?"

Tallie bit her lip as she silently closed the door. It seemed reasonable to assume that the "trouble" her boss alluded to was the basis for his abrupt holiday. And for Ron to leave his responsibilities at Parkbench, even temporarily, the trouble had to be dire.

On the walk back to her office, she nursed mixed emotions—concern for her boss, elation over her high-profile assignment, and fear that she would do something to alienate the company's biggest cash cow, Gaylord Cooper. She tingled with anticipation, thinking this could be a turning point in her career.

Watch your back, Tallie.

She worked her mouth from side to side, chalking up Ron's odd comment to his uncharacteristic state of mind. Then she released a dry laugh. Or perhaps he was talking about what Scary Kara might do when she discovered Tallie had been singled out to work with Gaylord Cooper. A gloating smile curled on Tallie's mouth, and she made a mental note to call her best friend Felicia to tell her the good news.

But meanwhile . . . back to the slush pile reading. Her phone rang and she smiled—a reprieve. "Tallie Blankenship."

"Hello, Tallie," said a deep, male voice—a hesitant deep, male voice. "My name is Keith Wages. We've never met, but our mothers are acquainted."

Tallie squinted—*Wages*. "Sheila Wages in Ann Arbor?" She had met her mother's childhood friend once, years ago. She vaguely remembered a son in the pictures the woman sent at Christmastime, but she couldn't place his face.

"Right." He gave a little laugh. "This is awkward, but I live in the city and when my mother found out that you live here, too, she suggested that I give you a call. You know . . . have lunch or something."

Red flags went up in her mind. WARNING: GEEKY SON OF MOTHER'S FRIEND DETECTED. PROCEED AT YOUR OWN RISK.

"That sounds nice," she said carefully. "But I'm really swamped for the next couple of weeks."

"Maybe we could grab a cup of coffee?" he suggested. "Something quick?"

Her mind raced, but she couldn't think of a polite put-off. And if she didn't meet the guy, her mother would eventually hear about it and pester her to death. "Okay," she said, checking her calendar. "How about Wednesday at twelve-thirty?" She'd learned a long time ago that having to get back to work was the best way to escape an encounter-gone-wrong.

"Sounds good—where?"

Someplace not too close to her office and not a regular hangout, in case he turned out to be a psycho. "Are you familiar with Suspicious Grounds coffeehouse on Lexington Avenue?"

"Yeah, sure. I'll see you there."

"Um, wait a minute," she said, her pulse suddenly picking up for no good reason other than the fact that he had a nice voice. "How will I know you?"

"I'll be wearing a Michigan State ball cap."

Oh, great—a sports nut, and obviously badly employed if he could wear a ball cap in the middle of the day. "Okay. See you then . . . Keith."

He hung up and she replaced the receiver, already dreading the meeting. The weirdo quota in her circle of acquaintances was full. With a sigh she picked up Mr. Wannamaker's cover letter for a quick skim to the end.

Many people don't realize how interesting the life of an IRS accountant can be. There was the time I had a hit put on me for nailing a congressman for tax evasion. And the time I killed a man, and got away with it.

Tallie's eyebrows shot up. She was accustomed to receiving outlandish letters from inmates trying to sell their life story, but this was a new one.

Suddenly, Mr. Richard Wannamaker's submission was a lot more interesting.

Chapter 2

Felicia Redmon dropped into her desk chair and sorted through her phone messages. Suze Dannon. Phil Dannon. Suze again, then Phil again. She sighed—the Dannons were determined to drive her and each other completely mad. Her best-selling husband and wife writing team had separated under nasty circumstances but had agreed to finish one last book together. Unfortunately, Felicia had soon found herself in the middle of not only their editorial squabbles but also their personal disagreements. Playing referee was wearing her nerves thin, but sometimes an editor had to go beyond the call of duty to make sure the book got in on time. Still, she was afraid that if the Dannons didn't find a way soon to put aside their differences, the hostile couple, known for their sensual murder mysteries, was going to wind up killing each other.

There was a message from her doctor's office—an appointment reminder, no doubt—and one from Tallie, who probably wanted to firm plans for getting together at their regular hangout. And Jerry Key had called. Her heart jerked a little, just like every time she heard the bastard's name.

She should have known better than to have gotten involved with a man with whom she would also have to do business, but literary agent Jerry Key had a way of making a woman forget little things . . . like consequences. He was probably calling on behalf of the Dannons, who were his clients. And whatever was wrong would definitely be her fault.

Might as well get it over with, she decided, and dialed Jerry's number—by memory, how pathetic.

"Jerry Key's office, this is Lori."

Felicia cringed at Lori's nasally tone. "Hi, Lori. This is Felicia Redmon at Omega Publishing, returning Jerry's call."

"Hold, please."

Felicia cursed herself for her accelerated pulse. A year was long enough to get over someone, especially someone as smarmy as Jerry had turned out to be.

The phone clicked. "Felicia," he said, his tongue rolling the last two vowels. "How are you?"

She pursed her mouth. "What's up, Jerry?"

"What, you don't have time for small talk anymore?"

Remembering the impending auction of one of his clients' books, which she'd be participating in, Felicia bit her tongue. "Sorry, it's been a long day. How've you been?"

"Never better," he said smoothly. "Except when we were together."

She closed her eyes. "Jerry, don't."

"Funny, I believe that's the first time you've ever said 'don't.' "

Her tongue tingled with raw words, but she reminded

herself that she was to blame for the predicament she'd gotten herself into. The bottom line was that Jerry Key represented enough big-name authors—some of them tied to Omega Publishing—that she had to play nice, no matter how much it killed her.

"Jerry, I'm late for a meeting, so I really can't chat. What did you need?"

He sighed dramatically. "Sweetheart, we have a problem. The Dannons are upset."

"Both of them?"

"Suze in particular. She said that you're siding with Phil on all the manuscript changes."

"Phil is the plotter, Suze is the writer, it's always been that way. Suze never had a problem with Phil's changes before."

"Suze said he's changing things just for the sake of changing them, to make more work for her."

"Have you spoken with Phil?" Felicia asked.

"Yes, and I believe his exact words were 'You bet your ass I am.' "

She rolled her eyes. "Jerry, the last time I checked, you represented both Suze *and* Phil."

"Yes, but editorial disputes are your responsibility, Felicia, and I rely on you to be fair."

She frowned. "I *am* fair."

"Then you need to be firm. Being assertive isn't your strong suit."

Anger bolted through her. "That's not true." She only had a problem being assertive with Jerry; he had a way of making her feel defensive and defenseless at the same time. "Don't turn this around, Jerry—you know that the Dannons are both hypersensitive right now."

"Which is why, Felicia, it would behoove both of us if

the Dannons find a way to patch things up and forget about this divorce nonsense."

"And you're telling me this because?"

"Because I think you should find a way to make this project more enjoyable, to make them realize how good they are together."

She summoned strength. "Jerry, I'm not a marriage counselor."

"But you're a woman."

A small part of her was flattered he remembered, but she managed to inject a bite into her tone. "What does that mean?"

"It means that . . . you know, you're all wrapped up in the fantasy of marital bliss. If I tried to talk to the Dannons about staying together, they'd know I was bullshitting them for the sake of money."

"Isn't that what I'd be doing?" she asked.

"No, you actually believe in all that happily-ever-after crap."

Felicia set her jaw. It wasn't enough that the man had broken her heart; he had to reduce her hopes for the future to the lyrics of a bad love song.

"What do you say, Felicia? Why don't you try to get the Dannons face-to-face and make them see that they're better together than apart? If anyone can convince them to work together, you can. After all, you almost convinced me to give up my freedom."

It was Jerry's idea of a compliment, and she conceded a shameful little thrill at his admission.

"I'll see what I can do," she said. "Oh, and Jerry— have you set a date for the Merriwether auction?"

"No, but you'll be the first to know."

"Good, because I finished reading the proposal and I

believe that Omega is the best publisher to take the book to market."

"We'll see," he said, his tone noncommittal.

Unease tickled the back of her neck, but she figured it was just another Jerry Key power play.

"Sweetheart, I got another call coming in," Jerry said. "Let me know after you've set up a meeting with the Dannons and I'll be there."

She started to say she couldn't promise miracles, but he had disconnected the call. Listening to the dial tone conjured up memories of when Jerry had phoned her to abruptly "cool things off." She had been in bed, still warm from their morning tussle, and had been caught completely off guard. Her cheeks still burned with mortification when she thought of it.

She called Phil Dannon first. "Phil, this is Felicia. How's it going?"

"If you mean the book, not so well, but that's Suze's fault."

Determined to keep her tone calm, she asked, "How so?"

"She refuses to make the changes that I want—you know that's the way we've always worked."

"Have you talked to Suze about it?"

"Talked, shouted, and screamed, in that order. She's impossible. She has a lot of nerve, giving me a hard time when she's the one—"

"Phil," Felicia cut in, not wanting to hear details about the breakup, "I know this is a tough time for you and Suze to think about work, but everyone has a lot riding on this book. I was thinking that you both should come in to the city, then we'll all sit down and work through these issues. How does that sound?"

"Fine with me," he said. "Of course, I'm not the one being unreasonable."

She decided not to bring up Jerry's comment about the ass-betting. "If I can get Suze to agree, would the day after tomorrow be okay with you?"

"Wednesday? Sure, just let me know."

"Meanwhile, could you fax me a list of the changes you asked Suze to make?"

"Will do. I'm sorry about all this, Felicia. I know this makes your job harder."

"It's okay," she said, experiencing a surge of affection for the man. Suze was the creative one, and Phil had always been the voice of reason. She suspected that Suze had initiated the breakup, although she couldn't be sure. And even though infidelity hadn't come up in the conversation when Phil had broken the news they were going to divorce, she had speculated that Suze, a flamboyant and attractive forty-something, had had an affair. But she could be wrong. People had fooled her before.

"We'll work through this," she promised. "I'll let you know about meeting on Wednesday."

She hung up, feeling another headache coming on. They had escalated in frequency and duration over the past few months, all stress-related, she knew. Which was only more frustrating because she hated the idea that, to all the emotional pain that Jerry Key had caused her, she could add a psychosomatic condition as well. She opened her desk drawer and removed a bottle of Imitrex, popped one, and washed it down with Water Joe, hoping the caffeinated bottled water would speed the drug to the site of her pain. She couldn't afford to go home with a migraine, not with all the work that had to be done this week.

She picked up the phone and dialed Suze Dannon's cell phone number. Suze answered on the first ring.

"Hel-LO."

Felicia blinked at the rather seductive tone of Suze's voice, then recovered. "Hi, Suze, this is Felicia. Did I catch you at a bad time?"

"Oh. Hi, Felicia. No, I can talk. I assume you're calling to plead Phil's case."

At the woman's brittle tone, Felicia touched her temple. "No, Suze. I understand that you two are having some editorial differences, and I was hoping we could all sit down Wednesday and work through some things."

"There's nothing to work through," Suze said. "Phil is being ridiculous. I'm not making the changes he wants."

"Why don't you let me see if I can come up with a compromise, Suze? The book is due in production soon and I need to know that both of you are happy with it."

"I don't know," Suze said, her tone suspicious. "No offense, Felicia, but you always side with Phil."

Felicia exhaled for patience. "I'm sorry if I've given you that impression, Suze, but believe me, I have only the best interests of this book in mind." Appealing to Suze's Achilles' heel—pride in her work—Felicia said, "Since this might be your last collaboration, don't you want it to be the best it can be?"

Suze sighed, and Felicia could feel the woman's resolve crumbling.

"Besides, Jerry will be there to make sure everything is decided fairly."

"Well . . . okay," Suze relented. "When and what time?"

"How is Wednesday afternoon at two, in my office?"

"Okay, but I'm telling you, Felicia, I'll kill Phil before I let him screw up this book or my career, got it?"

Felicia swallowed at the vicious note in Suze's voice, then glanced up to see a courier standing outside her door, holding an envelope. She waved to the courier and managed a laugh for Suze's sake just as the man stepped inside. "Well, let's reserve murder as a last resort, shall we? I'll see you Wednesday."

She hung up the phone and looked up at the bike courier, whose casual stance and blatant stare around her office struck her as annoying and too familiar.

"My assistant has the authority to sign for my packages," she said, her tone more sharp than she meant, but since her head had started to pound in earnest, she really didn't care if she embarrassed the man who, by the way, looked a little too old in her opinion to still be riding a bicycle for a living.

The wiry man jerked his thumb toward the door. "No one was out front. Besides, the package has specific instructions to be delivered to the addressee personally." He grinned. "So you're an editor?"

Felicia pressed her lips together and reached for the envelope. "That's right."

He handed it to her, still grinning. "So is this an important contract or something?"

"Where do I sign?" she asked, ignoring his attempt to chat.

He removed a handheld electronic device from a pouch on his belt that had JAG written on it in reflective tape. "Jag" handed over the unit, still grinning. "Have you read *The Immortal Class* by Travis Culley?"

She scrawled her name on the screen and handed back the device. "I can't say that I have."

"It's about his life as a bike messenger. Good stuff."

"That's nice."

From his blanched expression, Felicia saw that he realized she was dismissing him, but she refused to feel guilty for not engaging a deliveryman in conversation. "Is there anything else?"

He pursed his mouth, then lifted his hand. "No. Sorry to bother you. Have a nice day." He walked out of her office with a long, athletic stride, and she felt a pang of remorse. She could have spared ten words for the guy—with thousands of bike messengers in the city, it wasn't as if she would ever see him again.

With a sigh, she put the incident out of her mind and studied the return address typed on the plain manila envelope that was practically weightless. "Literary Associates," she murmured. With a generic name like that, the contents were either some kind of direct marketing campaign or a desperate attempt by an author to get her attention.

Using a letter opener, she sliced open the envelope, and out slid a 4x6 picture of herself, smiling . . . and naked from the waist up.

Felicia gasped and instinctively released the photo, which floated out of her fingers before gliding underneath her desk. She cursed and dropped to her knees on the prickly carpet, feeling for the photo while panic lurched through her chest. When and where had the photo been taken, and worse—who had sent it?

A rap on her door sounded, then she heard her assistant Tamara ask, "Felicia?" Felicia spotted the photo and slapped her hand over it, then pushed to her feet while palming the photo. "Yes?"

Tamara frowned. "Is everything okay?"

Felicia managed a little laugh and smoothed her mussed hair. "Just chasing down a paper clip."

But she suspected her casual tone belied her frenzied state, because her assistant stared at her curiously. "Okay, well, here's the mail," Tamara said, holding up a rubber-banded wad of envelopes.

Afraid that if she moved both hands, she would reveal the photo, Felicia nodded toward her desk. "Just drop it in my in-box. Please."

Tamara's eyebrows shot up in surprise, but she walked into the office and dropped the bundle in the tray a foot in front of Felicia. "There you go."

"Thank you."

"You're welcome." Tamara gave her a strange look, then said, "By the way, the lemon cupcakes you brought in were divine."

"Good. I'm g-glad everyone enjoyed them."

"When are you going to tell me the name of your bakery?"

"You know I don't reveal my sources." Felicia tried to smile past her burgeoning panic but failed. The hidden photo burned her hand. "Listen, Tamara, I'm really swamped right now—will you hold my calls?"

Tamara glanced down at Felicia's pristine desk, but pursed her mouth and nodded. "Sure." After a final inquisitive look, she left and shut the door.

With shaking hands, Felicia closed the blinds on the interior glass walls of her office to shut out the rest of the department and to thwart her assistant's curiosity. When she looked at the photo again, she was instantly nauseous. In the amateur candid, she was standing, wearing red bikini panties, slightly heavy-lidded, her blond hair tousled, her nipples erect.

Felicia's mind spun as she tried to place where the picture had been taken, but the background was dark, indistinguishable. The underwear was nothing special, she had always owned a few pairs of red bikini panties. Her hair, which she'd worn in the same long, straight style for years, gave no hint to time or place. She certainly didn't remember posing for the photo. . . . Had she been drunk? A month ago she'd had a one-night stand with a man she met at a holiday party—could he have taken the photo and was now playing some kind of sick game? His face floated in her mind, his features as hazy as his name—Jim? John? Her cheeks flamed, and she covered her mouth with her hand as bile backed up in her throat.

She searched the envelope for a clue to the sender's identity but found nothing other than the return address. A call to directory assistance revealed no such company at no such address, so whoever sent it had gone to lengths to remain anonymous.

She stared at the photo, willing it to disappear, then turned it over to check for processing information. It was printed on generic photo paper—on a personal printer? Her heart raced and her neck felt sticky with shame. What did it say about her that she'd been naked with enough men in her thirty-five years that she couldn't pinpoint the culprit immediately?

Who had sent the picture, and why would they have sent it to her at work with no message? Panic rose in her chest like a scalding tide—what should she do? What *could* she do? She pressed her lips together hard to stem gathering tears.

Nothing . . . except wait to see if the sender made another move.

 Chapter 3

Tallie stepped into The Bottom Rung at a few minutes past 6:00 P.M. She was immediately enveloped by the hum of voices and energy that fostered her excitement over the responsibility that Ron had entrusted to her. Editing an author as highly esteemed as Gaylord Cooper would mean having her name dropped at industry cocktail parties and mentioned in trade publications—in bold type. After years of harboring a "feeling" that her big break was just around the bend, she had finally rounded the proverbial corner. She had arrived.

Alone, her mother would point out.

Irritated that the thought had even wormed its way into her mind, Tallie threaded her way through vertical bodies, her bulky striped wool coat catching on everything and everyone she passed. It was that mortifying Christmas newsletter that haunted her. Her mother was the most wonderful, most maternal, most adept homemaker on the face of the planet. It was, Tallie knew, her mother's utter happiness with her role in life that fueled her worry that her daughter would become so wrapped up in pursuing success that she would miss out on the

things her mother found so fulfilling—a husband . . .
children . . . laundry.

Merrilyn Blankenship considered the state of her
family's clothing to be a personal reflection of her worth
as a person. Tallie's most enduring memory of childhood was wearing clothes so starched they crackled.
Even her sweatpants received knife-edge creases from a
sizzling iron. She didn't need a shrink to tell her that her
refusal to own an iron was a manifestation of her resistance to a life that resembled her mother's. Tallie acknowledged that she was fortunate to be the recipient of
her mother's mothering, but as soon as she'd been old
enough to read an atlas, she had plotted to escape the
confines of the sleepy town of Circleville and what she
perceived to be a preordained existence. Her deep-
seated fear of domesticity was undoubtedly the root of
her resistance to men in general. Oh, she dated occasionally, but no one had held her interest. She had her
own barometer for knowing when a man was getting too
close: As soon as he felt comfortable enough to help
himself to something in her refrigerator, he was history.

She smiled in vindication. Her dogged concentration
on her career had finally paid off. Wearing slightly rumpled clothing and sleeping alone were small sacrifices
compared to this drumroll beating in her chest.

Tallie scanned for a glimpse of Felicia or a free table.
The bar was more crowded than usual for a Monday, but
the previous Friday had blown up a blizzard that had
sent everyone home at lunch, and people who had
missed out on their regular Friday happy hour—like her
and Felicia—were making up for lost time. She spied a
couple of men leaving their table and sidled up to stake
her territory before anyone else noticed, grabbing one

chair for herself, hanging the straps of her purse and her manuscript bag over the back. Then she plunked her hairy coat in the other chair as a placeholder until Felicia arrived.

Tallie climbed into the chair at the tall table and drummed her fingers on the lacquered top. Felicia had seemed so preoccupied when she'd called back that Tallie had decided to wait until they got together to tell her about Gaylord Cooper. It was Felicia's opinion that she valued most because her friend was the epitome of cool, savvy, Urban Woman. Born and raised in Manhattan, Felicia knew every nuance of the city and every maneuver of the publishing industry. She was having cappuccino in the Rose Room of the Algonquin Hotel, rubbing elbows with the most powerful people in the business, while Tallie and the rest of the interns at Parkbench Publishing were grabbing bad coffee from street vendors on their dash into work. Felicia brought into the office delicacies from bakeries only she knew about and wowed the executives via the breakroom *and* the boardroom. Beautiful, smart, ambitious. It was no wonder she had been the first to be promoted, and the first to be wooed away by a bigger publishing house.

Tallie toyed with the Plexiglas stand containing the drink menu and marveled on the tenets of their friendship. Other people undoubtedly wondered why Felicia, who could spend time with just about anyone—male or female—of her choosing, would pair herself with Tallie, who was by just about every yardstick unremarkable. Yet Felicia had initiated the friendship all those years ago and, instead of being condescending about Tallie's rural upbringing, had seemed fascinated by it. She had appointed herself Tallie's big sister and had taken Tallie under her wing. For her part, Tallie's idolatry had evolved into genuine affection and admiration for Felicia. Theirs was a low-maintenance friendship, flying above short-term boyfriends, family crises, and sudden work commitments. They respected each other's privacy and shared a similar outlook on life: Success was power, and power was independence. Men were . . . distractions.

There was only once, about a year ago, that she'd thought Felicia had fallen in love, with agent Jerry Key. But that flash had burned out—Felicia had ended their affair because she'd been concerned about the career complications. Secretly, Tallie had been relieved because she'd heard some rather unsavory things around the water cooler about the self-proclaimed metrosexual.

Tallie looked up just as Felicia entered the bar. As always, her arrival was a study in human behavior. For a split second, everyone froze, looked, then moved aside. Felicia, clad in a long white cashmere coat, her golden hair flowing over one shoulder, could have easily passed for a supermodel. She glided through the opening, oblivious to the attention. It was Felicia's complete lack of vanity that allowed Tallie to remain friends with someone so beautiful without developing an inferiority complex.

Except today Felicia's normally flawless expression was marred by a wrinkle on her brow, and her mouth looked slightly drawn.

"Hi," Tallie said, removing her coat from the extra chair.

"Hey," Felicia said as her fingers moved over the pewter buttons on her fabulous overcoat. "Have you been waiting long?"

"Just a few minutes." Tallie leaned forward, but Felicia wouldn't make eye contact as she unshouldered her own manuscript bag and swung into the seat. "Are you feeling okay?"

Felicia looked up, and pain flashed in her electric blue eyes. "A little headache."

"Another one?"

"It's better," she said quickly. "I took a pill as soon as I felt it coming on."

Tallie was unconvinced. "Why don't you go home and get some rest?"

"No, I wanted to see you." Her smile didn't quite reach her eyes. "Have you ordered yet?"

"I haven't seen a wait—"

"How are you ladies doing?" a waiter cut in, clearing the glasses left by the previous occupants while beaming at Felicia.

Tallie lifted one side of her mouth; men materialized from thin air when Felicia was around. "We're fine, thanks. I'll have a Bacardi Silver."

Felicia wet her lips, then said, "I'll have a martini. Two olives, please."

Tallie waited until the man had left, then ventured, "Are you sure you should be drinking alcohol with your medication?"

"Probably not, but today calls for it."

Tallie's good news died on her lips. "Did you have a bad day?"

"Yes, but I don't want to bore you with the details." Felicia sighed. "How about you? What's going on at Parkbench?"

Tallie hesitated, unaccustomed to seeing her friend in anything but the best of moods. "Ron's going to be away for a few days."

"Oh, nice. Vacation?"

Tallie hesitated. "Actually, he didn't say, but I think he's in some kind of trouble."

Felicia frowned. "Trouble?"

"He's been so jumpy lately, I wondered if maybe he's going through a personal crisis. I overheard him talking on the phone to someone and he was angry that the person had called him at work—he said he was already in enough trouble."

"Maybe it's a boyfriend problem," Felicia said with a scoff that was so bitter that Tallie blinked.

"I suppose that's possible," she agreed slowly. "Or maybe it's an illness or something to do with his family."

"Could be. How long will he be out?"

"Possibly a few weeks."

"Does that mean extra work for you?"

The server arrived with their drinks and Tallie waited until she poured the Bacardi Silver into a glass over ice before smiling. "As a matter of fact, Ron asked me to edit Gaylord Cooper's manuscript while he's gone."

Felicia smiled in earnest for the first time since arriving. "Congratulations, Tallie! What a coup." She held up her martini and Tallie met her glass for a celebratory clink.

"I hope so."

Felicia took a deep drink and winced. "How did Scary Kara react?"

"She doesn't know yet," Tallie said. "But even Ron warned me to watch my back."

"Good advice," Felicia said, then her gaze clouded. "You never know who's out to get you."

Tallie frowned. "Did something happen today?"

"The Dannons are quarreling again, and Jerry Key wants me to play referee."

"Oh," Tallie said mildly. "You talked to Jerry?" That probably explained her taciturn mood.

"Yeah," Felicia said. "Tell me again why I got involved with him."

"Because he's a wealthy, charming, powerful, good-looking bachelor?"

"But he's such a bastard."

Tallie gave a dry little laugh. "Don't make me more nervous—I'm depending on him to smooth the way for me to work with Mr. Cooper."

"That's right, he represents Cooper. The guy is something of a kook, isn't he? I remember Jerry saying Cooper claimed to have worked for the government, thought everyone was gunning for him."

Tallie's stomach roiled. "The man has his eccentricities. I hope this assignment doesn't blow up in my face."

Felicia winked. "Ron's a smart cookie. He knows what he's doing." Then she glared. "Just stand your ground with Jerry."

Tallie nodded and took a drink from her glass, studying her friend. If she didn't know better, she'd think Felicia was still hung up on Jerry . . . not that it was any of her business, but she hated to see her go down that toll road again. Suddenly she touched her head. "I almost forgot—I found a gray hair today, can you believe it?"

Felicia phsawed. "Pluck it."

Tallie grinned. "My mother says that if you pluck a gray hair, seven will grow back in its place."

Felicia grew serious. "Really? I thought that was an old wives' tale."

"It is—my mother is an old wife."

"She is not," Felicia said, her tone sharp.

Tallie held up her hands defensively. "Hey, it was a joke." For never having met Merrilyn Blankenship, Felicia seemed almost protective of the woman. Tallie assumed it had something to do with Felicia's reserved relationship with her own mother, a securities attorney. At times she seemed envious of Tallie's mother, even though Tallie had tried to convince her that their relationship was far from ideal.

Felicia sighed and rubbed her temple. "Sorry . . . the migraine is making me cross."

"Let's finish our drinks and go home," Tallie urged. "I have a ton of reading to do, and you should get some rest."

Felicia nodded and seemed on the verge of saying something, then took a drink from her glass instead. But Tallie could tell that something was weighing on her mind, something heavier than a migraine.

"Felicia, Tallie—what a nice surprise!"

Tallie turned to see a familiar-looking olive-skinned woman walking toward them. Her memory stirred. "Jane?"

"Jane Glass," Felicia confirmed, offering a smile at the woman they had interned with years ago at Parkbench Publishing.

"Actually, I've added an accent to my name," Jane said cheerfully. "Now I go by 'Juh-nay.' I discovered my birth mother might have been French, so it seemed appropriate."

Tallie nodded awkwardly and remembered that when they had worked together years ago, Jane had been on an ongoing search for her birth parents and had sampled many ethnic customs, certain that she would sense when she happened upon the practices of her ancestors. The French connection probably also explained the jaunty beret sitting atop the woman's head. "Jané," she corrected herself, although the pronunciation sounded ridiculous leaving her tongue.

"So, *Jané*," Felicia said with the merest hint of sarcasm, "where have you been keeping yourself? Are you still at Bloodworth?"

"No. I'm working for Futurestar now," the woman said. "I think they're really going places."

A defense of the company's electronic publishing format, Tallie realized, before she or Felicia could say something negative about what was considered by industry pundits to be a second-tier book medium. "That's great," Tallie offered. "I've been reading good things about Futurestar."

"What are you doing for them?" Felicia asked, apparently unwilling to expound on Tallie's complimentary words about the start-up company.

"Well, it's a small shop," Jané explained. "Right now, we each do whatever needs to be done. Can I join you until my friends arrive?"

"Sure," they said in unison. While Jané stole a chair from a nearby table and dragged it over, Felicia gave Tallie a look that said she wished she'd gone home when Tallie had offered. Felicia had always thought Jane—er, Jané—an odd duck.

Jané settled herself and gave them a bright smile. "Tallie, I hear you're still at Parkbench, slaving away for Ron Springer."

Tallie blinked. "Well, I . . . yes."

"And Felicia, you're still at Omega?"

"Right."

"It's such a coincidence seeing you, Felicia. Your name came up in conversation today at work."

Felicia looked amused. "Really—how?"

Jané leaned in. "Well, I hate to be the bearer of bad news, but the president of our company, Seth Johnston, works out with Jerry Key."

Felicia's mouth hardened almost imperceptibly. "And?"

Jané squirmed in her seat. "And it seems that Jerry's been bad-mouthing you."

A pang of sympathy barbed through Tallie. She glanced at her friend, who was toying with the base of her glass, trying not to react.

"Can you be more specific?" Felicia finally asked.

Jané's hesitation spiked the tension, then she sighed and lowered her voice. "He told Seth that you were . . . well, *easy*. And that you were into all kinds of kinky stuff."

Felicia drank from her glass, then a little laugh escaped her. "Jerry is a dick. We were involved, but very briefly, so trust me, he's no authority on my preferences in bed." She lifted her chin. "How on earth did the subject come up between you and the president of your company?"

"Seth said that he was hoping to work out a deal for Futurestar to publish some of Omega's backlist, and I mentioned that I used to work with you." Jané looked apologetic. "Look, I told Seth you were a standup person, Felicia, but I thought that you'd want to know that your ex-boyfriend is talking behind your back."

Tallie felt compelled to jump to her friend's defense. "Jerry's just sore because Felicia dumped him."

Jané frowned. "He told Seth that he dumped *you*. What a jerk. Men are pigs."

Felicia nodded her agreement but seemed to turn inward. Tallie tried to fill in the uncomfortable silence with small talk, asking Jané where she lived (Soho) and if she was still single (yes, ergo the "pigs" remark).

"Listen, Tallie," Jané said, "I have a fiction author who writes fantasy murder mysteries, really great stuff. I'm looking for a print publisher who would be willing to release the book in tandem with the electronic edition. I was thinking of sending it to Ron—would you put in a good word when you see him?"

"He's going to be away for a few weeks," Tallie said, squashing her irritation at the implication that she didn't warrant consideration. "But I'd be happy to take a look." She paused, then couldn't resist adding, "Ron has passed along some of his high-profile writers to me—Gaylord Cooper, for one."

Jané looked impressed. "Okay, I'll have the manuscript couriered over tomorrow." She looked past Tallie's shoulder. "Oh, there are my friends. It was great catching up with you two—hopefully I'll see you both again soon."

They nodded and said good-bye, but when the woman was out of earshot, Felicia made a rueful noise. "*Juh-nay?* What a crock. And she played you, Tallie. She knows Ron wouldn't give that manuscript the time of day."

Tallie shrugged. "Maybe it's as good as she says."

"Maybe," Felicia agreed, then drained her martini. "I really should be going—but don't leave on my account."

"No, I'll walk out with you," Tallie said and, after leaving money on the table for the drink, pulled on her coat. "Hey, don't let what she said about Jerry get to you."

"I'm not," Felicia said, but her voice was tight, her forehead furrowed.

Tallie put her hand on Felicia's arm. "Are you sure something didn't happen today to upset you?"

Felicia looked up, and for a few seconds, Tallie thought she was going to divulge what was eating at her. But instead she shook her head and said, "Nothing that won't take care of itself."

 Chapter 4

Felicia's words stayed with Tallie as she climbed up three flights of stairs to her Chelsea apartment. The rickety elevator wasn't worth waiting for, and the spurt of exercise usually got her in the mood for a quick run before dinner. Usually. But a faint odor in the hallway made her a little queasy, and by the time she unlocked all three dead bolts on her door, she had convinced herself that it was too cold/late/dangerous for her to run, and she promised herself that having a salad for dinner would compensate for the calories not expended.

Nothing that won't take care of itself. It wasn't a fatalistic outlook but pure confidence that drove Felicia's belief that things generally turned out the way they were supposed to. Tallie walked into her tiny apartment, flipped on an overhead light that flickered frantically before it came on, and angled her head at her jumble of scavenged and distinctly uninteresting furniture. It was, she decided, the confidence of someone born on the Upper East Side and for whom things generally worked out well.

"The rest of us tend to be more skeptical," Tallie murmured as she turned to slide the dead bolts home again. *Thick, thack, whack.* She wondered again if whatever was eating at Felicia had something to do with Jerry Key. Anger sparked in her stomach: A woman was powerless to defend herself against a man's malicious rumors. It was bad enough that the guy was engaging in locker room talk about her, but even worse that Felicia— and she herself—had to work with the jerk. She wished she could find some way to teach the man a lesson . . . anonymously.

Tallie turned to survey the cluttered wood coffee table, the smooshed brown couch cushions, the pile of clean laundry in the green side chair that still needed to be folded. Her mother would have a heart attack if she could see the dust on the television, not to mention the dirty dishes in the sink. Deep down, Tallie felt bratty, because while she was no Heloise, she normally kept things halfway straight, though every time she returned from visiting her parents' home in Ohio, she regressed to Super Slob. As if she had to prove to herself that in no way did she resemble, desire, or have the talent to be a homemaker.

She stepped out of her shoes and padded to her bedroom, a mere three strides away, in her stocking feet. She stepped on something sharp and bent to retrieve a dropped—and now bent—earring out of the beige shag carpet. She didn't remember losing it, but it had been weeks since she'd run the vacuum, so for all she knew, her missing chunky metal belt could be hiding in the depths.

Her pint-sized bedroom was a disaster, her bed unmade, dirty clothes strewn everywhere, the gaping door to her tiny closet revealing another spectacular mess.

Tallie closed the door, then rummaged through bureau drawers and the piled-up chair next to the bed until she found a clean nightshirt. After stripping her sensible skirt and sweater and tossing them into an overflowing laundry basket, she wrapped herself in flannel, shoved her icy feet into sheepskin-lined slippers, and scuffed back to the kitchen to examine the refrigerator.

The interior reeked of something pungent and rapidly decomposing. The source, she discovered after much poking around, was a carton of soured orange juice. Yuck. The impossibility of making a salad began to sink in as she scanned the contents of her crisper: a soft tomato, a bag of dried-up midget carrots, and a stalk of celery so old it had turned white. She dragged over the garbage can and began tossing everything that looked suspicious, stopping when the bag was almost too heavy to lift.

That was the bad thing about cleaning—one thing led to another. She tied up the garbage, then grabbed the phone and ordered a burrito with a bushel of chips and a quart of salsa, telling herself she deserved to celebrate, considering the big boost her career had received today. A smile spread across her face, and she rose on her toes for a private little squeal. She picked up the phone again, eager to share the news with someone who would understand and would be happy for her, but her hand halted over the number pad.

Who?

Shari, her college roommate? They spoke every few months, and although Shari, who was a registered nurse, would be happy for Tallie, she wouldn't be able to grasp the significance of her news.

Chad, the guy she had most recently dated? He

worked in production for an entertainment magazine and he was a voracious reader, so he would certainly understand the magnitude of her news . . . but would he be happy for her? Probably not, considering she had ended their relationship rather abruptly over a carton of leftover shrimp chop suey that he had helped himself to in her refrigerator after a bout of sex that had been considerably less spicy than the food. The fact that she probably would have thrown out the chop suey hadn't been important—he had stepped over the symbolic line she had drawn in the sand around her relationships. He'd had to go.

Filching leftovers was simply too domestic for her to stomach. A man might as well say, "I'm hungry and I'm taking your food, woman." First he'd be foraging for food in the fridge, and next he'd be expecting her to cook for him, replace buttons on his shirts, and give up her job to have babies that looked like him.

There was Audrey, her former assistant, but she had eloped with one of their science fiction writers and now lived in Australia during the winter months. The phone call would cost her a small fortune.

There was Bradley, a guy she had dated a long time ago (stuffed manicotti had been his downfall) with whom she had managed to remain friends because they sometimes met on the running path in the park. But the last time she had seen him he'd mentioned that his girlfriend was moving in, so the woman might not appreciate a celebratory call from an ex-lover.

After a moment's hesitation, she punched in her parents' phone number. A couple of rings later, her dad's voice came on the line. "Hello?"

His baritone always put a smile on her face. "Hi, Dad, it's Tallie."

"Well, hi, sweetheart. This is a nice surprise. As much as your mother fussed over you during the holidays, I figured we wouldn't hear from you until Easter."

She laughed—her dad, an insurance salesman, understood the predicament of being caught between her mother and the real world. "I called to tell you some good news."

"I can't wait to hear it."

"Hi, Tallie," her mother broke in. "I picked up on the extension in the kitchen."

"Hi, Mom."

"Tallie has good news," her dad offered.

"Did Sheila Wages' son call you?"

Tallie blinked. Leave it to her mother to think that the good news involved a man. "Um, that's not why I called, Mom. My boss gave me a big assignment today."

"Your handsome boss, Ron, the one you have a crush on?"

She winced. "Yes, Mom, Ron—but I don't have a crush on him. Anymore."

"Don't worry, dear, he'll come around some day."

And to think she had hesitated before calling.

"What's the big assignment?" her father asked, bless him.

"Ron asked me to edit Gaylord Cooper's next book."

"Who?" her mother asked.

"You know," her dad said. "The successful author who writes those big thrillers. He's great." Her father had become a fan since Tallie had started sending him copies of Cooper's books.

"Is that safe?" her mother asked. "Doesn't he write about professional killers and perverts?"

Tallie pursed her mouth. "Mom, it's fiction. Just because he writes about those things doesn't mean he lives them."

"Well, it still sounds dangerous to me."

"I think it's great, honey, congratulations."

"Thanks, Dad."

"Tallie," her mother said, "I dropped a package in the mail for you today, an early birthday gift. I sent it parcel post—have you noticed how much postage has gone up? Now *that's* a crime somebody should write about."

"I'll be looking for the package, Mom, thanks." Tallie's doorbell rang, saving her. "Oh, there's my dinner."

"All that take-out food isn't good for you," her mother admonished. "You should cook once in a while. And when Sheila's son calls, be nice."

"Take care, sweetheart," her father said. "I'm proud of you."

"Thanks, Dad. I'll call again soon." She hung up the phone and shook her head ruefully—hadn't she known what would happen? And Keith Wages would give her mother something to obsess about for a few months.

The doorbell rang again, more insistently. She grabbed her purse on the way and counted out cash, then turned the dead bolts and opened the door the four inches the safety chain would allow. But instead of a burrito-bearing delivery person, Mr. Emory, the stout building super, stood outside her door wearing an unflattering black velour running suit.

"Something dead in there?" he asked without preamble, his big nose twitching.

"What? No."

"There's a bad smell on the stairs and it's coming from one of the apartments on this floor."

"Well, it's not coming from in here."

"Still," he said flatly, "I need to check it out."

Tallie frowned. "Give me a minute, okay?"

"Yeah, yeah, be brisk about it. I got eleven more apartments to check."

She closed the door and glanced over the disarray in her apartment; she couldn't make a dent in a minute's time. Resigned, she unlocked the chain and opened the door. "Sorry for the mess. I'm cleaning."

He took one look around and said, "Good. It needs it."

She squirmed. This was the equivalent of lying on a gurney in the emergency room wearing dirty underwear. And she hated feeling guilty about it—every guy she'd ever dated lived in worse conditions, yet it seemed to be men's God-given right to be untidy and women's God-given duty to care.

Mr. Emory poked in her garbage, then recoiled.

"Bad orange juice," she offered.

He opened and closed the refrigerator door, then stuck his head in her bedroom.

"Satisfied?" she asked.

"I suppose," he said. "But you'd better take out that trash. If you attract roaches, I'll have to charge you for the pest control service."

She swallowed and nodded.

He left shaking his head, and Tallie felt like a bum. On the spot, she decided to call Felicia's maid service and have them come over to give the place a good thorough cleaning. After that, upkeep wouldn't be so bad. She dialed Felicia's number, thinking it would also be a good excuse to check on her friend.

Just in case the situation Felicia thought would take care of itself needed a little nudge.

Chapter 5

Felicia wiped the flour from her hands on the hem of her vintage rose-patterned apron and leaned over the *Blankenship Bulletin*, reviewing the ingredients for Merrilyn's Best Carrot Cake to make sure she hadn't left out anything. The wonderful thing about Tallie's mother's cake recipes was the extra care required in preparing the ingredients, such as replacing a certain amount of the flour with finely ground hazelnuts; that kind of attention to detail was the difference between a homemade cake and a concoction worthy of the best bakeries in Manhattan. Felicia had learned early on that the foundation of being an accomplished baker was using only the best ingredients.

She dipped her finger into the thick, apricot-colored batter, dotted with fat golden raisins and shredded sweet carrots, and touched the dollop to her tongue. Mm— heaven. Tallie had no appreciation for her mother's genius in the kitchen. Over the years, Felicia had gotten some of her best baking tips through the Blankenship holiday newsletter, like the importance of sifting cake flour and how to remove a bundt cake from its pan with perfect results every time. Merrilyn Blankenship was a domestic goddess.

Felicia held the mixing bowl over the first of two round flour-dusted pans and, as carefully as one would handle an explosive substance, used a wooden spoon to dole out one-half of the lovely batter. The phone rang and she sighed. Once mixed, batter should never sit because the tiny air bubbles would begin to dissipate, resulting in a heavy cake (another newsletter tip). She glanced at the caller ID screen—Tallie—then picked up the receiver and jammed it between her ear and shoulder. "Hello?"

"Hey, it's me—did I catch you at a bad time?"

"I'm in the kitchen."

"Heating up a frozen dinner?"

A wry smile curved Felicia's mouth. "Yeah. Give me a minute to get this in the oven, okay?" She set down the receiver and carefully emptied the bowl into the second round cake pan, lightly tapped each on the counter to level the batter, then slid them onto the oven's center rack, positioning them two inches apart for best heat circulation. After setting the timer for thirty minutes, she picked up the phone. "Okay, I'm back."

"Microwaving those frozen entrees is much faster," Tallie said.

"But they don't taste as good," Felicia said breezily. "What's up with you?"

"I'm biting the bullet and calling to get the name of your maid service—my place is a total wreck."

Felicia glanced around her kitchen, spotless save for the cake-making supplies she had pulled from the glass-front white cabinets, and stalled. "Actually, Tallie, the service has been coming for so long, I don't remember the name offhand."

"Can you look it up?" Tallie pressed. "Your place always looks so great. If I'm going to spend the money, I want to go with a service I know does a good job."

"I'll look for it while we talk," she said, buying time.

"How are you feeling?"

"The migraine is gone," Felicia lied. But her head did feel better—baking always eased her stress level.

"Good. And I hope you don't let what Jane said about Jerry Key get to you."

Removing a yellow pages volume from a drawer, Felicia emitted a little laugh. "You mean *Jané*, don't you?"

"You said it yourself, Jerry's a bastard."

"True, but I thought even he had more integrity than to spread rumors about me."

"Felicia . . . you're not still hung up on the guy, are you? I mean, if you are, I wouldn't think badly of you."

Felicia stopped, then wondered what possible good could come from telling the truth. "No, Tallie, I'm not still hung up on him."

Tallie's sigh of relief whistled through the receiver. "Good. So what happened today to put you in such a bad mood? It couldn't be as bad as my gray hair."

The nude picture of herself rose in Felicia's mind. "No. Nothing as bad as your gray hair." But her voice sound high and false, even to her own ears.

"You know, Felicia, that you could tell me anything, that I would help you any way I could, don't you?"

Felicia's chest warmed with true affection, and she attempted a laugh to lighten the mood. "If I decide to put a hit out on Jerry Key, I'll give you a call."

"Deal," Tallie said, her voice equally light. "Oh, I didn't tell you—I'm supposed to meet the son of a friend of my mother's for coffee on Wednesday."

"Sounds promising."

"Are you kidding? The guy sounded like a dork on the phone. I'm hoping I get the flu so I can cancel. And my mother is already pestering me about it."

"Then you'd better get it over with," Felicia said, trying to remember the last time her mother had cared about anything in her life. She wasn't even sure if her mother was in town, or off on one of her "business" trips with a "client."

"Did you find the name of your maid service?"

Felicia looked down at the Cleaning Services page beneath her finger and selected the nicest ad. "Imperial Mother's Maid Service."

"Okay, thanks. Gotta run, there's my dinner at the door. Call me this week when you get a chance."

"I will," Felicia said, then disconnected the call slowly. She didn't like fibbing to Tallie, but her friend would never believe that she did her own cleaning and *enjoyed* it, no less. It was her own little secret; by all outward appearances, she was super career woman, but in the privacy of her own home, she preferred cotton house dresses and rubber gloves. It made her feel . . . nostalgic, like looking at the world through technicolored glasses.

While the cake finished baking, she ran hot water in the sink and added patchouli-scented dish-soap liquid from a glass bottle with a vintage-inspired label. She removed the Michael Graves-designed handled sponge and lovingly washed the mixing bowl, utensils, and measuring cups before rinsing them and setting them on a wire rack to drain. She took extra care with the German cutlery, since the blades of the knives that were precisely weighted could be dulled by aggressive cleaning, and downright ravaged in the dishwasher.

The sweet aroma of the specialty cleanser lingered after she polished the stainless-steel sink, blending beautifully with the cake that was, after she did a spring-back test with her finger, ready to come out of the oven. She placed both cake pans on a cooling rack and sat down at the table, satisfied at the sight and scents of the sparkling clean kitchen. If she closed her eyes, she could almost imagine a man's voice announcing, "Honey, I'm home. Mm, something smells *wonderful*."

She opened her eyes and listened instead to the hum of the overhead fluorescent light and acknowledged the chill of loneliness despite the warmth emanating from the oven. The only man she had ever loved was about as far-flung from a domesticated, adoring husband as a man could be.

Felicia touched a finger to her temple, which had begun to throb again. Not only was Jerry Key not the man she had dreamed he would be, but she was coming to the awful conclusion that he was the one who had sent the photo. Heaven knew she had been in a constant state of undress when they had dated—she wouldn't be surprised to learn that he had one, or even several, compromising pictures of her. The man had been insatiable in bed, and she had obliged. Sending a reminder of the hold he had over her was just the kind of thing that Jerry would do. Enough time had passed since he had dumped her for him to come sniffing around again. The fact that she hadn't responded like a lapdog was probably making him crazy. Crazy enough to resort to blackmail?

She walked over to the sink, pulled out a drawer, and thumbed through the comforting stack of snowy cotton dish towels before removing one. The faint scent of lemon wafted to her nose as she unfolded the cloth and carefully dried the splendid knives, then replaced them in their uniform slots in the hardwood block on her shiny kitchen counter. Felicia held up the last knife and caught her own reflection on the half-inch blade. Little did Jerry know, she could be crazy, too.

Chapter 6

"You can let me out here," Tallie told the cab driver.

"Suspicious Grounds is on the next block," the driver said, reminding her of the destination she'd given him.

"Here is fine," she said pointedly.

The cab stopped and, after paying, Tallie climbed out, hunched her shoulders against the bitter temperature, and walked slowly toward the coffee place. She was five minutes early, and she didn't want Keith Wages to get the idea that she was eager to meet him. A few strides down the street, she remembered why she had tossed these midi boots to the back of her closet—they were as uncomfortable as hell. Why she had decided to wear them today, she couldn't fathom. It wasn't as if she had dressed up for her pseudo blind date. In fact, she had deliberately selected a long skirt and sweater from the bottom of the stack of clothes in the green chair in her living room: They were clean but not particularly stylish. Certainly not sexy.

She winced when her calf muscles threatened to cramp—she'd run an extra mile and a half last night to make up for the missed run Monday night, and her body was letting her know she wasn't as young as she used to be. First a gray hair, and now inflexibility was setting in. At this rate, she'd be taking hormone replacement therapy before spring.

A cutting wind had blown up, effectively sweeping every piece of loose trash in Manhattan toward the East River. A McDonald's fries cup caught her on the cheek, and a newspaper page hugged her knees before whisking on its way. Her hair whipped painfully around her face, anchored by a knit cap that crept backward on her head. Behind the striped muffler wrapped around the lower part of her face, Tallie gritted her teeth. No man she *knew* was worth this, let alone a complete stranger.

She walked into Suspicious Grounds a couple of minutes late and caught a glimpse of herself in a Columbian coffee bean mirror. Pink of cheek and runny of nose . . . nice. She sniffled and unwound her scarf while she scanned the crowd for a Michigan State ball cap. Yankees, Yankees, Yankees, Red Sox, Yankees, Michigan State. She dropped her gaze, took in the view below the hat, and pursed her mouth. Not bad. Dark hair, neat sideburns, athletic build, gray sweater over a black turtleneck, burgundy wool scarf, new jeans, old sneakers. Leaning against the wall, the man had his hands in his pockets, seemingly lost in thought. Tallie had a momentary pang of regret that she hadn't worn a jacket instead of a schlumpy sweater, and that she hadn't looked harder for her nice emerald stud earrings that brought out the green in her eyes. Then she shook herself—the man hadn't even looked up and she was undressing and redressing for him.

He chose that moment to look up, and her mouth went

dry. Keith Wages, with large, distinct features and a hesitant smile, was not the average son of your mother's friend. One might even call him cute. Why hadn't she looked for the emerald earrings?

He straightened and walked toward her. She swiped at her nose and tried to smile. "You must be Tallie," he said. "I recognize you from the photos your mother's sent to our house over the years."

"And you're Keith," she said stiffly, her jaw practically locked from the cold.

He nodded. "Nasty day, eh? Let's get some coffee and warm you up."

Part of her was flattered that he noticed she was cold, and part of her was irked that he would take ownership of the remedy. She followed him to the counter and ordered a latte from a perky little blond who seemed taken with Keith. He angled plenty of teeth toward the young woman, asked for a tall black coffee, and pulled out his wallet to pay for both drinks.

"I'll pay for mine," she said quickly.

"You can get it next time," he said smoothly, which only perturbed her more. Who said there was going to be a next time? She relented because he was the one who had initiated the meeting, and she wasn't going to stand in the way of him looking macho in front of Blondie. While he paid, she studied him. Mid to late thirties, she guessed, and from the silver at his temples, he was ahead of her in the gray hair department. Of course he could be bald underneath the ball cap. In fact, he probably was.

"Are you sure you don't want a sandwich or something?" he asked.

"I'm sure," she said primly. "I don't have much time."

His dark eyebrows climbed, then a mocking expression came over his face. "Do you have time to sit down?"

She nodded sheepishly and followed him to a table in the back, then peeled off her winter garb. The knit cap came off last—a mistake because it had electrified her hair. The more she tried to smooth it down, the worse it crackled, and she was sure her lone gray hair stood up like a lightning rod. Not that Keith appeared to notice. His gaze kept straying past her shoulder—in the direction of the counter and the cute girl.

Tallie tingled over his obvious disinterest. "So, you're Sheila's son," she said to start the ball rolling.

"Mm-hm," he said, sipping from his cup and watching the counter.

She rolled her eyes. "How long have you been in New York?"

He glanced back briefly. "A couple of years now. You?"

"Almost ten years." She might as well have been talking to herself. She tried to guess at his occupation—deejay? Aspiring actor? Bartender? She took a deep drink from her coffee cup and scalded her tongue. Fitting.

It took him a few seconds to realize she wasn't talking. He looked back. "And you're a book editor?"

She nodded, no longer willing to make an effort.

He adopted an expression of feigned interest. "That sounds glamorous."

She gave him a flat smile. "It isn't."

He grinned. "Your mother makes it sound glamorous."

She blinked. "My mother? When did you talk to my mother?"

"I didn't, but I was at my parents' home in Ann Arbor for Christmas." His grin widened. "I read your family newsletter."

Mortification bled through her. "My mother fancies herself to be a writer."

"That was quite a headline."

Her face flamed. "I keep threatening to edit her."

"So you're still single?"

Four little words spoken with such amusement . . . a ringing condemnation of her life. No acknowledgement of her intellectual achievements, just a judgment on her marriageability. She knew her visceral reaction to his casual words was unreasonable, but this was the last thing she needed when the pressure at work had just been ratcheted up. And she was furious with herself for thinking about wasting her emerald earrings on him. Tallie's muscles bunched and her vocal cords constricted in preparation for lashing out at the man, but his attention had swung back to the girl at the counter. So much so that he was craning his neck, abandoning subtlety entirely, the creep.

"Look—" Tallie started but was cut short when in one motion Keith jumped to his feet and pushed her out of her seat with a shove to her shoulder.

"Get down!"

She got down, all right—landing hard, since she didn't have time to put out her arms to brace her fall. As pain blazed through her left shoulder, she was vaguely aware of Keith shouting, then screams ricocheting through the coffeehouse . . . and what sounded amazingly like gunshots. Glass shattered and Tallie floundered to her stomach, the pain forgotten as fear bolted through her chest—what the heck was going on?

With her heart galloping, she raised her head and looked around in the few seconds of charged silence. The coffeehouse was in chaos, people lying on the floor, tables and chairs overturned. Keith stood at the counter behind a man he had shoved *onto* the counter, holding a gun to the man's ear. Using one hand, Keith removed handcuffs from his waistband and secured the man's hands behind his back.

Tallie gawked. Sheila Wages' son was either a police officer or he was auditioning for a part on *Law and Order*.

"Is anyone hurt?" Keith shouted.

Everyone began to stir, helping each other to their feet.

"Anyone?" he repeated. "Tallie, are you okay?"

She pushed to her feet and patted vital areas, relatively sure a bullet couldn't have penetrated her chunky sweater. "I'm okay." With her heart still thumping, she watched him call for backup and direct people away from the broken glass, all while keeping an eye on the perp, who had apparently been trying to rob the place. The hardened criminal had a round baby face, shaggy blond hair, and baggy clothes. He was facedown on the counter, his head turned toward her. He stared at her, his eyes small and defiant. He looked so ordinary that it was easy to convince herself she'd seen him somewhere before. New York had a way of making a person feel that way—as if you had crossed paths with everyone in the city at one time or another.

She dragged away her gaze, and the shakes set in when she realized how easily someone could have been hurt if Keith hadn't been so alert—the reason, she now realized, he'd been so preoccupied with watching the counter. He must have spotted the man and suspected he was up to no good. And she'd thought Keith had been ignoring her. Shivering over her selfishness, she stared at him with something akin to awe. In the scuffle, he had lost his hat somewhere, and he wasn't bald underneath.

Everything about the man spoke of virility—his quick reaction, his calm control now that the danger had passed. And she'd never seen a man wield a gun in real life—it was kind of a turn-on to know that he had protected her. Of course he had protected everyone, but he *had* sort of singled her out by heaving her to the floor.

A crowd had gathered on the sidewalk to gape at the broken window. Within a minute, two police cruisers arrived, and the officers emerged, weapons drawn. They relaxed when Keith held up a badge, then began to confer. He handed over the robber's gun, pointed to the window and the wall behind where they'd been sitting—presumably the entry points for the stray bullets—then led the bad guy outside to a waiting car. Two officers fanned out across the street, and another one came into the seating area, checking with shaken customers one by one before sending them on their way.

"Are you all right, ma'am?" one of the officers asked her.

She nodded, started to tell them that she was with Keith, then realized that had nothing to do with anything. Through the window she watched as he tucked the robber into the backseat, then climbed into the front seat of the cruiser with another cop. The car flashed its blue lights, then pulled into traffic, signaling an effective end to her pseudo blind date.

"Make sure you have all of your belongings before you leave," the police officer said.

Tallie nodded again and, still in a state of near shock, pulled on her outerwear, piece by piece. Her latte had gone flying with her and had deposited a lovely brown stain on the front of her wool coat, although in hindsight, a coffee stain was better than a bloodstain. Rebundled, she headed toward the entrance, picking her way around glass. Near the counter, she spotted Keith's Michigan State ball cap on the floor, badly soiled, and on impulse, she bent to retrieve it. Her mother routinely washed her father's ball caps in the dishwasher. She, on the other hand, had never laundered a piece of clothing for any man she'd known . . . but then again, a man had never before saved her life.

It seemed like an even trade.

Tallie stuffed the cap into her coat pocket and walked outside to hail a cab, her chest still clicking with incredulity . . . and apprehension. Within a few minutes of meeting Keith Wages, she had been shot at and was contemplating household chores in his honor.

This couldn't be good.

 Chapter 7

Felicia looked up as Tamara stuck her head inside the door. "The Dannons are here." The young woman winced. "They're arguing."

"Has Jerry Key arrived?"

"No. Shall I call him?"

Felicia shook her head, which was starting its familiar throb. "I'll take care of it. Tell the Dannons I'll be with them shortly. Offer them a piece of yesterday's carrot cake, if there's any left."

Tamara touched her stomach. "Oh. My. God. That cake is *so* good. My mother's birthday is coming up, and I know she'd love that cream cheese icing."

"It's sour cream icing," Felicia corrected.

"You *have* to tell me the name of your bakery."

"Can't," Felicia said breezily. "Keep an eye on the Dannons."

"Okay, but if anyone throws a punch, I'm calling security."

Felicia smiled and after a few seconds' hesitation said, "Tamara?"

"Yes."

"There was a bike messenger here Monday who left a package with a return address I can't identify."

"What was in the package?"

"Nothing important," Felicia said quickly. "I wanted to track down the messenger to verify the return address, but I don't remember the name of the company."

"It's not on the envelope?" Tamara asked.

"The label is torn. It's green and I remember the word 'Jag' on a pouch around the courier's waist. Does that mean anything to you?"

"No. If you still have the envelope, I'll see what I can track down."

"No, thanks," Felicia said, picking up the phone. "It's not that important." After two days of poring over the photo and rehashing Jerry's recent flirtatious behavior, she was more and more convinced that he had sent that photo. When she saw him today, she was going to confront him.

After he helped her work things out with the Dannons, of course.

"Jerry Key's office, this is Lori."

"Hi, Lori. This is Felicia Redmon at Omega. Is Jerry on his way to our meeting?"

"Meeting?" Lori asked. "What meeting?"

Felicia pursed her mouth. "The meeting at my office right now with Suze and Phil Dannon. Jerry said he'd be here, and I left the details with you on Monday."

"Oh, right. Jerry said you could handle it."

She frowned. "Put Jerry on, please."

"He isn't here. He had an appointment with his chiropractor."

Felicia clenched her hand into a fist. When they had

dated, Jerry had told her that any time he needed to see his masseuse, he told his secretary that he had an appointment with his chiropractor. Right now she could think of at least a couple of Jerry's bones that she'd like to crack.

"Never mind," she said. "I'll page him."

"Jerry got a new pager number after . . . well, after you and he . . . um, split up."

Heat suffused Felicia's face—had he implied to his secretary that she had harassed him after their breakup? She swallowed and counted to five. "Lori, would you mind paging him and asking him to call me?"

"I'll page him," Lori said in a sing-songy voice, "but I can't promise anything."

"Just do it!" Felicia snapped and slammed down the phone.

At the sound of someone clearing his throat, she turned her head. Phil Dannon stood just inside her office door, the merest of smiles on his rugged face. "I sense a bit of tension in the air."

She exhaled to recover her composure and stood, pulling a wry smile from thin air. "Sorry to keep you waiting, Phil." She walked toward him and extended both her hands in genuine affection. "It's good to see you."

He smiled and captured her in a warm hug. His suede sport coat smelled of wood smoke, conjuring up images of sitting in front of the fireplace at the Dannons' vacation home in the Hamptons, where Phil was living full-time since the split. His big, powerful embrace was so comforting that Felicia stayed a split second longer than necessary, feeling a pang of anger toward Suze for belittling Phil's contribution to their books over the years. She stepped back, momentarily flustered over her reaction to her author's proximity. Phil was a very attractive man, but their relationship had remained strictly professional. Her response, she reasoned, was a by-product of the possibility that she might not be working with him after this project ended. And fallout from allowing Jerry to provoke her to behave unprofessionally toward his assistant.

Phil's dark eyes danced. "Suze is getting restless."

"Then let's get started," Felicia said, sweeping an arm toward the couch and chairs in front of her desk. "Grab a seat and I'll get Suze." She walked out into the reception area. Suze, dressed in red head to toe, including a flamboyant hat, sat in a chair, smoking a cigarette with a cell phone pressed to her ear and looking surprisingly happy. Either she had just received good news or she was talking to someone she liked . . . a lot. When she glanced up to see Felicia, her expression changed to guilt, reinforcing Felicia's thought that the woman was talking to her lover.

"I'll call you back," Suze said into the phone, then snapped it shut and stood. "Hello, Felicia."

"Hi, Suze." She spoke with as much warmth as she could inject into her voice. Suze Dannon was a very attractive woman, but she was so abrasive that Felicia couldn't imagine how she and easygoing Phil had gotten together in the first place, and more so, how another man would find her approachable enough to even suggest an affair. The woman emanated a chill lower than the temperature clinging to her voluminous coat. They hugged briefly and Felicia murmured, "I'm sorry to keep you waiting—it's been a busy morning."

Suze sniffed and took another drag from her cigarette.

Felicia cringed. "I'm sorry, Suze, but this office is a non-smoking environment."

Suze rolled her eyes, took another drag, and leaned over to stub out the cigarette in a potted plant. "Can't smoke anywhere in New York anymore. What about my rights? Where's the goddamned ACLU when *I* need them?"

Felicia tried to smile past her headache as she turned back toward her office. "How was your drive in?"

"Miserable," Suze said, picking up her red leather briefcase. "Traffic was a nightmare. I hope this won't take long, I need to be somewhere."

Felicia squashed her irritation at the woman's implication that her time was more important than anyone else's. "I hope we can reach a consensus quickly."

"Fat chance," Suze said.

When they reached Felicia's office, Suze marched in and settled herself on the couch, purposely ignoring Phil, who was sitting in one of the chairs. Felicia closed the door, marveling how two people who had once been so happy could scarcely stand to be in the same room.

"Is Jerry coming?" Phil asked.

"Something came up," Felicia improvised. "But he might call me if he has a chance, and perhaps we can conference him in on the speaker phone."

Suze made a scoffing noise. "I suddenly feel outnumbered."

"You aren't," Felicia assured her smoothly, claiming her own desk chair. "We're all on the same side here, we all want this book to be the best it can be."

"It's fine just the way it is," Suze said, her eyes growing hard.

"You always say that," Phil said patiently, "until you have time to think about my suggestions, and then you realize that the story can be improved."

"This time it can't," Suze snapped. "Besides, by the time I incorporate all the changes you suggested, I could write a new book!"

"It's not that many changes," Phil said, his tone more heated. "You're just being difficult, as usual."

Felicia leaned forward. "Why don't we—"

"Not that many changes?" Suze cut in, snorting. "Spoken like someone who doesn't know the first thing about writing! You have no respect for how hard it is to do what I do! You just sit back and criticize."

"—talk about this—"

"They're my ideas," Phil said, his face coloring. "*My* characters, *my* setting, *my* stories, *my* complexities— you're little more than a ghost writer!"

"—like reasonable, calm adults."

Suze leaped up from the couch. "Ghost writer? How dare you! You're afraid that when I get rid of you, I'll go on to be just as successful . . . maybe even more so."

"I've had a chance to review the changes in question—" Felicia said, rattling the papers in front of her.

Phil laughed harshly. "Suze, without me, you won't be able to get past the first page! You wouldn't know a plot if it were floating in your vodka!"

"—and I think we can reach a compromise—" Felicia continued.

Suze walked closer, her hat bobbing frantically. "You'll see—I'm going to make the name Suzanne Phillipo a worldwide commodity."

"—by all of us working together," Felicia finished cheerfully.

Phil stood and faced his angry wife. "No, you're not, because if you try to write another book under the name that I helped to build, I'll sue the pants off you." Then he gave her a disdainful look. "Assuming that you don't already have your pants off for someone else."

"*Okay,*" Felicia said, standing. Her uncharacteristic sternness got their attention, at least. In the ensuing silence, her phone beeped—Tamara. She sighed and punched a button. "Yes, Tamara?"

"Jerry Key is on the line."

"I'll take it," she said, then picked up the receiver so their conversation wouldn't be broadcast. "Jerry?"

"Felicia, how's it going?" His voice was the languid song of a man facedown on a massage table, being plied with oily female hands.

"Fine," she said tightly. "The Dannons are here."

His sexy laugh rumbled into her ear. "So if I tell you that I've been thinking about you all day, you can't chew me out, can you?"

Heat climbed her neck, and she tried to steer the conversation back to business. "We were expecting you, Jerry."

"Felicia, haven't you punished me enough? I'm dying to have you back. You know how good we are together."

She gripped the phone tighter. "So are you going to be able to join us later?"

"Maybe we can make a little trade. I'll cancel what I'm doing and drop by the meeting if you'll agree to have dinner with me this evening."

She set her jaw. "That's impossible."

"Nothing is impossible," he said, then sighed dramatically. "Felicia, I'm going to wear you down eventually. The sooner you give in, the sooner we can go back to the way things were."

Her gaze flew to the Dannons, who were staring at her expectantly. Her head pounded and her hairline felt damp. "Um, no," she said into the phone, her tone casual. "No, Jerry, that's okay. We'll get through this *alone*," she said pointedly. "Good-bye." She set down the receiver before he could respond and offered a shaky smile to the Dannons. "Now . . . where were we?"

Suze's eyes narrowed. "This asshole just threatened to sue me if I keep writing under the name that *I* invented!"

"It's a pseudonym we both came up with," Phil said, crossing his arms. "Using both of our names. And I helped to make it what it is today." He lifted his finger to Suze. "You can write whatever the hell you want to write, but you won't be doing it under the name Suzanne Phillipo."

Suze jerked her head toward Felicia. "He can't do that! Can he?"

Felicia sighed. "Phil has a point, Suze. The manuscripts were submitted with both of your names on the cover page, and you both signed the contracts."

The woman's face turned scarlet. "Of course you would take his side! You two are in cahoots!"

"No one is in cahoots," Felicia said calmly. "Please, Suze, let's sit down and talk about this like rational adults."

"Oh, and now you're saying I'm irrational?" Suze shouted, her eyes wild.

People outside Felicia's office turned to stare.

Phil touched Suze's arm. "That's not what Felicia said."

"Don't touch me!" she screamed, recoiling. She stumbled backward and snatched up her briefcase. "This meeting is over." She glared at Phil. "Just like this marriage!"

"And all of it your fault," Phil said calmly.

Suze stalked to the door, flung it open, walked through, and slammed it with enough force to shake the mini-blinds on the windows.

Felicia gave Phil an apologetic look. "I didn't handle that very well."

He made a rueful noise. "Give her a chance to cool off. You looked over the changes I suggested—what do you think?"

Felicia sighed. "It'll mean the difference between it being a good book and a great book. The basic idea of a serial killer murdering people through their e-book reading device is really intriguing, but the scenes seem forced."

He nodded. "That was Suze's idea, which is unusual. And it's a great commercial concept, but I can't get her to see that it isn't smooth." He emitted a long-suffering sigh. "For the record, I'm not going to sue her for the name, but if I have to, I'll use it to pressure her to make these changes. I want this last book to be our best."

"We're running out of time, Phil. If I don't get the manuscript into production in the next couple of weeks, the book will lose its fall spot."

"I understand," he said, nodding. "I'll call her later and try to smooth things over. I guess I'd better be going."

"Are you driving back today?"

"Actually, I'm staying in town for a couple of days, doing a little research."

She smiled. "For a book?"

He shrugged. "Something like that."

Felicia perked up, intrigued. "Promise you'll tell me about it."

Phil gave her shoulder a squeeze. "Someday, Felicia, I'll tell you all about it."

She watched him leave her office, his stride confident, his broad shoulders back, and thought with a start that perhaps Suze had underestimated Phil. Perhaps he was, at this very moment, working on a blockbuster. And heaven help her, she wouldn't want to miss the look on Suze's face if Phil struck gold on his own.

Her throbbing head necessitated slow movement back to her desk, where she downed another pill. Her mind slid back to the phone call from Jerry, and a slow burn started in her stomach. He was making it impossible to work with him. Not only did she need to set him straight but she also wanted him to know that she was on to him regarding the photo.

She shrugged into her coat and picked up her bag. When she walked out into the reception area, Tamara looked up from her desk. "Going out?"

Felicia nodded and gritted her teeth against the pain. "I need to see a chiropractor."

 Chapter 8

When Tallie returned to the office, she was still reeling from her hair-raising coffee date. She almost walked right past Jane Glass, who was standing in the reception area.

"Hi, Jane—er, Jané. This is a nice surprise."

Sans the beret, Jané's wiry hair was pulled back in a severe ponytail that left the spiky ends to fan around her head like a peacock tail. She was draped in yards of dark fabric, conjuring up images of séances and pots of boiling brew.

"Hi, Tallie." She smiled and held up a thick manila envelope. "I know I said I'd have this manuscript couriered over, but I was in the neighborhood and thought I'd drop in to see how things have changed around here." She scanned the dated décor and the dingy carpet, and her grimace said it all.

"Things haven't changed," they said in unison, then laughed.

"Come on in my office," Tallie invited, although Felicia's words about Jané playing her revolved through her head. Still, she owed her former colleague a certain amount of professional courtesy. "I have a few minutes to talk."

"Did you go somewhere fun for lunch?" Jané asked.

Tallie hung her coat behind the door, frowning at the large coffee stain. "Suspicious Grounds coffeehouse—and someone tried to rob the place while I was there."

"Are you serious?"

"Yeah—shots were fired, the whole bit."

Jané's black eyes widened. "Was anyone hurt?"

"No." Tallie shook her head. "Believe it or not, I was there with a cop, and he handled everything."

"Why were you there with a cop? Are you in trouble?"

Tallie laughed. "No. It was a blind date. Sort of." Pushing the episode from her mind, she sat down and invited Jané to do the same.

Jané nodded to Tallie's cluttered desk. "Slush pile reading?"

"A necessary evil," Tallie said, her mind momentarily flitting back to the partially-read-murdering-IRS-cost-accountant's manuscript. No murder yet, but either the man had led an extraordinary life or he'd dreamed up quite an imaginary existence while sitting behind a desk for forty years. Tallie sat back in her chair. "So tell me about this manuscript."

Jané slid the envelope across her desk. "It's a great story," she said, lapsing into sales mode. "This e-book is going to hit big, and I'd like to see Parkbench get in on the print rights."

Tallie lifted an eyebrow, removed the manuscript, and glanced at the cover sheet. "*Daymares* by J. P. Ames."

"An unknown," Jané admitted. "But not for long. It's a fantasy murder mystery, and it's great."

"So you said." Tallie tapped the manuscript. "Why are you shopping it instead of the agent?"

"A few agents have seen it, but no takers yet." She shrugged. "But we both know that good projects get overlooked all the time, especially if they can't be easily categorized."

"Okay, I'll take a look at it."

Jané glanced at Tallie's slush pile. "Can I get some priority?"

Tallie gave her a wry smile. "I'll get to it as soon as I can."

"Good enough," Jané said, standing. "Listen, Tallie . . . I've been having second thoughts about telling Felicia what Jerry Key said about her. Do you think I did the right thing?"

Tallie hesitated, studying Jané for signs of insincerity. The woman and Felicia had butted heads more than once when they had all interned together, with Jané's impulsiveness always being trumped by Felicia's level-headedness. But Jané's black eyes were unreadable, her full mouth set in a wince . . . or a half-smile?

A finger of unease tickled Tallie's spine, but she attributed the reaction to her recent brush with trouble. Shrugging lightly, she pushed to her feet. "Felicia can't defend herself if she doesn't know she's being maligned. Wouldn't you want to know if someone was spreading lies about you behind your back?"

Jané's demeanor changed almost instantly—for the worse. "Are you trying to tell me that someone is spreading lies about *me*?"

Tallie blinked. "No. It was hypothetical."

The woman recovered, then attempted a laugh. "Of course. Well, thanks for making me feel better about it."

With eyebrows raised, Tallie followed Jané to the door, suddenly eager for her to be gone; she felt almost disloyal to Felicia by simply talking to the woman.

"Call me when you've had a chance to read the manuscript."

"I will." Tallie watched Jané leave, wondering if the woman had any idea that some people thought she was . . . weird. Just the kind of person to edit the paranormal stories that were more popular among e-book readers. At least she'd found her niche. Tallie was about to close her office door when Kara Hatteras floated by, sporting a gloating smile.

"Tallie, everyone's gathered in the boardroom to see my spot on CNN. Chop, chop or you'll miss it."

She pranced on her way and Tallie murmured, "I'd like to chop, chop something of yours, Kara."

Her phone rang, and she gladly took the opportunity to answer it. The thought that Keith Wages was calling flitted through her head. She scoffed aloud, but she acknowledged a spike in her pulse. "Tallie Blankenship."

"Tallie . . . it's Ron."

A smile curved her mouth to hear her boss's voice. "Hi, Ron. How are you?"

"I'm okay," he said, his voice a little unsteady. "Are you okay?"

She laughed. "Sure, Ron—well, other than the fact that Kara is corralling us all to watch her CNN segment."

The line clicked.

"Ron?"

"—cell phone . . . dying . . . be careful . . . Gaylord's manuscript . . . fortune—"

She pushed the phone closer to her mouth. "Ron?

Ron, if you can hear me, don't worry about the manuscript. I'll take care of everything. Are you there?"

Static sounded, then dead air.

She frowned at the phone, then replaced the receiver.
He must be driving, perhaps on his way to his family in
Maine—or was it New Hampshire? She shook her head.
Poor Ron. Whatever the reason for his leave of absence,
he was still concerned about the company. His anxiety
was pushing hers higher, as if she wasn't already nervous about tomorrow's meeting with Gaylord Cooper
and Jerry Key. Especially now that she knew Jerry was
spreading gossip about her best friend.

When she slipped into the boardroom to join the
crowd gathered around the television mounted in the far
corner, the CNN segment was underway. Kara tore her
gaze away from her toothy self on the screen to glare in
Tallie's direction, presumably for being late. In the news
piece about the popularity of diet books, Kara gushed to
the reporter that when she had read the submission for
The Soup to Nuts Diet, she had been savvy enough to
recognize a best-selling book in the making. There was
little mention of the author or the medical merits of the
diet itself—just emphasis on the price point and the marketing push. Tallie took solace in the fact that everyone
standing in the room looked as uninterested as she felt.

At the end, Kara beamed at the halfhearted applause
and, in typical Kara style, wheeled in a sheet cake she
had ordered herself, featuring the cover of the book in
edible icing. Tallie felt a stab of remorse that she or
someone else hadn't thought to arrange refreshments—
the woman's lack of friends was really very sad. Tallie
suspected her pang of compassion was actually a mis-

fired signal from her brain meant to be a pang of hunger, considering the fact that she hadn't yet eaten lunch. Still, she hung back purposely to be the last served so she could work up some enthusiasm before she faced Kara, who was doling out wedges of yellow cake as if she had made it herself.

As if anyone in Manhattan actually baked. It was another thing she loved about the city: Domesticity was defined by how many times a week one watched *Trading Spaces*.

"Kara," she said when she stepped up to the table, "that was . . . great."

"Yeah," Kara said, cutting a wedge of cake with a fancy serrated knife. She dropped the piece upside down onto a Styrofoam saucer before handing it over. "Too bad Ron wasn't here to see it."

"Er, well . . . I'm sure he knows about it."

Kara looked past Tallie and seemed to hesitate until their last coworker left the room, then her attention snapped back. "I hear that Ron gave you Gaylord Cooper."

Tallie's mouth was full of dry cake. She chewed, then swallowed painfully. "I don't think 'gave' is the right word. I'm overseeing his manuscript until Ron returns."

"That assignment should've been mine."

Tallie blinked. "I don't know what you expect me to say, Kara. The decision was Ron's."

Kara rolled her eyes. "And we all know that he's been checked out lately."

Everyone had a theory about why Ron had taken time off, but Tallie refused to indulge in water cooler talk where her boss was concerned. Kara, however, who had contacts in the human resources department, was a more credible, albeit disliked, source. Tallie pretended to be absorbed in her next bite of cake. "Do you know why Ron took a leave of absence?"

The corners of Kara's mouth jumped. "I might."

Tallie waited for clarification, but Kara simply adopted a superior smile. "Let's just say that any decisions that Ron made before he left are subject to change."

Tallie's stomach contracted, the sickening sweetness of the cake only irritating it further. But she knew when it was time to speak up for herself. "Kara, I *will* be editing Gaylord Cooper's manuscript."

Kara stabbed the remaining chunk of cake with the elegant knife and twisted it, gouging a hole in the beautiful icing. "We'll see about that." Then Scary licked her fingers and stalked out of the room.

 Chapter 9

Wearing opaque sunglasses, Felicia settled into a comfortable chair with a bottle of Water Joe in a café across the street from the entrance to the Green Globe Spa. The Green Globe Spa was the choice of the rich and famous and the wannabes, like Jerry Key. One of his celebrity clients had gotten him into the invitation-only health club, and Jerry had managed to maintain his connections even after his celebrity client had dumped him for a more tony agent. She checked her watch. If memory served, Jerry normally scheduled a one-hour massage, so he should emerge, rejuvenated and horny, in about ten minutes. She leaned her head back and eased the muscles in her forehead to allow the painkiller to continue to diffuse the knot of pain behind her eyebrows.

Being in love with Jerry was killing her.

She sighed and considered phoning Tallie to see how her blind coffee date had gone. She should have called her last night and made her promise to wear something nice—knowing Tallie, she'd gone out of her way to look dowdy, to try to downplay her petite, natural beauty. It was as if she was challenging men to look past her contrived frumpiness to see the bright, savvy, career-minded woman that she was. Tallie denied her femininity and seemed irritated if the men she dated tapped into it. She was so afraid of turning into her mother that she over-compensated by cutting men out of her life the minute they got too close. Tallie was in denial about how lonely she was, which was why she buried herself in her work.

But, Felicia had to admit, being lonely was better than this emotional roller coaster she'd been riding for the past year. Her head knew that Jerry was a jerk, but her heart just couldn't seem to catch on. His escalating flir-tation was enough to make her crazy, but by sending the nude photo of her, he'd crossed the line.

The door to the spa opened and out strolled Jerry Key, blond, tall, and fashionably thin, a man bag over his shoulder for his necessities, like his camera cell phone with global positioning system or whatever techie op-tions were available. The man prided himself on owning the latest and greatest electronic equipment, from lap-tops to stereos. He had teased Felicia about her pen-chant for retro, from her vinyl collection and the old turntable she played them on to the big-button phone in her bedroom.

As always, her pulse increased at the sight of him, doubly so with the anticipation of confronting him. She stood and screwed the lid onto the bottle of caffeinated water. She was stowing the bottle in her purse when she realized that someone had joined Jerry on the street—a woman. Frozen, she watched as the two embraced, then shared a full-on kiss. Their meeting, it seemed, wasn't accidental. Felicia removed her sunglasses and bumped her nose against the window, flabbergasted. It couldn't be. But if the woman's long red coat wasn't enough to prove it was Suze Dannon pressed against him, the big red hat sealed the deal. And from their collective body language, it wasn't the first intimate kiss they'd shared.

Felicia covered her mouth with her hand, unable to believe her eyes. Hurt, anger, and, yes, jealousy squeezed her chest painfully. She wasn't foolish enough to think that Jerry hadn't taken lovers since their breakup, but seeing him with someone else . . . someone she knew . . . a client of his . . . an author of hers. Her mind raced. What should she do with this information—confront them, or keep quiet?

Jerry walked to the curb and hailed a cab, then helped Suze into the backseat. With one arm on the open door, Jerry stopped and scanned all around. For a split second, he seemed to look directly at her. Felicia jumped back from the window, her throat constricted. Then Jerry climbed in, and the cab pulled away. Felicia glared at the receding car; she had a feeling they weren't going back to Jerry's office to discuss strategy on the current book.

Feeling sick to her stomach, she dropped back into the seat she'd vacated, trying to get her mind around what she'd seen and the ramifications of the affair.

"Thanks, Jag. See you next time."

Felicia heard the words spoken behind her, and for a few seconds she couldn't figure out why something had clicked in her head.

Jag?

She turned to see a man at the counter. He was holding a package and was waving to someone who had just walked out the door. She lunged to her feet and ran to the door, opening it in time to see a tall, wiry man in a messenger uniform jump on a bike, bounce into the street, and pedal away.

"Wait!" she yelled. "Jag, wait!"

But her words were carried away by the bitter wind. Improvising, Felicia hailed a passing cab and swung into the backseat. "Follow that bike messenger!"

The cabbie turned around. "Is this a joke?"

She glared. "Am I laughing? Get going, and don't lose him!"

The taxi vaulted into traffic, and she stuck her head through the plexiglass sliding window between the seats to help keep the messenger in sight. "He turned right," she said, pointing. "There. There he is!"

The cabbie darted in and out of impossibly tight spots, causing her to dig her fingers into the seat. Then they were caught at an agonizing traffic light and she was sure they'd lost him.

"Sorry," the cabbie said with a shrug. "Do you want me to take you somewhere else?"

Fraught with disappointment, Felicia looked around to get her bearings, then she spotted a familiar bicycle chained to a sign about a half block away. "I'll get out here." She glanced at the meter, tossed the man enough for a good tip, and hopped out into the brittle air. Picking up her trailing scarf, she shouldered her bag and jogged down the sidewalk as fast as her high heels would allow. Her lungs hurt from the cold, and she turned an ankle dodging pedestrians, but she kept going. When she was a few yards away, "Jag" walked out, unchained his bike in a two-second sweep of his arm, and swung his long, Lycra-enclosed leg over the seat in preparation to take off again.

"Jag! Jag, wait!"

He turned his head and frowned past her.

Felicia waved her free arm. "Wait! I need to talk to you!"

He lifted his wraparound sports glasses and focused on her, his confusion and annoyance unmistakable. In another second, he'd be gone, and she was running out of breath.

"Jag . . . package . . . delivered . . . Omega . . . Publishing!"

At least she had his attention. She jogged up to his bike and gasped for breath. "I . . . need . . . to talk . . . to you . . . please." She removed her sunglasses and blinked up at him.

Beneath the rim of his helmet, his eyes narrowed, then he lifted his gloved hand. "Hey, I remember you—you're the editor, right?"

She nodded, her teeth chattering despite the warmth she'd generated beneath her coat from her impromptu sprint.

He gave her a sardonic look. "If memory serves, you weren't very talkative before—why the change of heart?"

Felicia's face was freezing, so a pained look wasn't a stretch. "I'm s-sorry if I was sh-short with you, I was having a b-bad day. The package you d-delivered to me—can you help me f-find out who sent it?"

"We require a return address."

"It was b-bogus."

He frowned. "Well, then sure, if you still have the bar code on the envelope."

She nodded eagerly. "I do. B-back at my office."

He removed his sunglasses, reached into the kidney-shaped bag hanging at his hip, and pulled out a slip of yellow paper. "Using a phony return address is serious business. Customer service will want to report—"

"No," she cut in, then hesitated before angling her

head. "I was hoping you could look into it f-for me. It's a . . . pr-private matter."

He squinted. "Look, lady, if someone is threatening you, then you need to call the police."

She lifted her chin and maintained level eye contact. He had hazel eyes, sparkling and clear. His face was chiseled, his cheeks and nose ruddy from windburn, his mouth shiny with some kind of balm that she suspected was necessary year round. She wet her own parched lips and submitted to another bout of chills. "Then you w-won't help me?"

He pursed his mouth and, after considering her up and down, sighed. "I can't make any promises, but I'll look into it if you get me the bar code number."

She smiled in between her chattering. "Th-thank you. How do I get in t-touch with you?"

He scratched his chin. "Got something to write with?"

She nodded and dug in her purse for a pen and paper, then wrote down the number he recited. "Is th-this your cell phone number?"

"It's my everything number," he said. "If I don't answer, leave a message and I'll be paged."

"Okay."

He shook his head, looking perplexed. "How did you find me?"

"I saw you at a café a few blocks back." She welcomed the warmth of a flush on her cheeks. "I had a cab follow you."

He laughed in earnest this time, a deep, hearty noise that sent a white cloud of breath into the air, then he nodded toward the street. "I have to get to my next stop."

She stepped back to give him plenty of room to maneuver the bike into the street between two parked cars. Then he looked over his shoulder. "What's your name again?"

"Felicia. Felicia Redmon."

"Nice name." Then before she could ask his, he was off, pumping his legs, bent low over the handlebars.

Struck with envy over his freedom, Felicia stood shivering until he disappeared into the traffic, then stepped to the curb and hailed a cab back to her office.

"Phil Dannon called," Tamara offered as she passed by.

Felicia walked into her office and closed the door behind her, then shut the window blinds. Poor Phil.

Poor Felicia. From the bottom of one of her desk drawers, she withdrew the envelope containing the photo, dismayed to find that the first half of the bar code had been torn off—purposely? It was a form of self-torture, but she removed the picture and stared at it, flooded anew with cold shame. She swallowed hard and returned the photo, then dialed the number the bike messenger had given her. After a few rings, it rolled to voice mail.

"Hey, this is Jack Galyon. Leave a message."

Jack Galyon. At the beep, she left her name and the partial number from the envelope, with instructions to call her direct number when he had information. What she would do with it was another matter.

She reburied the envelope in a drawer and downed another Imitrex. The only thing that could replace the image of the nude photo in her head was the image of Jerry and Suze locked in each other's arms and hurrying off together.

Her hatred for Jerry Key was now borderline pathological.

 Chapter 10

Tallie held her breath as she climbed the stairs to her apartment. The stench was getting worse—she hoped Mr. Emory tracked down the source soon. When she'd first moved in three years ago, a couple of rats had died in her bedroom wall. She'd heard their frantic scurrying, which had slowed painfully over time, until it had finally stopped all together. And then the smell had set in. . . . *Mercy.* Mr. Emory had told her that by the time he got a crew there to tear down the drywall, the dead critters would be dust. Instead, he'd given her a can of lemon air freshener and arranged to have twenty-five dollars taken off her rent that month.

Rats—dead *or* alive—were an aspect of city life that she could do without, and one she didn't dare share with her mother, or she'd never hear the end of it. She burst into her apartment and gasped for fresh air, getting a lungful of funky carpet and dirty laundry air instead.

She winced and decided on the spot that it was warm/early/safe enough for a run—anything to postpone dealing with the mess. The soonest the cleaning service could squeeze her in was Friday morning. Sometime between now and then she had to . . . straighten up.

She flipped through the mail, wryly noting the peach-colored pickup slip from the post office for a parcel from M. Blankenship—the promised early birthday gift from her mother. Something domestic, no doubt, destined to join other well-intentioned gifts from her mother stacked in the closet: the electrostatic duster with a 20-foot telescoping arm, the box of oxygenated cleanser, the miracle mop with a quick-change scrubbing head. Alas, a trip to the post office would have to wait until Saturday morning.

Tallie peeled off her gloves, and when she shoved them into her coat pockets, she found Keith Wages' ball cap. Turning it over in her hands, she worked her mouth back and forth, her chest filling with renewed wonder over her close brush with danger, and admiration over how he had sprung into action. She conceded disappointment that he hadn't called her at work sometime during the afternoon, if just to say that the incident was obviously a bad omen and they should simply leave well enough alone. It was for the best, she told herself—she couldn't picture herself dating a cop. She had nothing but the greatest admiration for men in uniform, but just a few minutes in Keith's macho company had left her feeling so . . . female.

With a frown, she dropped the soiled cap onto the coffee table. He probably hadn't even missed it . . . probably hadn't given her a second thought since he'd ridden off in that cruiser.

She shed her stained coat, then rooted around until she found her running shoes and enough clothing to keep her warm. Holding her breath against the odor in the hall, she walked out and locked all three dead bolts, then ran down the stairs. When she pushed open the door leading outside, darkness was pressing upon the city. She inhaled cold air and indulged in a good full-body shiver to warm herself, then jogged onto the sidewalk and set off.

The first half-mile was always the hardest for her. She wasn't a natural runner, not very efficient, and not very fast, but as exercise went, running was cheap and it went by faster than a video. Plus she always felt more connected to the city as her feet hit the concrete, brick, and tile of the eclectic sidewalks of Chelsea.

Tallie turned her head slightly to the right. Tonight, however, she wasn't alone. Behind her, loud, heavy footsteps sounded—running feet not shod in running gear. Her heartbeat picked up, reverberating in her ears. This was the same stretch where she'd been mugged last summer. There was no oncoming pedestrian traffic to lose herself in, and the warehouse storefronts were dark. A lone car coasted in the lane next to the sidewalk. Probably lost and looking for street signs, but a possible ally if need be. She patted her jacket pocket for the personal alarm she carried with her but winced when she remembered removing it when she'd tossed this jacket on top of the laundry pile last night. The irony was too much—her mother's warning that an untidy life was dangerous to one's health might just prove to be true.

"Hey!" a man's muffled voice sounded behind her. A ploy to get her to slow down—that scam had been circulated on the Internet. She picked up her pace, lengthening her stride and leaning forward. To her dismay, the footsteps behind her also increased in intensity. About fifteen yards back, she guessed, and closing. In her head she rehearsed the self-defense moves she'd learn at the YWCA: Scream *No!* then go for the soft tissue points— eyes, nose, neck, nuts. "Eyes, nose, neck, nuts," she murmured. "Eyes, nose, neck, nuts."

She reached the intersection, and the light was in her favor to turn right and cross. Bounding into the crosswalk, she heard the car rather than saw it and realized in a horrible split second that the cruising driver didn't see *her*. In a surreal, out-of-body experience, she had a vision of herself outlined by the car headlights blazing on high beam before she went flying backward. She landed on her back with a thud that jarred her teeth and stalled her lungs. Starbursts appeared behind her eyes, and pain ricocheted through her head.

Tallie opened her mouth and dragged air into her contracted lungs, wondering how badly her body was mangled. The ground beneath her moved, then moaned, and her muscles contracted in alarm. She flailed her arms, and when she met flesh, she realized that the ground moving beneath her was a person . . . or an angel. She rolled to her side and met cold, hard concrete, but she took that as a good sign because she was relatively sure the roads of heaven were not paved in concrete.

There was another alternative, however, considering the unkind thoughts she'd been having toward her mother.

A man's voice floated around her and she concentrated on the rhythm, the rise and fall of his urgent tone, until she zeroed in on what he was saying. "Tallie! Tallie, can you hear me? Open your eyes, Tallie. *Open* your eyes."

How could she ignore that nice voice? She opened her

eyes and blinked his face into view by the illumination of the streetlight. Familiar . . . yet elusive.

Mr. Familiar smiled, and her memory clicked—Keith Wages. His lips moved, but she didn't hear what he said. Her mind raced, clogged. "What . . . what are you doing here?"

"Saving your ass," he said wryly. "That car nearly ran you down. Are you okay?"

"I . . . think so."

"I'm going to check you for broken bones, okay?"

She nodded and lay still while he gingerly felt her arms and legs. Then he unzipped her jacket and ran his big hands over her collarbones, breastbone, and ribs. A clinical search, but her neglected erogenous zones didn't know the difference and leaped to attention. A crowd had gathered, and it occurred to her that this was as close to public sex as she might ever experience.

"Do you feel any pain in your back or neck?" he asked.

"No. I . . . just got the wind knocked out of me."

He looked relieved. "Can you sit up?"

She did, with his help, then stood and walked in a small circle. Everything seemed to be in working order, which brought her back to her original question. She looked him up and down—he wore an NYPD insulated jacket over jeans and boots. "What are you doing here?"

He lifted his hands. "I came by your place to say I was sorry about lunch. I saw you come out of your building, but by the time I parked, you were way ahead of me." He nodded toward his boots. "And these didn't help."

She frowned. "That was you behind me?"

"Didn't you hear me yelling?"

Despite the cold, a flush warmed her face. "I thought you were a mugger—that's why I ran out in front of the car. I wasn't paying attention."

He pulled his hand down his mouth, his eyes shadowed. "God, I'm sorry, Tallie. You could have been killed." Then he gestured toward the intersection. "But you had the right of way, which is probably why the driver didn't stop to see if you were okay." He grunted. "I missed the plate number."

"You yanked me to safety?" she asked, still trying to process what had happened.

One side of his mouth quirked. "All I could grab onto was your jacket hood."

She reached behind her neck and fingered the loose flap of fabric. Thank heaven her hoodless jacket had been even deeper in the dirty clothes pile. Then Tallie narrowed her eyes. "How did you know where I live?"

A sheepish smile crept up his face. "I *am* a police officer."

She crossed her arms. "So I gathered today, after the bullets started flying. Why didn't you say you were a cop?"

He shrugged. "You didn't ask."

"It's not as if we had a long conversation before the takedown."

"That's why I came by tonight," he said. "To see if you wanted to have a long conversation over a bite to eat." Then he made a rueful noise. "But I think we'd better get you back home. Do you feel like walking? I can get my car."

"No," she said quickly, irritated by his hovering. "I can walk." To demonstrate, she wheeled and set off toward her apartment building, although the first few steps were a bit unsteady. He caught up with her and seemed poised to catch her if she swooned. Tallie inched away, working up a slow fume over the fact that he needn't feel like her personal rescuer since he'd caused the incident himself. In truth, he had saved her from *him*.

"Nothing hurts?" he asked, his breath frosty white in the air.

"Only my shoulder," she said wryly. "From being shoved to the floor today at the coffeehouse."

"Sorry about that. I didn't realize how small you were under all those clothes." He winked. "You're not going to sue me, are you?"

She wasn't sure which comment offended her most. Tallie frowned harder. "What happened today, exactly?"

"I noticed the guy come in after you, and . . . I don't know—there was something about his body language that seemed off. He hung back and he seemed twitchy. I saw him pull a gun and when it swung in our direction, I reacted." He touched her arm. "Did I hurt you?"

She rolled her tender shoulder, then shook her head, feeling contrite. "I'm grateful to you . . . for saving my life." She swallowed. "Twice. In one day."

He scoffed. "I was just in the right place at the right time."

Coincidence, or fate? "By the way . . . I picked up your hat."

He grinned. "You did? Thanks. That's my favorite hat."

She dismissed his gratitude with a wave, lest he think she had put a lot of thought into the act. "Was the guy trying to rob the coffeehouse?"

"So it seems," he said. "Did you recognize him?"

Tallie turned her head to stare at him in the near-darkness. "No—why would you think that?"

"His address is in this zip code. I thought you might have seen him around."

"Not that I remember. What's his name?"

"Rick Shavel, lots of priors."

She shook her head. "The name doesn't mean anything to me."

They walked for a few minutes in silence, then he gestured to the shabby buildings they were passing. "So this is your neighborhood?"

She gave a little laugh. "It looks better in the daylight, although not much. But my apartment is decent-sized for the money. Where do you live?"

"Brooklyn."

Domestic. Tallie was grateful for the darkness that hid her inadvertent wince. "In an apartment?"

"No, I have a house."

Deeper wince. The suburbs. Yards, kids, dogs. "That's nice," she lied.

"I like it," he said easily.

But she could feel herself retreat from the man's easy voice, his easy good looks, his easy knack for being in the right place at the right time. It would be too *easy* to fall for a guy like Keith Wages and get sucked into a life that she knew she would eventually hate. She might be putting the cart before the horse—after all, he had shown no romantic interest in her as of yet—but why drive down a dead-end road? Why put on her blinker? Why even slow down?

"Hey, have a little mercy," he said with a laugh as he walked faster to keep up with her. "These boots aren't broken in."

"I'm cold," she said, which was not a lie. "Besides, that's my place up ahead."

"I'll walk you up," he offered.

"You don't have to," she said, walking faster.

"I'll get my hat and be on my way," he said pleasantly, and she couldn't think of an argument against that before they reached her building. He held open the door, and she decided to risk the rickety elevator to spare him the stairs. On the ride up, she alternately worried about the disarray of her apartment and told herself she didn't want to make a good impression on this man. When they stepped off the elevator, the mysterious stench hit them full force.

"Sorry," she said, covering her nose with her sleeve. "Someone has a dead rat."

Keith cringed. "That must be one big rat. Has anyone reported it?"

Tallie nodded as she unlocked the dead bolts on her door. "The super was here Monday night looking for the source, but I don't think he found anything."

When she swung open the door, she experienced a momentary spasm of embarrassment—the apartment, when seen through fresh eyes, was even worse than she realized. "Sorry for the mess," she said. "I'm doing some spring cleaning and everything is . . . out."

He nodded and glanced around, seemingly amused. He stepped into the tiny living room and leaned over to get his hat from the coffee table. "Thanks."

"No problem," she said, tingling with awareness of how dreadful she must look in her disheveled running clothes, soiled shoes, no makeup, and a knit cap. She stood with her arms crossed, caught between rudeness and her lack of desire to entertain Keith Wages in her messy living room. "I would offer you something to drink," she said, gesturing vaguely toward the kitchen area, "but I haven't been to the grocery . . . lately."

"Thanks anyway," he said with a laugh that made his dark eyes dance, and she felt like an idiot all over again. He was waiting for an invitation to sit, but she was loath to offer one, in a sudden panic about how quickly word would get back to her mother that she was the world's worst housekeeper. "I was going to wash your hat," she mumbled in a desperate attempt to redeem herself.

Keith laughed again. "That's okay." He folded the hat in his hands and nodded toward the stack of manuscripts on the coffee table. "I see you bring your work home."

She nodded warily, feeling a tug toward him. "I have so much reading to do, I can't possibly get it done during the day." Tallie hesitated, then unzipped her jacket. Her running clothes were like a second skin, but the man had already copped a feel, so what did it matter?

"I'll bet you hear from all kinds of crazies, don't you?"

She smiled. "You sound like my mother. Honestly, most submissions are just plain bad. I'm reading one now from a former IRS tax accountant who swears he killed a man and got away with it."

Keith's eyebrows went up. "Did you report it to the police?"

Tallie blinked. "Well . . . no."

"Why not?"

"Because he's probably making it up."

Keith pursed his mouth, then nodded agreeably and wandered over to her bookcase—a paint-chipped, rickety affair that listed to one side so badly, it appeared to defy gravity. "You read Gaylord Cooper?" he asked.

Astonished, she walked closer. "Actually, I'm his editor."

His eyes widened. "No kidding?"

A blush warmed her cheeks, and she felt compelled to

add, "I will be from now on. Are you familiar with his work?"

He nodded and pulled out one of Cooper's volumes. "I've read them all, although I think *Troubled Water* is his best work."

Tallie was impressed. "*Troubled Water* is a good one, but *Blood Trouble* was my favorite."

Another nod. "Does he have anything new coming out soon?"

She smiled, ridiculously pleased that he was interested in a topic on which she was knowledgeable. "As a matter of fact, he's delivering a new manuscript tomorrow."

"Really? What's it about?"

"I don't know, I haven't read it. Gaylord is . . . protective of his work until he turns it in."

He returned the novel to the bookshelf. "I've heard that he's a bit of a nut job."

She gave a little shrug. "The man has some hang-ups, but I suppose most creative geniuses do."

Keith patted the bookshelf, and it trembled violently. He leaned down and peered into the corners, where bowed nails spanned the separated joints. "I can try to repair this for you."

Tallie flinched. The man was five minutes into her private space and he was trying to fix things? "No, thanks," she said, a bit more sternly than she intended, although she didn't regret her tone. Who did he think he was?

He turned his head and caught her pointed gaze, then straightened. "Right. Well, I guess I'd better be going." He walked toward the door. "I just want to apologize again, Tallie, for the way things turned out today." He made a rueful face. "And I didn't mean to frighten you this evening, either."

"It's okay," she said, suddenly eager for him to leave. She strode to the door and opened it, conjuring up a congenial smile.

At the door, he turned, fingering his hat. "How about that long conversation over dinner sometime?"

Tallie studied Keith's open, masculine face and acknowledged a strong physical attraction to the man. Those broad shoulders were tempting as hell. But he was just the kind of guy her mother would want her to date—clean cut, gainfully employed, capable . . . macho. His association with her family would make things even more sticky when the relationship bombed because he didn't understand Tallie's long hours at work or her tolerance for dust bunnies . . . okay—dust *dragons*. She could see it now, her mother and Keith pooling forces to transform her into a minivan mom.

"Tallie?"

She blinked, then wet her lips. "The thing is, Keith . . . I don't think this is such a good idea."

His eyes clouded momentarily, but then he straightened. "Sure, I understand. It was nice meeting you. Take care."

Tallie nodded and closed the door behind him, squashing the flicker of regret in her heart, telling herself that nipping the attraction in the bud was the mature thing to do. Men like Keith Wages exuded some kind of pheromone that drove a woman to do crazy things, like . . . clean their nest.

She frowned at the mess around her and lifted her chin belligerently. She'd have time to straighten up Friday morning before the cleaners came. Another day or so of dirty dishes wasn't going to kill anyone.

 Chapter 11

"Good evening, Ms. Redmon," the doorman said to Felicia as she entered her building.

"Good evening, Del," she said, smiling at the portly man who had been the daily mainstay of her life for the past fifteen years.

"It's cold out there," he said cheerfully.

"Good for the skin," she said just as cheerfully, but her smile disappeared as soon as the elevator door closed and she was alone. She stabbed the button for the twelfth floor and leaned against the wall, feeling thoroughly miserable. She'd replayed the image of Jerry and Suze together in her head until she'd worked up a serious migraine. She still didn't know what she was going to do—confront Jerry? Suze? Tell Phil?

She was so glad she hadn't caved to Jerry's dinner invitation. She needed time to think.

With her chest and head aching, she unlocked her door and hung her keys on a hook, then swung to face her immaculate living room. Furnished with retro reproductions, from a boxy gray couch to a russet area rug and an orange leather ottoman, the room never failed to comfort her with its clean lines and suggestion of a simpler era. So unlike the fussiness she'd grown up with. Her mother, Julia Redmon-Clark-Gregg, had spent her exorbitant salary on French baroque décor. Heavy, ornate furniture, dark, depressing colors, velvet and brocade upholstery, fringe and swag embellishments, candles ad nauseum.

When Felicia had moved here from her mother's, she'd lived with a bed and one chair for nearly a year, reveling in the expansive room to breathe. Slowly she had filled it with simple pieces, but there was still more space that was empty than occupied . . . and she liked it that way.

She walked to her coat closet to deposit her outer wear, and her gaze went to the black-and-gray tweed scarf that Jerry had left at her place last year when their affair had been flaming hot. With a sigh, she reached out to touch the scarf, remembering how the soft wool would feel against her cheek when Jerry would walk through the door and pull her into his embrace. He would rock her back and forth and murmur against her hair that she was amazing and that he was a lucky, lucky man. They would undress on the way to the bed . . . if they made it that far.

Her eyes filled with sudden tears, because she had been so utterly fooled by him, by his loving words. Even now, she could close her eyes and conjure up the bliss of lying in his arms, inhaling the scent of his skin. Her chest swelled. On the heels of reminiscing always came the wave of anger at Jerry for his failing to realize what a good life they might have had together. She still believed that deep down, Jerry did love her but was afraid of the intensity of his feelings.

Felicia removed the oversized scarf from the closet and wrapped it loosely around her neck and shoulders, imagining that the warmth and weight were Jerry's embrace. She picked up the end of the scarf and breathed in the faint scent of his stock cologne, then walked to the bathroom and opened her medicine cabinet. A tiny white opaque sample bottle of Jerry's cologne remained where he'd left it on the top shelf. She caught a whiff of the heady musk every morning when she removed her toothbrush.

Curling her fingers around the bottle, she had a flashback of Jerry standing in her bathroom that last morning, boxers riding low on his lean hips, his hair still wet from the shower. He had sprayed the cologne on his neck with two neat pumps, then he'd winked at her where she'd lain on the bed watching him. In hindsight, he must have, at that very moment, been contemplating how he could end their relationship, and she'd been wondrously oblivious.

Felicia fingered the small bottle, noticing the glass had yellowed slightly. On impulse, she uncapped the top and sprayed two quick pumps onto the scarf around her neck. Actually, it was more like one and a half pumps, since the second time she depressed the button, the liquid spit and fizzled, diluted with air. With a bittersweet pang, she recapped the bottle and dropped it into the garbage can. The masculine scent permeated her nostrils as she caressed the scarf. She breathed deeply, like an addict, to pull the last vestiges of him into her lungs, then bit into her lip to stem the wretched tears that threatened to surface. *Jerry . . . why?*

The phone rang, startling in its shrillness, violating the quiet. She swallowed the lump at the back of her throat and cleared her voice of emotion before answering the unit on her nightstand.

"Hello?"

"Hello, dear. It's Mother."

Her heart squeezed with sudden pleasure. "How are you, Mother?"

"I'm fabulous," her mother said in her meowing Lauren Bacall voice. "I just got in from San Diego, and I realized that I haven't talked to you in ages."

Since the week before Christmas, but who was counting? "Maybe we could meet for dinner?" Felicia hated the pleading note in her own voice . . . and the hesitation at the other end of the line.

"Hm, well I was supposed to meet a friend, but I could reschedule."

"I wouldn't want you to break your plans," Felicia said hurriedly.

"No, that's okay." Her mother laughed lightly. "My daughter should take priority."

Felicia let the "should" part slide. "Do you want to get back to me?"

A rueful noise sounded over the line. "No, I'll meet you at eight, say—Braddock's?"

The trendy eatery wasn't exactly the place to indulge in cozy mother-daughter talk, but Felicia wasn't going to be choosy. "I'll see you at eight."

Her mother hung up without any niceties, but Felicia was accustomed to Julia's abrupt manner. She was simply happy at the thought of having her mother to herself and a few hours' reprieve from the trouble at hand.

Considerably cheered, Felicia unwound Jerry's scarf and placed it in the drawer in her nightstand. In deference to the falling temperatures, she changed to brown slacks and a warm pink sweater set. She smoothed her hair back with a wide headband and donned her grandmother's pearls. Given her mother's proclivity for the appearance of a woman's hands, Felicia freshened up her manicure with a slick of clear topcoat and smoothed cream onto her cuticles. She opted for a tan all-weather coat with tailored lines that smacked of Jacki-O, then pulled on brown leather gloves. As she descended in the elevator, Felicia realized that her heart was beating fast.

What did it say when a woman was nervous about having dinner with her own mother?

On the cab ride to Braddock's she compared what Tallie and her mother would talk about over dinner—Tallie's life—with what she and her own mother would talk about: Julia's job. Felicia's entire childhood had revolved around her mother's demanding legal position. At one point she had thought her mother actually had a second home that she went to when she left with a suitcase, and she'd once asked her mother if she could go with her to the "airport house."

As an adult she understood her mother's desire to have a career, and her childhood wouldn't have been so lonely if her father had been home to pick up the slack, but he had traveled more than her mother, gone for weeks at a time. When Felicia was nine, he had called from Germany and informed her mother that he wouldn't be coming home, or back to the States, even. He had met a woman, and they were going to have a baby. He had a new life, a new family. So long.

At first he had sent her cards and called sporadically, but over time the communication had stopped altogether. She couldn't even remember what he looked like. By now he was surely gray-headed, or maybe bald-

ing. And her half sister would be twenty-five years old. It
was a topic her mother refused to talk about; what's
more she would probably be angry if she knew how often Felicia thought about it.

"Ma'am?"

With a start, Felicia realized the cab had stopped in
front of Braddock's. She paid the fare and stepped out
into the cold, dodging a frozen puddle. Shivering, she
waited until a large party, dressed to the nines and obviously headed to a show, eked out of the restaurant entrance, then she ducked inside. Her mother hadn't
arrived, so she took a seat at the bar and ordered a glass
of wine. The bartender flirted with her, but she gave him
the brush-off, wondering idly if she'd ever meet another
man who would stir her emotions as much as Jerry Key
did. Disgusted that he was still dominating her thoughts,
she polished off the glass of wine and ordered a second.
Unbidden, Jack Galyon's hazel eyes flashed in her mind,
along with his voice. *"Nice name."*

She wondered if he'd been able to track down the
source of that package. She pulled out her cell phone to
see if she'd missed a call, then frowned at the empty
screen—the battery was dead. Felicia glanced at her
watch, slightly irritated that her mother was running late.

Forty-five minutes later, her irritation had shifted to
concern, so she asked the bartender for a phone. He
handed her a cordless unit, and she dialed her mother's
cell phone number, her heart thumping. Her mother was
rarely punctual, but she usually called ahead to say she
was going to be late. When Felicia received no answer
on the cell phone, she dialed her mother's home number.
On the third ring, her mother's sleepy voice came on the
line. "Hello?"

"Mother, are you okay?"

"Hm?" Her mother yawned.

Felicia's stomach fluttered with unease. "I thought we were having dinner. Are you sick?"

"Oh, shit," her mother murmured, then a man's voice sounded in the background. Her mother covered the mouthpiece, then came back on, stammering. "I'm sorry, dear, I lost track of time. Can we reschedule?"

Felicia's heart twisted. Her mother's "friend" must have come over after all. She tried not to imagine the state of undress on the other end of the phone as she adopted a casual tone. "Sure, just let me know."

"I will, dear."

Felicia set down the phone and tossed cash on the bar to cover her drinks, then shrugged into her coat. It wasn't the first time her mother had stood her up. The last time had been mere weeks ago, Christmas Eve—Felicia had spent the evening with her mother's maid before dismissing the woman early so she could go home and be with her own family. She'd left her mother's gift—a velvet quilt she had sewn herself—on the dining room table, and she'd yet to receive a thank you . . . or any acknowledgement at all, for that matter.

She hailed a cab and slumped in the backseat, huddled inside her coat. A good cry battled with a migraine for the right to claim her, and she prepared to yield herself to both. She shouldn't have had that second glass of wine. The only thought that cheered her was that she would be able to use her new rice pot and blanching basket to prepare a healthful dinner for one.

After paying the cabbie, she dragged herself out of the taxi, and for the first time that she could remember, the clean, stately front of her building did not look comforting, but instead seemed sterile and . . . lonely. But when she walked into the lobby, Del stood behind his desk, ready with a smile. "That was a quick dinner."

"Yes," she agreed with a little smile.

"You had a visitor."

She frowned. "A visitor?"

"A bike messenger, said his name was Gig, or something like that."

"Jag?"

"Yeah, that was it. He left something for you." He reached beneath the desk, withdrew a padded envelope, and extended it to her.

Felicia hesitated, wondering how Jack Galyon had found out where she lived.

"I hope that was okay, Ms. Redmon. The gentleman said he was an acquaintance of yours."

On the other hand, considering his job, the man probably had access to every address in Manhattan. "No, Del, it's fine." She took the envelope and gave him a reassuring smile. "Thanks." She boarded the elevator, pushed the button, and turned the envelope over in her hands. He had written her name in precise, block letters, all capitals. A man accustomed to filling out forms. For some reason, his handwriting struck her as . . . durable.

She slid her finger under the flap, tore against the glue, and peered inside. A book? She pulled out the worn volume and ran her fingers over the cover. *The Immortal Class* by Travis Culley. A memory surfaced—the book Jag had asked her about the day he'd been in her office. The first page was bookmarked with a slip of blue paper on which he'd written in stalwart script:

*No bookshelf is complete without this title. Am
closing in on the information you asked for. Will be
in touch. J.*

The elevator door opened and Felicia alighted, studying the book and working her mouth from side to side. If
she was going to eat alone, she might as well read. And
maybe the book would give her some insight into why a
full-grown man would want to ride a bicycle for a living.

 Chapter 12

Tallie's phone was ringing when she walked into her office Thursday morning. She picked it up, already feeling behind. "Tallie Blankenship."

"Where were you last night?" Felicia asked. "I called."

Shrugging out of her coat while juggling the phone, Tallie gave a dry laugh. "I went for a run, long story. Besides, I called back—where were *you*?"

Felicia sighed. "I went to meet my mother for dinner."

"How was it?" Tallie asked cautiously.

"She didn't show."

Tallie winced. "I'm sorry."

"Yeah, well, enough about me. I was calling to find out about your blind date yesterday."

"Hm, well, let's see, I was shot at and I have a huge honking coffee stain on my good coat."

"What in the world happened?"

"The place we went to was robbed."

"While you were there?"

"Yeah, but get this—the guy I met was a cop."

"That was convenient. Did he save the day?"

"Pretty much."

"That's exciting."

"Right. Then he decided to stop by last night to apologize for lunch, and he caught me leaving for a run. I thought he was a mugger chasing me so I ran out in front of a car, and he saved me from that, too."

"Are you making this up?"

"No."

"Is he cute?"

"Yes."

"Did he spend the night?"

"No."

"But you're going to see him again?"

"No."

"Why not?"

Tallie sighed. "Trust me, it just wouldn't work. I didn't want to start something, you know? And it kind of creeps me out to think that our mothers set us up to have sex."

"They didn't set you up to have sex."

"Sure they did—they set up their single children, hoping that things would go well, and generally when things go well, single people have sex."

"I'm sure your mother didn't think that far ahead," Felicia offered. "Mine doesn't seem to, but let's change the subject from my mother to something even worse— Jerry Key."

"What now?" Tallie asked, gripping the phone tighter.

"He's sleeping with one of his clients who just happens to be one of my authors—one of my *married* authors."

Tallie gasped. "That's appalling. I mean, I know that kind of thing happens, but what a mess. How did you find out about it?"

"I saw them."

"You were spying on Jerry?"

"No, he stood me up for a meeting, and I had a hunch where he'd be. When I went to confront him, I saw them together."

"Did he see you?"

"No."

"What are you going to do about it?"

"I haven't decided," Felicia murmured.

Tallie's chest blipped with panic over the dark tone in her friend's voice. The man was a jerk, but if her best friend threatened to reveal his uglies, he might hold it against *Tallie*, and she needed his cooperation to smooth the way with Gaylord Cooper. "I'm meeting with Jerry this morning," she said carefully.

"Well," Felicia said lightly, "don't let him bully you. Remember, you have Ron behind you, and even Jerry doesn't mess with Ron."

"Ron called me yesterday," Tallie said, glad to change the subject.

"How is he?"

"Worried about things at the office. But I didn't get to talk to him for long—we were cut off."

"He'll be back soon enough. Whatever the reason he's gone, this could be a boon to your career."

"Assuming things go well today."

"Will you have time to meet for a drink after work? We'll celebrate."

"Sounds good," Tallie said, sensing that Felicia didn't want to spend another evening alone. "I'll tell you all about this funky manuscript that Jane—I mean *Jané*—brought to me yesterday."

"Nice try—I want to hear all about your supercop."

"I'm hanging up," Tallie said, then set down the receiver. But she stared at the phone for long seconds, worried for her friend, whose life seemed strangely entwined with Jerry Key's a full year after their breakup. And judging by Felicia's brooding moods and increasing migraines, entwined in an unhealthy way.

A rap sounded at her door and she turned to see Norah, still wearing her coat and gloves, her eyes rounded. "Gaylord Cooper is here."

Tallie's heartbeat spiked. "Already? He's not supposed to be here until eleven."

Norah glanced over her shoulder, then put one hand beside her mouth and whispered, "He said he came early because his enemies wouldn't be expecting it."

"Ah, of course. I'll be right there." Tallie hung up her coat, stifling a yawn. She'd spent most of the evening finishing the IRS accountant's manuscript. (As it turned out, the man had killed someone "officially" through paperwork—clever.) And skimming the manuscript that Jané had given her. (Not bad, though not as fabulous as the woman had let on.) Then in preparation for today's meeting, she had surfed the Internet, reading anything she could find on the fifty-something-year-old Gaylord Cooper . . . little of it comforting.

She smoothed her hand over her jacket, grateful to have found one good suit in the back of her closet covered with dry cleaner's plastic. It was a warm-weather suit, but the dark green set off her eyes and gave her a reason to wear her emerald stud earrings. She looked better than usual.

Pasting on a brave smile, Tallie walked out into the reception area, where Gaylord Cooper stood holding a black briefcase and wearing a long black trench coat, fedora, and sunglasses straight out of the forties. Norah and passersby stared outright, but Tallie tried not to react to his outlandish getup. "Hello, Mr. Cooper. My name is Tallie Blankenship. I've worked for Parkbench for nine years, and I'm a big fan of your work." She extended her hand.

Gaylord stared at her, which was unnerving, since she couldn't see his eyes. "I don't shake hands, Ms. Blankenship. Germs can be deadly."

He spoke with a slight British accent, although according to his bio, he had been born and raised in Myron, Minnesota. Tallie dropped her hand and nodded curtly. "I understand, Mr. Cooper. Would you like something to drink—coffee perhaps?"

"I brought my own distilled bottled water," he said. "Where is Ron?"

She chose her words carefully. "I was under the impression that Ron had spoken to you about his temporary leave of absence."

"He left word through my agent that you, Ms. Blankenship, would be editing this manuscript, but that's simply unacceptable." He whipped off his glasses dramatically, and his bushy eyebrows came together over pale blue eyes. "How do I know that you can be trusted?"

Tallie blinked, then spoke in her most calming voice. "Mr. Cooper, why don't you come into my office and we'll discuss your concerns."

He pursed his mouth, and for a moment Tallie had a terrible vision of standing before publisher Saundra Pellum and explaining how she had single-handedly lost the company's biggest star.

Tallie made a rueful noise. "That is, if you'll give me a moment—I haven't had a chance yet to turn on the air filter in my office."

His expression turned to curiosity. "Is it an ionizer?"

She had no idea. The contraption was something her mother had sent her to sterilize evil city air. She'd only turned it on once, and the noise had nearly driven her mad. "Ionizer? Of course."

A glimmer of admiration flitted through the man's eyes. "Perhaps, Ms. Blankenship, we can discuss this matter after all."

She smiled. "Right this way, sir."

Tallie hurried into her office and scooped up the stack of papers sitting on top of the squatty air filter, searching frantically for the On button. Her fingers found a red toggle switch, and when she hit it, thankfully the machine whirred to life. She was glad she had tackled the slush pile this week; she had returned a mountain of manuscripts to the mail room since Monday, giving her office the appearance of being relatively neat.

"May I take your coat, Mr. Coop—?"

"Shhhh," he cut in, finger to lips. He closed the door, then crossed to her desk and set his black briefcase on the corner. After adjusting the combination with mani-cured hands, he flicked open the briefcase and withdrew a device that resembled a handheld piano tuner. Tallie watched in silence as he walked the perimeter of the room, sweeping the gadget over walls, outlets, vents, and furniture.

"It's clean," he barked finally, returning the tool to his briefcase.

Tallie squinted. "I'm sorry—what were you looking for?"

"Listening devices," he said curtly. "They're every-where, you know."

Tallie glanced up to the far corners of her office, then

back. "I can assure you, Mr. Cooper, nothing that goes on in this office would be interesting to eavesdroppers."

"I wouldn't be so sure," he said, unbuttoning his coat. "We're going to be discussing my manuscript, aren't we?"

"Oh . . . right." She reminded herself that they were in his fantasy world of conspiracy theories and espionage.

He removed his coat, revealing a pin-striped double-breasted suit, a white shirt with enough starch to make her mother smile, and a red ascot. He folded his coat carefully over the back of one of her mismatched visitor chairs before perching himself on the edge of the other. From his pocket, he removed a leather-bound notebook and clicked a pen into readiness.

"Now then, Ms. Blankenship, I'll need for you to answer a few questions."

Tallie lifted her eyebrows, a bit distracted by the fedora he still wore. "Questions?"

"Yes. Does anyone in your family work for the federal government?"

"Um, no."

"Are you of Russian or German descent?"

"No."

"Are you married?"

"No."

That rated a quick glance up. "Are you gay or simply picky?"

Tallie straightened. "Mr. Cooper, I don't think—"

"Have you ever been arrested?"

"Er, no."

"If you were a tree, what kind of tree would you be?" She squinted.

His mouth twitched. "That's a joke, Ms. Blankenship."

"Oh." Tallie managed a weak smile.

He snapped his notebook shut. "Ms. Blankenship, I'm not convinced that you're up to the task of taking on my manuscript."

Her cheeks warmed, and her mind raced for a noninflammatory response. "I respectfully disagree, Mr. Cooper. I've read all your books, and frankly, I'm good at my job."

"You've read all of my books?"

"That's right."

He narrowed his eyes. "What kind of car does my main character drive?"

"Griff drives a 1977 Chevy Nova, metallic green."

"What's his mother's name?"

"Gwendolyn."

"How many times has he been married?"

"Twice. Once before the series started to a woman named Alice. She died in a car accident—you showed that in a flashback in *Trouble Is*. Then he married Fiona in *Toil and Trouble*, but she left him because of his drinking."

He nodded, seemingly impressed. "Okay, so you know the books. But look what this job did to Ron."

She frowned. "What do you mean?"

The man scoffed. "Come on, you don't really think he took off for personal reasons, do you? It's obvious—Ron is afraid for his life."

Tallie shifted forward in her chair. "Afraid for his life?"

He nodded, his eyes huge and wild. A knock on the door circumvented any explanation he might have hatched in his confused mind, and frankly, Tallie was happy for the interruption. The door opened a few inches and Norah poked her head inside, her cheeks high with color.

"Jerry Key is here—" She jerked and emitted a little squeal, then Jerry appeared behind her and pushed open the door. "Thank you, Norah."

He walked in, his grin magnanimous. "Good morning, all. Gaylord, you're looking dapper as ever." It was clear Jerry knew his client, since he didn't extend his hand for a shake when Gaylord stood.

Still, Gaylord seemed agitated. "How did you know I was here?"

"Your secretary called my secretary."

Gaylord pulled his hand over his mouth. "I *told* her not to use the phone to report my travel patterns. There's no telling who followed me here!"

"Relax, Gaylord," Jerry soothed. "I didn't see anyone suspicious when I arrived."

Gaylord seemed somewhat relieved, and he pulled on his lapels as he reclaimed his seat. "Well, then. Ms. Blankenship and I were just getting to know each other."

Jerry turned his handsome face toward Tallie, and for a few seconds, she was mesmerized. The man was glorious, there was no doubt. Blond, with chiseled nose and chin, dressed in a gray cashmere coat with a pea green scarf around his neck, he might have walked off the front of any men's magazine. He grinned at her and stepped forward, removing his glove before extending his hand. "Ms. Blankenship, we meet at last."

"You two don't know each other?" Gaylord asked, his face wreathed with fresh concern over the revelation.

"Only by association, but I've heard good things about you," Jerry said, squeezing her hand and holding her gaze. "We have a mutual friend, and now I know why she kept you hidden away."

Feeling herself falling under the man's spell, Tallie replayed the conversation she'd had with Felicia only moments earlier and withdrew her hand. "So glad you could make it, Mr. Key."

"Call me Jerry," he said, unbuttoning his coat with long fingers. Underneath he wore a luscious navy suit that spanned his broad shoulders impressively over a deep cream-colored dress shirt and a tie that perfectly matched his wool scarf. The heavy musk of his cologne wafted to her nostrils. Intoxicating.

She gestured to the last empty chair. "Won't you have a seat?"

Jerry looked at Gaylord. "Did you sweep the place?"

"Yes, it's clean."

"Good." Jerry sat down, then rubbed his hands together. "Okay, let's have a look at the manuscript, Gaylord."

Gaylord paused for maximum effect, then reached into the briefcase to withdraw a thick manila envelope.

Tallie and Jerry reached for it at the same time, and their hands brushed. They both laughed awkwardly, and Tallie sat back. "Go ahead . . . Jerry."

"Only because I'm so eager to see it," Jerry said and opened the envelope. The manuscript looked to be a full ream of sparkling white paper, held together with a single red rubber band. Jerry read the cover page. "*Whole Lotta Trouble*." He looked up. "What's it about?"

A triumphant smile spread over Gaylord's face. "The CIA frames Griff for murdering Fiona."

"Fiona is killed?" Tallie asked with a squeak. "I thought she and Griff would get back together some day." When the men looked at her, she blushed. "I mean, I hoped they . . . would."

"That is out of the question," Gaylord announced crisply, then shifted in his chair. "There are two typographical errors—a misspelling on page one hundred twenty, and a dropped comma on page three hundred sixty-five." He glanced at Tallie. "I apologize. I didn't catch the mistakes until the last read-through, and my typewriter ribbon was fading."

"No apologies necessary," she assured him. Ron had warned her that Gaylord was a perfectionist. Revisions had to be worked out to the nth degree, every sentence powerful, every paragraph perfectly balanced. "I'm looking forward to reading it." She reached for the manuscript, driven partly by her fear that the men might yet change their minds and yank the project out from under her.

Jerry stared at her outstretched hand, then a glint of mischief came into his intense blue eyes. "Well, what do you think, Gaylord? Does Ms. Blankenship measure up?"

Gaylord adopted an indignant posture. "Does she know the rules?"

"Rules?" Tallie asked, dropping her hand.

Jerry cleared his throat. "Gaylord respectfully insists that no copies of his manuscript be made."

Tallie nodded slowly. Ron had mentioned that particular quirk of Gaylord's. Neither did the man keep a copy, or a digital file. "Okay."

"And that you are the only person who reads it," Gaylord added dryly. "No underlings, and not your boyfriend."

Tallie inhaled against his implication that she would be indiscreet. "I am a professional, Mr. Cooper."

"Besides," Jerry said with a sardonic smile, "Ms. Blankenship doesn't have a boyfriend."

Her mouth tightened. "No one other than I will read the manuscript." An impossibility after the book went into production, but of course Jerry knew that. The assurance was to assuage Gaylord's paranoia.

"No excerpts will be published, and no advance reading copies issued," Gaylord continued.

She nodded. His demands drove marketing berserk, but the fact that he could make such demands spoke to his remarkable success.

"If you need to reach me, you must call my secretary. She will get me the message and I'll call you back from a pay phone to arrange a time to meet. I don't use cellular phones, fax machines, scanners, or e-mail."

"That sounds agreeable," she said. For a reason she couldn't fathom, the air filter kicked into high, filling the air with a louder, more obnoxious hum.

"Ah, here come the negative ions," Gaylord said, nodding with approval. He looked over at Jerry. "I find Ms. Blankenship to be satisfactory, but I will defer to your judgment."

The smallest smile pulled at Jerry's mouth. "Gaylord, perhaps Ms. Blankenship and I should confer privately." He looked back to his client. "Besides, it might attract too much attention if you and I left together."

Gaylord popped up out of his seat. "Right you are, my boy." He closed his briefcase and gathered his coat. "Ms. Blankenship, is there a back or side exit I could use?"

"Down the hall and turn left at the dead end," she said.

"Dead end," he said, looking amused. "That's a good one." He retrieved his suitcase and gave her a mock salute. "Take care of my book, Ms. Blankenship."

"I will," she promised.

"You'd better," he said ominously, then turned on his heel and left.

Tallie looked at Jerry Key, whose gaze was riveted on her.

She shifted in her chair and crossed her hands primly to resist the urge simply to yank the manuscript out of Jerry's hands. "What did you want to discuss . . . Jerry?"

He pursed his beautiful mouth and sat back in his chair. "I want to discuss what's in this for me."

 Chapter 13

Tallie stared at the man sitting across her desk while a flush climbed her neck inch by inch. What on earth could Jerry Key want from her? "I don't understand," she said carefully. "What's in this for you is that Mr. Cooper's manuscript will be in good editorial hands."

Jerry angled his blond head and looked thoroughly amused. "I'm sure you're a fine editor, Tallie, but the city is full of fine editors." He lowered his gaze to her chest and caressed the manuscript on his lap. "But I'm looking for a fine editor with whom I can develop a really *good* business relationship."

Her breasts tingled under his scrutiny and a low hum started in her thighs that had nothing to do with the drone of the air filter. Tallie allowed the idea that Jerry Key found her attractive to wash over her, and for a few crazy seconds, her imagination leaped ahead, picturing them naked, writhing in tangled sheets, tapping into each other's psyches in a way no two people ever had. . . .

She snapped back to reality. This wolf in sheep's

clothing not only had single-handedly bedded most of the industry but he was also spreading vicious lies about her best friend. A tiny part of her was in awe that he was so thoroughly charming that even someone who knew about his exploits would be tempted, and for the first time, she understood the incredible power that beautiful-but-impossible women held over men.

Tallie wet her lips nervously, her mind racing with the decision at hand: Should she vault to her feet and blast his vulgarity? Deliver a well-deserved slap across his smooth cheek? Play along just to get along? Ron had handed her an enormous responsibility—didn't she owe it to herself and to the company to reach some kind of compromise?

She looked for her voice and found it cowering behind her fluttering heart. "What . . . what did you have in mind?"

A smile lit his remarkable eyes, then he immediately looked rueful. "I already have dinner plans tonight at the Highlander restaurant in the Hills Hotel, but how about coming by for a drink afterward?"

Her stomach pinched. The proximity of the hotel lent a more sordid slant to the situation.

"Just to talk about business," he said, lifting his hands. "Ron and I meet for drinks all the time."

She flushed—maybe she had misread his interest in her. After all, Jerry could have his pick of women, and if Felicia was correct, he was currently involved with someone. A drink in a public place . . . she met agents for drinks all the time. Shmoozing over alcohol was part of the business.

"Okay," she murmured.

"Great," he said so casually that she decided she *had*

misinterpreted his signals. Maybe Jerry Key oozed so much sex appeal that she had projected onto him a deep-seated fantasy. He stood and set the manuscript on her desk, then claimed his coat. From the look on his face, his mind was already elsewhere. He turned back and extended his hand again. "It was nice to meet you, Tallie."

She clasped his hand, and the shake was purely professional. She followed him to the door, feeling like an idiot.

He turned. "So I'll see you this evening, say . . . ten? Is that too late?"

She shook her head, stirred by his thoughtfulness. "No, but if your dinner runs later than you planned, we can reschedule."

"I don't think that will be necessary," he said. "My condo is being painted, so I have a room at the hotel. See you later."

She stood at the door and watched him walk away, her hand frozen to the knob. Red flags raised in her head as far as her mind's eye could see. It was a trap—her feet knew it because they took off after him. Jerry was stepping onto the elevator. She opened her mouth to call his name when a blur of blond blew past her.

"Hold the elevator!" Kara Hatteras yelled.

Jerry obliged and Kara glided inside, leaning into him with fawning gratitude. She gave Tallie a smirk just before the doors closed.

Tallie stood flat-footed until Norah walked by, her arms full of mail. "How did it go with Creepy Cooper?"

"Hm? Oh, fine . . . I suppose."

Norah blushed. "Jerry Key is so handsome, isn't he?"

"Yes," Tallie agreed absently, then walked back to her office, her stomach churning. Her gaze landed on the precious manuscript, and she almost wished that Ron hadn't given her the responsibility of the company's most valued writer. She consulted her Rolodex, then dialed Ron's cell phone number while drumming her fingers on the cover page of *Whole Lotta Trouble*. Her reader's instincts were kicking in. She couldn't wait to read the story, but first she wanted to talk with Ron about the best way to deal with Jerry Key.

The phone rang five times, then rolled over to voice mail. At the tone, Tallie hesitated. "Ron, hi, this is Tallie. Listen, I have Mr. Cooper's manuscript, but I'm having some, uh . . . *issues* with Jerry Key, and I was hoping you could give me advice on how to handle a situation. I'm supposed to meet him this evening, so if you could call me back today, that would be great. Talk soon . . . bye."

She put down the phone and sighed, thinking Ron probably didn't need her trouble heaped on top of his, whatever it was.

She moved aside the manuscript Jané had brought to her and pulled *Whole Lotta Trouble* to the center of her desk. With her heart beating in anticipation, she slid her finger under the rubber band just as a rap sounded on her door. Norah stuck her head in. "Crisis in production on one of your books—can you come?"

Tallie cast a longing glance at the manuscript but stood. "Of course. I'm expecting a call from Ron, so if he rings, will you find me?"

Norah nodded, and Tallie grabbed a pad of paper on the way out. At the last second, she pulled a key from her pocket and locked her office door—she wasn't going to take any chances that Gaylord's manuscript might walk off.

The day went downhill from there. While the hours

gave way to one emergency after another, Tallie's stomach grew heavier and heavier with dread over her late-night meeting with Jerry. When she returned to her office in the afternoon, Ron hadn't called, racheting up her concern over his mysterious predicament. Felicia had left a message saying she'd be at The Bottom Rung at 6:00. When Tallie thought about her best friend, about the anguish she had experienced at Jerry's hand, Tallie had a clear revelation that she simply couldn't meet with him. Even on the outside chance that he had no lascivious intentions, Jerry's reputation alone would put her in a suspect position.

She would cancel—what was the worst that could happen? After all, she had the manuscript in her possession.

Tallie straightened, feeling stronger and smarter. People like Jerry Key only had power if people like her allowed them to have power. She picked up the phone and was dialing Jerry's number when a knock sounded on her office door. Tallie looked up to see Saundra Pellum, the publisher, standing in her doorway. The phone slipped from Tallie's hand and landed on her desk with a deafening crash. She jumped to her feet, fumbling to right the phone and mumbling an apology. Saundra was a cross between Nancy Reagan and Leona Helmsley. Her appearance could mean only one of two things—someone was dead, or someone was fired. Tallie wavered between which news she wanted to hear least.

"Hello, Saundra."

The woman frowned. "Tallie, I just got off the phone with Jerry Key. He expressed concern about your ability to edit Gaylord Cooper in Ron's absence."

Tallie's head jerked back and her throat constricted in

shock. "I-I met with Mr. Cooper and Mr. Key just this morning, and everything seemed to go very well."

"That's not the impression that Mr. Key walked away with. He wants the manuscript to go to someone with more experience on high-profile assignments, and since he's Mr. Cooper's representative, we will comply with his wishes. You are to pass the manuscript to Kara Hatteras at your earliest convenience."

She could scarcely believe her ears. "Kara?" She swallowed hard. "With all due respect, Kara doesn't even edit fiction."

"Mr. Key assured me that Mr. Cooper's manuscripts require a light editorial hand. Mr. Key said he was impressed with Kara's do-it attitude with regard to marketing."

Tallie remembered Kara's timely appearance at the elevator and the woman's smirk. Ten dollars said the "do-it" attitude Kara had shown Jerry had nothing to do with marketing.

Tallie leaned into her desk, the edge cutting into the front of her thighs. She felt as if the opportunity Ron had given her was being plucked out of her hands. She glanced at the manuscript on her desk and had the crazy urge to grab it and run. She looked back to Saundra, who had already turned to go. "But Ron said—"

"Ron," Saundra cut in, her head whipping around, "is having emotional problems. He will have no say in this matter."

Tallie stood stock-still, her tongue paralyzed. She blinked her understanding, not that Saundra noticed or cared, since she was already halfway back to her office. Shell-shocked, Tallie turned her back to the door, every muscle in her body contracted with anger. The phone rang, and she took two deep breaths before answering. "T-Tallie Blankenship."

"Hi, Tallie," a woman's voice said. "This is Kara."

Tallie gripped the phone tighter. "I know what you did."

Kara scoffed. "I don't know what you're talking about, Tallie, but I assume from your nasty tone that Saundra has already spoken to you about the Cooper manuscript."

It was the first time in Tallie's life that she understood the true meaning of "seeing red." "How dare you go behind my back and steal this assignment!"

"I didn't steal anything," Kara said, her voice sing-songy. "More like . . . traded."

Tallie felt positively light-headed as revulsion rolled over her. "You won't get away with this," she said through clenched teeth. She heard a noise and looked up to see that Norah had stepped inside to say good-bye and that she'd overheard her comment. Norah gave a startled wave, then skedaddled.

"Really, Tallie," Kara meowed. "You shouldn't be so competitive. We're on the same team."

"What did Gaylord have to say about this?"

"That kook? As if he's capable of making a rational decision. Jerry said Gaylord would do what Jerry told him to do. Where is the manuscript?"

"I have it here," Tallie bit out.

"I left early. And I'll be working from home tomorrow," Kara said, ending on a yawn. "Would you be a dear and bring it by this evening?"

Tallie's mouth tightened. Kara lived in Chelsea, a few blocks away from her, but in a refurbished area of town—i.e., her hallways didn't stink of dead rats. "You expect me to *deliver* this manuscript to you?"

Kara sighed. "Look, you know Gaylord would have a stroke if I used a courier service."

"Then you'll just have to come in to pick it up," Tallie said, not bothering to keep the defiance from her voice.

"Fine," Kara said wearily. "I was trying to make this easy for you, but if you want me to come to your office tomorrow and get it, that's okay by me."

Tallie pursed her mouth—Kara would make a big honking scene for the office to gossip about for days. She pinched the bridge of her nose, scrunching her face in abject hatred, holding back a gurgling, primal scream. But the pressure must have broken something loose, because suddenly, a brilliant thought slid into her head: *Give Kara enough rope to hang herself.* She was out of her field when it came to fiction, and it was a good bet the woman knew nothing about Gaylord's books. Let her take this project and make a fool out of herself, in front of Saundra, no less.

And the sooner Kara got the manuscript, the better.

Tallie conjured up a contrite sigh. "No, you're right. It would be easier if I just dropped it by your place tonight."

"Great," Kara said. "603 Profitt, just leave it with my doorman. Bye now."

Tallie listened to the dial tone, and smiled, tongue in cheek. "Bye, Kara."

She set down the phone and stroked the manuscript sadly. Editing aside, she had been looking forward to reading the story. She picked it up and glanced toward the hall. For a few seconds, she considered going to the copy room and making a duplicate for herself, despite Gaylord's strict orders. Keith Wages' enthusiasm for the book had pushed hers to a higher level . . . strangely. It

was the power of sharing a good book, she reasoned, not
to be mistaken for an affinity with Keith himself.

Fingering the edges, she thought of the promises
she'd made to the strange, paranoid Gaylord Cooper this
morning when he'd sat in her office soaking up negative
ions. She couldn't betray those promises, no matter what
happened. Her integrity was why Ron had given her the
assignment in the first place.

Ron. Her thoughts moved to him as she slid the manuscript into its manila envelope. She set the envelope
aside, then reached for the beautiful cloisonné pen that
Ron had given her for Christmas. "Whenever you need
me, reach for this pen," he had said lightly. It had been
so out of character for Ron that she'd thought he was
teasing her . . . or, more foolishly, that he had been *flirting* with her. Had he known then that he was heading toward some kind of breakdown? Sudden tears filled her
eyes, because she couldn't imagine this place without
Ron. She sent up a brief prayer for his quick recovery—
a sobering reminder, she realized, that there were worse
things than having the career opportunity of a lifetime
ripped away by a sleazy superagent and a conniving
leg-spreader.

She worked her mouth back and forth. Jerry and Kara
deserved each other. Maybe hearing about this stunt
would cure Felicia of her fixation on the man. Tallie
wrote G.C. on the sealed flap of the manila envelope before stuffing it into her bag along with the manuscript
that Jané had given her. She glanced over at the envelope
that held the Wannamaker manuscript and decided to
print the lengthy editorial suggestions she'd written and
send it on its way before she left. If the former IRS cost

accountant wanted to make some serious changes and
agree (or admit) that the story wasn't an autobiography,
he might have a chance of turning *Journal Entry* into a
business thriller.

   While she waited for the letter to print, her mind went
back to Felicia. Something was eating at her best friend,
she could tell. Tallie narrowed her eyes. And after one
backstabbing encounter with Jerry Key, she would almost guarantee that whatever it was, it had something to
do with him.

Chapter 14

"Jerry Key's office, this is Lori."

Felicia assumed her most friendly voice. "Hi, Lori, it's Fel—"

"He's not here," Lori cut in. "Still."

Felicia closed her eyes briefly, trying to maintain her composure. "Did Jerry get my earlier messages?"

"Yes."

"And?"

"And perhaps you should send him an e-mail."

"I did." Three of them.

"Cell phone?"

Felicia pursed her mouth. "He isn't answering."

"Sounds like a hint," Lori said lightly.

Felicia bit her tongue—arguing with Jerry's assistant would get her nowhere. "When you see Jerry, would you please press upon him that I need to speak with him about some time-sensitive matters?"

"Sure thing," Lori said in a bored voice.

"Thank you," Felicia said stiffly and replaced the receiver. Too late, she realized she'd forgotten to ask Lori if a date had been set for the Merriwether auction. She groaned—just one more thing she had to get beyond before she confronted Jerry about his affair with Suze. And then of course there was the photograph. She glanced at the bottom drawer in her desk and ground her teeth. Like the other half dozen times today, she succumbed to temptation and pulled open the drawer. She'd taken the photo out of the envelope, so all she had to do was move aside a box of stationery envelopes to look at the sordid image. She'd considered tearing up the picture a hundred times, but she was afraid she would remember something to help identify who had taken it and not have the photo to prove it by. That was the only explanation . . . it simply wasn't possible that she enjoyed the self-torture.

"Is this a bad time?"

At the sound of a man's voice, Felicia jerked up her head. Bike messenger Jack Galyon stood in her office door, holding his helmet in one hand. She slammed the drawer and straightened with a guilty flush. "Um . . . no. Come in."

She stood and crossed her office, circling behind him to close the door. On the way back to her desk, she shut the blinds on her glass wall. Her heart pounded in her ears as she turned to face him. "Did you find out who sent the envelope?"

He hesitated a few seconds, studying her face, his eyes serious above ruddy cheeks. His hair was light brown and overlong, the top flattened and the sides winged by the helmet. His boyish looks belied the powerful build beneath his close-fitting cycling togs. "Whoever sent it covered their tracks. All I could find out was that it was dropped near Madison Square Park between

7:00 and 7:30 A.M., and the person paid cash. The teller doesn't remember anything special, doesn't know if it was a man or a woman. The signature was little more than a scrawl, unrecognizable."

"It's okay," she said, her stomach twisting. "That's enough." She turned away, hugging herself. Madison Square was two blocks from Jerry's condo. She'd assumed it was him, but deep down . . . good God, what kind of a scary place was she in if the idea of an unknown stalker had been more palatable?

"So, you had a good idea of who might have sent it?"

She turned back and looked up. Jack Galyon was very tall, his body even more elongated by the black Lycra pants and jacket. "I had my suspicions."

He nodded slowly. "Was it some kind of threat?"

His directness was comforting. Felicia wavered, overcome with the urge to unload on this stranger, yet too ashamed to reveal the details of the photo. Nonsense, really—what did she care what this man thought of her? A few days ago she hadn't even had words to spare for him. "Not a threat, exactly."

His eyebrows rose. "Do you want to tell me, exactly?"

She shook her head.

"Okay." He scratched his temple. "Are you going to get the police involved?"

His concerned expression made her chest feel crowded—he was getting too personal for comfort. Felicia straightened. "You're making too much of this."

He blinked. "I was asking only because I was going to offer to tell them what I know."

"I don't think that will be necessary." She heard the sting in her voice, and from the look on his face, he felt it.

"Got it." He put his helmet back on and turned to go.

Remorse barbed through her. "Mr. Galyon—"

"It's Jack," he said over his shoulder, securing the chinstrap.

"Jack," she conceded. "Thank you very much for helping me." She glanced back to her purse on her desk. "Wait, I have something for you." She stepped back to grab her bag, withdrawing her wallet.

He gave her a pointed look. "Are you giving me your home phone number?"

She looked down at the wad of cash in her hand, and her face warmed. "No. But I'd like to repay you for your time and trouble."

He met her gaze, and she was startled by the flash of disappointment she saw there. "Forget about it."

He was almost out the door when she remembered the package he'd dropped off the previous night. "Thank you for the book—I'm enjoying it."

"I'm glad," he said curtly.

"H-how will I return it to you?" she asked, trying to repair the insult of offering him money.

"Keep it," he said, then strode off down the hall.

She watched him walk away and was struck with a curious sense of loss, but it was quickly overridden with relief that the only other person who knew about the envelope was gone.

Of course, now that she knew that Jerry had sent the photo, her mind went back to . . . why? Was it just another level of harassment from the man who had dumped her yet couldn't seem to let her go? White-hot emotions bombarded her—after a year apart, Jerry could still trigger manic highs and lows. The headache she'd managed to hold at bay all day bloomed into a lit-

tle flower of pain. The sooner she got to the bar to meet
Tallie and get a drink, the better.

Considering the fact that traffic was at a standstill, she
opted to walk the eight blocks rather than hail a cab. And
she hoped a little fresh air might clear her head—not
that the fume-filled air of Manhattan was all that fresh,
but with recent filtering snows, January was a better bet
than any other month of the year.

She dug her hands deep into her pockets and sighed.
As a little girl, she'd trained herself not to dwell on the
past, to keep looking ahead no matter what, but at this
moment, she desperately wished she could turn back
time to the night she'd run into Jerry Key at a book-
launch party. Years of casual flirting had yielded to seriously good vodka screwdrivers, and he'd gone home
with her.

Within twenty-four hours, she had been head over
heels in love, and he had seemed equally smitten. The
rumors she'd heard about Jerry's proficiency in bed had
not been exaggerated. They'd been like-minded about
sex and nearly every other subject. For two months their
love affair had raged like a furnace, and then just like
that, he'd called and ended things . . . as if there had
been an expiration date on their fling that she'd been un-
aware of. The problem was, there seemed to be no expiration date on the feelings he'd dredged up from the
depths of her heart. But now something had to give. She
was losing her mind one baked cake at a time.

She picked up her pace, glancing toward the traffic,
wondering if Jack Galyon was still in the vicinity and
how many times he crisscrossed the city in a week's
time. So many businesses, but the publishing industry in

particular, relied on the fleet of bike messengers to move documents across town faster than the traffic moved. She saw messengers every day, yet she'd never given any thought to them as individuals, which was, on hindsight, quite snobby . . . and too much like her mother to sit well.

The man did have wonderful eyes.

A few minutes later she pushed open the door to The Bottom Rung, suddenly eager to see Tallie and hear about her blind date that had ended so bizarrely. Across the bar, Tallie lifted her hand, and Felicia noticed the furrow between her friend's eyebrows. And the fact that her friend had starting drinking without her . . . something was definitely up.

"Hey," she said, walking up to the table.

Tallie looked up, her eyes clouded. "Hey." She moved her coat, and Felicia grimaced at the sight of the coffee stain spread over the striped wool.

"Ooh, how did that happen?"

"Fallout from the coffeehouse shoot-out," Tallie said dryly. "I was hoping you could give me an idea of how to get it out. For what my dry cleaner will charge, I could probably buy a new coat."

Felicia enjoyed the challenge of a good stain, and coffee was right up there with blood. She was a whiz with blood. "The dry cleaner in my building will do it for next to nothing. I'll trade coats with you when we leave and take it home with me."

Tallie smiled. "You're so good to me."

"Yes, I am. Now, tell me about this superhero."

Tallie's smile flattened. "Scarily macho . . . *not* my type . . . let's leave it at that." She lifted her glass for a deep drink.

Felicia lifted her eyebrows at Tallie's vehemence. Hm. "Okay, so how did things go with the infamous Gaylord Cooper?"

Tallie's gaze dropped. "Um, he was fine, actually. Weird, but fine." Then she fingered the base of her glass. "But things didn't go so well with Jerry."

Heat flooded Felicia's face. "What did he do?"

Tallie looked up and squirmed. "He convinced Saundra Pellum to let Kara edit the manuscript instead of me."

Felicia gaped. "Kara? Why on earth would he do something stupid like that?"

Tallie took a drink and swallowed hard. "Because . . . Kara rode down on the elevator with Jerry when he left."

Felicia's stomach clenched. "Are you saying he changed his mind . . . afterward?"

Tallie nodded, looking miserable.

Felicia clenched her jaw, then reached across the table to squeeze her arm. "Tallie, I'm so sorry." Loathing backed up in her throat, choking her. "Jerry's behavior has gotten . . . out of control."

"Have you confronted him yet about the affair with your author?"

"Not yet," she admitted. "There are some . . . complications."

"What's going on?" Tallie leaned in. "I know something has been bothering you—is it Jerry? What did he do?"

To Felicia's horror, her eyes filled with tears.

"Felicia," Tallie gasped. "What did he do to you?"

"I thought I might find you two here," Jané Glass said over Felicia's shoulder.

Felicia blinked rapidly to get rid of the tears and manufactured a smile by the time the woman walked around to face her.

"Hi, Jané," Tallie said quickly, shifting in her chair to distract, like the good friend she was. "Good to see you again so soon."

"Mind if I sit?"

"No," they said in unison. Although Felicia wasn't crazy about the woman, she was grateful for the diversion from the serious conversation.

Jané pulled up an extra chair and smiled at Tallie. "Have you had a chance to read the manuscript I gave you?"

Tallie cupped her drink and nodded.

"Well, what do you think?"

A waiter stopped to take Felicia's and Jané's drink orders, and by the time he'd left, Tallie had pulled a manila envelope from her bag and pushed it across the table to Jané.

"The plot was really entertaining, but the writing . . . well, to be frank, the writing wasn't where I hoped it would be."

Jané looked crushed, then hopeful. "Maybe with some rewriting?"

Tallie nodded. "Sure. The whole thing about the serial killer murdering people through their e-book reader is really clever."

Felicia swung her head up. "What?" She held out her hand and gave a little laugh. "I'm sorry to interrupt, but I think I should mention that one of my authors has a book almost ready for production about a serial killer murdering people through their e-book readers." The waiter set down their drinks, and Felicia gave Jané an apologetic shrug. "I'm sorry—you know that synchronicity happens in this business."

But Jané looked understandably concerned when she gripped the envelope. "Are you sure it was your author's original idea?"

Felicia opened her mouth to say yes, then she recalled the conversation she'd had with Phil Dannon about the book after Suze had stormed out of her office. *"That was Suze's idea, which is unusual."* A finger of unease tickled her neck. "Jané, how many people have read this manuscript?"

Jané pressed her lips together and frowned in thought. "Me, of course, and my editorial assistant. And it's been out to half a dozen agents."

"Which agents?"

"Tony Barber, Lori Schaff, Diane Eso, Randy Jason, Jerry Key, and Vicki Carr."

Felicia and Tallie exchanged a nervous glance.

"What?" Jané looked back and forth.

"Nothing for certain," Felicia assured her.

Jané brought her hand down on the table, making their glasses jump. "Jerry Key—he's involved in this somehow, isn't he?"

"I don't know that," Felicia said carefully. "May I see the manuscript?"

Jané withdrew the manuscript and flipped through a few pages. "Here's the first murder scene."

Felicia skimmed the scene, her stomach sinking lower and lower as she recognized passages—different wording, but the same basic idea and execution. Suze Dannon could land herself and Omega in dire straits if she had submitted plagiarized material. And how could she have gotten it unless Jerry had given it to her? Felicia looked at Jané. "Did Jerry turn down this manuscript?"

Jané angled her head. "You mean the Simon Cowell of publishing? He wrote one of the most degrading rejection letters I've ever read. It was exactly two words: 'Torch it.'"

Felicia winced.

"Is the material the same?" Jané asked, pointing to the manuscript.

"It's similar," Felicia admitted.

"This author of yours—I guess they just happen to be represented by Jerry?"

Felicia hesitated, then nodded.

Jané's eyes blazed. "That bastard stole my story and gave it to someone else?"

Felicia put out her hand to calm Jané. "I'll talk to my author first thing in the morning, and I'll make certain that any similarities to your story are taken out."

"How can I be sure?" Jané asked, lifting her hands.

"Because I'm giving you my word," Felicia said evenly. "You know I don't want something like this to happen. The ethics aside, my author's reputation would be ruined, and Omega would suffer as well."

"Jané, you can trust Felicia," Tallie added. "At least this was caught before the book went to press."

Jané's mouth tightened. "Plagiarism is against the law, you know."

Felicia nodded solemnly and touched her temple. "I know. But this is completely out of character for my author—I'd venture that Jerry had something to do with it."

"Can't we report him to someone?" Tallie asked. "Isn't there an organization that oversees literary agencies?"

"Yes," Felicia said dryly. "And he's president. Besides, claims of plagiarism rarely result in charges. In the absence of exact duplication, it's too hard to prove."

Jané's face turned a mottled red. "So . . . what are we going to do?"

Felicia took a quick drink from her glass to try to calm her own elevated vital signs. "I told you, I'll speak to my author."

"I mean what are we going to do about Jerry?" Jané leaned in. "Look, Felicia, you know better than anyone that the man is a megalomaniac and a total ass. He can't get away with this!"

Tallie moved forward. "It *would* be nice to teach him a lesson."

Jané looked at Tallie. "You have a beef with him, too?"

Tallie nodded, and Felicia detected the same vengeful gleam in both women's eyes. Her heart started thumping faster when she realized that they were serious about getting even.

"Felicia, you know him better than we do," Jané said. "What can we do to put him in his place?"

Felicia shook her head slowly, loath to drag the girls into the big, fat mess of the photograph and Jerry's affair with Suze. "I don't think—"

"Hi, ladies." Bert Nichols, a chubby up-and-coming editor at Bloodworth, stopped next to the table. "Wow, you three look intense."

Felicia shifted guiltily and smiled a greeting.

Jané knew Bert from when she had worked at Bloodworth. She introduced the man to Tallie. "And I think you know Felicia."

"Sure," he said with a grin. "In fact, Felicia, I came by to say thank you."

She gave a little laugh. "For what?"

"You managed to outbid me on the last two books I wanted, and I was prepared to lose the Anne Merriwether book to you, too. So, I wanted to thank you for pulling out of the auction."

Acid bathed her stomach, but she managed to maintain her composure. "No problem, Bert. Um, when did the auction wrap up?"

"This afternoon."

The acid bubbled. "Oh. Well, congratulations. Don't think I didn't bid because I wasn't interested—it's a special book."

"Yeah, I think so, too," he said. "And hopefully will pave the way to work with more of Jerry Key's clients."

Jerry Key . . . Jerry Key . . . Jerry Key. His name revolved in her head until she thought her brain would explode. He was seemingly everywhere, taunting her, betraying her friends, and now sabotaging her career. Would she never be rid of him? After Bert waved and moved toward the entrance, she gulped down the rest of her drink and coughed lightly against the sting of vodka as it slid down her throat. Suddenly, getting loaded sounded like a very good idea. She signaled the waiter for another round, then ground her teeth. "Jerry deliberately excluded me from that auction."

Jané arched a dark eyebrow. "As I was saying, Felicia, you know Jerry better than we do. How can we get the bastard?"

"Some way to turn the tables, humiliate *him*?" Tallie asked, her gaze pointed.

Affection surged in Felicia's chest. Tallie was probably more motivated by what Jerry had done to her best friend than by the fact that he had ripped a high-profile assignment out from under her. And she didn't even know the entire story.

Felicia looked back and forth at the women, all of them wronged by a man who thought he could plow through people's lives with no consequences to his charmed career.

"Yes," Felicia murmured, buoyed by the thought of getting sweet revenge. "Humiliate him . . . on a large scale." A wicked thought popped into her head. "If there was some way we could lure him to a hotel room . . . get him in a compromising position . . . take a picture."

"Oh, that's good!" Jané said gleefully.

"We wouldn't have to lure him to a hotel room," Tallie offered, looking sheepish. "Jerry is, um, staying at the Hills Hotel while his condo is being painted."

Felicia observed Tallie's lowered lashes and wondered how *that* bit of information had been revealed.

Jané squealed with delight. "This is perfect! Do either of you have a digital camera?"

"Jerry has one on his cell phone," Felicia said. "He always has the latest gadgets."

Jané grinned. "Then we'll use his phone camera, download the picture, and send it to his entire e-mail list!"

Felicia burst out laughing at the mental image. "That would definitely bring him down a notch." Then she shook her head. "I swear, I'd be tempted if we could figure out how to pull it off without him knowing it was us."

The waiter brought the new round of drinks, and after he left, Jané lifted her glass. "Girls, we're fiction editors— we know how to plot, and we know how to cover our tracks. We can teach Jerry Key a lesson he'll never forget. And the best thing is that since he won't know who did it, he'll be on his best behavior around everyone!"

She laughed. "The entire publishing industry would be in our debt."

A delicious feeling worked its way through Felicia. An eye for an eye . . . or in this case, a picture for a picture. And while Jerry might suspect that she was behind the stunt, if they were careful, he wouldn't know for certain. And how excellent it would be to have Jerry walking on eggshells around her for a change.

She lifted her glass and clinked it against Jané's, then Tallie's. "To revenge."

"To revenge," Tallie and Jané chorused, and each drank deeply from her glass. Felicia decided they should plan their strategy before they got too drunk to see it through. Why delay? They knew where he would be . . . and she knew his weaknesses. She set down her drink, pulled a pen from her bag, and seized a cocktail napkin on which she wrote:

Step 1: Lay the trap.

 Chapter 15

Tallie walked out of the door of the Hills Hotel as casually as her thumping heart would allow. Her shoulders were tensed, waiting for the beefy hand of a security guard to clamp down and drag her back inside, but she moved down the stairs unimpeded. A uniformed valet stood at the bottom of the steps and turned to smile in her direction. She flashed a quick smile in return, hoping the low lighting obscured her face . . . or at least the man's memory. Then she veered away, striding down the sidewalk and around the block to the prescribed meeting place.

They all had taken separate exits as a precaution, and it looked as if she was the first to arrive. Feeling conspicuous for no good reason, she shoved her hands deep into her coat pockets and tried to lose herself in the milling crowd. A couple of minutes later, she was starting to get panicky, when Felicia rounded the corner, looking flushed. Tallie waved to get her attention, and Felicia hurried in her direction, a gleeful smile on her mouth.

"We did it!"

Tallie nodded, laughing. "We sure did."

"Where's Jané?"

"I haven't seen her."

Felicia's eyebrows pinched together. "I was held up behind a wedding party—I thought I'd be the last one here."

"Do you think she ran into trouble? Maybe we should go back."

Felicia chewed on her lower lip. "Wait here." She had taken two steps when Jané appeared, her color high, her eyes bright.

"What took you so long?" Felicia asked.

"The exit was blocked by a pallet of linens—I had to find another way out." Jané grinned. "Well . . . was that a kick or what?"

Felicia laughed and Tallie joined in, feeling eerily bonded. "Do you think he knew it was us?"

"No," Felicia said. "Thanks to Jané's performance on the phone."

Jané looked pleased. "He wouldn't have dared to defy Madame Penelope's order to blindfold and restrain himself before she arrived." She took a little bow. "And now, ladies, I hate to cut this little party short, but I have to be somewhere."

"I thought you said you had no plans," Felicia said, and Tallie detected a hint of suspicion in her tone.

Jané hesitated, and something akin to irritation flashed over her face. "I forgot . . . I have a group meeting with other people who are looking for their birth parents." She looked Felicia up and down as if to say that she wasn't lucky enough to have been born on the Upper East Side, then she jerked her thumb over her shoulder. "Besides . . . we probably shouldn't hang around. The maid could have found him by now."

Felicia straightened and nodded. "Right. And I was thinking . . . it might be a good idea if we weren't seen together for a while—you know, just in case this thing snowballs."

A strange look had come over Jané's face. Disappointment? "Sure." She looked from Felicia to Tallie, who squirmed and averted her gaze. "See you later," Jané said, her voice indicating that she wouldn't.

Tallie was suddenly assailed with the feeling that Jané would betray them, which was ridiculous since she couldn't finger them for the stunt without implicating herself. Tallie shook off the sensation, attributing it to nerves. They were all feeling a little high-strung.

"Come on," Felicia said, staring after Jané. "Let's go to the next block and get a cab."

Tallie fell into step with Felicia, whose mood seemed to have turned inward. Tallie wet her lips. "You don't think Jerry will lose his job when the picture gets out, do you?"

Felicia emitted a bitter little laugh. "Don't worry about Jerry. He'll probably find a way to put a spin on it that will only elevate his celebrity." She signaled an oncoming cab, which slowed. "Want this one?"

"No, you take it," Tallie said. "There's one behind it."

Felicia shrugged out of her coat. "Let's trade so I can see about that stain."

"Oh, right," Tallie said, unbuttoning her coat. She felt bad about exchanging her frumpy coat for Felicia's sleek one. "Thanks."

"No problem," Felicia said, taking the coat with a little smile. "Talk to you tomorrow?"

"I'm sure," Tallie said. While the cab took off and another slowed to pick her up, Tallie nervously glanced in the direction of the hotel, expecting to see Jerry Key tearing down the street, screaming obscenities. She scrambled into the taxi, gave the cabbie her address, then remembered she had to drop by Kara's first and corrected the street name.

Tallie smoothed her fingers over the fine mohair of Felicia's tan coat, thinking that she really should invest in a quality overcoat of her own at the end-of-winter sales. She noted with a start that her hand was still shaking slightly.

The plan had gone off without a hitch, better even than they had hoped. In hindsight, the three of them had worked together frighteningly well . . . Jerry Key hadn't stood a chance in the face of their collective wrath. At the memory of him trussed like a pig, she laughed aloud, covering her mouth when the cabbie gave her a strange look in the rearview mirror. She hoped her e-mail address was in Jerry's laptop address book so she could see the result of their efforts. If Jané was the technical whiz that she was purported to be, about three hundred of Jerry's closest associates would receive an e-mail message with the photo attached.

Tomorrow Jerry Key would be the laughingstock of the New York publishing world.

"Here you go, ma'am."

Tallie looked out the window to verify that she was, indeed, in front of Kara's building. She reached into her purse, then handed a ten-dollar bill over the seat. "Keep the change," she said magnanimously.

"Want me to wait?"

"No, thanks," she said, then slid out of the backseat and stepped up on the curb. She pushed the door closed, then hefted her purse to her shoulder and tilted her head back to take in Kara's building. Nice, with pointy ever-green trees in gigantic pots on either side of the entrance wrapped with tiny white blinking lights. But she was in such a powerfully good mood that she didn't begrudge Kara her nice building with the blinking trees. Now that she had exacted a measure of revenge against Jerry Key, she felt better about turning over the manuscript.

Without the Cooper manuscript to read, she planned to watch Lifetime Television until the wee hours. Be-cause she had to meet the cleaners in the morning, she could sleep in. Then she'd straighten up a bit, maybe do a load of laundry, and, after leaving the maid to work miracles, she would slide into work midmorning, where, upon arriving, she would act shocked when she heard the news that a hysterical photo of Jerry Key was mak-ing the rounds. And when she came home tomorrow evening, her apartment would be magnificently clean. All in all, it was shaping up to be a nice weekend.

Tallie walked into the small, well-appointed lobby and approached the suited concierge who stood at atten-tion. She smiled. "Hello, my name is Tallie Blanken-ship. I work with Kara Hatteras."

"She's not here, ma'am. You just missed her by a few minutes." He gave Tallie a rueful smile.

"I just need to leave a package for her," she said, reaching her right hand around her purse for the manu-script bag ever-present on her left shoulder.

Except her hand met with empty air.

She jerked her head down, and in the space of three stomach-dropping seconds, she realized that the bag was gone . . . and the manuscript therein. She gasped, then swung her head toward the door and tore outside, pray-ing the cab was still there or within sight. It wasn't. Tallie stood on the sidewalk staring down the street as pure, unadulterated panic seized her. The sole copy of Gaylord Cooper's manuscript, for which the company had paid a 1.1-million-dollar advance, was in the back of one of tens of thousands of Yellow cabs in New York City. Her stomach revolted, sending an acidic wash of tequila to the back of her throat.

"Ma'am?"

She looked back to the entrance, where the concierge stood in the open door.

"Is everything okay?"

Her mind raced frantically—she certainly couldn't leave word for Kara that she'd lost the package. She needed to buy some time until she could recover the manuscript. "Everything's f-fine," she stammered, then cleared her throat. "I think I'll wait and give it to her in person tomorrow."

"Very well, ma'am. Have a good evening."

She stared at him while hysterical laughter bubbled in her chest. A good evening? She was in so much trouble that she didn't know what to do first. The thought of telling Saundra Pellum that she'd misplaced the manuscript sent her running to one of the potted trees, where she threw up. Afterward, she sagged against a column and rinsed her mouth with water from a bottle in her purse. Fighting tears, she wiped her lips, then began walking the few blocks toward her building. Her legs moved automatically, her mind paralyzed with panic. By the time she reached her own block, her mind had recovered to the point that she had thought of calling the cab company to report the lost bag. Since it hadn't contained any money or obvious valuables, chances were, it would be returned.

She continued, slightly cheered, but her anxiety ratcheted higher as her building came into view, bathed in the blue lights of two police cruisers and an ambulance pulling away. She began to trot, wondering if Mr. Emory had finally keeled over with the heart attack that seemed inevitable. Inside she took the stairs, her heart beating faster when she saw the group of spectators on the third-floor landing.

"What's going on?" she asked, pushing through.

A guy whose face she vaguely recognized pointed to the hall ceiling, where a large vent trap hung down. "They found a dead guy in the HV/AC shaft."

Tallie gasped, then stared at the vent. A ladder stood beneath the opening, and a police officer stood on a top step, his torso obscured. When he climbed down, Tallie's eyes went wide. Keith Wages. He whipped off his dusty hat and banged it on his leg, then glanced toward the crowd and spotted her.

She mouthed, "What's going on?"

He made his way past the Do Not Enter yellow police tape and pulled her to the side of the crowd. "Hey, there," he said, then nodded toward the vent. "I had a hunch about the bad smell, so I came back to talk to the super this afternoon and asked him if I could look around."

"Someone said a guy had died up there?"

He nodded. "We're still investigating, but it looks like he was a burglar trying to gain access to apartments, and he either passed out from the heat, or simply got stuck."

She grimaced. "Ugh."

He nodded. "Yeah." He held up his blackened hands. "Can I borrow your sink to wash up?"

"Sure," Tallie said, although her mind bounced to the state of cleanliness of her sink.

"Let me break up the crowd and get another uniform up here to take over."

She watched as he spoke into his radio, then dispersed the crowd with calming reassurances that everything was fine and there was nothing left to see. Tallie didn't have to see the dead body to imagine the man wedged there, fighting for breath, knowing he was going to die. She felt a little light-headed and remembered that she had purged her day's nourishment into a potted tree. And there was the missing manuscript. She bit her tongue, assaulted with fresh panic. But when Keith followed her to her door, she realized suddenly that he might be able to help her, to contact the taxi company, maybe expedite her request.

It was her predicament over the manuscript and her nervousness about asking for his help that made her pulse race, she told herself. She unlocked the dead bolts and swung open her apartment door to encounter funky, but now frigid, air.

"The heat had to be turned off," Keith explained. "It might be a day or so before it resumes."

She walked inside, shivering, and realized that if anything, her apartment was in even worse shape than the previous evening.

"Still spring cleaning, eh?" he asked with a grin.

Her face warmed. "Yes." She shrugged out of Felicia's coat and noticed the flicker of admiration on Keith's face as he took in her green suit . . . and her legs.

"You look nice."

Her face grew warmer still. "Thank you." She opened the coat closet to stash Felicia's coat, and an avalanche of boxes of "as seen on TV" items her mother had sent over the years fell on her head, knocking her to the ground.

Keith fished her out of the debris and pulled her to her feet. "Are you all right?"

She nodded, mortified, and he burst out laughing.

"You're a mess," he declared.

She yanked her hand out of his and frowned at the corpse-in-shaft dirt that had rubbed off onto her fingers. "I happen to have had a very bad week. Yesterday I was shot at, and today I come home to find that a dead man has been in my circulation system for—"

"At least four days," he supplied.

"Great," she said, sidestepping the heap of boxes and heading toward the kitchen sink. "Between that news and the freezing temperature, I'm sure I'll sleep like a baby tonight." She took off her jacket and began to transfer the towering stack of dirty dishes from the sink onto the tiny counter so they could wash up. No way was she showing him her bathroom.

He came to stand next to her, rolling up his sleeves. "You could stay at my place tonight," he offered casually. "I'll be off-duty soon, and I can give you a ride."

A jolt of awareness shot through her at his nearness, but she busied herself squirting soap into the sink and locating the yellow scruffy thing to rid the supposedly "stainless" steel of stains as warm water tumbled in from the faucet. "Thank you, but I don't think that will be necessary. I wear flannel pajamas."

He made a rueful noise in his throat, then thrust his hands into the warm, soapy water. "Just trying to be friendly."

Beneath the suds, his fingers slid on top of hers, tickling, teasing . . . not accidental. Her breath caught in her chest, and she couldn't bring herself to look at him.

"I have a guest room," he continued easily. "Two of them, in fact, but only one has a bed."

His fingers were even warmer than the water, his soapy touch somewhere between a massage and a caress, sending chills up her arms. And it didn't help that they were standing there talking about beds.

"I'll be fine," she said, then pulled her hands out from under his. She gave him a flat smile as she shook her hands, realizing suddenly that she had no clean dish towels and the cardboard paper towel roll was bare. "Let me . . . find something . . . to wipe . . . oh, hell, what does it matter?" She pulled her blouse out of her waistband and wiped her hands on the tail. Keith worked lather between his hands, then stuck them under the running water for a rinse. He shook most of the water from his hands and looked at her, eyebrows raised.

"Go ahead," she said, offering the damp tail of her cotton shirt.

He moved in front of her and considered her shirt, unbuttoned at the bottom. The damp fabric touched her bare stomach and, in the room's chill, brought her nipples to bud. Keith noticed, and for a few seconds, the thought crossed her mind that if he ripped open her shirt, he was going to be mighty disappointed to find a gray sports bra—the only bra she'd been able to locate this morning that had been clean.

For a few seconds, their breathing was the only sound in the room as they both acknowledged with loosened mouths the electricity zinging back and forth between them. Finally the *drip, drip* of water from his fingertips to the linoleum floor brought them around. Instead of using her shirttail, he pulled his own from the waistband of his uniform pants to wipe his hands, giving her a glimpse of a ribbed white undershirt stretched taut over the flat planes of his stomach.

Her body hummed with awareness, sending indicators to long-neglected places. "The next time you're here, I'll be more prepared," she murmured, then, realizing how stupid she sounded, added, "I mean . . . I'll have towels." She swallowed and took another stab at sounding rational. "Paper towels, I mean."

He laughed. "Oh, so I'm going to be invited back?"

She had walked into that one. "Well, I mean if you're ever in the building . . . or in the neighborhood . . . on a call . . ."

One side of his mouth lifted. "Don't tell me I might find more dead bodies if I stick around."

She laughed. "I hope not."

His dark eyes danced. "You have to admit that trouble seems to follow you around."

She was forming a retort on her tongue when the missing bag popped into her mind. He had a point. She crossed her arms over her own points and said, "Speaking of trouble, I . . . could use your help with something."

He looked surprised. "Sure."

To her humiliation, tears pushed at the back of her eyes when the enormity of what she'd done descended on her shoulders. "I . . . lost something important."

His expression immediately sobered. "Okay. Do you know where?"

She blinked rapidly. "I believe I left it in a cab a little while ago. It was a black nylon bag that I carry my manuscripts in."

"I gather it held some rather important work?"

She swallowed past a lump in her throat. "Gaylord Cooper's newest book."

He sucked air through his teeth. "And you don't exactly want an extra copy of the man's book floating around in this city."

"It's not an extra copy," she said miserably. "It's *the* copy."

"*The* copy—you mean there's only one? In this day and age?"

She sighed. "Gaylord has all of these conspiracy theories about this agency or that agency trying to get their hands on his manuscripts, so he uses a typewriter and he doesn't make copies. He's a little . . . flaky."

"I'll say. Have you called the cab company?"

"Not yet."

"Then we'll start there," he said. "Was there any ID in the bag?"

"Um, no. Just the one manuscript, in a manila envelope."

"Do you happen to remember the cab number?"

"No."

"How about the cabbie's name?"

She shook her head, starting to feel panicky again.

"Can you describe the driver?"

She lifted her hands, as if the movement would somehow jog her memory. "Graying hair, heavyset, Brooklyn accent."

He winked. "Sounds like me in a few years."

She tried to smile—did men actually wink these days?

"Do you remember seeing anything in the cab that might help identify the driver, maybe something hanging from the rearview mirror?"

"No." She inhaled deeply to calm herself. "Keith . . .

my job is on the line—can you pull any strings with the cab company?"

His eyes grew solemn. "I'll try. Can I use your phone?"

She nodded, then spent the next five minutes trying to unearth the portable unit. She finally found it under a pile of mail and handed it to him, her cheeks flaming. "I really appreciate your help."

"No trouble," he said, then dialed information.

She watched, nibbling on her nails, still out of sorts over the physical attraction that had sprung up between them. Keith Wages filled out his tall, broad uniform well, and his powerful physique made her think of immoral activities. She reminded herself, however, that big, strapping macho guys were like liquid diets—they were great for emergencies, but she wouldn't want to be on one all the time.

A few minutes later he had a customer service representative on the line. He identified himself as a police officer and emphasized that the item missing had no retail value (not exactly true) but was of "great sentimental value" (she was, she reasoned, pretty sentimental about her job).

"The item was a black nylon bag," he said. "It contained an envelope with a manuscript inside." He paused, then looked back to Tallie. "Where did the taxi pick you up?"

She had to think. . . . She and Felicia had walked a couple of blocks away from the Hills Hotel before going their separate ways. "Um, I think it was Third and Twenty-first Street—around Gramercy."

"What time?"

She hesitated, although she wasn't sure why. "Around ten."

"And did the cab drop you off here?"

"No—at 603 Profitt, about four blocks from here."

He repeated the information into the phone, then said, "I would very much appreciate you giving this matter high priority . . . and there is a reward."

She lifted an eyebrow—it couldn't be a big reward. Although on second thought, it would be in her best interests to offer the difference between her paycheck and unemployment wages.

He covered the mouthpiece and addressed Tallie. "What number shall I give them to call if they find the bag?"

She recited her home number, her work number, and her cell phone number. Keith murmured a few niceties, then disconnected the call. "They have shift changes every hour, and that's usually when the drivers turn in items to lost and found." He glanced at his watch. "The longest shift is eight hours, so if the guy had just clocked in before he picked you up, he'll be clocking out at six A.M." He gave her a little smile. "So, chances are, you'll hear something in the morning."

She exhaled . . . he was right. She'd already told Norah she'd be coming in late, so she'd have time to pick up the manuscript and drop it off at Kara's before going into the office, and no one would be the wiser . . . except Keith, of course. She smiled. "I owe you one."

He grinned, and her heart tapped against her breastbone. "I have to warn you—I always collect."

Tallie shivered, and she suspected it had little to do with the cooling temperature in the room.

He rolled down his sleeves. "Are you sure you don't want to use my guest room tonight?"

She wet her lips. "But then I'd owe you twice, wouldn't I?"

His laugh was a sexy rumble. "I see you're on to me. Seriously, though, I'd be happy to offer you a safe, warm place to sleep."

Next to him. The words hung in the air, and the tiny hairs in Tallie's inner ears picked up on them. He was tempting, standing there with that I'll-take-care-of-you look on his handsome face. Her body strained toward him, and for a few seconds she actually considered grabbing her flannel jammies and following him home. Then all the reasons she shouldn't came flooding into her head—at least one of them legitimate. "I . . . really should stay here in case the taxi company calls."

"Right," he said, although he looked disappointed. "Well, I need to go and file reports."

She followed him to the door. "Thanks for calling the cab company for me."

"No problem." His smile returned. "I'm a big Gaylord Cooper fan, remember? I have a vested interest in making sure that book goes to print."

She opened the door and nodded toward the hall. "Oh, and if you don't mind, um, don't mention the whole dead-man-in-my-ductwork thing to your mother. It'll get back to *my* mother, and I'll have to move. Back to Circleville."

He laughed. "Understood." Then he pulled out his wallet and withdrew a business card. "Let me know if that manuscript turns up."

She took the card and nodded. "I will."

Keith touched his finger to his hat, then strode away. Tallie stared after him, feeling a curious sense of trust and indebtedness. It was scary, really, that in the space of two days the man had positioned himself firmly as a protector . . . and that his persona had very little to do with the uniform.

She closed the door and shivered, heading toward the bathroom in search of a long, hot bath. Then a thought popped into her head that stopped her cold . . . as cold as the air in her cramped, unkempt apartment.

What if she hadn't left the bag in the cab? Her mind raced backward, trying to remember the last time she'd seen it . . . she'd lifted the strap from the back of her chair when she and Felicia and Jané had left The Bottom Rung on their way to . . .

Her hand flew to her mouth.

If she'd left the manuscript in the hotel room, Jerry Key would know exactly who had set him up.

Chapter 16

Felicia laid her head back against the bathtub and sank up to her neck in the thick head of bubbles. By now Jerry surely had been discovered by a maid, thanks to a message they'd left with the front desk. The image sent a wide smile sliding across her face. But his humiliation would be complete once he realized that everyone he worked with had a photo of one of his fetishes in their in-box. She laughed, sending bubbles into the air.

"That'll teach you to mess with me, Jerry," she murmured, remembering the heady power of securing the ropes on his wrists. She'd surprised herself that she could be so exacting, so vengeful. Secretly she'd been afraid that she would lose her nerve when she saw him. Instead, the sight of him blindfolded and vulnerable had stirred an inner demon. In that moment, all the suppressed rage she'd felt toward the people who had abandoned her—her father . . . her mother . . . Jerry—had surfaced and she was very, very glad she hadn't had the means to truly hurt him . . . because she might have.

The knowledge was scary . . . and oddly empowering, because she felt as if she had exorcised Jerry from her system for good. For the first time in months, her head felt clear and pain-free without the aid of medication.

She reached for the glass of chardonnay on the tub surround and sipped the cool liquid, holding it on her tongue before swallowing with satisfaction. She used a remote control to dim the lights, then closed her eyes and listened to Dusty Springfield, an album she'd picked up on her last visit to Final Vinyl. From "Just a Little Lovin' " to "In the Land of Make Believe," she massaged every inch of her body with a soapy slough sponge and finished the wine. Her breasts and thighs were tingly and heavy—the episode with Jerry had heightened her senses and left her with no outlet.

After opening the drain, she climbed out gingerly and sat on the edge of the tub to rub her skin with a warmed towel. She opened the vanity door and surveyed the stock of jewel-toned bottles and jars. She ran her hand over the lids, flushed with pleasure at their orderliness and prettiness, then selected a jar of vanilla-scented body butter. She twisted off the lid and drew the sweet, nutty scent into her lungs, then dipped her fingers into the lotion and smoothed it over her skin in long, creamy strokes.

Julia Redmon-Clark-Gregg wasn't the best mother in the world, but Felicia would be eternally grateful for the good genes she'd passed down. Three weekly sessions of Pilates and salads for lunch was all it took to maintain her figure . . . and abstaining from all the baked treats she created in her kitchen, of course.

From her lingerie drawer, she chose turquoise silk tap pants and a matching camisole, then slipped into a long pink jersey robe and soft rose-colored leather slippers. Felicia carried her empty wineglass through the living area, where Tallie's coffee-stained coat lay across a chair—her weekend project.

The phonograph arm had returned and switched off automatically, so she stopped at the stereo long enough to flip the arm to continuous play. A detour by the glass-fronted bookshelves was usually a boost for her ego, but the numerous titles featuring the name Suzanne Phillipo made her pause. She would have to confront Suze about the plagiarism tomorrow. Even though she knew she now had the leverage to force Suze to make those changes to the manuscript and others that Phil wanted, the conversation would not be pleasant.

On the other hand, explaining to Suze the consequences of plagiarism might be enough of a jolt for the woman to realize that her lover Jerry Key did not have her best interests at heart . . . not even close.

The phone rang, and she noticed from the caller ID screen that the call was from the lobby phone. "Yes?" she answered.

"Ms. Redmon," Del said. "A visitor for you."

Her first thoughts jumped to Tallie or Jané—had something gone wrong? Then her mind flitted to her mother—Julia was known for showing up unannounced, especially on the heels of bad behavior. And unbidden, Jack Galyon's face came to her, although she couldn't fathom why the man would stop by after their awkward exchange this afternoon.

"Who is it, Del?"

"A gentleman—Mr. Phillip Dannon. He says he has something for you."

Phil? Her eyebrows rose in surprise. "Thank you, Del. Mr. Dannon is a business associate—please send him up."

"Will do, Ms. Redmon."

Felicia glanced down at her robe but decided that everything was covered, and chances were that Phil was dropping off something work-related and wouldn't be there long. She worried her bottom lip, wondering whether to mention the plagiarism to him. When the doorbell rang, she decided she'd play it by ear. She answered the door and smiled up into the rugged face of her favorite author.

Phil Dannon was a powerful figure standing in her doorway wearing jeans, western boots, and a cream-colored turtleneck under his trademark suede jacket. His eyes looked a little bloodshot, as if he'd been drinking, and his thick hair looked hand-ruffled. In one hand he held a blue file folder. He straightened as he took in Felicia's robe. "It's late, I know. I'm sorry to bother you, Felicia."

"No, Phil, it's fine," Felicia assured him, then stepped back. "Would you like to come in?"

He stepped inside. "I won't keep you long."

"Let's sit down," she suggested, then led the way to the living room. She sat on the gray couch while Phil paced restlessly around the room.

"Nice place."

"Thanks." She sat with her hands folded as he walked around the room, picking up small items and setting them down. "Is something wrong, Phil?"

He turned and laughed lightly. "Only everything." Then he stopped in front of her. His gaze dropped, and she realized that her robe had parted below her knees.

Felicia shifted and discreetly closed the opening. "Do you want to talk? How about a cup of coffee?"

He pulled his hand down his face. "Do you have any made?"

She knew bleak when she saw it. "No, but it'll only take a few minutes. Come with me." She stood and headed toward the kitchen, wondering if he'd had another run-in with Suze. She flipped a light switch, illuminating the spotless, gleaming kitchen. "Have a seat," she said, gesturing toward the table. She pulled out the coffeemaker. "Decaf?"

He shook his head. "Full-strength, if you don't mind. I'm heading back home when I leave here."

She nodded and pulled out the good stuff—Island Lava Java. "Have you spoken to Suze?" she asked over her shoulder.

He sighed. "No. She won't return any of my calls."

Too wrapped up in her lover, Felicia mused, then smirked to herself. No doubt Suze would feel differently toward Jerry after he lost some of his powerful footing.

Phil placed the blue folder he'd been holding on the table in front of him.

"What's that?" Felicia asked.

He looked sheepish. "Just an idea I've been tossing around . . . I don't know if it's any good."

She sat down in the adjacent chair and reached for the folder. "Let me be the judge."

He put his hand over hers. "Later. I'd be a nervous wreck if you read it while I was sitting here."

Felicia glanced down at Phil's large hand over hers, and desire stirred in her belly . . . an extension of the tension that had been fermenting all evening. She looked up and realized the bewildered expression on Phil's face mirrored what she was feeling. He had been betrayed . . . she had been betrayed. The loneliness they felt was a tangible entity in the room. His hand tightened over hers, and Felicia felt her mouth open, felt herself lean forward until their lips touched. His were warm and firm and comforting. Then he curled his hand behind her neck, and the kiss intensified.

Dusty Springfield's "Just a Little Lovin' " sounded in Felicia's head. She and Phil were grown-ups . . . they deserved this indulgence. She opened her mouth and let him in.

 Chapter 17

        Tallie slept with the telephone…when she
slept. Mostly she tossed and turned, freezing, and stared
at the clock radio ticking by agonizing minute after
minute. After Keith had left, she'd finally broken down
and called Felicia to see if she'd seen her bag and if not,
to confess that she might have left it at the hotel. But
when Felicia hadn't answered, Tallie had set down the
phone and told herself that Felicia didn't need to be burdened; if Jerry found the bag and traced the incident
back to her, so be it. Meanwhile, she hoped against hope
that she'd left the bag in the cab and that it would be
turned in.

Except now that she had time to think about what
they'd done to Jerry, she was starting to have some serious misgivings, which, admittedly, probably had something to do with her worry that she'd be fingered.

They hadn't really done anything illegal . . . had they?
Jerry had left the hotel room door ajar and had donned a
blindfold voluntarily. He'd even gone so far as to fasten
restraints around his own ankles, presumably to save
time when his mystery dominatrix arrived. The photo

couldn't be considered slanderous because it wasn't a misrepresentation. Besides, Jerry would probably be willing to forgo any legal charges in hopes of quieting the situation as quickly as possible.

Around 3:00 A.M., she decided she couldn't lie there any longer. She swung her legs over the side of the bed and stood, promptly tripping over a pile of dirty clothes. Mr. Emory had offered space heaters to residents, but she had passed, fearful of sparking an inferno. After she turned on the light, she glanced around at the disarray and, shivering, conceded that 3:00 A.M. was probably a good time to have the laundry room all to herself. She pulled on a pair of jeans, slipped her feet into tennis shoes, and proceeded to stuff as many clothes and towels as would fit into the laundry basket. She gathered quarters for the machines, soap powder and fabric softener dryer sheets, and, distrustful of the range of her cordless phone, tucked her cell phone into the pocket of her flannel nightshirt in case the cab company called at this ungodly hour. She unlocked the dead bolts and scooted the basket into the hallway, looking over her shoulder at the vent in the ceiling with a scrap of police tape dangling down.

If possible, it was even colder in the hallway. The hairs on the back of her neck tingled, and her pulse picked up. It was deadly quiet. Her gaze darted to the dark corners of the dingy, poorly lit space, knowing her fear that someone was skulking around was unreasonable but unable to stop the dark possibilities from entering her head. The dead man hadn't been after her personally, she reminded herself, and if he'd managed to enter her apartment, he probably would have been so appalled by the mess that he would have moved on to cleaner fare.

Tallie hurriedly locked the dead bolts, scuttled to the elevator with laundry in tow, and stabbed the button for the basement. But the elevator's normal thumping and bumping sounded like tolling bells in the still night. By the time she reached the bottom floor, she was starting to rethink her witching hour urge. The doors opened and she was relieved to see the glow of a night-light leading to the gaping, black-hole doorway into the moldy laundry room. She lowered the basket to the floor and approached the darkness with trepidation, then held her breath, reached around the corner, and slapped at the wall until she found the light switch. The three rows of overhead lights came on one by one, sending six- and eight-legged creatures running for cover. Tallie winced and looked away until all was clear. The room held four mismatched washers and seven hodgepodge dryers, three of the machines highlighted with Out of Order signs. But no boogeymen. She shook her head at her silly fears . . . she was letting the events of the week get to her.

She retraced her steps to get her laundry and set about sorting the items into separate machines. She made a return trip upstairs to get another basketful and to strip her bed linens, figuring she might as well take advantage of all of the machines being free. The scent of bleach and soap powder tickled her nose, reminding her of home. Merrilyn Blankenship was most happy when everyone's eyes stung from antiseptics in the air.

After Tallie had the washers chugging along, she traipsed back to her apartment. Fully awake now, she decided to get a jump on straightening up for the cleaners so they could concentrate on the heavy-duty jobs. She sorted junk mail, tossed disposable food boxes, and threw away empty toiletry containers. Before long, five bulging garbage bags sat next to the door. Once she began to see floor and furniture surfaces again, her energy level kicked higher. Keeping busy meant keeping warm. If she dusted, she reasoned, the cleaners could concentrate on the floors. And if she cleaned the bathroom sink, they could spend more time on the bathtub. If she washed the dirty dishes, they could put real elbow grease into the furry appliances. At various times during the dish-washing, Keith Wages came to mind, and she could almost feel his hands fondling hers in the water. Okay, the man was sexy as hell with his big . . . everything (one could assume). And if she were inclined to have a hot fling, she'd pick him out of a lineup. But did she really want to risk that the man would report back to his mother that Tallie was a "fun" girl?

Nooo.

She pushed Keith Wages from her mind and ran back to the basement to transfer wet clothes to the dryers. Later she folded shirt after shirt, towel after towel. All the while, she kept her ear angled toward the phone, which refused to ring. She hummed and kept moving to take her mind off her burgeoning panic. She vacuumed the shag carpet until the nap stood up, cleaned the refrigerator until it didn't reek, and scrubbed the stove until her triceps objected. Suddenly she realized that dawn was peeking through her living room windows—which were quite dirty.

Tallie frowned. She couldn't do anything about the outside glass, but she hadn't washed the inside of the windows since . . . never. She found a trigger bottle of blue liquid cleaner under the sink whose label was so faded that she had no idea what it was, but it smelled like ammonia and seemed to cut through the smoky grime on the windows well enough. She stood back and gazed upon the blackened cloth and the sparkling glass, impressed with the results.

Her mother would be so proud.

The thought stopped her in her tracks, and she glanced around her clean apartment, realizing that she'd left very little for the maid service to do. But the cleaning had taken her mind off the trouble at hand, and the realization opened the way for a question to worm its way into her head: Did her mother clean to avoid unpleasantries?

Tallie's mouth quirked sideways. If so, and if she'd inherited that pathological tendency, and if the *Whole Lotta Trouble* manuscript was truly lost, she'd be cleaning until her fingerprints wore off.

She remade her bed, cleaned her closet, organized her dresser drawers, and even matched all the odd earrings in the Tupperware container that doubled for a jewelry box.

By 7:30 A.M., she couldn't take the suspense any longer. She phoned the cab company, told her story to two different people, and was on hold for twenty minutes before being told that yes, they had her claim on file, but since found items were turned in at various terminals across the city, processing could take a while and she shouldn't expect to hear anything for oh, maybe a day or two.

Tallie disconnected the call and grasped the clean kitchen counter for support. A day or two? How could she put off Kara for a day or two? Hot, choking tears materialized, and she felt light-headed. She slid down the cabinets to sit on the floor and put her head on her knees. This was payback for delighting in the humiliation she'd doled out to Jerry Key last night. Other people did terrible things all the time and got away with it. The first time she did something truly vindictive, it came back to hit her in the face like a big, spiky boomerang.

Jerry Key would probably find some way to turn the picture into a publicity stunt. Meanwhile, she'd be on the street looking for a job. And if Parkbench Publishing or Gaylord Cooper decided to hold her responsible for the lost manuscript, her grandchildren would be working off the $1.1 million advance.

She concentrated on breathing deeply and telling herself not to jump to conclusions—chances were, the bag had been found and was at this moment working its way through the claim system. She lifted her head and pressed against her temples. She'd simply tell Kara that something came up and she'd get the manuscript to her later . . . on Monday. That should be plenty of time to recover the manuscript from the cab company. Tallie stood up and gave herself a mental shake. She simply refused to consider that the manuscript was elsewhere.

Until she had to.

A glance at the clock told her she had an hour before the cleaners arrived, and a whiff of herself told her that she could benefit from a shower. She wiped the remnants of her tears with the heels of her hands, then pushed to her feet carefully. Lack of sleep combined with lack of food made for a shaky stance, but she downed a glass of water to give her a push toward the bathroom. She stripped her nightshirt and jeans and, while the water ran warm, gave the ancient bathtub a good scrubbing. She then gave herself a good scrubbing, and turned her thoughts toward a plausible excuse for not delivering the manuscript to Kara.

She could be sick, she decided—which, considering the knots in her stomach, wouldn't be a lie. She hadn't used a sick day in . . . never, so she probably had a stack of them coming to her. She had no meetings scheduled today, and Ron wasn't there to call on her. She could stay near the phone and be ready to go to the cab company at a moment's notice. She had plenty of reading she could do at home. Tallie turned off the water and frowned.

The only thing she'd miss would be the hoopla over the Jerry Key photo, and she had been looking forward to that . . . of course now she was having mixed feelings.

After drying off and wrapping her hair in a towel, she dressed in clean, comfy sweats. She moved toward the phone to call Norah at the office but was interrupted by the doorbell. The peephole revealed two women on the other side of the door carrying cleaning supplies. Tallie unlocked the dead bolts and ushered them inside. "Hello," she said, introducing herself.

The women stood holding brooms, mops, and buckets, looking around. The one that smelled like cigarette smoke said, "Looks pretty clean to me—what did you want us to do?"

Tallie followed the woman's gaze and realized that indeed, her apartment was cleaner than the day she'd moved in. "Well . . . there are a few spots on the carpet— can you take care of those? And maybe some air freshener?"

Smoker looked at her with thin eyebrows raised. "That's it? You ain't going to get your money's worth."

Tallie glanced at the bags of garbage lined up by the door. "And take the trash to the Dumpster?"

The women looked at each other, then nodded and set to work on the food stains that had matted areas of the shag carpet—stuffed manicotti here, shrimp chop suey there. The women were fast and efficient. Thirty minutes later they were on their way out the door, laden with the overflowing garbage bags she had accumulated. Tallie waved good-bye and turned to inhale the air freshener—"new car" wasn't her first choice, but it beat "dead man."

The heat suddenly kicked on, and she took that as a good omen. She picked up the phone and dialed Norah's number. After a few rings, she was prepared to leave a message, but Norah picked up.

"Tallie Blankenship's office, Norah Mennon." She sounded breathless.

"Norah, hi. It's Tallie. Listen, the heat to my building was turned off last night and I woke up not feeling good, so if anyone asks, I'm taking a sick day."

"Okay," Norah said. "Jane Glass called."

Tallie frowned. "This morning?"

"Yes. She said she needed to talk to you right away."

Tallie's chest tightened. "Okay. Anything else?"

"Well," Norah's voice lowered, "have you heard the news about Jerry Key?"

This was important . . . she had to act completely surprised. Tallie wet her lips. "Jerry Key? No . . . what happened?"

"He's *dead*."

Everything in the room tilted. Tallie's lungs compressed painfully. Her vision dimmed.

"Tallie, are you there?"

Tallie gasped for air. "What . . . what did you say?"

"Jerry Key is dead. He was murdered last night in a hotel room."

The phone slipped from Tallie's hand and crashed to the floor.

Chapter 18

Felicia stepped off the elevator and rushed through the reception area, incredibly late for work. Her neck was raw from whisker burn, and her leg muscles were tight. Parting with Phil this morning had been so awkward, she couldn't bear to think about it . . . what had she been thinking last night?

Heads turned when she walked in, and she noticed that everyone was standing around computers in clumps, heads together.

The photo, she realized with a rush of adrenaline, was making the rounds. But the hushed whispers were a far cry from the raucous laughter she'd expected. In fact, no one was laughing.

Tamara glanced up from her desk. Two interns standing behind her scampered on their way.

"What's going on?" Felicia asked carefully.

"Um, well," Tamara stammered, "a friend of mine forwarded this note to me this morning." She rotated her monitor, and Felicia blinked.

Seeing the photo she'd taken of Jerry on a two-inch-by-two-inch cell phone screen was one thing, but seeing it on a seventeen-inch, high-resolution monitor was something else altogether. It was a glossy page out of an S&M magazine—from the strip of black leather tied around his eyes to the chains and buckles crisscrossing his torso. Below the note read the words, "Jerry, Jerry quite contrary"—Jané's idea and handiwork. The man looked like a complete idiot.

"It's Jerry Key," Tamara whispered, her eyes wide.

"I gathered as much," Felicia said. Triumph zigzagged through her, and she tried to hold back a smile. "Well, he's certainly coming out of the closet in a big way." She gave a little laugh.

Tamara stared. "You don't know, do you?"

Felicia frowned. "Know what?"

"Felicia . . . Jerry's . . . well, he's . . . *dead.*"

Disbelief hit Felicia like a gong. Her mouth twitched down, then up in an incredulous smile. "No . . . you're joking."

But Tamara shook her head, her eyes pained. "I'm not. He was found murdered in a room at the Hills Hotel."

Felicia's knees buckled, and she leaned into Tamara's desk. She couldn't speak, couldn't think. *"Murdered?"*

Her assistant nodded. "Stabbed . . . or so that's the rumor going around." Tamara pointed to the computer screen. "Apparently the murderer took this picture and sent it to a bunch of people before he killed Jerry. How godawful creepy is that?"

Felicia's jaw loosened, and she felt the blood drain from her face. Horror rolled over her.

"Felicia," Tamara said, standing and reaching out. "I'm so sorry. I know that you and Jerry used to . . . date."

"Yes," Felicia murmured. "A long . . . time ago."

"This must be a terrible shock for you."

Felicia nodded and staggered into her office, where she dropped into the nearest chair and covered her mouth with her hand.

Tamara hovered near the door. "I'll get you some water."

Felicia nodded and swallowed, tentatively. She was numb. White noise buzzed in her ears. Jerry couldn't be dead . . . he simply couldn't be. The phone rang, piercing the air and causing her nearly to jump out of her skin. She exhaled and pushed to her feet, realizing when she reached for the phone that she was still wearing her coat. "Yeah," she croaked, business protocol going by the wayside.

"It's Tallie," a barely recognizable voice said on the other line. "H-have you heard . . . about Jerry?"

Bile rose in Felicia's throat, but she choked it down. "Y-yes . . . I just walked in, and Tamara told me." The anguish in her own voice terrified her. "She . . . she said that he was st-stabbed?"

"That's what I heard, too," Tallie said.

Felicia closed her eyes briefly, striving to keep her voice calm. "Everyone here has the photo pulled up on their computer."

"I haven't seen it, but Norah said she'd forward it to me."

"They're saying . . ." Felicia swallowed. "They're saying that the murderer took a picture of him and sent it out before killing him."

Silence sounded on the other end.

"Tallie?"

"Oh, my *God*," Tallie said tearfully. "We have to go to the police, Felicia."

At the sound of Tamara returning, Felicia lifted her head. Her assistant set a plastic cup of water on her desk and gave her a tentative smile.

Felicia covered the mouthpiece on the phone. "Thank you."

"There's a Jané Glass on the phone," Tamara said. "I asked her to leave a message, but she said you'd want to talk to her."

Felicia schooled her face into mild surprise. "Yes, I'll take it." She waited until Tamara left and closed the door before she spoke to Tallie. "Hold on—Jané is on my other line. I'll conference her in."

"Okay," Tallie said in a broken whisper.

Felicia pressed her second line button. "Jané?"

"Holy shit, Felicia . . . have you heard what happened to Jerry?"

Felicia pinched the bridge of her nose and struggled for composure. "Um, yeah. Listen, Jané, Tallie's on the other line. I'm going to conference us all in." She fumbled with the buttons, finally managing to push the right ones. "Tallie? Jané?"

They chimed in, and Felicia expelled a shaky sigh. "Jané, what have you heard?"

"*Holy shit* . . . the word around the office is that Jerry was *stabbed in his hotel room*!"

"Same here," Felicia said.

"I'm at home," Tallie said, "but my assistant just told me the same thing when I called in."

"Holy shit!" Jané said. "What the hell happened after we left? *Holy shit!*"

Tallie moaned.

"Let's calm down," Felicia said, mostly to soothe her

own nerves. "Someone was obviously there after we left."

"He could have stabbed himself," Jané said. "Maybe he logged onto his laptop, saw the picture had been sent, and couldn't take the humiliation."

Tears gathered in Felicia's throat at the suggestion, but her mind violently rejected that idea. "No," she whispered. "He wouldn't have."

"Everyone says he was murdered," Tallie said. "If he'd committed suicide, wouldn't that information have been released?"

Felicia inhaled painfully . . . this conversation was surreal. Her mind raced . . . facts. They needed facts. "Tallie, can you call your cop friend and find out what happened?"

Tallie made a rueful noise. "I think we should go to the police right now and tell them what we did."

"Are you insane?" Jané practically shouted. "We're not involved in this."

"We set him *up*." Tallie retorted, her voice breaking. "We took a picture and sent it to everyone in his address book. We're *involved*, Jané!"

"If we go to the police," Jané said, "they'll haul us in for murder."

"But we didn't kill him," Tallie insisted.

"And you think the police are going to believe that? This isn't Pleasantville, Ohio, Tallie. This is New York fucking City. They will arrest us first and ask questions later."

"Okay," Felicia said, trying to regain control. "For all we know, the police could have someone in custody, right?"

"Right," they chorused, contrite.

"So," she continued, "Tallie, can you call your cop friend and find out what happened?"

After a few seconds of silence, Tallie sighed. "Okay. I'll see what I can find out. But . . ."

"But what?" Felicia asked.

"There . . . might be a complication. I got home last night and didn't have my manuscript bag. My first thought was that I left it in the cab, but now I'm afraid—"

"You left it in the hotel room?" Jané roared.

"I don't know," Tallie murmured.

"It wouldn't be unusual for Jerry to have manuscripts," Felicia said, realizing suddenly that she was siding with Jané about not going to the police. "Is there anything in the bag to lead back to you?"

"No . . . unless you count the sole copy of Gaylord Cooper's latest book," Tallie said, her voice ending on a sob.

Felicia touched her temple—if possible, things were getting worse.

"But doesn't Jerry represent Gaylord Cooper?" Jané asked.

"Yes," Tallie got out.

"Then it would make sense that Jerry would have the manuscript," Jané said. "Look—we planned this down to the last detail, and we're still okay if everyone just chills out and keeps their mouth shut. Okay?"

Felicia's mind reeled, unable to absorb the enormity of the situation. She could feel the pull of her subconscious, the temptation to shut down . . . to cover her head . . . to run. But one end image kept her functioning— the image of the three of them in prison (or worse) for something they didn't do. Her career, gone. Her life, ruined.

"Okay?" Jané repeated, then she knocked on the receiver.

Felicia sighed. "I think Jané is right, Tallie. See what you can find out from your cop friend, and let's sit tight while things settle. We could be overreacting."

"Okay," Tallie said finally, although it was clear in her tone that she didn't completely agree. "I'll see what I can find out from my cop . . . friend."

The weight of guilt settled on Felicia's shoulders like a thick mantle. She knew that Tallie was following her lead . . . she just hoped she wasn't leading her best friend into even deeper trouble than they were in already.

 Chapter 19

Tallie disconnected the call and stared at her silent computer monitor, feeling sick. She didn't want to see the picture that Felicia had taken of Jerry, but the pull was irresistible, and she had to face it sooner or later. Like a snake striking, she tapped the power button, then started the coffeemaker while the machine booted up. She rubbed her arms, trying to keep the burgeoning panic at bay. A few minutes ago, she'd been worried the manuscript could link her to having sent the digital picture; now she was dealing with the possibility of being tied to a murder.

Murder. She closed her eyes, trying to soak in the awfulness of the word. Who would murder Jerry Key?

A lot of people, she acknowledged a split second later. Angry authors, irritated editors, pissed-off peers—not to mention a long line of cuckolded men and scorned women.

Like Felicia.

Who had been astonishingly calm last night while they'd executed their plan. At the time, Tallie had attributed her irreverent demeanor to the alcohol Felicia had consumed, but now . . .

Tallie shook her head to halt her train of thought. Felicia had wanted Jerry to get his comeuppance, but she wouldn't have killed the man. Besides, she had heard her best friend's voice on the phone. Felicia was on the verge of coming apart.

The computer chimed, then the screen vibed to life, displaying her cluttered electronic desktop. She frowned wryly—more cleaning to do. Since her apartment building was light-years away from installing a digital subscriber line and she hadn't coughed up the money for a cable modem, she was stuck with plain old dial-up. After much nervous leg-jumping and finger-drumming, she successfully connected to the server at Parkbench and pulled up her e-mail. The note with the subject line "Jerry, Jerry quite contrary" was on the top line of her inbox.

By the multiple "forwarding" notations, the original e-mail had made the rounds. With her heart tripping overtime, she double-clicked on the note. The first half of the note was addresses of people who had forwarded it and the addresses of people it was being forwarded to, along with individual commentary like "Look at this!" and "I know this guy!" At the bottom of the note was the imbedded digital image of Jerry, which loaded very slowly, one horizontal slice at a time. His yellow hair . . . the black blindfold . . . the gag . . . his naked torso, crisscrossed with painful-looking chains . . . his wrists enclosed with leather cuffs . . . his long legs stretched out on the bed spread-eagle . . . his ankles bound. When the three of them had made their escape, they had laughed their asses off about how ridiculous he had looked.

They'd left him trussed up to be found by a maid. Instead he had been found by a killer and had been helpless to do anything about it.

Tallie started shaking uncontrollably and covered her mouth with her hand. They were responsible. *She* was responsible. This was not the kind of headline she'd been hoping to give her mother this year:

OUR SPINSTER DAUGHTER IS SPENDING CHRISTMAS IN ATTICA!

She gulped air, and her mind spun wildly. Desperation welled in her chest, and she stood abruptly, sending the chair crashing to the floor. She backed away from the computer and hugged herself, choking back tears. What had they done? What *had* they done?

The ring of her doorbell jolted her out of her panic. The cleaners returning for some reason? She sniffed mightily and walked over to look through the peephole.

Keith Wages—in uniform—stared back.

She jumped back from the door and glanced around the apartment in panic. The police already knew . . . he was here to take her away. Ridiculously, she looked for an escape route but finally acknowledged that she'd rather be hauled off in handcuffs than picked off a fire escape with a tranquilizer gun, or whatever the police did to subdue fugitives. She breathed into her hand, ending on a sob.

The doorbell rang again, and she realized she had to get a grip. She hadn't killed Jerry—they couldn't lock her up for embarrassing a man to death.

She inhaled deeply a few times, then unfastened the chain and sundry dead bolts and swung open the door.

Keith looked up and smiled . . . not exactly the reception she'd expected. "Hi," he said.

"Hi," she responded tentatively.

He pointed to the hallway vent with the hat he held in his hands. "I thought I'd stop by to see if everything was okay this morning. Did the super turn the heat back on?"

Tallie hung on to the doorknob, weak with relief. "Um, yes . . . a few minutes ago."

"Good. Did the cab company call?"

"I called them, but they said it could be a day or two before I heard about my bag."

He winced. "Sorry to hear that."

Her mind swirled, trying to figure out how she could bring up the subject of Jerry without it sounding contrived.

"Is that coffee I smell?" he asked, craning his neck toward the inside of her apartment.

"Yes," she said, pouncing on the opening. "Do you have time for a cup?"

"Just one," he said with a smile. "It's really cold out there."

She opened the door, conscious of her rumpled (but clean) jeans and wrinkled (but clean) sweatshirt, both of which could have spent a little less time in the dryer. Her hair, on the other hand, could have used a little *more* time under the dryer—it was still damp and no doubt suctioned to her head. But Keith was so surprised by the state of the apartment that he didn't even notice her.

"Wow, that was some spring cleaning," he said.

Tallie squashed the urge to accept a compliment on

cleaning—the man was already getting coffee. She closed the door just shy of a slam.

"I didn't think I'd catch you at home," he said, staring at the leaning bookshelf, as if he longed to repair it. Then he looked back to her and flashed a smile. "I figured you editor types went in to the office early and stayed late."

"I wanted to check with the cab company this morning," she said. "And make sure the heat came back on."

He nodded, then suddenly turned his attention on something behind her.

The computer. Panic ballooned in her chest.

"That picture is all over the Internet," he said. "Did you know the guy is dead?"

"Um, yes . . . he worked in publishing," Tallie said, rushing to explain why she'd have something so graphic on her computer. It shouldn't matter what he thought since they weren't going to . . . *get involved*, but she wouldn't want something like that getting back to her mother via *his* mother.

"You knew this guy Key?" he asked, walking over to the computer. He leaned down to casually right the chair she'd overturned, then scrutinized the screen.

She stared at his large hand wrapped around the back of the chair. The symbolism of him making things right again wasn't lost on her. Was it a sign that she should collapse into him, regurgitate her lurid tale, and beg for his help?

But to do so would mean involving Felicia and Jané . . . not to mention that every cell in her body railed against the thought of falling into the habit of Keith Wages coming to her rescue.

In her silence, he looked back. "Did you know him?" he repeated.

She paused to select the best words to represent their relationship. "Jerry Key. He's Gaylord Cooper's literary agent."

He arched a dark brow. "So you worked with him?"

"Briefly." She walked to an overhead cabinet and removed two matching and squeaky clean coffee cups, glad to have her back to him. "Do you know what happened to him?"

"His body was found this morning in a room at the Hills Hotel. Apparently, it was a kinky scene and things went too far."

She wet her lips, torn about using their . . . *acquaintance* to glean information while keeping her involvement in the situation from Keith. It made her feel smarmy. "My assistant—she's the one who sent me the picture—told me that he was, um, stabbed." She poured coffee into both cups.

"Yeah. And whoever killed this guy had a sick sense of humor. I'm just glad he sent a 'before' photo instead of an 'after.' "

Her hand jerked, and she spilled coffee on the pristine counter.

"Need some help over there?"

"No," she said, using one of her clean dish towels to mop up the mess, scalding her hand in the process. "Ow!"

He strode over and inspected the red welt on her hand.

"It's okay," she said, pulling back.

But he resisted her movement, then turned on the cold water faucet and held her hand underneath the cool water. "I've had first-aid training," he said, his dark eyes teasing. "You have to bring down the temperature of the skin."

While the temperature of her fingers went down, the temperature around her pulse points ratcheted higher. She squirmed at his closeness—if Keith Wages knew what she'd done, he'd be slapping cuffs on her hands instead of making them all better.

"That's good," she said with a little smile, retracting her hand and shutting off the faucet. "Cream and sugar in your coffee?"

"No, thanks," he said, helping himself to the cup closest to him.

She blew on the top of the dark liquid in her cup, then took a sip. "You said 'he' sent the picture—has someone been arrested for Jerry Key's, um, murder?"

"Figure of speech," Keith said. "No one's been arrested, but I'm working with the detectives on the case so I really can't say much more than that."

"But it wasn't a suicide?"

"No." He sipped the coffee, then swallowed hard and knocked on his chest with his fist. "Wow. Maybe I'll have some cream after all."

Despite the tension wound tight in her chest, she angled her head. "I said I had coffee . . . I didn't say it was good."

He laughed and dumped in two of the fast-food brand creamers she pulled from the back of a drawer. While he stirred his coffee, she tried to reopen the subject as casually as possible, considering her desire to scream. "Well . . . do you at least have a suspect?"

He looked up. "No." He lifted his chin slightly. "Tallie, do you know something about this case?"

"No," she said . . . too quickly? "You mean about Jerry Key? No, of course not." She busied herself drinking from her coffee cup. Tallie grimaced—the stuff was pretty vile.

Keith was silent for a few agonizing seconds, then took a drink of his diluted coffee, his face unreadable. "The crime scene is still being processed."

Tallie averted her glance—would they find her manuscript bag? Keith knew she'd lost it. If it turned up, he'd be the one to make the connection. Her hairline grew moist.

"And detectives will start conducting interviews today," he continued. "Can you give me names to add to the list?"

"Um, not really," she said. "I mean, I didn't know him that well . . . just by reputation."

"He had a bad reputation?"

"I didn't say that." She swallowed hard. "I . . . truly don't—er, *didn't* know him that well."

"Just through your author?"

She hesitated, loath to mention Jerry's connection to Felicia and her connection to Felicia. "I only met Jerry Key once, and it was with Gaylord Cooper." Not counting last night when she'd been in his hotel room.

"You met him this week, when you received the manuscript that you lo—er, I mean that is missing?"

She nodded. "Y-yesterday."

He pursed his lips. "I can see why you're upset—you were probably one of the last people to see him alive."

The breath froze in her lungs. "I'm sure that's not true," she croaked.

He pulled a notebook from his pocket. "Do you know how to reach Mr. Cooper?"

She heaved what was supposed to be a cleansing sigh. "It's complicated . . . the man is a paranoid recluse. If I want to talk to him, I have to call and leave a message with his secretary, then he calls back from a random pay phone and arranges a time and a place to meet."

His eyebrows rose. "O-kay."

"He's certifiable," she agreed.

"How did he and Jerry Key get along?"

She shrugged. "Fine. In fact, Jerry seemed to be the only person Gaylord trusted. Jerry and my boss, Ron, who's on vacation."

He made a few notes. "Anyone else you would suggest that we talk to?"

She shook her head. "I'm sure Jerry's assistant and coworkers can be more helpful."

He nodded and put away the notebook. "Right. I'm sure the detectives will cover all the bases. Don't be surprised if they contact you, since you saw him yesterday."

The phone rang and she glanced at it, not wanting to answer in case it was Felicia or Jané. But it would be worse, she realized, if the machine kicked on and they left a message. *"Tallie, remember, don't tell your cop friend that we were the ones who took that picture of Jerry. . . ."*

"Excuse me," she said, then dove for the phone. "Hello?"

"Hi, Tallie, it's Mom."

And, as usual, her timing was impeccable. "Hi, Mom. Is everything okay?"

"Everything is fine here. I called your office to see if you'd received my package, and Norah told me that you'd called in sick."

"Oh, just a little cold," she said, then coughed to give

her claim some validity. She glanced across the room to find Keith watching her with a little smile and sipping his coffee as if he belonged in her kitchen. She frowned and straightened. "And I received the parcel pick-up slip, but I haven't had a chance to get to the post office."

"Oh," Merrilyn Blankenship said, disappointment clear in her voice.

Tallie closed her eyes briefly. "But if I go into the office later, I'll try to stop."

"That would be nice," her mother said. "Now, have you called Sheila's son?"

She glanced up, and when Keith grinned at her, her face flamed. "Um, Mom, this isn't a good time."

"Do you have morning company?"

Tallie rolled her eyes. "Morning company" was her mother's code for a guy sleeping over. "It's not like that."

"I didn't realize you had a special friend," her mother continued, "or I would have told Sheila to tell her son that you were . . . involved. Is it that handsome boss of yours?"

"No, Mom. It isn't Ron; it isn't anyone, okay?" Keith was now laughing. She shot daggers at him. "I'll call you later, okay?"

"Okay. Bye."

She hung up the phone and sighed.

Keith was rinsing his coffee cup. "I can guess the gist of that conversation."

"God, I hope not."

He grinned and wiped his hands on a towel, then folded it just as nice as you please and put it back on the counter. "I need to get going. Will you be okay?"

She nodded and followed him to the door, with a myriad of emotions pulling at her—gratitude for his presence and guilt for deceiving him. But in the back of her mind she kept telling herself that the killer would be caught, and no one needed to know that she, Felicia, and Jané had ever been in the hotel room.

At the door he turned. "I'm sorry about your business associate. Even if you don't know someone well, their death can still affect you."

He had no idea. She was suddenly antsy for him to leave.

A small smile lifted his mouth. "I guess I'll see you the next time you're in trouble."

She conjured up a matching smile. "Don't take this the wrong way, but I hope I don't see you any time soon."

He put on his hat and winked. "Don't take this the wrong way, but I hope you do."

As he walked away, Tallie wondered which one of them would get their wish.

Chapter 20

Halfway to her office, Tallie realized that she'd forgotten the parcel pick-up slip to retrieve the package her mother had sent her. Somehow in the midst of the lost manuscript worth millions and Jerry Key's murder, the package had slipped her mind.

She had tried to call Felicia after Keith had left, but she'd gotten Felicia's voice mail. And she didn't feel right talking to Jané without Felicia . . . the moody woman made her nervous, and she had a feeling that if given the chance, Jané would join one of them to gang up on the other.

Not that that would ever happen—she and Felicia were fast friends and would never betray each other.

Her thoughts slid to the unease nudging her conscience this morning regarding Felicia hurting Jerry. If Felicia *had* returned to the room and done something to the man, he had deserved it.

Although stabbing someone while they were in restraints did smack of mental instability. Was it possible that Jerry had driven Felicia over the edge? Her friend was a pillar of strength, but occasionally even pillars shook.

When Tallie walked into the editorial department of Parkbench, it was close to 11:00 A.M., and the noise level was definitely higher than usual. Jerry Key's name rode on the air in a swirl of conversation so titillating it practically pulsated.

"You decided to come in," Norah said as Tallie approached.

Tallie nodded. "My heat came back on and it seemed like a day I should be here."

"Just so you know, Kara has called for you, like, a dozen times. Said you were supposed to drop off Gaylord Cooper's manuscript to her last night." Norah frowned. "I thought you were editing Mr. Cooper's book."

"Change in plans," Tallie said wryly, although technically, now that Jerry was out of the picture . . .

She winced at her own train of thought. Besides, chances were good that the manuscript would come back to her once Ron got wind of what was afoot, or when Kara made a mess of things.

Considering, of course, that she located the manuscript. "Thanks, Norah. I'll call her this afternoon."

Norah's chin dipped. "What did you think of the picture?"

"Oh . . . it's . . . pretty wild."

"Yeah. And to think he was here, alive and well, just yesterday."

"Yeah."

Norah leaned in. "So, who do you think did it?"

Tallie's throat squeezed. "I wouldn't have any idea, Norah."

"There's a theory going around."

Her breath came faster. "What . . . what's the theory?"

Norah looked all around, as if she might be over-heard. "Everyone thinks it's a serial killer."

Tallie's shoulders dropped in relief at the ridiculous-ness of the statement. "Well, I'm sure the police are on it."

"The police are in Saundra's office right now."

Tallie felt her eyes go wide. "What? Why?"

Her assistant shrugged. "I don't know, but I assume it has something to do with Jerry Key."

They were onto her. She broke out in an instant sweat. "Tallie, are you okay?"

She nodded woodenly, but she couldn't speak. She simply gestured to her office, walked inside, and closed the door. Moving like an automaton, she shrugged out of her second-best coat and hung it behind her door, then walked to her desk and picked up the phone to dial Feli-cia's number. Her hand shook violently, and she consid-ered getting sick into her garbage can. Before her body could oblige, there was a knock on her door. When she looked up, her worst fear was confirmed . . . Saundra Pellum stood in the doorway with two suited gentlemen behind her. Neither of them looked as accommodating as Keith Wages.

"Tallie, I need a few minutes of your time," Saundra said.

Tallie replaced the phone unsteadily and clasped her hands in her lap beneath her desk. She sensed she should stand, but she didn't trust her legs. "S-sure, Saundra. What can I do for you?"

Saundra waved in the two men and closed the door be-hind them. "These are Detectives Riley and McKinley. Gentlemen, this is Tallie Blankenship, one of my editors."

They each murmured a greeting and she nodded, unable to speak. Her teeth were literally chattering.

Saundra stepped forward, and if possible, her expression grew even more stern. "Tallie, we have a little . . . *issue,* and the detectives would like to talk to you."

Tallie blinked, now unable to even nod.

Saundra's mouth tightened. "It seems that Ron is missing."

Tallie opened her mouth to confess, then squinted. "Excuse me?"

"Ron didn't make it to his parents' house in Maine. They contacted me this morning, and have already filed a missing person report."

She shook her head, trying to make sense of what Saundra was saying—at the moment, the rush of relief that she wasn't being arrested was overriding every other sensation. "Maybe Ron simply made another stop first."

"His rental car was found abandoned," Detective Riley said.

"On the highway?" Tallie asked, suddenly fearful.

"In Hoboken," Riley said.

Across the river? "But Ron lives in Greenwich."

"Precisely," Detective McKinley said. "When was the last time you heard from Mr. Springer?"

She touched her head, trying to remember, then looked at Saundra. "It was the day we were in the boardroom watching Kara's segment on CNN—was that Wednesday?" It seemed like a year ago.

Saundra nodded. "Did Ron call you?"

"Yes, but we really didn't talk. The reception on his cell phone was bad, his voice kept going in and out. He mentioned Gaylord Cooper, so I think he was just checking in to see if things were going okay."

"Gaylord Cooper is one of Ron's authors," Saundra explained.

"What time was the call?" Riley asked.

"Around one-thirty."

"Did Mr. Springer say where he was, or where he was headed?"

She thought a moment, replaying the broken conversation in her head. "No."

"Ms. Blankenship, do you know if Mr. Springer was involved with anyone—a woman . . . or a man?"

She squirmed. "No. Ron was a very private person."

"Ms. Pellum says that Ron hasn't been himself lately. How did he seem to you the last few weeks that he was here?"

"Preoccupied," she said. "Distracted."

"Do you know why?"

"No. Like I said, Ron was very private."

"We understand that he worked with Jerry Key," McKinley said.

At the sudden veer in the conversation, her pulse skyrocketed. "Y-yes."

"Do you know the extent of their relationship?"

Tallie frowned. "Ron and Jerry? What are you getting at?"

"Did Mr. Springer like Mr. Key?"

"I've never heard Ron say anything bad about Jerry, just that Jerry had a reputation."

"A reputation for what?"

Tallie shrugged carefully. "For being difficult, arrogant."

"A playboy?"

"I guess that too."

"Do you know if Mr. Springer had any . . . fetishes?"

"Fetishes?" she asked, incredulous.

"You know . . . leather, whips and chains?"

She stared, and it began to dawn on her that they were trying to connect Ron's disappearance with Jerry's murder. "Did I mention that Ron was a private person?"

"Is that a 'no'?"

"Yes, that's a 'no.' If Ron had fetishes, he didn't talk about them."

"Do you know if the two men ever disagreed about anything?"

"Not to my knowledge. I believe that Gaylord Cooper was the only author they had in common, and Jerry seemed to be respectful of the working relationship that Ron had with Mr. Cooper. From what I saw, Jerry was very hands-off and let Ron take care of everything where Mr. Cooper was concerned."

McKinley grunted. "I understand that Jerry Key was here yesterday to see you, Ms. Blankenship."

The moment of truth . . . or untruth. She squeezed her hands together in her lap until they hurt. "That's right. Ron asked me to look after Mr. Cooper while he was away. Jerry met me and Mr. Cooper here for the delivery of a manuscript."

"How did Mr. Key behave?"

She lifted her eyebrows. "What do you mean?"

"I mean, did he seem normal?"

Tallie unclenched her hands and lifted them. "It was the first time I'd met Mr. Key, so I'm not really in a position to know how he was normally."

"Ms. Pellum said that your meeting didn't go well."

Tallie's gaze flew to Saundra, whose expression remained stoic. "Actually, that's not true. I was under the impression that the meeting went very well."

"But after the meeting, Jerry requested that his author be handled by another editor," Riley said.

She wet her lips. "Yes."

"So the two of you must not have hit it off."

She swallowed and tried to affect a casual tone. "Apparently Mr. Key decided he preferred an editor he perceived to have better skills in . . . marketing." She flicked her gaze to Saundra to see if the woman understood. From the quirk of her mouth, she did.

"So would you say that Jerry Key was a likable person, Ms. Blankenship?" Riley asked.

"I really couldn't say—"

"Just your general perception," McKinley cut in with a shrug. "What did you think of the guy, having just met him?"

She considered both of the men and Saundra, and realized that she could help paint a picture of Jerry Key as a man who had many enemies. "The truth? I thought that Jerry seemed like the kind of guy who would stab you in the back."

McKinley nodded thoughtfully. "Interesting choice of words, considering that's almost exactly what happened to Mr. Key."

A hot flush climbed her neck, then her face. "Will that be all?"

Riley gave her a flat little smile. "Can you tell us what time Mr. Key left yesterday?"

She shrugged. "Between nine and nine-thirty, I

think." *Don't ask me if I saw him again,* she prayed. *Don't ask . . .*

"Just one more thing, Ms. Blankenship."

She held her breath.

"Can you think of anything else that might help us to locate Mr. Springer?"

Tallie exhaled and shook her head, then stopped. "Wait . . . there was one thing." She pressed her lips together, trying to remember details. "Ron called me to his office Monday to talk about handing over responsibility for Mr. Cooper's manuscript. As I was leaving, his phone rang and when he answered it, he seemed agitated at the person on the line."

"Was it his desk phone or his cell phone?"

"Desk phone."

"Did you hear what he said to the caller?"

"He said that he was in enough trouble without the person calling him at work."

The detectives looked at Saundra. "Trouble?"

She shook her head. "I don't know what he was referring to unless it was his state of mind. Ron was a stellar employee. He requested a leave of absence because he recognized that his emotional problems were affecting his job."

Riley looked back to Tallie. "Do you have any idea who he was talking to?"

"No."

"If you hear from Mr. Springer, will you let us know right away?"

"Of course." She bit her lip. "Do you really think something happened to Ron?"

Riley gave her a rueful smile. "We have an unsolved

murder and a missing man, and the two people knew each other. If the cases aren't related, it's a pretty big coincidence."

Tallie sat back in her seat, boneless. Ron? *Her* Ron? Could he really be involved in Jerry's murder?

 Chapter 21

"Bye," Felicia said, then waited for Tallie and Jané both to hang up before she did. A click sounded, and the light next to the line Tallie was on went out.

"Felicia," Jané said, "are you still there?"

"There" was a relative place, Felicia thought. She was sitting in her chair holding the phone, but her mind had been all but absent from her bodily experiences since this morning. *Jerry's dead . . . Jerry's dead . . . Jerry's dead . . .*

"I'm here," she murmured.

"Felicia, listen—I'm afraid that Tallie is going to spill her guts to this cop friend of hers."

Felicia massaged her temple. She couldn't take another Imitrex for an hour. "Why do you think that?"

"Because Tallie's not like me and you, Felicia. Deep down, she's still a country girl—naïve enough to think that if we tell the truth, nothing will happen to us."

Felicia frowned. "Tallie's not going to say anything."

"Are you sure? How well does she know this cop—is she sleeping with him?"

"No, he's like . . . the son of her mother's friend, or something like that."

"Oh, great—he's a bumpkin, too?"

Anger sparked in Felicia's stomach. "Tallie's not a bumpkin—she deserves more credit than that."

"Look, all I'm saying is to keep an eye on her—her boyfriend might convince her to tell everything in return for immunity."

"But we didn't kill Jerry, Jané."

"And are you so sure about your friend Tallie?"

Felicia's stomach bottomed out. "Are you insinuating that Tallie might have done this?"

Jané made a rueful sound. "Haven't you wondered how Tallie knew that Jerry would be at the hotel last night?"

"She said he mentioned it to her in their meeting yesterday morning."

"And I guess that just came up in casual conversation? Are you sure they weren't having an affair?"

Felicia clamped her mouth shut. She knew firsthand how irresistible Jerry could be.

"And now Tallie tells us that the police suspect her boss might be involved . . . what if she and her boss did it together?"

Felicia gave a little laugh. "That's just crazy, Jané. Tallie didn't have as good a motive as—" She stopped herself.

"As you or I?" Jané finished with a harsh laugh. "Bingo. So if she and her cop share a little pillow talk and everything comes out, it'll look worse on us. You used to sleep with Jerry and you took the picture of him. I set up the message and hit the Send button. Tallie just stood back and watched."

"That was her job, Jané—to keep watch."

"And she managed to leave a bag on the scene!"

"We don't know that for sure," Felicia said stubbornly.

Jané sighed. "Mark my words, Felicia . . . Tallie will talk."

Felicia's mouth tightened. "Jané, it seems to me that you're the one who's doing all the talking."

Silence, then, "*Fine*. But just so you know, Felicia—if word gets out, it's every woman for herself."

A click sounded, and the light for the second line went out. Felicia replaced the handset with a very bad feeling rolling around in her empty stomach. She didn't entirely trust Jané, but the woman had brought up some valid points. If their story came out, things would look worse for her and Jané . . . for her in particular since she'd once been involved with Jerry.

Although she hadn't witnessed his S&M fetish first-hand, she'd been aware of it. Frankly, she'd been glad that with her, Jerry had been all about meat-and-potatoes sex—she was of the mind-set that props were for one-night stands and marriages past their prime. It had made her feel special that their lovemaking had needed no artificial stimulants. Indeed, the sight of him blindfolded and restrained on the bed had struck her as rather silly and a little pathetic. And it had enraged her all over again that he hadn't been the man she'd thought he was.

She bit her tongue to stem a pool of sudden, hot tears. Had he shared and acted out his fantasies with Suze Dannon? Felicia allowed a thought that had been fermenting all day in her aching head to materialize: Had Suze murdered Jerry? Had she shown up at his room and their hurt-me play had gone too far? Or had Jerry broken off their affair and Suze had retaliated?

The woman didn't seem capable of murder, but she did make a living writing about it. Felicia closed her eyes. And she herself was living proof that a scorned woman was capable of shocking behavior—from humiliating a former lover to having revenge sex with an author.

At the knock on her door, she looked up to see Tamara standing there with a pained look on her face. "Suze Dannon is here—do you have time to see her?"

Felicia blinked. "Um, yes, I'll see her." But her heart was tripping fast when Suze walked in, looking a little less willful than the last time she'd been there, her obnoxious red coat billowing behind her.

"Oh, Felicia," she cried, her face crumpling. "I just heard about Jerry—it's so awful!"

Felicia embraced the woman reluctantly and released her quickly. "Yes, it's a tragedy. I'm sorry, Suze, that I didn't call to tell you personally, but frankly, I'm still trying to acclimate myself."

Suze nodded, her face now red and puffy. "I'm in total shock. I can't imagine how you must feel since you and Jerry"—she stopped and took a well-placed swallow— "have known each other for so long."

"Yes," Felicia said, nodding. She had to avert her gaze to gather her composure—she couldn't look at Suze without remembering her in Jerry's welcome embrace on the sidewalk.

"Oh, I'm a mess," Suze whimpered, wiping at her eyes. "Do you have a tissue?"

"Of course." Felicia opened the bottom drawer of her desk and rooted around for a purse pack of tissues. Her gaze landed on the photo of herself, and she inhaled sharply. Jerry shouldn't have done it . . . he shouldn't have done a lot of things, but he hadn't deserved to die. Felicia slammed the drawer and handed the tissues over the top of her desk.

She waited while Suze blew her nose heartily and mopped up most of the moisture around her eyes. "Do you know anything about the funeral arrangements?"

"No," Felicia said. "But if I hear anything, I'll make sure you and Phil know."

"Thank you," Suze murmured.

"I'm a little surprised you're still in town," Felicia said. "Have you been visiting . . . friends?"

"Consulting with my attorney," Suze said with a sniff. "About the separation and all this nonsense of Phil trying to stop me from using my writing name."

Felicia sat forward, clasping her hands in front of her. "Suze, I'm glad you stopped by, because I needed to talk to you about something else. This isn't exactly the best timing, but it can't be helped."

Suze lifted her gaze, and Felicia saw a flash of fear in the woman's weepy eyes—did she suspect that Felicia knew about her affair with Jerry? Felicia maintained her silence a few more seconds for the sheer satisfaction of tormenting the woman who had gone from being a likable and competent writer to an unlikable and difficult diva. "I know about the plagiarism in the current manuscript."

A multitude of emotions passed over Suze's face—relief, shock, remorse, then denial. "I don't know what you're talking about."

"Don't do this," Felicia said. "The publishing industry is a small world. Editors talk about manuscripts that cross their desks, and last night an editor friend told me about a manuscript of one of her writers in which the victims are murdered through their e-book reading devices. They read about their own murder, and then it happens. Sound familiar?"

Suze lifted one shoulder. "Coincidence. There's no such thing as an original idea."

"I would ordinarily agree with you," Felicia said. "Except I read passages in her author's manuscript, and they were *very* similar to the passages in your manuscript."

A flush stained Suze's face. "That's impossible," she said with a little fake laugh.

"It would be," Felicia agreed, "except that Jerry had read and rejected the manuscript." She gave Suze a pointed look. "So I think we both know how the material wound up in your manuscript."

Suze shook her head stubbornly.

"Phil told me that the e-book element was your idea, and that you were especially resistant to changing any of those scenes."

Suze narrowed her eyes. "When did Phil tell you that?"

Panic blipped in Felicia's chest . . . did Suze know about her and Phil? "He told me Wednesday, after you stormed out to mee—" She stopped herself and exhaled. "After you stormed out of the meeting." She pursed her mouth. "The bottom line is, you have to take out the material."

Suze stood and paced to the window, then looked back, her expression utterly defeated. "Okay, you're right . . . Jerry gave me the idea, and a few photocopied pages, but he swore it was a book that would never see the light of day."

"It doesn't matter, Suze—it's someone else's work. It's stealing. Plagiarism is a *crime*."

"A crime?" Suze laughed harshly and walked back to Felicia's desk. "How ironic, because I came to talk to *you* about a crime."

Felicia's mouth went dry. "What . . . what are you talking about?" She was struck with terror that Suze somehow knew what she and the girls had done . . . but if so, then Suze must have murdered Jerry. Was she about to confront . . . or confess? Felicia stared up at the woman who seemed to be weighing her options.

Finally Suze shook her head. "It's so awful, I can't even say it."

Felicia took shallow breaths. "What, Suze?"

"I think I know who killed Jerry."

Felicia felt light-headed.

Suze pressed her lips together, then murmured, "Phil."

Felicia thudded back to earth. *"Phil?"*

Suze nodded tearfully. "I tried to reach him all last night and he didn't answer his phone. When he called me back this morning, he was very evasive about where he'd been all night, and . . . I don't know, call it a wife's intuition, but I just got this feeling that he'd done something *wrong*."

Oh, God, this wasn't happening. "Suze," Felicia said, holding out her hand, "you're jumping to a big conclusion. Phil could have been out drinking all night, or gambling, or, or, or . . . at a strip club."

"Or he might have killed Jerry," Suze said evenly.

Felicia paused, then gave Suze an equally pointed look. "And what possible motive could Phil have had to kill Jerry?"

She could see the wheels turning in Suze's head. If she admitted to having an affair with Jerry, she could implicate herself in the murder . . . especially if Phil wound up having an alibi. "None," she murmured finally.

"Right," Felicia said. "So I think you'd better let the police handle this. They'll put the right person behind bars." She stood and walked over to a tall file cabinet, opened a drawer, and withdrew the folder containing the changes that Phil had faxed to her. "Meanwhile, you have some revising to do."

After a few seconds' hesitation, Suze took the folder. "And no one will ever know about this conversation?"

Felicia crossed her arms. "What conversation?"

Suze nodded. "Okay then . . . I'll send a revised manuscript as soon as possible."

"Good enough."

A knock sounded at the door and Felicia looked past Suze to Tamara, who had stuck her head in. "I'm sorry to interrupt, but the police are here to ask you a few questions about . . . Jerry."

One more hurdle. She clenched her jaw, then smiled. "Suze was just leaving, weren't you, Suze?"

"Yes," the woman said and practically jogged past Tamara, who then ushered in two suited gentlemen with loosened ties and knowing eyes—Detectives Riley and McKinley. Felicia did a double take—Martin McKinley reminded her of her father, thick-shouldered and square-jawed. The two men would be about the same age. Is this how her father looked now—a slight paunch and a receding hairline?

"Sit down, gentlemen," Felicia said, then reclaimed her seat behind her desk. "What can I do for you?"

"We're investigating the murder of Jerry Key," Riley

said, "and we're asking routine questions of people who knew him. His secretary gave us your name."

Good old Lori. "Yes, I knew Jerry. We've worked together on various projects over the years."

"Word is you two used to be an item," McKinley said.

She nodded slowly, trying to shake the natural defiance she felt toward McKinley simply because he looked like the man who had walked out on her when she was nine. "We were involved for a couple of months about a year ago."

"Who ended the relationship?" Riley asked.

"I did," she lied.

"Really? We heard different. In fact, Mr. Key's secretary told us that he had to change his pager number after you split up because you kept calling."

Anger bubbled in her chest, but she managed a sad little noise. "That's simply not true. But I'm not surprised that Jerry wanted people to think that he broke it off."

McKinley leaned forward. "Cocky SOB, was he?"

"Yes," she said, then tamped down her anger. "But it was his job to be cocky. He was a salesman."

"An ethical salesman?" Riley asked.

She gave them a mild smile. "Jerry made deals happen any way he could."

"Like sleeping around?"

She shifted in her chair. "That happens in this industry, but it didn't figure into our relationship."

"Your relationship was different?" McKinley probed.

It was crazy, but she wanted this man to think well of her. "I believe so—we cared about each other."

"So why did you end it?"

She wet her lips. "It was too intense, dating someone in the same business. I didn't want it to affect my career."

"So you weren't obsessed with Jerry Key?"

Felicia battled to remain calm, but her face felt warm. "Absolutely not."

McKinley seemed satisfied. "When was the last time you saw Mr. Key?"

Last night in his hotel room, and before that, Wednesday in Suze's arms. Felicia frowned, then shook her head. "I can't recall. Probably at a party during the holidays?"

"Which party?"

"I'm sorry—there are too many to keep track."

"When did you last talk to him?"

"That would have been Wednesday. He was supposed to be here for a meeting with me and two of his clients, a writing team that I edit. He didn't show, and I called his secretary. She paged him, and he called me back."

"Where was he?"

She gave them a flat smile. "At his club, getting a massage."

"What's the name of his club?"

She hesitated, then realized she had no reason not to tell them. "The Green Globe Spa—at least, that's where he used to belong."

"So he blew off the meeting," Riley said.

She shrugged. "He said he thought I could handle the meeting without him—it was no big deal to him."

"Was it a big deal to you?"

Felicia splayed her hands in front of her. "Only because I was trying to mediate a problem between the writers. I thought his presence might make things go more smoothly."

Riley nodded again and looked as if he wanted her to say more. She didn't.

"Who were the authors?"

"Suze and Phillip Dannon—they are a married couple who write as Suzanne Phillipo."

"Yeah, I've heard of them," McKinley said. "Don't they write kinky murder mysteries?"

"Sensual crime novels," she corrected.

Riley looked back to his notebook. "That was Wednesday . . . so why did you call Mr. Key yesterday, let's see—four times?"

She lifted her chin. "The same reason—the matter wasn't yet settled when the Dannons left my office. I was hoping Jerry could help me expedite a solution, else the release date of the book was going to have to be pushed back."

"Did you ever hear back from him?"

"No."

"Ms. Redmon, do you know if Mr. Key was involved with anyone romantically?"

The image of Suze wrapping him in her big ridiculous red coat was burned into her retinas. "No, I don't."

McKinley opened a file and held up the photo of Jerry bound to the bed . . . the photo she herself had taken using his phone. The print resolution wasn't great, but simply seeing it again was enough to take her breath away. He'd been alive when she'd snapped the photo . . . *alive and healthy . . . his heart beating . . . his body long and splendid . . .*

"Ms. Redmon, are you familiar with this picture?"

"Yes. I'm in Jerry's address book, which is—I assume— why I received the e-mail message containing the picture."

"Were you shocked by the S&M getup?"

"Jerry had quite a reputation, but it wasn't a side that he ever revealed to me."

"Ms. Redmon, do you have any idea who could have taken that photo?"

Felicia channeled all of her energy into looking perplexed and sad, then shook her head slowly. "No."

McKinley pushed to his feet and Riley followed suit. "Thank you for your time, Ms. Redmon. We'll let you get back to work."

She walked them to the door . . . she was almost over the hurdle.

"Oh, just one more thing," McKinley said, turning back. "Where were you last night, Ms. Redmon?"

She gave a little laugh, then touched her temple. "I left here about six o'clock, met some friends for a drink, and then I went home."

"Do you live alone?"

She nodded.

"Were you at home alone all evening?"

Panic barbed through her as she tried to decide what to say. "Yes . . . except for a brief time when my author Phillip Dannon came by to drop off some paperwork."

McKinley raised an eyebrow. "What time was that?"

"I'm not sure . . . maybe around ten-thirty."

"Kind of late for a business meeting." His words sounded almost . . . fatherly.

"He was headed out of the city back to his home in the Hamptons."

"I see. And can Mr. Dannon corroborate your story?"

She swallowed. "Of course."

The detective stared at her, as if he were sizing her up for the truth. "Thank you."

Felicia maintained a flat smile until her door closed behind them. Then she strode to her desk drawer and downed another Imitrex with a swallow of caffeinated

water. She bit down on her tongue to tuck the tears behind the veil of numbness that had descended this morning when Tamara had first told her that Jerry was dead.

She dreaded the moment when the numbness lifted.
She never wanted to feel again. . . .

Chapter 22

The phone jolted Tallie awake Saturday morning. She did a vertical leap out of her bed and landed with the receiver in her hand. After pushing her hair out of her eyes, she stabbed the Call button and croaked, "Hello?"

"Mrs. Tallie Blankenship?"

"Miss," she corrected, shielding her eyes from the blinding daylight streaming through her abnormally clean windows. "Who's speaking?"

"This is Mr. Hooks down at Yellow Cab. You reported leaving a bag in one of our taxis?"

"Yes," she said, then held her breath.

"Black, twelve inches by eighteen inches with straps?"

"Yes," she said, then held her breath again.

"With an envelope inside?"

"*Yes,*" she said, then held her breath again.

"Well . . . we found it."

Unspeakable relief flooded her body. She whooped with joy and did a little dance, thanking the man profusely. "You are my hero! Where can I pick up my bag?"

He gave her directions to the terminal and advised her she'd have to show a picture ID to retrieve the item at lost and found. She thanked him until he hung up on her, then she ran around her apartment, screaming with joy. After the week she'd had, she was due some good news.

A knock sounded at her door, and she frowned in the direction of the clock—8:35 A.M. If it were Keith Wages, he was going to get an eyeful of what she looked like just rolling out of bed . . . in fact, she thought, tromping to the door, it just might be enough to extinguish any thoughts he could be having about them hooking up.

She unlocked the dead bolts and opened the door as far as the chain would allow. Mr. Emory stood there and, from the disheveled state of his—gulp—*Finding Nemo* printed pajamas and his wiry hair, he also was not long from the rack.

"Someone dying in there?" he asked.

"What? No."

"Then what's with all the screamin'?"

She blanched. "Oh . . . I . . . was happy." She gave him a wry smile. "*Was* being the operative word."

"Yeah? Well, keep it down. The residents got me jumping at every little noise since that man crawled up in the ceiling and died." He stomped off down the hall, muttering under his breath.

Tallie closed the door—her good mood would not be compromised. She'd scarcely slept a wink last night, which was actually preferable to the nightmares that had dogged her the few times she had managed to doze off.

She stepped into a lukewarm shower and hummed to try to keep troubling thoughts at bay—Jerry's murder, their involvement, Ron's disappearance. It was almost too much to comprehend. Yesterday seemed surreal . . .

cartoonish. She desperately hoped that finding her bag was a good omen. Maybe the police had found the killer . . . or maybe someone had confessed. Either way, her mother was right: By the light of day, things did seem better.

Her mother. Guilt tugged at her—she had to remember to pick up her mother's package at the post office. And she needed to set aside an hour to call and listen to her mother's stream of consciousness with good-daughter patience.

She turned off the water and dried quickly, eager to get to the taxi terminal and put her paws on the manuscript. Dressing was harder now that she had so many clean clothes to choose from, but she opted for soft corduroys and a sweater that she'd picked up at the Salvation Army. Her shopping at Goodwill made her mother crazy—it was all dead people's clothes, Merrilyn declared, and who knew what kinds of plague germs could be lurking in the yarn, just waiting to infect cheapskates who didn't properly disinfect the garments before wearing them. In deference to her mother, she sprayed the sweater with Mountain Breeze Lysol and pulled it over her head.

She called Kara Hatteras before she left. After four rings, the woman's groggy voice came on the line.

"Hel . . . lo."

"Oh, Kara, did I wake you?" Tallie asked, smiling.

"Good God, Tallie, this has to be you. No one else has such deplorable timing."

"I'll be there with the manuscript in a couple of hours."

"Well, fucking finally—did you have to bond with it first? You'd better not have made a copy, for Christ's sake. Gaylord Cooper is a psycho just waiting for a lame reason to fucking snap."

"Good-bye, Scary." Tallie disconnected the call and opened the coat closet to find a hat. Her gaze landed on Felicia's beautiful coat, and she felt a rush of affection for her friend for offering to have her cleaners get the coffee stain out of the chubby striped wool coat that Tallie loved. One of these days, Felicia was going to make someone a great wife—she knew all the best service providers, from maids to dry cleaners to bakeries to seamstresses.

On her walk to the train, she called Felicia, who was an early riser for some ungodly reason.

"Hello," Felicia said, her voice thick with sleep.

"Oh, I woke you . . . I'm so sorry."

"It's okay," Felicia whispered, obviously trying to rouse herself.

"Are you sick?" Tallie asked, immediately concerned.

"Just tired," she said. "I didn't get much sleep . . . can't imagine why."

"I hear you," Tallie said, although she sensed Felicia was hurting over Jerry's death more than she was letting on. "But I have some good news."

"Well, let's hear it."

"The taxi company found my bag with Gaylord's manuscript, and I'm on my way now to get it."

"That is good news . . . I know you're relieved."

"Yeah," Tallie said. "I just might be able to keep my job . . . if I can stay out of prison."

"Don't even joke about it," Felicia said. "What did you do last night?"

"Alphabetized the books on my bookshelf."

"Hm?"

Tallie sighed. "Let's just say my apartment is benefiting from me lying low and trying to keep my mind off . . . things."

"Have you talked to your cop since yesterday?"

"He's not *my* cop," Tallie said. "And no, I haven't talked to him. I don't want him to think that . . . I'm interested. But I'll probably call him today or tomorrow just to see if there have been any developments."

"I don't suppose you've heard from Ron?"

Tallie's stomach clenched. "No, I haven't, and I'm really worried about him. Do you think he could have had anything to do with Jerry's death?"

"Are you asking me if Jerry was bisexual?"

"Well . . . was he?"

"Not to my knowledge," Felicia said dryly. "But it has been a year since we were together, and I guess things change."

"Did you ever hear rumors about Ron being into S&M?"

"No," Felicia said, then made noises as if she were rearranging herself in bed. "But it's strange . . . I always suspected that Ron had this secret life, you know a side that no one else knew about. He was such a contradiction in terms—he was an intellectual, but he preferred to work on genre fiction. He was in the Army, but he collected midcentury chairs. He was like this . . . chameleon."

"Did you ever meet any of his lovers?"

"No, but Ron was very private. I ran into him once after I left Parkbench—I was in Albany with my mother for some sort of legal symposium, and when we went to dinner one night, I looked across the restaurant and there was Ron, having dinner with a distinguished-looking gentleman."

"Did you say hello?"

"Sure—and Ron literally came out of his chair. It was obvious he didn't want anyone to recognize him, he didn't even introduce me to his dinner companion. I kind of got the idea that the guy was military, so I figured it was someone Ron knew from the Reserves."

"So why would he care that you saw him?"

"Because the other guy was wearing a wedding ring."

"Oh."

"Right. He called me at work the next day and tried to make light of the whole thing, said he'd appreciate it if I didn't mention to anyone that I'd run into him."

"What did you say?"

"I told him that was cool, and I didn't mention it . . . until now."

"So, do you think this 'secret' life of his had something to do with Jerry's death? The police don't think it's a coincidence that no one can seem to find him."

Felicia's sigh whistled across the line. "I have no idea, Tallie. The truth is, Jerry knew a lot of people personally and professionally and eventually pissed off nearly every one of them . . . anyone could have done it. Or it could have been a complete stranger."

"The serial killer theory?"

"Or someone he met at a club or online."

Felicia sighed. "Tallie, I have something to tell you."

Hearing the dread in her friend's voice, her stomach clenched. "What?"

"The other day I received something in the mail . . . something disturbing."

"What was it?"

Felicia hesitated for so long, Tallie thought she might not even answer. "It was a picture . . . of me . . . nude."

.

Tallie gasped. "What? Who sent it?"

"I don't know for sure, but I think it was Jerry."

A sick, sick feeling pooled in Tallie's intestines. "But . . . why?"

"Who knows why Jerry did half the things he did?"

Felicia's blasé tone worried Tallie the most—she sounded . . . *disconnected.* Unease roiled in her stomach as the implication became clearer. "Felicia, is that why you suggested we take the photo of him?"

"Yes," Felicia murmured, her voice anguished.

"You should have told us," Tallie said, her voice more angry than she'd intended. She felt betrayed that Felicia hadn't told her everything . . . as if she'd been set up.

"Would it have made a difference?" Felicia asked.

"You're still in love with him, aren't you?"

Felicia's silence spoke volumes.

Tallie pulled her hand over her mouth, sickened by the revelation.

Tallie looked up and saw the subway sign. "I'm almost at the station. I need to go."

"Tallie, when you talk to your cop . . ."

"Yeah?"

"I know you wanted to tell the police everything when this first happened, but you realize, don't you, that if we come forward now, we're definitely going to look guilty."

Tallie frowned, puzzled. "Are you afraid that I'm going to tell Keith what happened?"

"All I know is that sometimes it can be tempting to trust someone . . . to trust a man and to believe that he's going to fix things."

Tallie stopped abruptly, and a guy behind her clipped her shoulder as he dodged her suddenly stationary body. He glanced back, then kept walking, but a sense of déjà vu struck her like a whip. It took a few seconds for her memory to catch up. A sweatshirt hood obscured his hair, but she was sure it was the baby-faced shooter from the coffeehouse. A chill traveled up her spine . . . coincidence? Keith had said the guy lived in her neighborhood, so it wasn't out of the question that he would be walking down the same street. Was he already out of jail? He kept walking and didn't look back, disappearing in the crowd a few seconds later.

"Tallie, are you there?"

"Yeah," she said, craning her neck, but she didn't spot him again.

"Are you angry?"

She blinked and tried to remember what Felicia had said . . . something about a man fixing things? Oh, right—Keith Wages. "Felicia, you of all people know that the last thing in the world I want to be is a damsel in distress."

"I know that," Felicia said. "I'm sorry."

"It's okay," Tallie said. "We're all under a lot of stress right now. I have to go, but I'll call you later."

"I'm glad you found your bag."

"Me, too."

Tallie disconnected the call and cast another glance in the direction the hooded man had taken. Nothing. She sighed, telling herself that she was reading too much into every situation. True, this week had been a doozie—the shooting, almost being run down by a car, the dead guy in the HV/AC shaft, losing the manuscript, Jerry's death, then Ron's disappearance. But New York was a dangerous place with dangerous people walking around, and this week she seemed to be separated only a degree or two from the danger.

Shaking off the heebie-jeebies, she descended the stairs to the train station and waited on the platform, studying the cross section of people around her—grungers, punkers, skaters, tourists, artists, athletes, bankers. Tattooed and pierced, swathed in cultural clothing, all colors and languages . . . it was what she loved about New York, and if she had to live with a little danger in her life in order to experience it, it was worth it.

A train came quickly (another thing she loved about New York), and a few stops later, she was climbing the steps to the taxi terminal, her heart thumping in anticipation of getting the manuscript back. Mr. Hooks at the lost-and-found counter remembered her from the exuberance of thank-yous. She showed her picture ID, then with no pomp and circumstance whatsoever, was handed her manuscript bag. She glanced inside to make sure the envelope was intact, then clasped it to her chest and breathed a lung-emptying sigh of relief.

"Says here that there's a reward," Mr. Hooks said.

Tallie blinked, then remembered that Keith had added that tidbit for incentive. She pursed her mouth, then opened her purse and scrutinized her slim wallet—twelve dollars and a book of stamps. She handed over the ten and the stamps, then tossed in a free drink coupon from Starbucks. "Thanks." Then she turned and fled.

While waiting for the train, she reached inside the bag and withdrew the thick manila envelope. On the back flap, over the wide piece of clear packing tape, were the letters G.C. in her handwriting. No one had tampered with it, no one had read the manuscript. She sent a thank-you skyward and returned the envelope to the bag.

In deference to the sunny day, she walked from the train station to Kara's, welcoming the bite in the air. She hoped the cool air would clear her head, help her come to grips with the decision she'd made yesterday to go along with Felicia and Jané about not going to the police immediately. Her stomach contracted painfully. Operating under a state of shock, the consequences of coming forward had seemed too costly to contemplate. She had assuaged her guilt with the knowledge that they were innocent of Jerry's murder.

But what if their story could help with the investigation? What if one of them had seen something or someone that had seemed insignificant at the time but in fact could lead the police to the killer?

And she hadn't counted on the weight of her conscience, which seemed to grow heavier with each breath . . . breaths that Jerry Key had been denied. Trying to sleep last night had been pure torture, and she wasn't exactly looking forward to it again tonight.

Felicia had suggested that the three of them not be seen together in public for a while. She had said it might look suspicious, or might jog the memory of someone who had seen them together at The Bottom Rung the night of Jerry's murder. Felicia was especially concerned that Bert Nichols would recall their conversation about Jerry and become suspicious. But Tallie wondered if Felicia was simply afraid that if they got together, tempers would flair and something incriminating might be overheard. Or if Felicia was trying to distance herself from Tallie and Jané altogether so she wouldn't have to face what they'd done.

For now, it was probably the smart thing to do, but Tallie felt secluded . . . lonely. She didn't mind being alone when things were going well, which was most of the time—until lately. But with the ground shifting beneath her feet, she conceded the advantage of having someone . . . *substantial* to grab onto.

A woman race-walked by her on the sidewalk wearing a coat that reminded Tallie of her striped wool standby—she hoped that the coffee stain wasn't set in. If so, she thought wryly, it would be a lasting reminder of Keith Wages after his attention moved on to a more adoring woman. She was very grateful for his assistance . . . and even for his company. It was nice to know that there was someone in town whom she could call if she was in trouble.

Again . . . or more.

Tallie shivered in her lighter-weight coat and considered taking a shortcut or two to get to Kara's building. She glanced up to get her bearings and saw a bicyclist barreling down the sidewalk toward her, paying no heed to the pedestrians leaping out of the way. The woman who had bustled by her didn't move fast enough. The bicyclist reached out and ripped a dark bag from the woman's arm, then the purse snatcher, his face obscured by a full-face knit cap, sped past Tallie, who barely had time to fling herself in the bushes.

She lay facedown in prickly landscaping, trying to process what had happened. Cold wetness seeped through her gloves and clothing. She groaned and slowly pushed to her feet, managing to grind elbows and knees into the muddy mulch in the process.

She slung her hands to free as much of the debris as possible, then collected the manuscript bag and her purse and hurried over to help the woman who had been knocked down.

"Are you okay?" Tallie asked, relieved to see the woman was trying to stand.

The young woman nodded, although tears ran down her cheeks. Tallie's heart squeezed with sympathy—the woman couldn't be more than twenty-two, and to have your purse stolen was a life-altering experience. And she felt a tad guilty, too, because she was so damned thankful it hadn't been her. Gripping the seemingly cursed manuscript bag a little tighter, she was antsy to give it to Kara and be done with it.

She used her phone to call 911 and stayed with the woman—who had been hurrying to get to the bank before it closed and happened to have had a wad of cash in her wallet, unlike Tallie, who had a whopping two bucks left—until a police cruiser arrived. She ignored the barb of disappointment when Keith Wages didn't emerge from the car, then reminded her silly self that he wasn't her personal police force. She and the young woman tried to describe the purse snatcher and his bicycle, but they couldn't give the officer much to go on. He offered them both a ride home, but Tallie explained she was almost at her destination and said good-bye to the poor woman.

She jogged all the way to Kara's building holding the manuscript bag with a death grip. She was panting by the time she sprinted past the tall pointy potted evergreens and flung open the door. The doorman sitting at the desk was startled by her sudden appearance, dropping the newspaper he was reading.

Tallie stopped to catch her breath, then walked over to the desk. "My name is Tallie Blankenship, and I have a package for Kara Hatteras."

He frowned at her appearance, and she realized she looked a mess. "I was almost mugged," she offered.

His face reflected zero sympathy. "You were here Thursday night."

"That's right."

He smirked. "Feeling better?"

He'd found the puke in the potted plants. Warmth crept over her cheeks. "Um, yes, thank you. Kara is expecting me."

He dialed a number, and spoke in low tones, then hung up and gave her a placid smile. "Fifth floor, apartment 512."

"Thank you."

She soaked in the snazzy décor and muted music while she waited for the elevator. The building reminded her of Felicia's, and while it was probably doing wonders for the property values of the neighborhood, she felt a twinge of sadness that the area was becoming gentrified. She worked her mouth from side to side, realizing that she was starting to sound like a native.

The elevator door opened. She walked in and punched the 5 button. The silent ride up reminded her of the one in the elevator of the Hills Hotel, the three of them on their way up to exact revenge on Jerry Key, laughing nervously, flush with a slight buzz and the anticipation of doing something naughty and getting away with it.

Except they hadn't gotten away with it—someone else might have gotten away with murder.

The elevator door slid open. Tallie stepped off and found apartment 512. She knocked, and a few seconds later, Kara swung open the door. She wore a sulky pout and a skanky tank top . . . with no bra.

"It's about fucking time," she said. "I was starting to think you were going to try to pull a fast one now that Jerry Key is out of the picture."

"Hello to you, too," Tallie said wryly. "I assume you heard about Jerry?"

"Yeah. Too bad—we sort of got along." She leaned on the door frame and smiled. "Emphasis on 'long.' "

Tallie winced. "Jeez, Kara, have a little respect."

Kara smirked, then looked her up and down. "What the hell happened to you?"

"I was almost mugged."

Kara *tsk*ed. "You really should move to a safer part of town." Then she angled her blond head. "Maybe if you ever get your promotion." She smiled, then flipped her hand over and waved her fingers in a "gimme" motion.

Seething, Tallie reached into the bag and withdrew the manuscript. "You might want to read up—"

"Thanks, Tallie," Kara cut in, then yanked the envelope out of her hand. "I don't mean to be rude, but I'm expecting company, so I'll see you Monday." The door swung closed with a bang.

Tallie gaped, incredulous, then trudged back to the elevator, feeling icked out. If she hadn't needed a shower before, she certainly needed one now. The doorman, who was standing outside near the curb stealing a smoke, gave her a parting glare. Tallie shrugged it off and turned toward her apartment, feeling somewhat less burdened now that the manuscript was where it was supposed to be.

She was climbing the stairs to her apartment when she realized she'd forgotten to stop by the post office to pick up her mother's package, and the post office had already closed.

Chapter 23

Tallie dragged herself to the grocery Saturday afternoon, then spent Saturday night the way she always pictured a swinging single in New York City would: surfing the Internet for news stories about the life and death of a supersleaze literary agent.

The sheer volume of stories returned by the search engine, she decided, was due to Jerry's many media contacts. The tone varied, however, depending on whether the byliner was shocked, gleeful, or philosophical. There were articles about his career and writers he had made famous. There were articles about his reputation and the gruesome way he'd died. There were spin-off articles on the inappropriate use of cell phone cameras, the underworld of S&M, and how many murders occur in New York City hotel rooms.

The photo of Jerry had gone global, appearing in nearly every news item she could find, including many written in foreign languages, because Jerry had been a popular personality at the annual London and Frankfurt book fairs.

She felt compelled to print the articles that contained

details of the crime scene—Jerry was stabbed once in the chest with a serrated knife, estimated time of death between 8:00 P.M. and midnight. A maid arrived the next morning to find him lying in blood-soaked sheets. Tallie closed her eyes, trying to drive that horrific scene from her mind.

They had left an anonymous message with the desk for a maid to come to Jerry's room within minutes after they left so he wouldn't be bound all night. Either a maid hadn't gone to the room, or she had gone, then left at Jerry's request and then the murderer had arrived. Tallie pressed her lips together. Or what if a maid had gone to the room, but the killer had answered the door and sent her away?

Tallie sighed, once again plagued by the thought that they could provide the police with information that at least might help narrow down the time of the murder. She toyed with the idea of making an anonymous tip, but she'd have to use a pay phone across town, and with all the video cameras in use today, she was afraid the call still somehow would be traced back to her.

Around one in the morning she turned off her computer and, still too wired to sleep, walked over to her rickety bookcase. Keith Wages' face and proffered hammer floated into her mind. She'd left a message for him on his voice mail, a breezy note about retrieving her bag, but she hadn't heard back. Then she glanced toward the computer and cringed—he might have tried to call while she'd had the phone line tied up. On the other hand, it was Saturday night and the man was probably out on the town, looking for someone desperate enough to drive all the way out to Brooklyn with him to get laid.

She frowned and leaned over to browse her newly alphabetized book collection. After fingering the spines of several good friends, she pulled out *Blood Trouble*, her favorite Gaylord Cooper book. The story took place after retired CIA agent Griff Edwards had met Fiona White, but before they were married. Their relationship had just begun to evolve, subtly affecting Griff's willingness to accept risky assignments. She thought the romance had added much-needed depth to Griff's hard-nosed character, and personally, she had delighted in his late-night calls to Fiona after a long, hard day of kicking terrorist/communist/serial killer ass.

She settled onto the couch and pulled a lap quilt that Felicia had given her around her legs, hoping the reading would make her sleepy. She opened the book and thumbed past the copyright page, her gaze landing on the dedication page.

For A.C. in Albany

Her mouth quirked; she wondered if A.C. could be Ron's mystery man in Albany. Then she laughed at her musings . . . as if Ron would share something that personal with someone as unstable as Gaylord. And as if Gaylord would dedicate his book to a friend of Ron's. And as if there was only one Albany. Besides, the book was three years old.

She flipped to the first page and began to read. Despite knowing the plot line of the story, she was quickly absorbed in the characters and their interactions. But somewhere after chapter three, she started to nod off. With great relief, she switched off the lamp and wiggled down in the cushions. Imbedded in the softness was almost like sleeping in someone's arms. . . .

But her dreams were troubled, fraught with graphic, violent images and dark, desperate fear that she couldn't pinpoint or outrun. She woke late Sunday morning with a stiff neck and a sense of impending doom. An icy rain blew against the windows, the day as gray and thick as potter's clay. Her head felt just as dense, muddled from the bad dreams that, unfortunately, hadn't ended simply because she'd woken up. She slogged to the kitchen for some bad coffee, then gazed out the window longingly. A run would help to work out some of her sleep kinks, but risking hypothermia to ease muscle stiffness seemed rather counterproductive. When she had cleaned, however, she had found her long-lost jump rope, which seemed like a good way to release some pent-up energy and get in a short workout. About ten minutes into the jumping, her doorbell rang.

Her traitorous thoughts instantly flew to Keith, but she squashed them. Good thing, too, because when she opened the door, Mr. Emory stood there glaring at her.

"What?" she asked, panting from the exertion.

"Someone reported a loud thumping noise," he said in a monotone. "Like jumping."

"Not *like* jumping," she said, holding up her jump rope. "It *was* jumping."

He scowled. "Knock. It. Off." He turned on his heel and strode away, fists clenched.

Tallie frowned after him, then closed her door and sighed. She opted for a quick shower and was contemplating braving the weather to see a matinee when the phone rang. She hesitated, knowing it was more likely to be bad news than good, and picked it up on the third ring.

"Hello?"

"Hi, Tallie, it's Mom."

She closed her eyes briefly, then remembered her pledge to be more patient with her mother. She smiled into the receiver. "Hi, Mom. How are you?"

"Fine, your father and I just got back from church. Did you go this morning?"

"Um, no." Although, in hindsight, it would have been a more productive use of her time.

"Oh. Well, Jacqueline Berry asked about you. I told her you were getting a big promotion."

Tallie winced. "The promotion isn't a sure thing, Mom."

"Still . . . if that handsome boss of yours is handing over one of the company's biggest authors—what did you say his name was?"

"Gaylord Cooper."

"Right—then a promotion can't be far behind."

"One can hope," Tallie said painfully. Ron missing and Jerry dead—when did things get so crazy?

"How did you like the gift?"

She winced again. "Well, I got busy yesterday and didn't make it to the post office before it closed."

"You know, they'll only keep it for a couple of days, then they'll send it back to me or it'll go to one of those dead mail facilities. There's one in Alabama that has a website offering items for sale. Your dad bid on a socket wrench set."

Tallie dropped into her green chair and laid her head back. "Oh?"

"He needs a certain size wrench to fix the washer properly and said the washer is so old, they don't make that size anymore, but this particular socket wrench set has the right size."

"Good."

"Yes, because I don't want to get a new washer with all those newfangled features. Just more to tear up, if you ask me."

"Right."

"How are you feeling—did you get over your cold?"

"Yes, I'm feeling better."

"You should take a multivitamin, you know."

"I do, Mom."

"But does it have extra Vitamin C?"

"I'll check the label."

"And calcium. You're getting older now. You need to pay attention to your bones."

At a twinge on her scalp, Tallie rolled her eyes upward. Was that another hair turning gray? "How's the weather, Mom?" Always a safe subject.

"Dreary—I can't wait for spring to get here so I can give the house a really good cleaning."

Like it needed a really good cleaning. "Yeah."

"Speaking of which, have you talked to Sheila Wages' son?"

Tallie frowned—was there a connection? "Well, Mom, actually Keith and I have seen each other . . . a few times."

"Oh," her mother said in that universally hopeful mother singsong.

"But only as friends," Tallie added quickly. "He's really not my type."

"Is he ugly?"

"I didn't—"

"Because Sheila's husband is no movie star, letmetell-you. But Henry is a nice person and that's what matters. And he has good teeth."

"Right. Well, actually—"

"Besides, Tallie, the lights will be off most of the time."

Tallie blinked—was her mother talking about what she thought she was talking about? Ew. "Mom, Keith isn't bad looking."

"*Oh?*"

Tallie sighed. "He's just not my type."

"Really?"

"He's a cop."

"So Shelia told me. Did he tell you that he owns his own home?"

"Yes."

"Three bedrooms, and Sheila said it is *nice*. He has a room set up for her and Henry so they can visit."

"It's in Brooklyn."

"So?"

"So . . . he's just not my type, that's all."

Her mother expelled a long-suffering sigh. "All right—call me crazy for thinking my daughter would want to be set up with a nice-looking man with a respectable job who owns his own home."

Tallie pushed her tongue into her cheek. "Mom, please don't do this."

"Do what?"

"Worry. Fret. Fuss."

"I'm your mother, Tallie. That's my job. So I want to see you settle down before I die, so sue me."

Tallie gripped the phone. "Mom, are you sick?"

"No, my doctor says I'll live to be a hundred."

"Well, I promise, I'll settle down before you're a hundred."

"You get that sharp tongue from your father's side."

"Well, tell Dad I said hello. I'll call you later in the week."

"Okay. Tallie?"

"Yes?"

"Be careful."

Tallie frowned. "Careful?"

"Call it mother's intuition, but I've had this feeling all week that you were in some kind of trouble." Her mother gave a little laugh. "You probably think that's stupid."

Tallie's chest suffused with affection. "No, I don't think that's stupid. But don't worry, Mom, I'm fine."

"If you say so. Call me when you get your package."

"I will." Tallie disconnected the call slowly, buzzing with renewed appreciation for a mother's bond with her children. She pressed her hand over her heart until she could feel the even thumping beneath her fingers. Could her mother telepathically sense that something was wrong with her child's universe, or did she sense Tallie's stress in her voice, in her forgetfulness? Regardless, knowing that her mother was constantly putting those "feelers" out there made Tallie feel blessed. And knowing that her mother would be devastated if she knew what her daughter had done to humiliate another human being made Tallie feel vile. But beyond what her parents would think of her, Tallie was feeling rotten all on her own. The ever-present gnaw in her gut was why people walked into police stations and confessed to crimes they'd committed years earlier.

Massaging her stomach, Tallie noted that the rain had slacked off. She glanced at her watch and moved to her coat closet; she had to get out of this apartment, and a matinee would be a good way to pass the afternoon. For a half second, she was tempted to wear Felicia's coat, but considering her penchant for accidents lately, she decided to pass lest she ruin hers too.

Tallie considered calling Felicia and inviting her to go, then changed her mind. Felicia had made it clear that it wasn't a good idea for them to be seen together until things died down.

Er . . . bad choice of words.

 Chapter 24

Felicia decided that the pain she'd been referring to over the past few months as "migraines" was in fact baby headaches compared to the true sparkling torture currently hammering at her brain. The weight of the wet cloth on her forehead was almost too much to bear. Under different circumstances, she might believe that she was having a stroke, but she was utterly certain that the agony in her head was a manifestation of her guilt, disbelief, and anguish over what she'd done to Jerry. The picture of him was seared indelibly into her brain, with phrases from the newspaper attaching and revealing themselves at will.

A source in the NYPD insinuated there's no sense of urgency in solving the Hills Hotel murder because it was committed during rough sex play. "The murder will be investigated, of course, but we have other cases pending that merit priority."

In other words, the pervert had gotten what he deserved.

Considering her involvement, she should have been glad that the crime seemed to have sunk beneath the police department's radar. Instead, it made her feel even more despondent about Jerry's death.

Her head vibrated. It was as if all the pain she had wanted to inflict upon Jerry had been inflicted upon her instead, and on some bizarre level, she welcomed it. Being incapacitated on her couch was better than pretending everything was okay when the only man she'd ever loved was lying on a slab somewhere waiting to be dressed in a suit cut up the back.

She covered her mouth with her hand to smother a sob, and the reverberation in her head felt as if she were riding the clapper of a huge, tolling bell. *Gong . . . GONG.* A moan escaped her.

"Felicia, sweetheart?"

It was her mother's voice, and at first she thought she was hallucinating. But then fingers wrapped around hers, and she recognized Julia's dry, cold touch.

"Felicia?"

She heard a click, and even through her eyelids, the light was too much to bear. She sucked in a breath and shielded her eyes with her hand. "Turn it off," she said past a clenched jaw.

"I'm sorry, sweetheart!" her mother yelped, her voice stirring more inflamed receptors in Felicia's brain. "Do you have a headache?"

"Migraine," she whispered, hoping her mother would follow suit.

Julia sighed. "I suppose that's why your phone ringer is off. I called Del, and when he said you hadn't left your place all weekend, I knew something was wrong. Why didn't you call me?"

Felicia would have laughed if it wouldn't have hurt so much. Call Julia? Why? So her mother could talk non-stop about Rick or Steve or whoever was the flavor of the week? Instead of speaking, she opened her eyes one sliver at a time until she could make out Julia standing next to the couch in the darkened room, her face pinched with uncharacteristic concern. Rather than speaking, Felicia moved her head slightly back and forth on the pillow.

Julia shrugged out of her coat. "I'm going to snoop in your bathroom," she murmured, her voice more hushed this time.

Felicia didn't respond, just glad to be able to close her eyes again.

A few minutes later, her mother returned, then Felicia felt a hand on her side, nudging her.

"Roll over, sweetheart. Onto your stomach."

Felicia lay immobile a few seconds longer, working up the effort to turn herself over. She slowly lifted the wet cloth, now tepid, from her forehead. Her mother helped her, and soon she was lying facedown, her head turned in the direction of the open room. She opened one eye enough to see her mother roll up the sleeves of her silky blouse, then undo small vials. The aromas of lavender, peppermint, and eucalyptus essential oils rode the air, distracting her from the pain almost instantly as her brain processed the pleasing scents.

Her mother poured some of each into her palm, then rubbed her hands together, blending the floral and mints into a relaxing perfume. Then she placed her hands on Felicia's shoulders and began to knead very gently between the straps of her cotton tank.

At first the sensation of touch was intense, but Felicia

set her jaw against the jolt, and after a few seconds, the pressure on her shoulders seemed to draw the pain from her head. Incredulous, she yielded to her mother's ministrations. Julia massaged across her shoulders and the back of her neck in a slow rhythm, again and again until Felicia was sure her mother's hands must be aching. Then she pressed the pads of her fingers against the base of Felicia's skull to the point just shy of new pain and released, triggering a buoyant rush of relief. Felicia groaned with gratitude.

"I'm going to rewet this cloth," her mother said, then padded toward the kitchen.

Felicia lay in stunned silence. Never had her mother tended to her when she was sick—there had been maids and day nurses for that kind of thing. And how had she known what to do anyway? Felicia was still marveling over her mother's skill when Julia came back into the room, carrying the folded cloth.

Feeling much improved, Felicia turned over on her own accord, straightened her tank top, and reached up to position the now-cool cloth her mother placed on her forehead.

"Better?"

Felicia nodded and gave her mother a bewildered smile. "Thank you. How did you learn to do that?"

Julia eased into a midcentury harvest gold recliner. "Your father used to have terrible migraines."

Felicia blinked. They never spoke of her father . . . ever. "He did?"

"You don't remember?"

"No."

Julia nodded. "He'd get them a couple of times a

month. I did some reading and learned that some doctors suggested massage." She smiled. "It always seemed to make your father feel better." She expelled a little laugh. "Either that or he just liked the attention."

Felicia breathed in and out. She didn't know what to say, she was afraid to break the spell of her mother talking about her dad fondly. "Do you know what caused his headaches?"

"Stress. Peter hated his job."

Surprise filtered through Felicia. "I never knew that."

"We were good at keeping things from you . . . and Peter was good at keeping things from me." Julia's voice suddenly sounded broken . . . old.

"I'm sorry, Mother."

Julia looked up. "What are you sorry about?"

"That Peter wasn't a better man."

Julia was quiet for so long that Felicia thought she wasn't going to answer. "I'm sorry about that, too. I'm sorry that I picked Peter to be your father. And I'm sorry that we didn't have another child so you wouldn't have been so lonely."

In the semidarkness, Felicia couldn't see her mother's eyes, but she saw the sheen that suddenly developed there. Revelation shot through her. "You loved him, didn't you?"

After a few seconds' hesitation, her mother nodded. "Fiercely. I was stunned that he could just walk away from me . . . and you. It took me years to get over him." She looked down at her hands and smoothed her thumb over her bare left finger. "Sometimes I think I never did."

Felicia's heart squeezed for her mother's enduring heartache, but she sensed an ulterior motive to the purposeful confession. "Mother, why are you telling me this . . . now?"

"Because of Jerry Key," Julia said, then gestured to the couch. "Isn't that what all this is about? Isn't that why you're prostrate with grief?"

Panic crowded Felicia's chest—had her mother heard something through her friends in the DA's office? Is that why she was being so nice, because she knew her daughter was in big trouble? "What do you mean?"

"I read the papers, I know that Jerry is gone, and under what circumstances." She gave Felicia a sad little smile. "I know you were crazy about the man, honey, even after he left."

"I broke it off," Felicia insisted.

Julia angled her head. "You couldn't have . . . you loved him too much. That's why you're hurting, isn't it?"

Tears filled Felicia's eyes. "I don't feel like talking about this right now."

"No . . . you're right," Julia said matter-of-factly, then reclined the chair she sat in. "You need to get some rest. I'll sleep here tonight."

"That's not necessary," Felicia said.

Julia dismissed her with a motherly wave . . . an *actual* motherly wave. "When is the funeral, sweetheart?"

Felicia exhaled slowly. "There's a memorial service tomorrow morning."

"Do you want me to go with you?"

It was a very generous offer, but Felicia was going to have to ease into receiving emotional support from her mother. With the guilt of the photo of Jerry yoked on her shoulders, she didn't feel as if she deserved it. "Thank you, but I need to be alone when I say good-bye."

Julia nodded. "I understand. How about we have dinner tomorrow night and you let me make up for Braddock's?"

"That would be nice, but . . . can we go somewhere else?"

"How about Carlinda's?"

Felicia smiled. "Perfect." She settled back on her pillow, immensely grateful for the layer of ease that her mother had spread over the ugliness of Jerry's death. Felicia glanced at her mother, and her heart swelled with love. Julia wasn't going to pass judgment on Felicia's feelings for Jerry . . . she understood what her daughter was going through.

With the possible exception of withholding information about a serious crime.

But Felicia marveled that she and Julia were sitting quietly in the same room, behaving just like any other mother and daughter might. "You can turn on the lamp by your chair, Mom, if you want to read. It won't bother me."

Julia did, then picked up the blue folder that Felicia had left on the side table. "What's this?"

"New material from one of my authors. I haven't had a chance to read it yet, but I'm hoping it's good."

"Man or woman?"

"Man," Felicia said, pushing thoughts of sex with Phil to the farthest-flung areas of her mind. While she had been romping with an author, Jerry might have been lingering . . . drawing his last breath. She hadn't slept in her bed since it had happened.

"Looks like he put some blood, sweat, and tears into it."

Felicia turned her head on the pillow. "What do you mean?"

Julia held up the folder and pointed to a dark discoloration the size of a thumbprint on the back. "This looks like blood to me."

Chapter 25

"Miss?"

Tallie moaned. Yes . . . *miss*, as in unmarried and unlikely to be in the near future.

"Miss?"

She jerked awake, arms flailing as she stared into the face of a strange man. "What?"

The uniformed usher nodded toward the front of the theater. "The movie's over."

She pivoted her head, and sure enough, the white screen was blank and the theater lights were on. She was the only person left in the entire place. Tallie jumped to her feet, fully awake now and tingling with embarrassment. "Thank you," she said primly, and fled. She was eight dollars poorer, but as least she was a bit refreshed.

The rain had stopped, but the January skies were still leaden and low-hanging, promising more soup to come. Full darkness was less than an hour away. Tallie picked up her pace, but during the walk back to her apartment, Ron was weighing heavy on her mind—probably because she had subconsciously absorbed the military element in the thriller she'd just slept through.

What had happened to him? What kind of trouble was he in? Had he suffered a mental breakdown? Was he connected to Jerry Key's murder? If so, what had caused him to snap? And where was he now?

The questions kept swirling, and she replayed in excruciating detail the last conversation she'd had with him in his office, his preoccupation, his nervousness. On some level, she was disappointed that he hadn't come to her for help; she had always thought that she was Ron's favorite underling, that they shared a respectful, if not friendly, bond. She thought that he trusted her. On an even more fundamental level, she simply couldn't get her mind around the idea that Ron would do something so terrible, but Felicia insisted there was another part of Ron that he kept hidden from everyone else.

For that matter, she thought as she climbed the stairs to her apartment, didn't everyone have a side of their personality that they kept hidden from everyone else? She did . . . her random slovenliness, her preoccupation with a sleazy reality television show, a shoebox of sex toys under her bed.

That provocative recollection still lingered in her mind when she reached the landing and looked up to see Keith Wages with his back leaning against her door. She blinked. "What are you doing here?"

He was out of uniform, dressed in jeans and a rugged coat, wearing his Michigan State hat and an expression of concern on his handsome face. "Tallie, I need to talk to you."

Panic flooded her limbs. "What's wrong?"

He nodded toward the door. "It probably would be better if we went inside."

She fumbled with the keys and finally managed to unlock the dead bolts. She swung open the door, and he followed her inside. Taking off her coat, she draped it over the back of a chair, then turned, her heart pounding against her breastbone. "What's this all about?"

He took off his hat and folded it idly in his hands. "I've been looking into some things, following a few hunches."

She crossed her arms and hugged herself. *He knows.*

He unfolded the hat and folded it again. "I think you're in trouble."

Tallie inhaled sharply, and words stuck in her throat. *I'm sorry. I'm innocent. Don't tell my mom.*

"But before I can help you, you're going to have to confide in me. Just remember that even though I'm not in uniform, I still have a duty to report crimes that I'm made aware of."

We didn't mean it. Something went wrong. I need an attorney.

"But if you're involved in something illegal, I'll try to help you." He winced. "Is it drugs?"

Tallie squinted. "Hm?"

"This is touchy because our mothers know each other, but I'm not going to judge you."

She shook her head, utterly confused. "What are you talking about?"

"The guy in the coffeehouse, Rick Shavel—you said you didn't know him."

"Right," she said, nodding. "Although it's weird—I saw him yesterday."

His shoulders stiffened. "Where?"

"I was walking to the train and I stopped suddenly, and he bumped into me from behind."

"He was following you?"

She frowned. "Why would he be following me? You said he lived in the neighborhood, so I just assumed he was going somewhere like me. He kept walking."

"You're positive you've never met this guy?"

"*Yes*. Keith, what's going on?"

"The other day at the coffeehouse—I don't believe he was there to rob the place." He pressed his lips together. "I think he was there to shoot you."

She gaped, then laughed in incredulity. "That's crazy. Why would a stranger want to *shoot* me?"

"I was hoping you could tell me," Keith said, not laughing.

Tallie sobered. "You're serious, aren't you?"

"Dead serious. And there's more."

She reached behind her until her fingers touched the back of the chair at the table. "I have to sit down."

He helped her with the chair, then took the other one for himself. "Later that same day you were jogging and that car almost hit you."

"I remember."

"I don't think it was an accident."

Her eyes went wide. "You think the driver was trying to run me down?"

"If I remember correctly, the car was moving slowly and hugging the curb. Then when you stepped out into the crosswalk, it sped up. At the time, I thought perhaps the driver mistook the gas for the brake, but now I'm not so sure."

A shiver crawled over her arms. "But why would someone try to run me down?"

"I don't know. Can you remember anything about the driver?"

"It was a man, I think, but I was too busy looking at the grill of the car bearing down on me." Then Tallie scoffed and shook her head. "No, this is preposterous. Keith, look—I barely know you, but you seem like the kind of guy who . . ." She trailed off, hesitant to say what was on her mind.

His dark eyebrows came together. "What kind of guy am I?"

Here was her chance to establish proper distance between them. "The kind of guy who enjoys . . . saving people."

He pursed his mouth, nodding slowly. "And that's a bad thing?"

"No. But in this case, I think you're trying to make connections that just aren't there." She laughed. "Trust me, my life isn't interesting enough for anyone to bother trying to kill me."

He stared at her a minute, then pulled his hand over his mouth. "Let me get this straight—you think I'm making something out of nothing so I can come out looking like a hero?"

She swallowed. "I didn't say that."

"But that's what you think?"

"I think it's ridiculous to think that someone would want to kill me!"

He nodded, his mouth tight. "Okay, well, there is one more thing."

Her heartbeat ratcheted up. "What?"

"The M.E. report is back on the guy who died in your HV/AC shaft."

"And?"

"Cause of death was a heart attack. Time of death was sometime Monday morning."

She lifted her hands. "Okay, that's pretty terrible. But what does that have to do—"

"The guy had tools and equipment on him to install telephone bugging devices."

She frowned. "He was bugging the building?"

"Probably an individual apartment," Keith said. "And since he was on his way back out when he had the heart attack, he probably had finished his job."

Tallie laughed. "Sounds like a domestic issue to me— someone snooping on their ex."

"That's usually the case," he agreed. "So at first I didn't think anything about it."

She waited, breathing harder.

"And then I found out the man's name was also Shavel—he's a brother to the guy who shot up the coffeehouse, who, I discovered, has a pretty powerful attorney for a common street thug. The guy was out of jail practically before the police report was filed."

Her heart thrashed. "Coincidence?"

"I don't think so." He got up and walked over to her portable phone, where it sat in its base unit. He popped off the receiver cover and looked inside, then he reached in with thumb and forefinger and withdrew a disk about the size of a quarter, holding it by the sides. "Bingo."

The blood drained from Tallie's face as her mind reeled with questions—who the hell would bug her phone? And worse . . . how many incriminating conversations had been overheard since Monday?

She stared at the tiny device in Keith's hand. This couldn't be happening. She was the daughter of Merrilyn and Bernard Blankenship of Circleville, Ohio. Until this week the only experience she'd had with serious crime was in the books she edited.

He wrapped the bug in a paper towel and put it in his pocket. "Do you have any other phone units in the apartment?"

She shook her head.

He walked back to where she sat at the table. "So . . . do you have any idea why someone would want to put a tap on your phone?"

She shook her head again, speechless. "Can't . . . can't you tell anything from the bug?"

"I'll have it dusted for prints, but they'll probably match up to our dead guy. He's a middleman, I'm almost certain. And this model looks fairly generic." Keith scratched his head. "Well, let's start with the obvious—do you have a boyfriend?"

"No."

His mouth quirked slightly. "How about a former boyfriend who might do something like this?"

"No."

"Someone you went out with only once or someone you met that gave you the creeps?" He smiled. "Present company excluded."

She appreciated his attempt at humor but made a painful admission. "Meeting you for coffee Wednesday was the closest thing I'd had to a date in months."

He pursed his mouth but made no comment. "Okay, have you been involved in a court case lately?"

"No."

"Dispute with a neighbor?"

"No."

"A crime of some sort?"

She touched her temples—a phone tap installed on Monday couldn't possibly have anything to do with the Jerry Key incident on Thursday . . . they hadn't even planned it until Thursday after work. What the heck was going on?

"Tallie?"

She looked up to find Keith studying her, questions in his eyes.

"I was mugged last summer . . . and there was the incident in the coffeehouse Wednesday with you."

He nodded slowly, but he still had that suspicion in his eyes.

Tallie looked away. "That's all."

"Okay," he said. "How about work? Any issues there?"

"Nothing that would warrant a wiretap." Then she frowned. "Wait—do you think this could have anything to do with Ron's disappearance?"

"Anything is possible. What is your relationship to him?"

"He's my boss."

"Were you . . . romantically involved?"

She glanced up.

He looked sheepish. "Your mother might have mentioned to my mother that you had a crush on your boss."

She pursed her mouth. "Ron is gay."

One dark eyebrow shot up. "Got it. Did he share details with you about his personal life?"

"No."

"When did you see him last?"

"Monday he asked me to his office to tell me he was

going to be away from the office for a while. He didn't explain why except he said no when I asked if it had something to do with the Reserves. I told Detectives Riley and McKinley about the phone call I overheard when I left his office." She repeated the conversation and the fact that she didn't know who he'd been talking to.

"And that was on Monday?"

"Right. About midmorning."

"Maybe the person who planted the bug was someone who knew that your boss was leaving. Maybe they were trying to keep tabs on him and thought he might be calling you at home."

She shook her head. "Ron has never called me at home. He has my cell phone number, but he's only called me on it once or twice."

He pulled a notebook from his coat pocket. "So we'll need to check your phone at work, too." He smiled. "And it might be a good idea to give me your cell phone number."

She lifted her eyebrows. "What, police officers don't have access to that information?"

He winked. "Since I might use it for personal business, I thought I should ask."

Tallie was suddenly struck by a bolt of full-body awareness of his good looks and solid body. A man offering refuge from the scary unknown was a powerful aphrodisiac. Sexual energy leaped between them, and Tallie knew instantly that they would be compatible in bed. Desire moved deep in her midsection, but she realized that wanting to sleep with Keith probably had much to do with her desire to escape from the bizarre situation in which she found herself, to feel safe.

His mouth opened slightly, and she knew that similar

thoughts were going through his head. He had the instinctive urge to protect . . . and comfort. He averted his glance, and his chest expanded with an inhale. When he looked back, he was all business again. "Do you have someone you can stay with until we can figure out what's going on?"

"Do you think that's necessary?" she asked, her body still humming with attraction for the man.

"Tallie, you could've been killed . . . twice. And someone invaded your apartment to plant a bug. This is serious."

Renewed fear shot through her. "You're right. I'll call my friend Felicia."

"I'll stay and give you a ride."

She retrieved her cell phone from her purse and punched in Felicia's number, dreading heaping more trouble on her friend when she was already strung so tight. After a couple of rings, a woman's voice came on the line.

"Hello?"

Tallie frowned. "Felicia?"

"No, this is Julia, Felicia's mother. Who's this?"

"Oh, hi, Ms. Redmon. This is Tallie."

"Hi, Tallie. Felicia's in bed with a terrible migraine—can I take a message?"

Her friend was definitely too ill for company. "Um, no, there's no message. I hope she feels better."

"I suspect she will . . . after the memorial service tomorrow."

A slight frown crossed Tallie's forehead. Did Ms. Redmon know something? Had Felicia broken down and confided in her attorney mother? Was Julia Redmon at this moment negotiating a deal for her daughter? Then

Tallie pinched the bridge of her nose. Would she continue to be suspicious of everything her friend did? "Er . . . yes. Goodnight, Ms. Redmon." Tallie disconnected the call, plagued with new doubts, then turned a wry smile toward Keith. "Well, there's always a hotel."

"Or you can stay at my place," he said smoothly.

Tallie wet her lips. "Not to sound ungrateful, but that's just so . . . far."

He laughed. "No, it isn't."

"I should stay in Manhattan," she said. "I need to be at work early so I can leave to attend the memorial service."

"Okay." Then he spread his arms. "So, how about I sleep on the couch?"

She blinked. "Um . . . well—"

"Your mother and my mother would never forgive me if something happened to you." He grinned. "So in truth, you'd be doing me a big favor."

That sexy hum started up again, pushing a slow smile across her mouth. "A big favor, huh?"

"Yeah, and don't worry—I'll behave myself."

It was the ideal solution, she reasoned. And he didn't seem to mind. . . . "It's very nice of you to offer. And I accept."

"Good."

"But my couch is kind of lumpy."

He grinned again and took off his coat. "Is there any other kind?"

The sight of him removing clothes made her warm in various womanly places. "When is bedtime?" she blurted.

His dark eyebrows arched. "Bedtime?"

The warmth spread. "I mean . . . what time do you normally go to bed?"

He grinned. "That depends."

Her nipples hardened. "I . . . I . . ."

"On my work schedule," he clarified, then his eyes danced. "And other considerations. How about you?"

"Um, well . . . same," she said idiotically, then cast around desperately for a new subject. "Have you eaten?"

When the words left her mouth, they hung in the air in unfortunate juxtaposition to the previous topic. He wiped his hand over his mouth to smother a grin.

"Dinner?" she squeaked.

"Um, no," he said pointedly. "I haven't eaten . . . dinner."

To cover her gaffe, she plowed ahead. "What are you in the mood for?"

Unfortunately, it only pushed the tension in the room even higher. Tallie crossed her arms, hopelessly tongue-tied and fearful, frankly, to say something else lest she have an orgasm on the spot.

Keith stepped in front of her, his face angled down, a smile playing on his mouth. "How about I kiss you so we can get past this awkwardness?"

Chapter 26

Keith was over a head taller than her, his body half again as wide. His eyes were dark and playful, his jaw tinged with tomorrow's beard. He was so male and so damned sexy, she . . . what was the question? Oh, yeah—a kiss.

She swallowed hard. "I think that would be . . . constructive."

He slipped his hand behind her neck and lowered his mouth toward hers. Tallie arched upward to meet him, and their mouths jarred together in a kiss that went from strong to intense in a matter of seconds. He moaned into her mouth, sending sensual vibration through her tongue. Her nipples peaked, driving her to press her body against his. She slid her hands around his waist, skimming a hard bulge that she realized with a start was his gun. He pushed his fingers into her hair and smoothed his other hand down her back. She inhaled his skin scent into her lungs and felt her control begin to slip. Panicked, Tallie pulled away from the kiss and stepped back, her breath coming fast and hard. She put her fingers to her puffy lips and gauged Keith for his reaction.

His eyes were slightly hooded, his chest rising and falling, his erection a definitive bulge. He cleared his throat. "Yes, that was . . . constructive."

"Right," she said, gasping. "I don't feel awkward at all." A big stinky lie—she knew they'd just opened Pandora's box.

"Me neither," he said, his tone strained.

"Shall we order in?"

"Sure."

"Chinese?"

"Perfect."

"Spicy?"

"Absolutely."

She put some distance between them and picked up the phone. Staring at the receiver, she laughed wryly. "Well, whoever tapped my phone knows that I don't cook." She hit the speed-dial button for her favorite Chinese delivery place and ordered three times as much food as normal. By the time she hung up, at least her hormones were back under control. "Beer?" she asked.

"Sure," he said.

She withdrew two bottles of Michelob Light from the refrigerator and rummaged in a drawer for an opener. After popping the caps, she handed him a bottle, noticing that he, too, seemed to have recovered physically.

"Thanks," he said, then turned up the bottle for a drink. They reclaimed the seats at the table, Keith stretching his long legs out in front of him.

The man took up a lot of room. She eyed the couch, realizing that some part of him was going to be hanging over when he stretched out. She took a drink, her mind sorting through the poor appendages that might be neglected.

"So other than your fast-food orders," he said casually, "what other kinds of conversations did the phone tapper hear this week?"

Tallie squirmed and tried to make light. "Nothing too interesting . . . a couple of frustrating conversations with my mother. Why?"

He shrugged. "If we can't link the tap to you, we might have to look at the people you've been talking to."

She laughed. "Maybe my mother, Merrilyn, is secretly a crime lord."

Keith laughed, a nice noise that she wanted to hear again. "I see a lot of strange things in this line of work. Sometimes the ones you least suspect commit the most serious crimes."

A spasm hit her stomach, and she practiced a few openers in her mind. *Keith, there's something I want to tell you. . . . Keith, if you think this phone tap thing is weird, have I got a story for you. . . . Keith, remember when you said that trouble seemed to follow me around?*

He pivoted his head and glanced at her computer monitor sitting on the end of the table against the wall. "Doing some research?" He picked up the top couple of pages she'd printed about Jerry Key's murder and gave her a quizzical look.

Her heart thudded and she opened her mouth to draw in more air. She studied his face, trying to guess how he might respond to the perfectly unbelievable story that she and her two girlfriends had duped Jerry on the phone, had arrived and finished strapping him down, had taken a photo and sent it out over e-mail, then left and had a big belly laugh.

"Horrible way to go," he said. "The worst thing is, no

matter what the man achieved, people are always going to remember him as the poor shmuck in the photo."

Because of us. Tallie took a drink from the cold bottle, suddenly wishing she was drinking something stronger. For whatever sins Jerry Key had committed, he didn't deserve to be remembered like this.

"How's the investigation going?" she asked.

He made a rueful noise. "There aren't too many clues to go on. The hotel is old and traditional—no security cameras. There were at least three private parties going on, so the foot traffic was heavy and security more lax than usual." He sighed. "Unless we get a break, it might go down as another unsolved case. In this city, there are more of those than you could imagine. Detective McKinley told me that they've been handed four murder cases since this one."

God help her, a little bud of hope and relief bloomed in her chest—the murder, as tragic as it was, might simply fade into time. She closed her eyes, glad beyond relief that she hadn't opened her big mouth.

"Are you okay?" he asked, reaching over to cover her hand with his.

His fingers were warm and comforting and sexy. It occurred to her again that Keith Wages would be very easy to fall for.

He squeezed her fingers lightly. "Have you ever known someone who was murdered?"

She shook her head.

"To see a person alive one day, and know they're dead the next day . . . it can be disconcerting."

A stone of guilt settled in her stomach—guilt for what she'd done to Jerry Key, and guilt for the reassurance that Keith was offering her, thinking he was talking to a woman who was simply upset over the death of a colleague. She was such a hypocrite.

Her doorbell rang, to her great relief.

"That was fast," he said.

"The Chinese place is just around the corner," she explained, then emitted a self-deprecating laugh. "And the deliveryman knows his way here."

"I'll get it," he said, standing and reaching for his wallet.

"No—you're my guest."

"You can get it next time," he said in a voice that brooked no argument, then he strode to the door.

He'd said the same thing in the coffeehouse . . . and she had to admit it was nice that a man offered to buy her a meal. She'd forgotten the name of the guy she'd dated last fall—he would live forever in her mind as "Dutch."

Keith returned with two bags and set about pulling out steaming carton after steaming carton of great-smelling food. She retrieved plates and utensils. He opted for chopsticks, and she joined him. He asked about her family and she relayed stories about growing up in Circleville in a bubble of contentment. He had similar stories—his parents had grown up in Ohio but had moved to Michigan for the job market. Still, the Wages family had not forgotten their Midwestern roots. He spoke of his parents and two siblings with a warmth that she appreciated.

"What brought you to New York?" she asked.

"Nine-eleven," he said. "I came as a volunteer to help with the cleanup." He shrugged. "And I decided to stay."

They talked about how the event had affected both of their lives, and somewhere between coconut chicken and pineapple fried rice, Tallie realized that she liked this son of her mother's friend . . . a lot. In fact, it was rather frightening how good Keith Wages looked sitting across from her at the table, all relaxed and . . . *right*.

He helped her clean up the leftovers, and when she realized they had a couple of hours to kill before "bedtime," she decided it would be best to keep her hands busy.

"I need to do some work," she said, gesturing to the table. "I hope you don't mind."

"Not at all—can I steal a book to read?"

"Sure."

She settled at the table and opened a file folder of miscellaneous paperwork—cover blurbs to review, marketing plans to examine—but her eyes strayed to him across the room. He frowned slightly as he touched the compromised joints of the dilapidated shelf, but he moved on to the books, finally selecting one and settling into her green chair. The color suited him, she thought, and wondered if he had a shirt that color. If not, he should.

"Is me being here a distraction?" he asked.

She blinked, realizing that she was staring across the room and had unconsciously dragged a red felt-tip marker across the page she had been reading. "Um . . . no."

He smiled. "Good." Then he went back to his book.

Tallie forced herself to concentrate on her work and was soon engrossed, looking up only occasionally at the swish of a turned page or an unconscious murmur that he made while he read. A couple of hours later, her back was stiff from sitting in the same position for so long. She stood up and yawned, getting his attention. "I think I'm ready to turn in," she said. "I'll get you some sheets and a pillow."

"Okay," he said, closing the book on his finger. He was a fast reader, since he was near the end of the book.

"You can take the book home with you if you don't finish it tonight," she said.

"I will, thanks. It's good."

She stood there nodding like an idiot, mesmerized by the sight of him folded into her chair, seemingly so at home. It unnerved her and thrilled her . . . which unnerved her. She pointed toward her bedroom. "I'll get you some sheets and a pillow."

He grinned. "So you said."

"Right." A flush spread over her cheeks. She turned and walked into her bedroom, where she took one pillow from her bed and bounced it against her forehead. She had to get a grip . . . she was only turned on to him because of the stressful situation . . . and the proximity . . . and the camaraderie. Tallie winced. These sensations bouncing around in her chest for a Brooklynite did not mesh with her plans to remain a swinging single in Manhattan.

She changed the pillowcase and pulled an extra set of sheets from a drawer, then removed a quilt from her bed—since her internal thermometer seemed to be running higher than normal, she could spare a layer tonight.

When she walked back into the living area, Keith was removing his gun from his belt. "Okay if I set it on the table?" he asked.

She nodded, staring at the holster. "Do you wear it all the time?"

"Yeah, it's part of the job," he said with a little smile. "Does it make you uncomfortable?"

"Not as long as it isn't pointed at me."

He laughed and reached for the covers.

"I'll help you make up the couch," she said. "It might be a little . . . short for you."

"I promise I've slept on worse," he said.

They worked in tandem, tucking the sheet under the pillows.

"So, um, Keith . . ."

"Yeah?"

"Is your girlfriend going to be sore that you're bunking on my couch?"

He glanced up. "She might be."

Discovering that he had a girlfriend shouldn't have been a surprise, but it was . . . and it bothered her . . . some.

"*If* I had a girlfriend," he added with a grin. "Which I don't."

Exasperated, her mouth quirked to the side. "Goodnight."

He winked. "Goodnight."

"I'm getting up early," she called over her shoulder.

"Whatever time it is, I'll already be up," he said.

"If you take a shower, leave me some hot water."

"No worry . . . I'll probably take a cold shower."

Tallie stopped, feeling his gaze on her back. The man was tempting. She gritted her teeth and counted to three, then said, "Goodnight," walked into her bedroom, and closed the door.

A lot of good the door did. The man's pheromones oozed through the keyhole and the crack underneath the paneled wood. Tallie pulled the sheet over her head and tried to quiet the parts of her body that strained toward him, but she couldn't dispel the feeling that she was letting something slip away. . . .

Water. She needed a glass of water. Then she'd be able to sleep.

She opened the door as noiselessly as possible and walked out. She glanced toward the couch, and from the moonlight streaming through her clean windows, she could make out his sprawled form on the couch. Then he moved—first pushing up onto his elbow, then swinging his legs over to sit up. "Tallie?"

His broad shoulders were outlined, and his head was tipped slightly in question. He stood and she walked closer, irresistibly drawn to him. He wore pale-colored boxer shorts, his torso solid and spectacularly bare.

"I was thinking," she said, her voice wavering.

"Yeah?" His voice was hoarse and held a note of anticipation.

She wet her lips and summoned her courage. "How about we sleep together so we can get past this awkwardness?"

Ten seconds of agonizing silence went by. She was wondering how she could pass off her forward behavior as sleepwalking when he said, "I think that would be constructive."

She went to him, and they found each other for a kiss that began as a tender exploration but quickly increased in intensity because they both knew where it was leading. He caught her up in his arms, pulling her against his warm body, molding her hips to his. Through the thin layers of fabric between them, his erection burned into her stomach. Tallie moaned, and moisture pooled between her thighs in answer to his call. She splayed her hands over his warm, smooth back, reveling in the expanse.

He kissed her thoroughly, sliding his hands up and

down her back until she lifted one leg and hooked it around the back of his knees. He picked her up and lowered her to the couch, easing himself on top of her. Tallie moaned and ran her hands down his lower back, slipping her fingers inside the elastic waistband of his boxers, pushing down his shorts with her hands and feet, then pulling him into the vee of her knees. His sex surged against the fabric covering her and he kissed her hard, thrusting his tongue against hers, as if sampling the rhythm she enjoyed.

He skimmed his hands over her stomach and lifted the skimpy top over her head. Her nipples budded instantly, and she inhaled in anticipation of his touch.

"Tallie, you're beautiful," he said, his voice thick with lust.

Her body shook with a shiver of pleasure. He captured her hands in his, entwining their fingers and raising them over her head, obliging her to arch, pushing one breast into his waiting mouth. She gasped as he drew in the nipple, and urged him to apply more pressure, to take more of her. He was sensitive to her noises and seemed content to devote himself to her breasts, sucking, biting gently and flicking his tongue against her nipples.

Then he kissed her jaw and her mouth, sliding his chest over hers, squeezing her fingers between his into the pillow behind her head. She lifted her hips to rub against his erection, and he moaned into her mouth. He broke the kiss long enough to whisper, "You're killing me."

"I want you inside me," she murmured.

"Not nearly as much as I want to be there."

"Do you have protection—other than your gun?"

"Give me a minute to find my wallet." He pushed himself up with a grunt.

"I don't know if I can wait that long," she said, immediately missing the weight of his body.

"Don't start without me."

"Too late," she said, pushing down her pajama pants and panties and toeing them off. Her curls were damp with wanting him.

He exhaled forcefully, keeping one eye on her while he searched for his wallet, his hands growing frantic. She welled with feminine satisfaction and admired his solid profile, his powerful chest and legs, his jutting erection. He found the prize and rolled it on in record time, then strode back to her and lowered himself on top of her again, sliding skin on skin, sex to sex. She stretched like a cat and opened her knees. He reached down and stroked her with his hand, delving into her folds. Their moans mingled when he encountered the wetness collected for him. Her body jerked when he found her pleasure site. He stayed there until he proved his point, sending her into a fierce orgasm, at the height of which he thrust into her, sending her to another level of pleasure-pain.

He held himself in check until she recovered, then slowly began to pump his hips. She gasped and sank her fingers into his arms and back, then urged him into a faster and harder rhythm. The fullness of him inside her, rubbing, sliding against already sensitive flesh sent her into another wave of orgasms, this one deeper than the last. In the throes of her release, he stiffened and groaned, burying himself inside her, murmuring her name against her neck as he spent himself.

Slick with perspiration, they lay together until the
chill of the air settled onto their bodies. Then he gingerly
disengaged and stumped his way to the bathroom. Weak
from exertion, Tallie sat up and patted around until she
found her underwear and tank and pulled them on with
shaking arms, her heart skipping like a scratched record.

So that's what all the fuss was about.

She was in big, big trouble.

Chapter 27

Felicia walked into the crowded chapel wearing dark sunglasses and stopped, allowing the lenses to adjust to the low lighting. No way were the wire-rimmed Guccis coming off, lest everyone know she'd been weeping all night for the man in the casket.

The casket.

At the front of the chapel sat a closed casket the color of steel, covered with a huge spray of red roses. At the thought of Jerry lying inside, bile backed up in her throat and her feet were paralyzed. It was simply unimaginable that someone with his youth and zest could be dead. Her heart thudded in her ears, and she felt light-headed.

"Take my arm," a man said.

She looked up to see Phil Dannon, his arm extended, his expression one of gentle concern. Her mind flew to the bloodstained folder that he'd given her Thursday night, but Felicia couldn't reconcile the handsome gentleman next to her with a cold-blooded killer. And it was nearly inconceivable that he would do such a thing and then come to her bed.

Then a thought struck her like a thunderbolt: unless he'd come by looking for an alibi.

"Felicia?"

She swallowed, and because she didn't want to make a scene—or fall down—she tucked her hand beneath Phil's arm and allowed him to lead her near the front to a pew where Suze sat, looking like she'd been white-washed. Felicia hesitated but slid into the pew next to Suze. Phil sat next to her. She was sandwiched between her warring writers, either of whom might have killed Jerry.

Suze sat erect and unmoving, except to occasionally tap a tissue to her nose or eyes. She had traded her red for black and looked ten years older than when Felicia had last seen her. Phil seemed equally inert, staring straight ahead, although not at the casket. Was he nursing a guilty conscience about Jerry? About their lapse? Had he and Suze gotten back together?

Remorse hit Felicia like a slap in the face. She had condemned Suze for having an affair with Jerry, yet her own behavior was ten times worse . . . Jerry had rubbed off on her. Felicia inhaled deeply and glanced around the chapel, recognizing the partners from Jerry's agency, and midlevel editorial representatives from most of the major publishing houses—the top brass had obviously opted to stay away in view of the way Jerry had died. She spotted Jané Glass sitting next to her boss, Seth Johnston, Jerry's workout partner. Jané fidgeted nervously, gnawing on her nails like a preteen. Unease tickled the back of Felicia's neck—the woman was a time bomb.

More people entered the chapel, and Felicia saw Tallie, looking hurried and flushed. Felicia's heart welled with affection—Tallie was so fundamentally honest, the guilt had to be killing her. But hopefully, when the memorial service was over, the worst would be behind them.

It had been the only thought that could compel her to get out of bed this morning.

The audience, she wryly noted, was about eighty percent teary-eyed females. No doubt most of them had slept with Jerry, or had wanted to. He had left an acre of broken hearts in his wake . . . hers wasn't so special. She glanced from face to face—slender redhead, petite blond, lush brunette . . . had one of them killed Jerry? Considering how many people Jerry had crossed personally and professionally, it could be anyone in this room . . . or a total stranger.

She pushed the thoughts from her mind—she didn't want to work up another migraine, not after her episode over the weekend. Julia's caretaking notwithstanding, Felicia didn't want to experience that kind of physical pain again.

A suited man came out of a side door and walked to the front pew to shake hands with a man and woman in their sixties in the front row. Felicia presumed they were Jerry's parents. She recalled that they lived in a Chicago suburb. They had to be devastated, first by their son's death, then doubly so by the manner in which he'd died. Her thoughts went to his personal effects. They were likely to find all manner of sex paraphernalia, maybe even drugs—maybe even nude pictures of herself—in his possession unless the police had already taken everything away.

She put her thumbnail between her teeth and bit

down, then remembered Jané's nervous habit and clasped her hands in her lap.

The minister started the ceremony by asking everyone to stand and bow their head in prayer. Since Jerry had been more devilish than saintly, she wondered what he would think of people praying in his honor. Knowing Jerry, he'd be much more concerned about the turnout than the ceremony itself, and what he was wearing, even if the casket was closed.

It was the typical Manhattan memorial service—prayer, eulogy, message, prayer—all in less than thirty minutes. She didn't shed a tear. It was easy to remain stoic in public . . . it was when she was by herself that the debilitating grief descended.

But when she filed past the casket at the end of the ceremony, she wavered. She couldn't stop picturing him inside the casket, a placid smile on his powdery face, his eyes closed forever, his hands crossed over his abdomen. A photo of Jerry sat on the head of the casket—tanned and beautiful, he was smiling into the camera. Her camera. She had taken the picture when they had gone to the shore for a long weekend, then she'd had it blown up and framed for his birthday. Her knees buckled slightly and she tripped. To her horror, she fell against the casket, rocking it on its pedestal as she ended up face-first in the god-awful roses.

A collective gasp created a vacuum in the chapel, and even the organist missed a note. Felicia flailed for footing, and someone grasped her by the arm and righted her—Phil. "Are you going to be all right?" he murmured, patting her shoulder.

It occurred to her that he—and probably everyone—thought that she'd thrown herself onto the casket. Indeed, people were looking at her as if she'd lost it. Her face flamed. "I'm fine," she whispered.

She wanted to evaporate, or at least run out of there, but she made her feet keep moving with the flow of people, toward Jerry's parents. They were smartly dressed and polished, although their faces were lined with grief. In Jerry's tall, distinguished father, she saw what Jerry would have looked like as an older man . . . if they had built a life together. When it was her turn to greet them, they shook her hand warily, and she had the crazy urge to explain herself . . . to admit that she'd hoped some-day to be their daughter-in-law . . . to tell them how much she'd loved him. But they looked past her to the person behind her, and the moment was gone.

Swallowing the lump in her throat, she made her feet move forward and down the aisle toward the exit, dis-creetly noting where Jané and Tallie were in the line. She'd wait outside the chapel; no one would think it un-usual to see them together at the service. She wanted to check Tallie's state of heart and Jané's state of mind.

Suze and Phil came out together and walked toward her. Felicia summoned a small smile—she still had to work with them.

"This is so awful," Suze said, holding a shredded tis-sue to her red nose.

Felicia nodded, murmuring appropriate words.

"How are you holding up?" Phil asked.

Some of her irritation with him, she knew, was irrita-tion with herself for sleeping with him. He was only try-ing to be nice, but right now she wanted to be left alone. "I'm fine," she said, then decided to turn the conversa-tion in the direction of business. "How's the book com-ing, Suze?"

Suze blinked, then gave a little nod. "Fine."

"We're working on it together," Phil added, telegraphing a message to Felicia with his eyes.

They were back together . . . well, thank God for small miracles. The sooner they returned to firm professional footing, the sooner she could put what had transpired between her and Phil behind her. "There's time, but you should be thinking about representation—if you're going to stay with your agency or shop for another one."

Suze frowned. "Felicia, Jerry isn't even in the ground."

Felicia bit her tongue. Suze wanted to lecture her about protocol? She wanted to scream at her that *she* was the one who had loved Jerry. . . . *She* was the one who was pained over the thought of Jerry going into the ground. "I'm only looking out for what's best for you," she said stiffly, then gave Suze a pointed look. "We need to move on."

Suze shifted uncomfortably, then pulled on Phil's arm.

He hesitated. "Felicia, are you sure you're okay?"

"No," she snapped, then inhaled. "Phil, could I speak to you for a moment . . . privately?"

He squirmed, but nodded. "Suze, why don't you wait for me in the car?"

Suze looked back and forth between them, but nodded and walked away.

"Is this about the other night?" he asked. "Because I think we can both agree that it was a one-time event, best to be forgotten."

"Yes," she agreed quickly. "But Phil . . . the file folder you left at my house—"

"Yeah, what about it?"

She looked him squarely in the eye. "There was a bloody fingerprint on the back."

His expression clouded. "Blood? Where did that come from?"

"I was wondering the same thing."

He looked confused, then his eyes widened. "Wait a minute . . . you don't think that I . . . Felicia . . . I didn't kill Jerry."

Felicia pressed her lips together. "Where did the blood come from, Phil?"

He shook his head slowly, then looked away, as if searching his memory. Suddenly he looked back, his expression clear as he held up his hand. "I remember. I got a bad paper cut on the folder, here between my finger and thumb."

Felicia glanced at the web of flesh, but the cut would have healed by now.

He gave a little laugh. "Listen, Felicia, Jerry was an SOB, but I had no reason to kill him."

She searched his eyes and realized that he didn't know about the affair between Suze and Jerry. "Right," she said with a little smile, then sighed. "I'm sorry . . . my imagination has been in overdrive lately."

"It's a tough day for all of us," he said gently. "Everything is okay between us, right?"

She nodded. "Right. Call me later this week to let me know how the revisions are going."

He nodded and walked toward Suze, who was standing next to their car.

Felicia averted her gaze. God, what a mess she'd made of things. Several people she knew spoke as they passed, giving her pitying looks. She ignored them, scanning the milling crowd for Tallie and Jané, craving a cigarette for the first time in years. A police car and an official-looking dark sedan sat at the curb—escorts for the family, she supposed. Jané came out of the chapel and spotted Felicia, then made a beeline in her direction. Real subtle.

The woman was a frenzied mess, her wiry hair on end, her garb looking like she'd been to a garage sale and worn it all away. She looked exasperated. "What's with throwing yourself on the coffin?"

Anger sparked in Felicia's stomach. "I tripped."

"Yeah, whatever," Jané said. "Have you heard anything new?"

"Just what I read in the papers."

"I heard from a friend that Ron Springer might be involved."

"Apparently Ron is missing," Felicia said. "And the police are looking for a connection."

"Well, at least it takes the pressure off us," Jané said.

Felicia frowned and glanced around. "Would you like to say that a little louder?"

Jané glared and lifted her hand to gnaw on her nails.

Felicia narrowed her eyes. "Jané, where exactly did you go after we left the hotel?"

Jané stopped biting. "Why?"

"Curiosity."

Jané spit out a bit of nail. "I went home. Where did you go?"

"Home."

Jané pursed her mouth. "Then I guess we're in the same boat if either one of us needs an alibi."

Felicia had that uneasy feeling about Jané again. Had the woman gone back to the hotel room and finished off Jerry? There was no doubt the woman was . . . different. But while Jerry scheming to plagiarize from one of her authors was abominable, it wasn't exactly worth killing over.

"Have you talked to Tallie?" Jané asked.

"Briefly, on Saturday. She's worried about Ron, too."

Jané glanced at the police car sitting at the curb. "*I'm* still worried she's going to spill the beans to her boyfriend."

"She won't," Felicia said, although she, too, was worried. "There she is now." Felicia raised her hand to get Tallie's attention. Tallie saw her and began to thread her way through the crowd, but Felicia saw the pinched expression on her friend's face and experienced a momentary stab of panic. Had Tallie confided in her cop friend?

"Uh-oh," Jané said, staring at the curb.

Felicia turned to see Detectives Riley and McKinley emerge from the dark car and head in their direction. A tall, stern-faced uniformed officer climbed out of the cruiser and followed the detectives. Felicia's heart dropped into her stomach. This couldn't be good. But as the men drew closer, she realized they weren't focused on her or Jané . . . they were trying to intercept Tallie.

Chapter 28

        Tallie made her way nervously toward Felicia and Jané, knowing they were going to freak out completely when she told them about the phone tap: Somewhere, someone knew what they'd done. It was time they went to the police and admitted everything. They were innocent; they had made a mistake by not coming forward immediately. But what worried her as much as anything was what Keith would think of her when he found out what she'd done.

    Then, as if she had conjured him up from thin air, she saw him in uniform striding toward her. Her heart jerked, belying the fact that it had been only a few hours since she'd seen him. They had indulged in an early-morning romp, then they'd taken a shower and left at the same time, with him extracting promises that she would be careful until he could get to the bottom of the wiretap. He'd said he would come by later to check out her business phone, then he'd said good-bye with a wink.

    Tallie smiled, but he didn't—if anything, his expression turned darker. Then she noticed Detectives Riley and McKinley in front of him.

"Ms. Blankenship," Detective Riley said.

"Yes," she whispered.

"We need for you to come with us."

She swallowed hard, feeling sick. In her peripheral vision, she saw Felicia and Jané join the group.

Grasping at the straw that this somehow concerned something other than Jerry Key, she said, "Is this about the wiretap on my phone?"

"Wiretap?" Felicia asked, her eyes rounded.

Riley looked annoyed. "We're still looking into the wiretap. But we were finally able to access Ron Springer's cell phone voice messages."

"You found Ron?" she asked, hopeful.

"No," McKinley offered. "But we did find a message that you left on Thursday for Mr. Springer asking for his assistance. You said you were having some 'issues' with Jerry Key, and that you needed his advice. You said you were supposed to meet Mr. Key later that night . . . the night he was murdered."

Tallie felt faint. She'd completely forgotten about leaving that message for Ron. Her vision blurred. She reached out to brace herself against something . . . anything, and met with a solid arm. She blinked Keith's face into view. The hurt and betrayal she saw there took her breath away. "Keith—"

"Don't say anything," he cut in, his jaw hard. "Not here."

"This way, Ms. Blankenship," Detective Riley said.

"Wait," Felicia said, stepping up. "I'm going with Tallie."

"Felicia, don't!" Jané hissed.

Felicia wheeled on Jané. "You're going too, Jané. We're not going to let Tallie face this alone."

The detectives looked at each other, eyebrows raised.

"We didn't kill him," Felicia said. "Jerry was alive when we left the hotel room."

"Felicia, shut up!" Jané said.

"We'll talk about this more down at the station," Riley said. "But Ms. Blankenship has worse trouble."

Tallie looked up—how could this situation possibly be worse?

"Your coworker Kara Hatteras was found strangled in her apartment, and her doorman says you were the last person to see her."

Her jaw loosened and she gasped for air. "Kara . . . is . . . *dead*?"

"Yep. Ms. Blankenship, you'll ride with Lieutenant Wages." He looked back to Felicia and Jané, who were equally slack-jawed at the news. "You two, come with us."

"Wages," Riley said, and Tallie watched as Keith made eye contact with the man. "Advise your friend here that anything she says to you can be used against her."

Keith's mouth tightened. "Yes, sir." He swung his gaze to Tallie, but his eyes were flat and hard. "You heard him. This way, please."

 Chapter 29

It was smart thinking, Tallie concluded, to equip the police cars in New York City with barf bags. She filled one on the way to the station. At different times, Keith looked frustrated, sympathetic, sick, and angry. He didn't speak except to tell her that if she needed for him to pull over, she should say so. But he did hand a handkerchief through the barrier for her to wipe her face.

She arrived at the police station purged and petrified, and Keith led her to a room for questioning, where she was given a bottle of water and made to wait alone. Her eyes kept darting to the dark mirrored windows covering two walls, wondering which was the two-way mirror that allowed her to be observed from the other side. And was Keith watching? God only knew what he thought of her.

"Sometimes the ones you least suspect commit the most serious crimes."

While she waited, she kept thinking about Kara, strangled. Tears welled in her eyes. Ron . . . Jerry . . . Kara . . . why was this happening?

The door burst open, admitting McKinley and Riley, both of them looking somber.

"Where's Felicia and Jané?" she asked.

"They're being questioned," Riley said. "And now it's your turn. Do you want to tell us what happened Thursday night?"

"Yes," she said. "I'll tell you everything."

And she did. How she had met Jerry that morning in her office, how he had invited her to meet him later and she had agreed. "But I was having second thoughts, which was why I left the message for Ron."

"Why were you having second thoughts?"

"Because I had the feeling that Jerry had more in mind than business cocktails."

"He was hitting on you?"

"It's hard to say, but I was uncomfortable."

"So why didn't you just cancel your meeting?"

"I was going to," she said. "Then the publisher came to tell me that Jerry had requested that Gaylord Cooper be moved to another editor. I assumed that meant the meeting was canceled."

"The other editor was Kara Hatteras?"

She swallowed against a constricted throat. "That's right."

McKinley consulted handwritten notes. "We're told that you and Kara Hatteras didn't exactly get along."

"Kara was . . . difficult. She didn't get along with very many people."

"Why do you think that Mr. Key asked that the manuscript be given to her instead of you?"

She told them about Kara's elevator ride down with Jerry.

"You think she traded sex for an assignment?"

"I really don't know."

"Well, what do you think?"

Tallie sighed. "From the remarks Kara made Thursday on the phone and Saturday when I was at her apartment, I'd say yes."

"You spoke to Ms. Hatteras Thursday?"

"Yes, before I left the office. She asked me to bring the manuscript to her that night at her apartment."

"Hm. That must have been when your assistant overheard you say something to the affect of 'you won't get away with this.' "

A guilty flush climbed her face. "I might have said something like that . . . but I wasn't threatening her life."

"Hold that thought. Let's get back to Thursday night. What happened after you left work?"

Tallie told them that she'd met Jané and Felicia, and after a few drinks and airing grievances toward Jerry, they had concocted a plan to humiliate him.

"Whose idea was it?" Riley asked.

Tallie squinted and replayed in her head as much of the conversation as she could recall. "Jané's, I think."

"What was her grievance toward Jerry?"

"She found out that he had conspired with one of his clients to plagiarize from one of her authors."

"And Ms. Redmon—what did she have against Jerry?"

"They were involved for a couple of months about a year ago," she said. "But Felicia broke it off. A few nights ago, Jané told Felicia that Jerry was engaging in locker room talk about her. Then she found out that he had excluded her from a book auction."

"Anything else?"

Tallie hesitated. There was so much between Felicia and Jenny . . . how much should she tell?

"Speak up, Ms. Blankenship."

"Felicia told me that Jerry was having an affair with

one of his clients, who was also one of her authors . . . a married author."

"Did she say who it was?"

"No, and I didn't ask."

"And your grievance against Mr. Key?"

She sighed. "Just that he had pulled the Cooper manuscript."

"Was that going to hurt your career?"

"Not enough for me to commit murder over," she said dryly. "We only planned to humiliate him, get him in a compromising situation and take a photo, then send it to his e-mail list."

"And is that what happened?"

"Yes, that's all."

"What happened, exactly?"

She pulled her hand over her mouth. "Jané called Jerry's cell phone from a pay phone and said she was a dominatrix and she wanted to come over with a friend. She told him to leave the door propped open and that he had to be blindfolded when she got there."

"And was he?"

"Yes." She wet her lips. "I don't know a lot about the subculture of S&M, but Jané said that she'd heard some things about Jerry and that he wouldn't dare 'disobey.' "

"Jané Glass—is she into S&M?"

"You'll have to ask her."

"How well do you know her?"

Tallie told him about the three of them interning at Parkbench together. "We were friendly, but we weren't friends."

"And does she know Ron Springer?"

"Yes."

McKinley heaved a noisy sigh. "This just gets stranger and stranger."

"How do you think it looks from this angle?" Tallie asked.

He frowned. "Let's get back to the hotel room. Mr. Key is blindfolded and strapped to the bed . . . then what?"

"Then Felicia used his cell phone camera to take a picture of him. Jané booted up his laptop, downloaded the picture, and sent it to his address book."

"And all this time you were just watching?"

She swallowed. "I guess."

"And what was Mr. Key doing?"

"He kept asking what was going on, but he thought it was all part of the game."

"None of you spoke?"

She shook her head. "Jané was the only person who talked. She can change her voice and do all these accents."

"He didn't know it was the three of you?"

"Not to my knowledge."

"Okay, the picture was sent—then what?"

"Then Jané called the front desk and asked that towels be delivered in thirty minutes so he would be found. And we left."

"What time was that?"

"Around nine-thirty, I think."

Riley checked his notes and twirled a pen in his fingers.

She lifted her hands, and her eyes filled with tears. "We thought it was going to be a big joke. Instead the next morning when we heard what happened . . ." Her voice broke off on a sob.

Riley scowled. "If you were so broken up about it,

why didn't you go to the police? Or tell us what happened when we first questioned you?"

"We were scared," she said. "We knew how bad it would look."

"It looks bad," Riley agreed, then sighed. "But your stories match up. Are you willing to take a lie detector test?"

"Absolutely," she said, exhaling with relief that they seemed to believe her.

McKinley grunted. "Ms. Blankenship, when you left the hotel, did you go straight home?"

"No. I was supposed to drop the manuscript off at Kara's building. But when I got there, I realized I'd left my bag in a taxi, so I told her doorman I'd give it to her the next day, and I walked home, which was only a few blocks." She bit her lip. "Keith—er, Lieutenant Wages can verify that part of my story. He was at my building when I arrived."

"Now we're to the part about the dead guy in the ceiling?"

She nodded. "I told Keith about my lost bag. He called the taxicab company for me and reported it lost. And he said he'd also file a police report for me."

"I see. How well do you know Lieutenant Wages?"

"We met last Wednesday. Our mothers are old friends and they . . . thought we should meet."

Riley waved to one of the mirrors. In a couple of minutes, the door opened and Keith walked in, his face unreadable. Tallie pressed her lips together to hold back tears.

"Lieutenant Wages, can you verify Ms. Blankenship's story about Thursday night?"

He nodded. "It's just as she said."

"Did you notice any blood on Ms. Blankenship's clothing?"

"No, sir."

"And how was her demeanor?"

"She was upset about the missing bag."

"But she wasn't hysterical?"

"No, sir."

"And what can you tell us about these two Shavel guys?"

Tallie listened as he told about the episode in the coffeehouse and the guy in the HV/AC unit, the men's relationship, and the phone tap. He was so articulate and handsome that her chest swelled with admiration . . . and maybe something else.

Riley swung his gaze back to Tallie. "When was the last time you saw Kara Hatteras?"

She retraced her steps on Saturday, giving time estimates as best as she could remember. "Kara wasn't very friendly," she said. "She was smug about getting the assignment, and she made a crass remark about Jerry."

"Did you think that she might have had something to do with his murder?"

Tallie frowned. "No . . . although when I arrived at her building Thursday night, her doorman said she had left a few minutes before."

Riley scribbled on his notebook. "Did you go into her apartment Saturday?"

"No. She met me at the door, we talked for less than five minutes, and she told me she had to go because she was expecting someone."

McKinley perked up. "Did she say who?"

"No."

"The doorman said he doesn't remember any other visitors for Ms. Hatteras that afternoon."

"The doorman was outside by the curb smoking when I left," she said, "and the desk was unmanned. Depending on how much the man smokes, he could have missed something."

"Do you know why anyone would want to hurt Ms. Hatteras?"

"No. But she was a volatile person."

Riley tossed down his pen. "Ms. Blankenship, have you heard from Mr. Springer?"

"No. Not since his call on Wednesday, like I told you before."

"Was there history between Mr. Springer and Ms. Hatteras?"

"History?"

"A romantic liaison? Problems at work?"

"Not to my knowledge," she said. "I don't think they were good friends, but Ron recognized that Kara was adequate at her job."

The men made frustrated noises and looked at each other, shaking their heads. Riley grunted. "Ms. Blankenship, we got thugs and wiretaps and bodies and a shitload of unanswered questions—what the hell kind of trouble have you gotten yourself into?"

She glanced up at Keith, who looked as if he didn't know what to believe. Her heart thudded in her ears and she swallowed hard. "A whole lot of it?"

 Chapter 30

Bored with sitting, Felicia stood and paced the small room in which she'd been questioned. She glanced at her watch—2:00 P.M. Why were they keeping her? For the umpteenth time, she glanced at her purse and considered calling her mother. Julia would be furious if she didn't, but frankly, she didn't want to drag her mother into her mess . . . not when they'd just begun to gain ground on the mother-daughter front.

She'd told the detectives everything . . . almost. She'd told them everything about the night at the hotel . . . just not all of the events leading up to it. The fact that Jerry had excluded her from an auction and had conspired with one of her (unnamed) authors to plagiarize was plenty of background; she didn't have to mention the fact that he'd broken her heart so cruelly, or that he'd sent a nude picture of her to taunt her, or that he was sleeping with one of her authors. If possible, she wanted to keep the Dannons' names out of this; the book that Suze was revising was Felicia's best bet for a big fall hit, and the best chance for all of their lives to get back to normal.

The door opened and she turned to see Detective

McKinley enter. "Thanks for your patience, Ms. Redmon. Just a few more questions and you can be on your way."

"Okay," she said, although she didn't entirely trust this man who reminded her of her father.

"You said that after you left the hotel, you went home and you were alone until Phillip Dannon came by to . . . drop off some paperwork, I believe you said."

She crossed her arms, trying to keep her face passive. "That's right."

"Well, I spoke with Mr. Dannon . . . and he backed up your story."

Relief bled through her. "Of course."

"Unfortunately, the way your doorman remembers it, Mr. Dannon didn't leave that night, but early the next morning."

Del. The man had a memory like a steel trap. She lifted one hand in a vague gesture. "My doorman remembered incorrectly, that's all."

He nodded, his mouth pursed.

"Is that all, Detective?"

"Actually, no. Your friend Ms. Blankenship said you told her that your old boyfriend Jerry was having an affair with one of your authors, who was married. What can you tell me about that?"

Felicia set her jaw against the flare of anger toward Tallie for opening a can of worms that would ultimately only make Felicia look more guilty. Then she affected a casual expression. "Oh, that. It turned out to be innocent. I saw them together and because of Jerry's reputation, I jumped to the wrong conclusion, that's all." She shrugged. "My mistake."

McKinley's eyebrows shot up. "Your mistake, huh?

Well, maybe you should give me the name of this woman so we can check it out ourselves."

Her mind raced. "I'd rather not," she said finally. "I don't want my silly mistake to affect my working relationship with the woman. I'm sure you understand."

The detective nodded slowly, but his eyes were lined with suspicion. "Sure, I understand. After all, if you thought this woman had something to do with the murder, you'd say so, right?"

"Right," she said lightly.

"Especially since you're so torn up about Mr. Key's death that you threw yourself on the coffin at the memorial service."

She crossed her arms. "I tripped. Is there anything else, detective?"

"No . . . that's all for now. You're free to go."

She picked up her purse and coat on the way to the door.

"Ms. Redmon?"

Felicia turned back. "Yes?"

"This isn't over, you know. We could still charge any or all three of you, and we will if we find any discrepancies in your stories."

She didn't react, just gave him a curt nod and strode out of there. Her next stop was her office, where she asked her boss of six years for a private conference. Then she told her what part she'd played in the photo being taken and sent. "I'm not proud of what I did," she said, "but I wanted to tell you everything I told the police, I know this could reflect poorly on Omega, and I apologize."

Her boss was disappointed but said she appreciated

Felicia's honesty. "And while you didn't exercise the best judgment, you didn't break any laws. Still, maybe it would be best if you took vacation until this matter with the police is settled. We'll talk again after I've had a chance to confer with the executive board."

Felicia nodded in resignation and thanked her. Dry-eyed and numb, she went back to her office, and while she was loading up her manuscript bag, Felicia thought of the nude photo. In case the police searched her office for some reason, she didn't want that tidbit to be found and traced back to Jerry. She opened the bottom drawer and withdrew the picture, then retrieved a pair of scissors from her desk and proceeded to cut it into tiny slivers. With each slice, she felt as if she were cutting some kind of hold that Jerry had had over her. When the last unrecognizable scrap fell into her trash can, she exhaled the breath she didn't realize she'd been holding.

Apprehensive, but more clearheaded than she'd been in weeks, Felicia took a taxi home and wondered if Tallie and Jané both had cast guilt her way during their interview. Jané . . . Felicia tapped her finger against her lower lip. Something about the woman had always bothered her. The whole searching for her identity gig—it was so . . . eighties. When she got home, she was going to do a little research . . . make a few calls. Perhaps Jané was hiding something. They had gone years without seeing her, and then she'd shown up at The Bottom Rung with a grudge to grind against Jerry. And a few days later, he was dead.

Maybe she'd set *them* up.

Her mind clicking, Felicia barely glanced at Del as she walked past and onto a waiting elevator.

"Ms. Redmon, the police—"

But she allowed the doors to close—she didn't want to talk about the police questioning him about Phil. She was doing everything in her power to block that event from her memory. But when she opened her door, she realized that Del was trying to tell her something else . . . that the police were searching her condo.

Frustration and a sense of violation welled in her chest at the sight of a half-dozen gloved officers systematically turning her neat-as-a-pin home upside down.

"You'd better have a search warrant," she said to the officer standing in the kitchen with a clipboard. He handed her a copy of the form and went back to cataloging the items that were bagged on her counter—her German knives!

"You can't take my cutlery," she said. "Those cost me a fortune."

"Sorry," the guy said, clearly *not* sorry. Then he pointed to the smallest set of serrated knives—her favorites. "There's one missing, do you know where it is?"

She counted them . . . seven. "They should all be there."

"I checked the dishwasher," he said.

"You don't put good cutlery in the dishwasher," she admonished.

He gave her a "diva in the house" look, then went back to writing.

She rubbed her temple, her heart pounding faster. Where could the other knife be? Had someone taken it? Used it to kill Jerry?

"Found this in the bedroom," a man said in the doorway. She turned to see him holding up Jerry's scarf by a pencil. Her pulse kicked even higher. The black "JK" monogram was undeniable. Mr. Clipboard joined him in the next room, but she could hear them talking. "From the strength of the cologne on the fabric, I'd say he left it here within the past week or so."

She closed her eyes—that one little relapse was going to land her into even bigger trouble. *Damn you, Jerry.*

"Bag it. What else you got?"

"I found this wool coat with a stain on the front, looks like it could be blood."

Tallie's coat. "It's coffee," Felicia said loudly. "It belongs to a friend of mine—I offered to try to get the stain out for her."

The men looked her up and down, from her caramel-colored kid boots to her black suede dress jacket with richly embroidered lapels. One guy scoffed. "Yeah, right."

She folded her arms, thinking they'd probably never believe that she'd done all this embroidery herself. "How do I know what you're taking?"

"I'll give you a copy of the list," Mr. Clipboard said.

"And when will I get my things back?"

"When it's determined that the items are no longer relevant to this case."

"Ballpark estimate?"

"A year—two years, tops."

She pressed her lips together. Jerry's scarf she had planned to throw out, and she could buy Tallie another coat . . . but taking her German cutlery—that stung.

"Here's your copy of the items we're taking, ma'am." Mr. Clipboard handed her an almost unreadable carbon copy. Then they gathered up the bagged items and left, not bothering to straighten anything. Tears filled her eyes—it would take her days to get her condo back to

normal. On the heels of Jerry's memorial service, the
sense of being violated was overwhelming.

She stared at the list—knives, monogrammed scarf,
stained coat. Collectively, she admitted the items were a
tad on the incriminating side. And Detective McKinley
had made it clear that she was still a suspect. For a few
seconds, she gave in to a feeling of resentment toward
Tallie—if she hadn't left that message on Ron's cell
phone, the police probably would never have connected
them to the crime. She bit down on the inside of her
cheek, hating herself for blaming Tallie. If their friendship dissolved, she would be so . . . lonely.

The phone rang, breaking into her thoughts. The
caller ID displayed the lobby. She sighed. "Hello, Del."

"Visitor for you, Ms. Redmon. Says his name is Jag?"

Jack Galyon? Felicia pursed her mouth—what could
he want? Probably his book back, she thought . . .
maybe he'd given it to her for an excuse to see her again.
One side of her mouth lifted. The man deserved points
for planning. "Send him up, Del."

"Will do."

She opened the door as Jack Galyon was walking up,
dressed in full courier garb, his chin strap swinging.

"Hi," she said, realizing with a start that her smile
wasn't forced—she was glad to see him.

"Hi," he said, then made a rueful noise and reached
into the large courier pouch at his side. "This was addressed to you at Omega so I tried you there, but your assistant said you'd gone home. I thought it looked . . .
suspicious, so I thought you'd want to see it right away."

A tiny part of her was discomfited that he was there
on business and not a made-up excuse to see her.

He pulled out an envelope that had the same bogus address that had been listed on the first envelope containing the nude photo. She took the package with a shaky hand and used the pull tab to tear open the envelope. Turning discreetly, she parted the cardboard envelope so she could see what was inside. Her stomach flipped—another photo. She opened the envelope wider to see the photo—her again, nude again. She inhaled sharply—a message from the grave?

She snapped the cardboard envelope shut and turned back to Jack, who stood waiting patiently, concern on his handsome face.

"When was this dropped?" she asked breathlessly.

"Friday."

"Not Thursday and mailed on Friday?"

"Right—it was dropped at the same location on Friday for overnight delivery next business day."

She covered her mouth with her hand as a terrible realization dawned.

Jerry couldn't possibly have sent this photo . . . so he probably hadn't sent the first one, either.

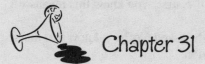 Chapter 31

"Lieutenant Wages will give you a ride home," Detective Riley said.

Tallie sat still for a few seconds and considered asking them to lock her up on the spot rather than face Keith. He didn't look any happier with the prospect than she felt, and the only conversation he offered on the way out to the car was, "You can ride up front."

She did, but they had to roll the windows down for the first few minutes to dispel the faint odor of throw-up in the air.

"I'm assuming you don't want to go back to your office," he said.

"The day's almost shot anyway," she said, wondering if she would have a job to go back to.

"There was a bug in your phone at work, too," he said.

She laid her head back. Of course there was. "I'm sorry."

There was a pause, then, "About what?"

She turned her head to study his profile. "About not confiding in you."

One of his big shoulders lifted. "I told you that I'd

have to report knowledge of a crime being committed. I would've had to turn you in." He stopped for a red light, then glanced over. "Of course, you know this means we can't . . . er—"

"Sleep together?" she asked wryly. "I know that much from watching television."

He nodded. "The detectives are only letting me stay on the case because they know they can trust me."

She frowned—just like a man. "I'm not going to try to *tempt* you to compromise your ethical duty, Keith. Last night was fun, but let's don't make a big deal out of it."

A muscle ticked in his jaw, but he didn't respond.

She stared out the window, feeling slightly nauseous and mostly miserable. She needed to talk to Felicia, to apologize for bungling everything, and to thank her for not having thrown her under the bus when the police had shown up. Her heart squeezed with affection for her friend—she had risked her own job and reputation by coming forward. And Jané . . .

Anxiety knotted her stomach. The woman had been willing to let her face the firing squad alone. Upon closer examination of everything that had happened that night, Jané had been the driver. She and Felicia weren't any less to blame for the outcome, but when she started re-playing that night's conversation in her head, it had been Jané who had been intent on retaliation, Jané who had made the phone call, Jané who had been late to their meeting place.

"Tallie?"

She started out of her reverie.

"We're here," he said, nodding toward the windshield.

And so they were. A police van sat in front of her building, parked on the sidewalk. "What's going on?"

He made a rueful noise. "They might be executing a search warrant."

"On my place?" she asked, incredulous. "I thought the detectives believed our story."

"Tallie, they have to do their job. I'm sure the other women's apartments are being searched, too."

She opened the door and climbed out, feeling a little woozy. Little sleep, unaccustomed physical activity, scant nourishment, and a police grilling were a poor combination. "What are they looking for?"

He closed the driver's door. "Primarily, the murder weapon. Outside of that, maybe a calendar or photographs." His mouth was a thin line. "Your office will probably be searched, too."

"Maybe they'll confiscate some of my slush pile," she said wryly.

When she opened the door to her apartment, she gasped. Two uniformed officers were systematically going through every drawer, shelf, and container. Furniture sat askew, the tabletops and counters were jam-packed, with papers hanging out of drawers. It looked worse than before she had cleaned. Mr. Emory stood surveying the action, dressed in a tight, yellow sweat suit and holding a thick ring of keys. He pointed at her as he walked out the door. "*You* are too much trouble."

She closed her eyes. Great—now she'd probably have to find a new place to live, too.

The officers acknowledged Keith and said they were almost finished. She sidled through the living area and peeked into the bedroom, grimacing at the chaos.

"I realize it looks bad," Keith said behind her, "but I know these guys and they're pretty gentle." His gaze fell on the open shoebox on her disheveled bed containing a lifelike vibrator, a nicely identified set of Ben Wa balls, and various "hotstuff" lotions.

Tallie reached over to replace the lid. "This would only be better if my mother were here." She turned to look at Keith. "Would it be too much to ask you not to—"

"Don't worry," he said. "Your mother won't find out from me."

"Thanks."

"All done," one of the cops said from the doorway.

She and Keith walked out, and she surveyed the bin of items they had amassed.

"My computer?" she cried. Along with all the print-outs of the news stories about Jerry's death. Then she saw they had bagged Felicia's nice coat. "Wait—that's not even mine."

"It's ours now," one of the guys said with a shrug.

Why they would want Felicia's coat was a mystery to her until she saw another item in a small baggie . . . the cocktail napkin on which Felicia had written out their step-by-step plan to humiliate Jerry. She must have left it in her coat pocket. Once again, Tallie had inadvertently handed more evidence to the police. Her stomach twisted.

Keith walked the officers to the door, then came back with a copy of the list of items they'd taken. "Well, at least they didn't find the murder weapon," he said lightly.

She stared at him. "You didn't think they would . . . did you?"

He gave a little laugh, then shook his head. "No. I don't think you're capable of that kind of violence."

Her heart dipped a little, and she gave him a sardonic smile. "If provoked, I could take a man down."

His expression changed subtly, and he nodded. "You certainly could." Then he straightened. "I guess I'd better be going."

"Actually," she said, "there is one more thing I could use your help with."

"What?"

She sighed. "I need the Gaylord Cooper manuscript that I took to Kara Hatteras. I don't mean to sound crass and I'm terribly sorry about what happened to her, but I need to get that manuscript before some well-meaning friend or relative cleans out her apartment and tosses it in the trash."

He shook his head. "I don't know, Tallie. As far as the detectives are concerned, that manuscript is the link between you and Kara Hatteras. It's probably considered evidence."

She heaved a sigh and closed her eyes briefly. "Okay, if we find the manuscript, you could arrange to have a copy made and delivered to my boss if you don't want to give it to me, and keep the original for evidence. Would that work?"

He hesitated.

"Keith, this manuscript is worth over a million dollars. I'm already in enough trouble without adding that kind of liability to the list." She swallowed her pride. "Please help me."

His shoulders dropped an inch. "Let me make a phone call."

While he talked on the phone, she brushed her teeth, splashed water on her face, reapplied powder and liptick, and ran a comb through her hair. The gray hair refused to lie down, and to her horror, she noticed another one nearby—it was gathering recruits!

"Ready?" Keith called.

She walked out and nodded. "It's okay?"

His glance was admiring of her improvements. "Yeah, as long as we don't disturb anything at the scene."

But "the scene" was disturbing all on its own— apparently Kara had been working. The items on her desk were askew . . . a coffee cup overturned and the stain soaked into the blotter, a tumbled pencil holder and its contents on the floor. A straight-back chair lay on its side. A few feet away from the desk was a crude outline of the woman's body in white tape on the dark carpet. Tallie had to cover her mouth. It was easy to visualize what might have happened—Kara had probably been sitting at her desk and the attacker had come up behind her. They'd struggled and she'd fought for a few seconds, moving away from the desk before falling to the floor. A shiver shook Tallie's insides.

"They don't have any suspects?" she whispered. Then she frowned. "Other than me?"

"They're looking into old boyfriends," Keith said, then scratched his temple. "Apparently, she had a few . . . including the doorman."

Tallie wasn't surprised, although she was still sorry that the woman had met such a violent end.

"Let's get this over with," Keith said, stepping toward the desk.

Tallie followed, surveying the stacks of manuscripts, reference books, advance reading copies, galleys—there was a lot to go through. But hopefully, the Cooper manuscript was somewhere close to the top of the pile. The outside envelope would be the most telltale item, but Tallie didn't see it. She pulled out the trash can and poked around, finding a piece of packing tape with manila paper fibers still attached and the letters G.C. written on it in her handwriting. "This came from the envelope," she announced. "So the envelope and the manuscript have to be here somewhere."

Two hours later, they conceded defeat. Keith even allowed Tallie to poke around in Kara's bedroom, bathroom, kitchen, and various large purses. "It's not here," Tallie said.

"Could it be at her office?" Keith asked.

"What was the estimated time of death?"

"Sometime Saturday afternoon."

"I can't see Kara going into the office on Saturday, but I guess it's possible," Tallie murmured as they left the apartment. Anxiety billowed in her chest. On top of everything else, this was the last thing she needed. That cursed manuscript was going to be the death of her.

The death of her.

She looked up at Keith, her eyes wide. "That's it."

"What's it?"

"The manuscript . . . that's why Kara was killed . . . someone wanted the Cooper manuscript."

Keith frowned. "Enough to kill for it? Why?"

"I don't know," Tallie said, shaking her head, trying to process all the thoughts flooding her brain. "But it might explain why my phones were bugged—maybe someone knew that Ron was giving me the manuscript and wanted to keep tabs on me." A memory clunked into place, and she touched her forehead. "Omigod."

"What?"

"That Shavel guy . . . when I saw him the other day, I was on my way to pick up the manuscript from the taxicab company."

From Keith's expression, Tallie could tell he was starting to buy into her theory. "So if he had been listening to your conversations, he would have known you were on your way to get it."

"Right." She grabbed Keith's arm and squeezed. "I was almost mugged on my way to Kara's. A guy on a bike snatched the purse of this woman in front of me—" *A woman wearing a coat that reminded her of her own striped wool coat.* "Omigod—the guy mistook her for me. She was carrying a black shoulder bag and wearing a coat like mine!"

"Then you delivered the manuscript to Kara," Keith said in a rush, "and she was strangled."

"And now we can't find the manuscript," Tallie said breathlessly. "It has to be it!"

He looked bewildered. "But what value would the manuscript have? Could someone sell it?"

"Sure," Tallie said. "What a coup for the black market to get a copy of a book before it's even published . . . especially for an author on Gaylord's level. Plus this is supposed to be his last book in the series, so there would be a lot of interest."

"Could you sell enough books on the black market to make any money?"

"With the Internet, absolutely."

Keith pursed his mouth and nodded. "You just might be on to something here. Didn't you say that Jerry Key was Gaylord Cooper's agent?"

"That's right."

"So Key is connected to the manuscript. And Ron Springer?"

"He's been Gaylord's editor up until now."

"And now he's missing." Keith's pace picked up as they walked back to the cruiser. "That Shavel thug could be some kind of middle man."

As she fastened her seat belt, Tallie's heart was pounding like crazy, and she felt decidedly ill: If she had kept the manuscript, it might have been her body outlined in tape instead of Kara's. Her cell phone rang, and she dug it from the depths of her purse. The caller ID showed Felicia's name. Tallie hit the Call button.

"Hello?"

"Are you okay?" Felicia asked.

"I'm fine," Tallie said, then glanced at Keith. "In fact, I'm better than fine."

He lifted one eyebrow.

"I mean, I think things are going to be okay. Keith and I are looking into something that might explain everything."

"That's great," Felicia said. "Does it have anything to do with Jané?"

Tallie frowned. "Jané?"

Felicia sighed. "You know I've had a bad feeling about her from the beginning. When I got home today, I did some checking around, made a few phone calls."

"And?" Tallie asked, rife with anticipation.

"And it seems that Jané was fired from Bloodworth for passing a copy of a manuscript of a hot book to a website that printed the titillating details and gutted sales for the book."

Tallie's pulse raced, and she covered the mouthpiece. "Jané could be in on this," she said.

"And there's more," Felicia said. "Remember the manuscript she had you read that Jerry plagiarized?"

"Sure. Ames, I think was the name on it. J. P. Ames."

"J. P. Ames is *Jané*," Felicia said. "*She* wrote that manuscript."

And would have been more than furious with Jerry for lifting her own work. Tallie swallowed hard at the thought of having shared drinks with a cold-blooded killer. "Meet us at the police station."

 Chapter 32

The next day, Tallie was still reeling over Jané's arrest while she tried to deal with the aftermath of the lost manuscript. The woman had denied everything, from the murders to knowledge of the Cooper manuscript, but Tallie suspected that the book was, at this moment, in the hands of some smarmy publisher who would have pirated copies of *Whole Lotta Trouble* in every English-reading country by the end of the week, and elsewhere within a couple of weeks.

She picked up the phone and dialed the number Ron's assistant Lil had given her. Gaylord was not going to be happy about this, and after all the legal dust settled, would probably own Parkbench Publishing. It would serve Tallie right if she had to crawl back to Circleville and beg for a job. She waited nervously as the phone rang once . . . twice . . . three times . . . four— A tone sounded. "We're sorry. The number you called has been disconnected."

Tallie sighed at her clumsiness, then redialed Gaylord's secretary's number. She tried not to ponder Ron's involvement in all of this. Had he been in cahoots with

Jané? Tallie simply couldn't accept the fact that he'd sell out an author and a job that he loved so much . . . but where was he?

The tone sounded again. "We're sorry. The number you called has been disconnected."

She frowned at the receiver, then called Lil to see if she had the right number.

"That's the right number, Tallie. The woman would always take a message, then Gaylord would call Ron later."

"It seems that the phone has been disconnected. Do you have another way to reach him?"

"Actually, no, I don't."

Frustration welled in Tallie's chest. "Okay, give me his address and I'll try to find him that way."

"We don't have his address."

"What do you mean we don't have his address? Accounting has to have his address to send royalty statements and 1099s."

"I have a PO box in Hoboken."

Tallie frowned. "Hoboken? Okay, let me have it." She copied it down, then—not unhappy to have a reason—called Keith.

"Hi," he said. "How's it going?"

"Surprise . . . I need your help again."

He laughed. "Okay. What is it?"

"I need to reach Gaylord Cooper and his phone has been disconnected. The only address we have for him is a PO box in Hoboken, and I'm kind of at a dead end."

"I'll need his Social Security number."

She put him on hold and got the number from accounting, then recited it to him. "I really appreciate this," she said.

"No problem," he said. "I'll see what I can come up with."

When she hung up the phone, she worked her mouth back and forth, considering the man who had inserted himself into her life so easily. Yes, it was nice to have someone with his expertise around in light of everything she was experiencing, but she didn't like the idea of picking up the phone and asking for his help all the time.

It could get to be habit-forming.

She frowned and vowed that the next time, she would exhaust every possible avenue before calling Keith Wages for his assistance.

She called to find out arrangements for Kara's memorial service and noted the time on her calendar. Memorial services . . . another bad habit. She prayed this one would be the last one, then thought of Jané. New York was a capital punishment state.

Pushing aside that disturbing train of thought, she buried herself in the work that had piled up while her head had been elsewhere, and pushed through lunch. Around 2:00, Norah announced Tallie had a visitor. She looked up to see Keith standing in her door, and she smiled. "Come in."

Norah grinned and gave Tallie a thumbs-up behind Keith's broad back.

Tallie gave her a look. "Will you please close the door, Norah?" She smiled at Keith. "Sit down. Did you find Gaylord's phone number for me?"

He eased into one of the chairs in front of her desk and set his uniform hat on his knee. "Actually . . . no. In fact . . ." He gave a little laugh.

"What?" she asked, concerned now.

He lifted both hands in the air. "There is no such person as Gaylord Cooper."

She scoffed. "What? That's crazy, of course there is."

"Not according to the federal government. The Social Security number is bogus, and the PO box in Hoboken belongs to some international commodities company. I couldn't find a mention of him in the DMV, property taxes, or voter registration records."

Her mind swirled. "That's impossible—the man has been writing for this company for fifteen years."

"Somebody has been writing for this company, someone you know as Gaylord Cooper, but that's not his legal name. Is it a pseudonym?"

"No." She touched her forehead. "There's some mistake."

She called Lil again to verify, then accounting, then legal. She hung up the phone. "Everyone insists that Gaylord Cooper is the man's real name."

Keith shrugged. "I don't know what to tell you, Tallie. The guy must be some kind of con man."

She gave a disbelieving laugh and sat back in her chair. "Or a spy."

He laughed. "Right."

Then a thought crawled into her head . . . and another . . . and another. A nervous shiver overtook her body as the pieces of info chained together in her mind. She lunged forward in her chair. "What if he *is* a spy?"

Keith laughed again. "Come on, Tallie."

"I'm serious. The man walks around dressed like Elliot Ness, talking about his secret work for the government. He's always worried about being followed—he even swept my office for bugs."

"Well, he obviously missed the one in your phone,

didn't he?" Keith said sarcastically. "Tallie, from everything I've read about the man, he's a paranoid schizo-
phrenic. The trench coat and all that is just an act, part of
the fantasy in his head."

She stood up, walked around the front of her desk,
and leaned against it. "But what if it's not an act? What if
it's real?"

He shook his head. "You're losing me."

She leaned over to pick up the phone. "Norah—would
you please go to the library and bring me one copy of
every Gaylord Cooper novel? Thanks." She set down the
receiver and turned back to Keith. "Humor me. Ron
Springer is in the Reserves—supposedly. He's gone one
weekend every month for duty. It's the perfect cover."

Keith looked from side to side. "For what?"

"For being a secret agent!"

"Oh, so now your boss and Gaylord Cooper are *both*
secret agents?"

She sighed. "Hear me out—Ron arrived at Parkbench
fifteen years ago. Shortly thereafter he discovered Gaylord Cooper in the 'slush pile.' Gaylord will work with
no one but Ron, and Ron is very protective of Cooper—
he goes to great lengths to make sure that no copies of
the book are in existence until the very end of the publishing cycle. Don't you see? They could have created
this Gaylord Cooper character with all his idiosyncrasies so they could protect the work until it was ready
to be received."

He frowned. "Wait a minute . . . are you saying that
the books themselves are some kind of vehicle for secret
messages?"

She lifted her hands. "Why not? What better way to
get a message to an agent in a remote part of the world

than for them to go into a bookstore and buy a book off the shelf? It's brilliant."

He looked unconvinced. "That would mean that remote parts of the world would have access to Gaylord Cooper books."

Tallie nodded, feeling more and more excited. "Actually, that's practically the case. Gaylord's books are printed in nearly every language. His books have more foreign sales than any author on our list. Early on, Ron arranged for the foreign editions to be printed simultaneously with the North American edition. That's almost unheard of. It was earmarked as a global marketing strategy, but it would be an ideal setup if the books are a communication vehicle to far-flung government agents."

Keith looked less impressed, pulling his hand over his mouth. "This sounds pretty weird to me, Tallie. I think your imagination is in overdrive."

She gave a frustrated sigh, then lifted her finger as a memory came to her. "Felicia told me that she saw Ron once in Albany, having dinner with a distinguished older man who looked like he might be in the military. She said that Ron almost freaked out when she said hello, that it was clear he didn't want anyone to recognize him. She said he didn't introduce the man he was with and that he called her the next day and asked that she not mention to anyone that she'd seen him there."

He shrugged. "Sounds like a secret affair."

"That's what Felicia thought because the other guy was wearing a wedding ring. But what if it was someone in the FBI or CIA, someone that Ron reports to?"

He shook his head. "I don't know, Tallie."

"Isn't there an FBI office in Albany?"

"Sure. There's an FBI office in every state capital."

"And in every major city in the world?"

"Usually through the American embassies."

Norah knocked on the door and Tallie waved her in. Her assistant wheeled in a little bookshelf cart. "Here you go—thirteen in all."

"Thank you, Norah."

When the door closed, Tallie picked up the first book and turned to the dedication page. " 'To B.A. in D.C.' " She handed it to him, then picked up the second one. " 'To M.E. in Berlin.' " And down the line. " 'To A.K. in Atlanta. To E.K. in Tel Aviv.' " Every book bore a similar dedication.

"Don't you see?" she asked. "It's a code. The initials are probably for an agent who's based in that city. What do you think?"

He handed the last book back to her and stood, shaking his head. "Tallie, you accused me once of trying to connect dots that weren't related. I think you're so eager to explain away what happened to your boss that you're grasping at straws. I know you've been under a lot of stress lately, and I can understand why you're upset about losing this manuscript, but I just can't see the FBI or the CIA or any government agency using the *New York Times* list as a way to distribute a message to one individual." He put on his hat. "I'm sorry, but I have to get back to work."

He stopped at the door and flashed her an apologetic smile, then walked out.

Tallie dropped into her desk chair, feeling spent. Either she was on to something, or she was an idiot. Maybe Keith was right . . . maybe she wanted so much for Ron not to be crazy or underhanded or murderous that she *was* grasping at straws. But her mind persisted in trying to tie pieces together.

Her gaze landed on the cloisonné pen that Ron had given her for Christmas, and she smiled sadly. She picked it up, remembering how flattered she'd been because Ron had never given her anything before, had never given a gift to anyone in the office that she knew of, not even to Lil. •

Never. Until a few weeks before he disappeared.

His rental car was found in Hoboken, where the phantom PO box was located.

Tense excitement flowered in her chest as she stared at the pen. She looked all around, then back to the pen, prickling with embarrassment at what she wanted to do. Then she shrugged—what the hell . . . were there really degrees of idiocy?

She held the pen about six inches from her mouth. "Ron, if you're listening, this is Tallie. Please call my cell phone at 555-2543. I desperately need to talk to you."

A chill rose on her arms in the ensuing silence. She stared at her cell phone sitting on the corner of her desk. The drone of her computer sounded like an industrial fan. She could scarcely breathe, and her heart flapped in her chest. A minute ticked by, then two, then three . . .

She sighed. "Keith was right," she said aloud. "I'm losing my freaking mind."

And then the cell phone rang.

 Chapter 33

Felicia shouldn't have been nervous waiting in the sitting room of the house she grew up in, but she was. And when her mother walked in, her vital signs increased despite the smile on Julia's face.

"This is a nice surprise," her mother said, planting a kiss on Felicia's cheek.

"I thought it was time I came and explained my behavior—the whole mess with Jerry. I'm sorry you had to read about it in this morning's paper."

Her mother spread her hands. "So am I. When you canceled dinner, you might have mentioned that you had been questioned for murder."

Felicia exhaled and held up a box. "I brought a cake—can we have some coffee?"

"Well, you know I'm not much on sweets, but I'll have some coffee with you."

Felicia followed her mother into the kitchen, fighting a feeling of being hemmed in by the heavy draperies and ornately framed landscapes. She set the cake on the counter and opened the box, folding it down on the sides so that if they didn't eat the cake, they could at least look at it.

"Hm, pretty," her mother said as she poured coffee in dainty cups. "And it smells wonderful—coconut?"

Felicia nodded. "Three layers."

"My bridge club would probably like it . . . where did you buy it?"

Felicia wet her lips. "I didn't buy it . . . I made it."

Her mother's laugh tinkled. "Oh, go on. Where did you buy it? Franco's?"

"No, Mother, I made it. I . . . bake quite a bit, actually. It's a hobby of mine."

Julia's mouth opened, then she recovered. "Well, apparently, there's a lot I don't know about my daughter. Let's sit."

Felicia took a chair adjacent to her mother's at the café table in the breakfast nook. "Mother, I'm not going to try to justify my behavior, because there's no excuse for it. I'm very sorry if it has caused you any embarrassment among your peers."

"Well, I'm still sore you didn't call me before you talked to the police," Julia said. "But I'm just so relieved that they have that woman in custody—what's her name?"

"Jané Glass. She interned with me and Tallie at Parkbench when we first started." Despite Jané's arrest, Felicia still had unanswered questions, such as the knife missing from her kitchen. And who had sent these photographs.

Julia shook her head. "It's sad what a man will drive you to do . . . things you wouldn't think yourself capable of."

Felicia nodded agreement, but her mother wasn't paying attention—she had drifted off in thought. Felicia sipped coffee from her cup, but after a few seconds, when Julia hadn't returned, Felicia reached forward to clasp her mother's hand. "Are you okay?"

Julia snapped back. "Yes."

"Again, Mother, I'm so sorry—you don't need the added stress."

After setting down her coffee cup, Julia heaved a long sigh. "It's not what you've done that's causing me stress . . . it's what I've done."

"We don't have to rehash anything, Mother." Felicia patted her hand. "Let's just start fresh."

"I have something for you," Julia said. "Wait here." She disappeared in the direction of the library, then returned with a small slip of paper.

"What is it?" Felicia asked.

"It's the name and number of your sister, Isabella."

Felicia's head jerked up. "My sister?"

Julia nodded. "She's twenty-five now and living in Boston. She wrote me several months ago asking my permission for her to contact you." Julia's mouth tightened. "I did a terrible thing. I wrote her back and told her that you weren't interested in meeting her. But what I did was wrong, and I want you to have this so you can make up your own mind."

Emotion crowded Felicia's chest as she looked at the slip of paper. Isabella, the daughter her father had wanted, had raised. She considered telling her mother she had done the right thing, that she wasn't interested in meeting the girl.

"I know you're lonely, Felicia, and I blame myself for

not having more children, for not spending more time with you. But I'm not going to be around forever, and I want you to know that you have a sibling out there who is interested in having a relationship with you."

As if on its own volition, Felicia's hand reached out to take the slip. A sister. Someone to share with . . . to love . . . "How will you feel if I contact her, Mother?"

A sad little smile curved her mother's mouth. "Relieved."

 Chapter 34

　　　　　Tallie stared at the cell phone, unable to believe it was ringing. It was probably Felicia or Keith or . . .

She picked it up and jammed it to her ear. "Hello?"

"Tallie, I always knew you were the smart one," Ron said.

She fell forward in abject relief. "Ron, omigod, Ron—where are you?"

He laughed mildly. "Tallie, considering the conversation I just overheard with—Keith, is it?—you know I can't tell you that."

Incredulity washed over her. "I was right?"

"Yes, on just about all accounts. I was an FBI plant, and the man you know as Gaylord Cooper was one of my co-agents. Parkbench was the perfect publishing house for the pilot program—I don't think the government had any idea what a logistical and financial success the program would become. It was a win-win situation—Parkbench made money, the government made money, and readers were part of a plot bigger than they even realized." He made a rueful noise. "Everything was fine until this last book, then I got called away on an assignment. I knew I could trust you to protect the work: Not messing with the wording was essential so the field agents could crack the code. But what I didn't know was that a terrorist group in Tel Aviv figured out what we were doing—not the code, but the delivery vehicle. They hired a mercenary to infiltrate, and the guy latched on to our weakest link, Jerry Key."

She blinked. "Jerry was in on this?"

"Actually, no. One thing we knew would blow our cover in this industry was if Gaylord didn't have a good agent. Jerry was perfect—high profile and hands off. Unfortunately, the man had a few . . . vices. The counteragent probably got impatient when he found out that Jerry didn't have the manuscript."

"Jané Glass has been arrested for his murder."

"I'm working on that. And I can't tell you how sorry I am, Tallie, that you were in danger—if I'd known about the counteragent, I would have never left town. Gaylord told me that your phone was bugged, but I risked calling to warn you."

"The day your phone went out?"

"Right. Then I caught wind of a tail and had to lie low. But Gaylord dropped a few hints."

She squinted. "I do remember him saying that you were afraid for your life."

"Yes, I heard him through the pen."

"Did he know about the pen?"

"Yes, he found it and the phone bug when he swept your office. I'm sorry to have planted a bug in the pen, Tallie, but I was worried—I needed some way to keep tabs on you. If you disassemble it, you'll find the bug. Just toss it in the river or something."

"Okay," she said, her mind in turmoil. "This . . . counteragent . . . do you know what he looks like?"

"No, I've never seen him, but my sources tell me he looks very unassuming, very young."

The baby-faced guy. "I've seen him," she said. "He took a shot at me in a coffeehouse."

"He probably thought you were in on this. I'm so sorry."

She swallowed. "You know that Kara is dead."

He made a regretful noise. "Yes . . . horrible, I'm sick about it. But if it had to happen, better her than you, my friend."

"The counteragent got the manuscript," Tallie said. "I went to Kara's and looked all over for it, but it's gone."

He sighed. "We figured as much from piecing together conversations. And it's a real setback—having to end the program is bad enough, but having to end it when a field agent is counting on those instructions is even worse. But we're taking solace in the fact that even though the manuscript has been intercepted, the code would be extremely difficult to crack."

She swallowed hard. "You're not coming back, are you?"

"No. I have to go under for a while. No one at Parkbench knows about this—they'll probably write me off as a mental case who simply disappeared. And I have to ask you not to share this information with anyone unless it's a life-or-death situation."

"I won't. You can trust me."

"I know," he said. "One thing I did leave behind was a recommendation that you be promoted as soon as possible. And you can have my Eames chairs."

She grinned. "Thank you, Ron."

"I have to say good-bye now. If you need me, here's a contact." He recited a number. "Call from a pay phone or a cell phone. Someone will answer and take a message, then I'll get back to you when I can."

"Okay," she said nervously, overwhelmed with information to process, and loath to hang up.

"Take care, Tallie."

"You too, Ron. Is that your real name?"

"No," he said with a laugh. "But I like it."

The call disconnected and she sat in her chair, utterly limp, wondering if anything that she'd believed about the man was true . . . was he even gay? Her face burned with a flush, and she tingled all over. Had that phone call really just happened?

A knock on her door sent her leaping to her feet. Norah looked at her as if she'd gone mad. "Um, want me to take the books back now?"

"That would be great."

"Are you okay? Your face is all red. Do you have a fever?"

"Um, maybe. In fact—" She glanced at her watch. If she left now she could pick up that package that her mother had sent. "I think I'll roll on out of here."

"Okay. See you tomorrow." Norah laughed. "Don't worry—it'll all still be here, as boring as ever."

Tallie gave a little laugh. "Yeah . . . boring as ever."

Still marveling over the conversation, she caught a taxi to the post office and, after standing in an unbelievably long line, presented the pick-up slip to a lady at the counter. The woman disappeared for twenty-five minutes and came back carrying a box the size of a toaster. It probably was a toaster, although it was kind of heavy.

"We almost sent it back," the woman said in a threatening voice.

Tallie frowned. FBI agents had nothing on the United States Postal Service workers.

She walked home, itchy to call Keith, to rub in his face that she had been right! Then she winced. She'd promised Ron that she wouldn't tell anyone about their conversation unless it was life or death, so she wouldn't . . . even if it killed her.

Chapter 35

        Tallie climbed the stairs to her apartment, trying to decide if she felt like running. If truth be told, she'd rather have sex, but it seemed as if the flame with Keith had burned out. Or perhaps *doused* would be a better word, considering how much she'd thrown up during the ride to the clink.

He probably still was shaking his head over her nutty theory about Ron and Gaylord being secret agents. And no doubt thinking she was much more trouble than she was worth.

She unlocked the dead bolts on her door and stepped inside to survey the mess that the police had left, which she still needed to clean up. She closed the door behind her and refastened the locks, thinking Chinese food sounded good again tonight. Chinese for one, this time.

She placed her order, then went in search of a knife to open the box her mother had sent. What a remarkable day it had been. She replayed the conversation with Ron over and over, wondering how many federal agent programs were at this moment operating in plain view— covert messages on toilet paper packaging, or on billboards? She still could scarcely believe it; at this moment, the men she knew as Ron Springer and Gaylord Cooper were being briefed on a new assignment that would consume another chunk of their lives . . . amazing.

It wouldn't be difficult to explain the sudden disappearance of Gaylord Cooper from the literary scene— the man was known to be so eccentric that no one would be surprised. Indeed, it would probably increase his backlist sales.

She opened the box and withdrew the white envelope on top of the paper. It was a card for a kid, complete with cartoon animals and big wobbly sun. " 'Happy birthday from Mommy and Daddy,' " she read aloud. Inside was a twenty-dollar bill and a handwritten note.

Tallie,

I know this package is early, but I always say if you have a gift for someone, why wait to give it to them? They might be able to use it and there it is, sitting on your shelf in a box waiting to be given. Where's the caring in that? Anyway, I hope you can use this money and gift for something special.

Love, Mom and Dad

Tallie smiled and opened the box, then she cringed. An iron. Oh, good grief, and it looked like a nice one, too. She hefted it out of the box and stared at the dials and water chambers and wondered what on earth she'd do with it.

The doorbell rang, and she set down the iron in favor of the twenty-dollar bill, which would pay for her dinner. She unlocked the dead bolts and had a ready smile for the deliveryman, and instead got a glimpse of the baby-faced man before he shoved the door hard, knocking her to the floor. Pure terror bolted through her as she gasped for breath . . . the man did not look so young and innocent when his face was scrunched in fury.

"Where the fuck is the manuscript?" he screamed.

Tallie scuttled backward like a crab until she hit the couch. "I don't know what you're talking about."

He pulled a handgun from his waist and pointed it at her. "Don't be stupid—that thing is worth more to me than it is to you." He spat on the floor. "I killed that blond, and she wasn't half the trouble that you've caused me. I'd be glad to put a bullet in you."

Tallie gulped air . . . she had no doubt the man would kill her. Stupid things went skating through her mind— she'd never told her mother how much she loved her chocolate cupcakes . . . or Felicia what a kind friend she'd been . . . or Keith that it was cool and mature that he owned a house, even if it was in Brooklyn.

"Now," the man said, punctuating his words with a jerk of the gun. "I'm going to ask you one more time. Where—*oomph*!"

The door slammed into him from behind. The gun went off, and a bullet imbedded into the couch next to her arm. Babyface landed practically on top of her, and Keith Wages landed on top of him. The air was driven from her lungs like an explosion. She wanted to scream . . . she simply couldn't.

Babyface was being ground into her as the men wrestled for the gun. He head-butted her twice, and she was thoroughly jabbed. Keith rolled them off of her, and she lay there for a few seconds wheezing for breath, then pushed to her knees.

"Get out of here, Tallie," Keith yelled, pounding the man's wrist on the end table so he would release the gun.

She scrambled to the door just as Babyface swung his knee into Keith's back, and Keith momentarily sagged. Babyface yanked his arm free, then took an elbow to the eye. The men lunged into another wrestling match, but this time Babyface was on top. Tallie looked for something to throw, but considering the fact that she threw like a girl, she dumped that plan in lieu of grabbing her new iron and swinging it like a bowling ball between the bad man's legs, where it connected with a nauseating *thunk*.

Babyface stiffened, then went limp, dropping the gun. Keith grunted in surprise, then rolled the man off him. Picking up the gun and pushing to his feet, Keith glared at Tallie. "I told you to get out. You could've been killed." He scoffed. "Stubborn woman."

She set the iron down on the kitchen counter. "Something you're going to have to get used to, I guess."

He looked back to the man curled on the floor, drool oozing from his slack mouth. "Damn, you really clocked him."

"I told you I could take a man down."

"You made a believer out of me." He radioed for backup.

"Um, you might want to call the FBI, too," she said mildly.

Keith frowned, then his eyebrows went up.

She adopted a smug expression and nodded.

He pressed the radio button again and asked for the captain while he fastened handcuffs on the flaccid prisoner.

The door swung open and Mr. Emory stood there, smoke coming out of his big, hairy ears. "Someone dyin' in here?"

"As a matter of fact, yes," Tallie said. "But we're on top of it."

Mr. Emory scowled. "You are a whole lotta trouble, you know that?" Then he stomped off down the hall.

"Are you hurt?" Keith asked, coming over to cup her face. "Your forehead is bleeding."

"Just a scratch," she assured him. "Where did you come from?"

"I was feeling bad about the way I walked out of your office." He hauled her into his arms and kissed her hair. "I should have believed you."

"Well, I admit it was a pretty unbelievable story." She nodded at Babyface. "And I didn't expect this—I thought he'd be long gone with the manuscript, but apparently he doesn't have it."

"Do you think someone else killed Kara Hatteras?"

"No, he told me he'd killed a blond, but she must not have had the manuscript."

Keith pursed his mouth. "Wonder where it is?"

"Good question."

There was a knock on the doorframe, and they looked up to see a wide-eyed delivery guy. "Did someone order Chinese?"

Chapter 36

Felicia sat at her desk, replaying in her mind the unbelievable top-secret story Tallie had told her—Jerry had simply been in the wrong place at the wrong time . . . a pawn in a government game. The irony was that Jerry would have loved the notoriety, yet only a handful of people would ever know how he'd died. She looked up as Tamara stuck her head into her office. "Suze Dannon is here—do you have time to see her?"

"Sure," Felicia said, although she wasn't particularly looking forward to it. She and Suze had some unfinished business.

"By the way," Tamara said, "here's your knife." She held up the serrated knife missing from Felicia's collection.

Felicia took the knife and squinted. "Where did you get this?"

"You brought it in with that yummy carrot cake, remember?"

Felicia closed her eyes briefly. She did remember slipping it inside the box. "Of course. Thanks, Tamara."

"Oh, and your sister called while you were in the staff meeting . . . she said she'd call you back this afternoon."

Felicia smiled, happy for that new bit of warmth in her life. "Thanks."

Suze walked in dressed in a demure camel-colored coat. "Hi, Felicia," she said, patting the envelope in her arms. "The revisions are all finished."

"Great. Are you and Phil both happy with the book?"

"Yes. It might not be as intriguing without the e-book element, but it's good. In fact, we think it's our best book yet."

"Good."

"And Phil shared with me an idea that he's working on . . . it's rather good. He said he'd given it to you to read. What did you think?"

Felicia paused, wondering if Suze knew about their brief affair, if this was her way of bringing up the fact that Phil had been by Felicia's apartment. "I thought it showed a lot of promise," she admitted. "Have the two of you decided to work on separate projects?"

"No," Suze said. "In fact, Phil and I are going to renew our wedding vows."

Felicia smiled, relieved. "That's wonderful."

"But first I want to get something off my chest."

Felicia clasped her hands together and squeezed hard. "Okay . . . what is it?"

"I sent those photos to you."

Felicia blinked. "*You* sent them?"

Suze nodded, tearing up. "Jerry and I were having a fling, and I found them at his place. I demanded that he get rid of them and he refused, saying that he loved you."

Her heart unfolded. "He loved me?"

Suze nodded. "He said he knew he was a jackass and

not the marrying kind, but that he had really loved you, and he was going to keep the pictures. I took them from his apartment after he temporarily moved to the hotel, and I mailed them to you out of spite." Tears rolled down her cheeks. "I'm so sorry, and I'm begging you . . . please don't tell Phil about the affair . . . it would break his heart."

Felicia shook her head slowly. "I won't."

Suze sniffed and stood, extending the envelope. "Thank you. Let me know when you've had a chance to review the changes."

Still a little stunned, Felicia nodded. "I will." She sat in her chair, so grateful for the gift of Suze's words. Jerry had loved her—she hadn't imagined the intimacy, and she knew she would be able to recognize it again if she was lucky enough to find it. She held the envelope for a few minutes as an idea unfurled in her head. After consulting her Rolodex, she dialed a number.

"Futurestar," a voice said.

"Jané Glass."

"Just a moment."

"Hello—this is Jane speaking."

Felicia frowned at the dropped accent on the woman's name—she was back to plain old Jane. "Jane? This is Felicia Redmon."

The woman paused, probably wondering about the purpose of the call. Felicia hadn't talked to Jane since the murder charges had been dropped.

"Hi, Felicia," she said, her voice wary. "What can I do for you?"

"I've been thinking about that manuscript, the fantasy murder mystery with the e-book reader element."

"Yeah, what about it?"

"Are the print rights still available?"

"Yes."

"Will you have a copy couriered over to me?"

"Sure," Jane said, clearly surprised. "But, Felicia, I have to be honest with you. I wrote that book."

"Even better," Felicia said cheerfully. "When should I expect it?"

"This afternoon," Jane said, her voice buoyant.

"Looking forward to reading it. Bye, Jane."

"Bye."

Felicia set down the phone, feeling good about offering an olive branch to Jane. And it was crazy, but she was hoping against hope that the courier would be a familiar tall man with excellent hazel eyes. But when the package came later that afternoon, the courier wasn't Jack Galyon. Felicia tried not to read too much into her disappointment; she had finished reading the book he'd given her, so she could always use it as an excuse to call him. It was strange how much she'd thought of him lately, realizing that no man had ever come to her aid like he had, without question. He fascinated her, especially after reading *The Immortal Class*. And she wanted to know more.

After dinner she was feeling nostalgic, so she dropped by Final Vinyl on the way home to see what they had to soothe her soul. She was looking at Etta James' *Stickin' to My Guns* when a voice next to her said, "Her best one, in my opinion, is *Red Hot and Live*."

Felicia looked up and did a double take—Jack Galyon, not in courier garb, but in jeans and a lovely olive green sweater. Had she conjured him up, or was he, once again, simply where she needed him to be? "Hi . . . I almost didn't recognize you."

He grinned. "I'm not on my bike twenty-four/seven. I have to admit, I'm surprised to see you here."

"Oh, I love this place," she said. "Do you have a big collection?"

"Getting there," he said. "You?"

She smiled. "Getting there."

"I'd love to see yours sometime," they said in unison, then laughed.

Jack grinned. "If you'll show me yours, I'll show you mine."

A little electric jolt went through her heart. "Sounds like fun."

"What are you doing right now? Have you had dinner?"

She nodded ruefully. "Yes."

"Me, too—but there's a great dessert place around the corner."

She smiled. "Dessert place?"

"Yeah, I kind of have a sweet tooth," he said sheepishly.

Her smile widened, and her heart beat happily. "Really? That's . . . wonderful."

 Chapter 37

Tallie picked up her ringing phone. "Tallie Blankenship."

"Mrs. Blankenship?"

"Um, miss," she corrected gently.

"Miss Blankenship—this is Richard Wannamaker."

A memory chord stirred, but she couldn't place his name.

"I sent you a manuscript a few weeks ago about my life as a tax accountant."

"Oh! Yes, Mr. Wannamaker. I mailed the manuscript back to you with some suggestions for revisions."

"That's why I'm calling," he said. "The cover letter is addressed to me, but this isn't my manuscript."

She squinted. "Pardon me?"

"My manuscript was called *Journal Entry*, and the one I got back was—let's see—*Whole Lotta Trouble*."

Tallie's breath stalled in her lungs. Her mind reeled—she must have switched the manuscripts and the envelopes . . . no wonder the counteragent had come looking for her.

"Are you there, Miss Blankenship?"

"Mr. Wannamaker, listen to me very carefully . . ."

Keith looked up from fixing the bookshelf and shook his head. "What do you know? It was a simple mistake that might have saved the world."

Tallie grinned. "Well . . . I wouldn't go that far. Lives, maybe . . . but not the entire world."

He gave the bookshelf a final shake to make sure it was solid, then he came over and gave her a long kiss. "You're my hero."

She grinned up at him. "What a coincidence. You're *my* hero."

He pulled her close against his hardening body and groaned. "I knew when I first laid eyes on you that I was in big trouble, and that was before the bullets even started to fly."

She laughed and melted into him, loving that tingly anticipation of knowing they were going to have great, heaving, noisy sex. They undressed each other slowly, and Keith wound up sitting in the green chair, with her astride. A much better use for the chair, she decided as he thrust into her, than a holding place for laundry. He kissed her breasts and brought her to a great crashing orgasm with his hands, then drove himself into her until he climaxed, gathering her around him and moaning into her hair. When she fell forward on his chest, Tallie was struck by a heady sense of rightness. It was scary how much she wanted to be close to this man, to see him, to talk to him. Scarier still . . . what would she do if he changed his mind . . . decided to leave? A small voice inside of her said that she couldn't lose herself, couldn't relinquish control. That was how women became pathetic.

"That was . . . incredible," he said. "You wear me out, Tallie."

She gave a little laugh and climbed off him gingerly, then fell onto the couch. "Does that mean you're staying here tonight?"

"I was hoping I could get you to come home with me," he said, standing to stretch. "Don't you want to see my house sometime?"

The voice, the voice, the voice. "I'll think about it," she murmured.

"Well, while you're thinking about it, I'm starving." He headed toward the kitchen. "Got any leftovers?"

Tallie stared at him, naked and silhouetted in the light of her refrigerator. Her stomach pitched—and not from hunger.

"Oh, wow, ravioli," he said, holding the bowl high. "Mind if I have it?"

She averted her glance, her heart pounding. He was moving in . . . to her heart . . . crowding her . . . their parents would expect . . . things. Then her gaze landed on the bookshelf he had so thoroughly repaired and her heart opened wide.

Tallie looked back and laughed at how ridiculous he looked, and how ridiculous her fears had been. "No, go right ahead."

 Epilogue

THE BLANKENSHIP BULLETIN

OUR BEAUTIFUL, SUCCESSFUL DAUGHTER
IS FINALLY GETTING MARRIED!

If Women Ruled the World . . .

Everyone knows that if women
ruled the world, it would be a better place!
And everyone also knows that in romance,
women do rule . . .
making the hero a better man.

Now read ahead to discover
how the heroines of the
Avon Romance Superleaders—
as created by Jacquie D'Alessandro,
Stephanie Bond, Samantha James, and,
as an added treat, the four stellar authors
of Avon's newest anthology collection—
tenderly, but most definitely, take matters
and men into their own hands . . .

Coming September 2004

If Women Ruled the World . . .

Sex would definitely be better

In Jacquie D'Alessandro's *Love and the Single Heiress* we discover what happens when a young woman anonymously— and scandalously—publishes her thoughts on love, marriage, and a woman's place in Regency society. Needless to say, the men are flummoxed . . . and one *particular* man is intrigued.

> *Today's Modern Woman should know that a gentleman hoping to entice her will employ one of two methods: either a straightforward, direct approach, or a more subtle, gentle wooing. Sadly, as with most matters, few gentlemen consider which method the lady might actually prefer—until it's too late.*
>
> *A Ladies' Guide to the Pursuit of Personal Happiness and Intimate Fulfillment*

*T*onight he would begin his subtle, gentle wooing.

Andrew Stanton stood in a shadowed corner of Lord Ravensly's elegant drawing room, feeling very much the way he imagined a soldier on the brink of battle might feel—anxious, focused, and very much praying for hopeful outcome.

His gaze skimmed restlessly over the formally attir guests. Lavishly gowned and bejeweled ladies swir around the dance floor in the arms of their perfectly turned-out escorts to the lilting strains of the string trio. But none of the waltzing ladies was the one he sought. Where was Lady Catherine?

His efforts to seek out Lady Catherine this evening had already been interrupted three times by people with whom he had no desire to speak. He feared one more such interruption would cause him to grind his teeth down to stubs.

Again he scanned the room, and his jaw tightened. Blast. After being forced to wait for what felt like an eternity finally to court her, why couldn't Lady Catherine—albeit unknowingly—at least soothe his anxiety by showing herself?

He reached up and tugged at his carefully tied cravat. "Damned uncomfortable neckwear," he muttered. Whoever had invented the constraining blight on fashion should be tossed in the Thames.

He drew a deep breath and forced himself to focus on the positive. His frustrating failure to locate Lady Catherine in the crowd *had* afforded him the opportunity to converse with numerous investors who had already committed funds to Andrew and Philip's museum venture. Lords Avenbury and Ferrymouth were eager to know how things were progressing, as were Lords Markingworth, Whitly, and Carweather, all of whom had invested funds. Mrs. Warrenfield appeared anxious to invest a healthy amount, as did Lord Kingsly. Lord Borthrasher who'd already made a sizable investment, seemed interested in investing more. After speaking with them, Andrew had also made some discreet inquiries regarding the matter he'd recently been commissioned to look into.

But with the business talk now completed, he'd reted to this quiet corner to gather his thoughts, much as he did before preparing for a pugilistic bout at Gentleman Jackson's Emporium. His gaze continued to pan over the guests, halting abruptly when he caught sight of Lady Catherine, exiting from behind an Oriental silk screen near the French doors.

He stilled at the sight of her bronze gown. Every time he'd seen her during the past year, her widow's weeds had engulfed her like a dark, heavy rain cloud. Now officially out of mourning, she resembled a golden bronze sun setting over the Nile, gilding the landscape with slanting rays of warmth.

She paused to exchange a few words with a gentleman, and Andrew's avid gaze noted the way the vivid material of her gown contrasted with her pale shoulders and complemented her shiny chestnut curls gathered into a Grecian knot. The becoming coiffure left the vulnerable curve of her nape bare . . .

He blew out a long breath and raked his free hand through his hair. How many times had he imagined skimming his fingers, his mouth, over that soft, silky skin? More than he cared to admit. She was all things lovely and good. A perfect lady. Indeed, she was perfect in every way.

He knew damn well he wasn't good enough for her.

Coming October 2004

If Women Ruled the World...

Office relationships would be a whole lot easier

In Stephanie Bond's *Whole Lotta Trouble* three young editors are bound together when the smary creep they all dated is discovered ... dead. Who could have done it? And, more important, how do they all get out of being the prime suspects?

$\mathscr{F}$elicia Redmon dropped into her desk chair and sorted through her phone messages. Suze Dannon. Phil Dannon. Suze again, then Phil again. She sighed—the Dannons were determined to drive her and each other completely mad. Her bestselling husband-and-wife team had separated under nasty circumstances, but had agreed to finish one last book together. Unfortunately, Felicia soon found herself in the middle of not only their editorial squabbles, but also their personal disagreements. Playing referee was wearing her nerves thin, but sometimes an editor has to go beyond the call of duty to make sure the book gets in on time. Still, she was afraid that if the Dannons didn't soon find a way to put aside their differences, the hostile couple, known for their sensual murder mysteries, were going to wind up killing each other.

There was a message from her doctor's office—an appointment reminder, no doubt—and one from Tallie, who probably wanted to firm plans for getting together at their regular hangout. And Jerry Key had called. Her heart jerked a little, just like every time she heard the bastard's name.

She should have known better than to get involved with a man with whom she would also have to do business, but literary agent Jerry Key had a way of making a woman forget little things . . . like consequences. He was probably calling on behalf of the Dannons, who were his clients. And whatever was wrong would definitely be her fault.

Might as well get it over with, she decided, and dialed Jerry's number—by memory, how pathetic.

"Jerry Key's office, this is Lori."

Felicia cringed at Lori's nasally tone. "Hi, Lori. This is Felicia Redmon at Omega Publishing, returning Jerry's call."

"Hold, please."

Felicia cursed herself for her accelerated pulse. A year was long enough to get over someone, especially someone as smarmy as Jerry had turned out to be.

The phone clicked. "Felicia," he said, his tongue rolling the last two vowels. "How are you?"

She pursed her mouth. "What's up, Jerry?"

"What, you don't have time for small talk anymore?"

Remembering the impending auction of one of his clients' books that she'd be participating in, Felicia bit her tongue. "Sorry, it's been a long day. How've you been?"

"Never better," he said smoothly. "Except when we were together."

She closed her eyes. "Jerry, don't."

"Funny, I believe that's the first time you've ever said 'don't.' "

Her tongue tingled with raw words, but she reminded herself that she was to blame for the predicament she'd gotten herself into. The bottom line was that Jerry Key represented enough big-name authors—some of them tied to Omega Publishers—that she had to play nice, no matter how much it killed her.

"Jerry, I'm late for a meeting, so I really can't chat. What did you need?"

He sighed dramatically. "Sweetheart, we have a problem. The Dannons are upset."

"Both of them?"

"Suze in particular. She said that you're siding with Phil on all the manuscript changes."

"Phil is the plotter, Suze is the writer; it's always been that way. Suze never had a problem with Phil's changes before."

"Suze said he's changing things just for the sake of changing them, to make more work for her."

"Have you spoken with Phil?" Felicia asked.

"Yes, and I believe his exact words were 'You bet your ass I am.' "

She rolled her eyes. "Jerry, the last time I checked, you represented both Suze *and* Phil."

"Yes, but editorial disputes are your responsibility, Felicia, and I rely on you to be fair."

She frowned. "I *am* fair."

"Then you need to be firm. Being assertive isn't your strong suit."

Anger bolted through her. "That's not true." She only had a problem being assertive with Jerry—he had a way of making her feel defensive and defenseless at the same time. "Don't turn this around, Jerry—you know that the Dannons are both hypersensitive right now."

"Which is why, Felicia, it would behoove both of us if the Dannons find a way to patch things up and forget about this divorce nonsense."

"And you're telling me this because?"

"Because I think you should find a way to make this project more enjoyable, to make them realize how good they are together."

She summoned strength. "Jerry, I'm not a marriage counselor."

"But you're a woman."

A small part of her was flattered he remembered, but she managed to inject a bite into her tone. "What does *that* mean?"

"It means that . . . you know, you're all wrapped up in the fantasy of marital bliss. If I tried to talk to the Dannons about staying together, they'd know I was bullshitting them for the sake of money."

"Isn't that what I'd be doing?" she asked.

"No, you actually believe in all that happily-ever-after crap."

Felicia set her jaw—it wasn't enough that the man had broken her heart, but he had to reduce her hopes for the future to the lyrics of a bad love song.

Coming November 2004

If Women Ruled the World . . .

Dating would be a whole lot easier

Even in Regency society, men had a habit of somehow slipping away . . . out of your life. But now, in *The One That Got Away*, four delightful heroines discover that the men of their dreams have never forgotten them. Written by three *New York Times* bestselling authors—Victoria Alexander, Eloisa James and Cathy Maxwell—and one rising superstar, Liz Carlyle, this is an anthology you'll never forget.

Much Ado About Twelfth Night
by Liz Carlyle

*I*n fair weather, the vast estate of Sheriden Park lay but a half day's journey from Hampshire, and this particular day was very fair indeed. Still, the cerulean sky and warm weather did little to calm Sophie's unease. Seated beside Aunt Euphemia, she found her apprehension grew with every passing mile, until their coach was rolling beneath the arched gatehouse and up the rutted carriage drive. And suddenly the stunning sight of Sheriden Park burst into view, snatching Sophie's breath away.

Despite the rumors of ruination, the sprawling brick mansion seemed outwardly unchanged. Row upon row of massive windows glittered in every wing, and already the door was flung wide in greeting. Sophie saw Edward long before they reached the house. He would have been un-mistakable, even in a crowded room. But he stood alone on the bottom step like some golden god, his shoulders rigidly back, his eyes hardened against the sun. Sophie's heart leaped into her throat.

A footman hastened forward to put down the steps. "Get out first, Will," instructed Euphemia, prodding at his ankle with her walking stick. "Go 'round and tell Edward's servants to have a care with my hat boxes. I'll not have any broken feathers, do you hear?"

"Yes, ma'am." Will leaped down.

At once, the new marquess took his hand. "Good afternoon, Weyburn," said Edward, using her brother's title. He gave Will a confident handshake, but strangely, his eyes remained on Sophie.

Will turned away to greet Sir Oliver Addison. In the carriage door, Sophie froze. Edward was staring up at her, his gaze dark, and his jaw hard, as if newly chiseled from stone. Well, he did not look quite the same after all, did he? He seemed taller, broader—and anything but glad to see her.

A Fool Again
by Eloisa James

A well-bred lady never ogles a man from behind her black veil, especially during her husband's burial. But Lady Genevieve Mulcaster had acknowledged her failings in ladylike deportment around the time she eloped t Gretna Green with a bridegroom whom she'd met thre hours earlier, and so she watched Lucius Felton with r attention throughout Reverend Pooley's praise of her ceased husband—a man (said Mr. Pooley) who rose before his servants and even for religious haste went unbuttoned to morning prayer. Felton looked slightly bored. There was something about his heavy-lidded eyes that made Genevieve feel thirsty, and the way he stood, almost insolently elegant in his black coat, made her feel weak in the knees. His shoulders had to be twice as large as her husband's had been.

Recalled to her surroundings by that disloyal thought, Genevieve murmured a fervent, if brief, prayer that heaven would be just as her husband imagined it. Because if Erasmus didn't encounter the rigorous system of prizes and punishments he anticipated, he would likely be discomfited, if not sent to sizzle his toes. Genevieve had long ago realized that Erasmus wouldn't hesitate to rob a bishop if an amenable vicar could be persuaded to bless the undertaking. She threw in an extra prayer for St. Peter, in the event that Erasmus was disappointed.

Then she peeked at Felton again. His hair slid sleekly back from his forehead, giving him an air of sophistication and command that Genevieve had never achieved. How could she, wearing clothes with all the elegance of a dishcloth? The vicar launched into a final prayer for Erasmus's soul. Genevieve stared down at her prayer book. It was hard to believe that she had lost *another* husband. Not that she actually got as far as marrying Tobias Darby. They were only engaged, if one could even call it that, for the six or seven hours they spent on the road to Gretna Green before being overtaken by her enraged father. She never saw Tobias again; within a fortnight she was married to Erasmus Mulcaster. So eloping with Tobias was the first and only reckless action of Genevieve's life. In prospect, it would be comforting to blame champagne, the truth was yet more foolish: She'd been smitten by an untamed boy and his beautiful eyes. For that she'd thrown over the precepts of a lifetime and run laughing from her father's house into a carriage headed for Gretna Green.

Memories tumbled through her head: the way Tobias looked at her when they climbed into the carriage, the way she found herself flat on the seat within a few seconds of the coachman geeing up the horses, the way his hands ran up her leg while she faintly—oh so faintly— objected. 'Twas an altogether different proposition when Erasmus stiffly climbed into the marital bed. Poor Erasmus. He didn't marry until sixty-eight, considering women unnecessarily extravagant, and then he couldn't seem to manage the connubial act. Whereas Tobias—she wrenched her mind away. Even *she*, unladylike though she was, couldn't desecrate Erasmus's funeral with that sort of memory.

She opened her eyes to the breathy condolences of Lord Bubble. "I am distressed beyond words, my lady, to witness your grief at Lord Mulcaster's passing," he said, standing far too close to her. Bubble was a jovial, white-haired gentleman who used to gently deplore Erasmus's business dealings, even as he profited wildly from them. Genevieve found him as practiced a hypocrite as her late husband, although slightly more concerned for appearances.

"I trust you will return to Mulcaster House for some refreshments, Lord Bubble?" Since no one from the parish other than Erasmus's two partners, his lawyer, and herself had attended the funeral, they could have a veritable feast of seed cakes.

Bubble nodded, heaving a dolorous sigh. "Few men praiseworthy as Erasmus have lived in our time. We condole each other on this lamentable occasion."

A sardonic gleam in Felton's eyes suggested that *he* didn't consider Erasmus's death the stuff of tragedy. But then, Genevieve had studied Felton surreptitiously for the past six months, and he often looked sardonic. At the moment he was also looking faintly amused. Surely he hadn't guessed that she had an affection for him? Genevieve felt herself growing pink. Had she peered at him once too often? *Think like a widow*, she admonished herself, climbing into the crape-hung carriage.

Nightingale
by Cathy Maxwell

A soft rap sounded on the door.

"What is it?" he said, his voice harsh. He wanted to be alone. He *needed* to be alone. Tomorrow, he was going to run Whiting through, and then . . . *what?* The word haunted him.

"There is someone here to see you, sir," the footman's voice said from the other side.

At this hour? "Who the bloody hell is it?" Dane demanded. He went ahead and poured himself another whiskey. To the devil with temperance or being a gentleman. Tonight was for exorcisms, although the whiskey didn't seem to be having any effect. He was feeling everything too sharply. He lifted his glass.

"I'm sorry, Sir Dane, I don't have her name," the footman answered. "She refused to tell me or give me her card but asked to see you on the most urgent of business. I let her in because she is obviously a Lady of Quality."

Lady of Quality? Out and alone at this hour of the

Curious, Dane set down the glass without drinking. "Send her up."

There was silence at the door as the footman went to do Dane's bidding. Dane sat quiet. Who would be coming to see him at this hour? It couldn't be a mistress. He had the last—what was her name? Something French. Always something French . . . although none of them had been French any more than he was. *Danielle*. He had signed Danielle off three months ago and had not had the energy or interest in searching for another.

In fact, for the past year, since he'd returned to London, he had been weighed down by a sense of tedium coupled with a restless irritation over the every day matters of his life. He'd been going through the motions of living without any clear purpose or desire.

Perhaps he should let Whiting run *him* through?

The idea had appeal. Dane picked up the glass and drained it of the precious amber liquid.

The footman rapped on the door to signal he had returned with this uninvited guest. Dane pushed both the will and his whiskey glass aside before calling out, "Enter."

The door opened slowly and the footman, dressed in blue and gold livery with a powdered wig on his head, stepped into the room. "Sir Dane, your guest."

He moved back. There was a moment's pause, a space of time, three ticks of the clock, and then the woman walked into the room—and Dane stopped breathing.

Before him stood Jemma Carson, the widowed Lady Mosby, looking more beautiful than ever.

The Trouble With Charlotte
by Victoria Alexander

"*B*loody hell." Hugh Robb, formerly Captain Robb and now, thanks to his resurrection, Lord Tremont, stared at the figure of his wife in a crumpled heap on the floor. "She dropped like a stone."

"Not unexpected under the circumstances." A man Hugh had scarcely noticed upon entering the room moved toward Char, then hesitated. "We should probably, or rather, one of us should—"

"Probably." Although Char certainly wasn't going anywhere and it might well be best first to know exactly who his competition was. "And you are?"

"Pennington. The Earl of Pennington." The man— Pennington—stared. "You're Captain Robb, aren't you? Charlotte's husband. Charlotte's *dead* husband."

"Indeed, I am the husband." Hugh narrowed his eyes. "And are you her—"

"No!" Pennington paused. "At least not yet."

"Good." Hugh nodded with a surprising amount of relief.

He bent beside his wife and gathered her into his arms, ignoring the flood of emotion that washed through him at the feel of holding her again. The last thing he needed was to have Char's affections engaged right now. Not that it mattered. From the moment he'd decided to return home, he had vowed not to consider anything she might have done while believing him dead to be of any importance whatsoever.

"You might put her down now," Pennington said firmly.

"Of course," Hugh murmured.

He deposited Char carefully on a sofa and knelt beside In repose, she was peaceful and serene but she'd always had an air of restlessness about her. It had drawn them together and led them along the edge of scandal. And they had reveled in it. She'd been only eighteen when they'd wed and he a bare two years older. Neither had known anything of life save fun and excitement and high, heady passion.

Had she changed? He was certainly not the same man who had stalked out that very door seven long years ago. He had left a selfish, stupid boy and returned as . . . what? A man at long last willing, even eager, to live up to the responsibilities of his life? Dear God, he prayed he had indeed become man enough to do so. And prayed as well he had not lost his wife in the process.

Her long, lush lashes flickered and her eyes opened, caught sight of him, and widened.

"Char?"

Char's gaze searched his face as if she were trying to determine if he was real or nothing more than a dream. Slowly, she raised her hand to his face and rested it upon his cheek. Her dark eyes met his and he read wonder and awe and . . . fury.

She cracked her hand hard across his face.

The sound reverberated in his head and around the room, and he jerked back on his knees. Even Pennington winced.

"You're alive!" She stared in shock and disbelief and struggled to sit up.

"Indeed I am." Hugh rubbed his cheek gingerly. "You do not appear quite as pleased as I thought you'd be."

"You thought I'd be pleased? Pleased? Hah!" She scrambled off the sofa and moved away from him as if to keep a safe distance between them. "How—"

"It's a very long story." Hugh searched for the right words. "Some of it is confusing and some rather unpleasant and"—he drew a deep breath—"much, if not all of it, is my fault."

"*That* was never in question." She shook her head. "This is impossible. You simply cannot be here looking so . . . *alive!*" Char turned on her heel and paced. "You must be nothing more than a dream—"

"A good dream?" A hopeful note sounded in Hugh's voice.

"Hardly," she muttered. "Marcus, is there a man standing in this very room looking suspiciously like my husband? My *dead* husband?"

Pennington nodded reluctantly. "I'm afraid so, Charlotte."

"I am flesh and blood, Char." Hugh stepped closer. "Touch me."

She stared at him for a moment, then once again smacked her hand across his face.

"Yow!" Hugh clapped his hand to his cheek and glared. "Bloody hell, Char, why did you do that?"

Char stared at her reddened palm. "That hurt."

Hugh rubbed his cheek. "Damned right, it hurt."

"The first time I scarcely felt it," she murmured. Her gaze shifted from her hand to Hugh's face. "You really are alive. Real."

"I daresay there were better ways to prove it," Hugh muttered, then drew a deep breath. "However, you may slap me again if you need additional proof."

"Thank you, but no." She shook her head slowly. "I do appreciate the offer and I should like to reserve the right to smack you again should I need to do so."

Coming December 2004

If Women Ruled the World...

There'd be a whole lot less gambling.
And houses would be cleaner too.

In Samantha James's *A Perfect Groom* we discover what
happens when a young man believes he can seduce anyone . . . and puts his money where his ego is. But when
he's given the challenge of enticing the one known as "The
Unattainable" he knows he's in big trouble . . .

A pleasant haze had begun to surround Justin, for he
was well into his third glass of port. Nonetheless, his
smile was rather tight. "Don't bother baiting me,
Gideon," he said amicably.

Gideon gestured toward the group still gathered around
the betting book. "Then why aren't you leading the way?"

Justin was abruptly irritated. "She sounds positively
ghastly, for one. For another, no doubt she's a paragon of
virtue—"

"Ah, without question! Did I not mention she's the
daughter of a vicar?"

Justin's mind stirred. A vicar's daughter . . . hair the
color of flame. Once again, it put him in mind of . . . but no.
He dismissed the notion immediately. That could never be.

"I am many things, but I am not a ravisher of innocent
females." He leveled on Gideon his most condescending
stare, the one that had set many a man to quailing in
boots.

On Gideon, it had no such effect. Instead he erupted into laughter. "Forgive me, but I know in truth you are a ravisher of *all* things female."

"I detest redheads," Justin pronounced flatly. "And I have a distinct aversion to virgins."

"What, do you mean to say you've never had a virgin?"

"I don't believe I have," Justin countered smoothly. "You know my tastes run to sophisticates—in particular, pale, delicate blondes."

"Do you doubt your abilities? A woman such as The Unattainable shall require a gentle wooing. Just think, a virgin, to make and mold as you please." Gideon gave an exaggerated sigh. "Or perhaps, old man, you are afraid your much-touted charm is waning?"

Justin merely offered a faint smile. They both knew otherwise.

Gideon leaned forward. "I can see you require more persuasion. No doubt to you Bentley's three thousand is a paltry sum. So what say we make this more interesting?"

Justin's eyes narrowed. "What do you have in mind?"

Gideon's gaze never left his. "I propose we double the stakes, a wager between the two of us. A private wager between friends, if you will." He smiled. "I've often wondered . . . what woman can resist the man touted as the handsomest in all England? Does she exist? Six thousand pounds says she does. Six thousand pounds says that woman is The Unattainable."

Justin said nothing. To cold-bloodedly seduce a virgin, to callously make her fall in love with him so that he could . . .

God. That he could even consider it spoke to his character—or lack thereof. Indeed, it only proved what he always known . . .

was beyond redemption.

He was wicked, and despite Sebastian's protestations otherwise, he knew he'd never change.

"Six thousand pounds," Gideon added very deliberately. "And worth every penny, I'll warrant. But there's one condition."

"And what is that?"

"She must be yours within the month."

A smile dallied about Justin's lips. "And what proof shall you require?"

Gideon chucked. "Oh, I daresay I shall know when and if the chit falls for you."

He was drunk, Justin decided hazily, perhaps as drunk as that fool Bentley, or he wouldn't even give the idea a second thought.

But he was a man who could resist neither a dare nor a challenge—and Gideon knew it.

There had been many women in his life, Justin reflected blackly. Having reached the age of nine-and-twenty, thus far no woman had ever captured his interest for more than a matter of weeks. He was like his mother in that regard. In all truth, what was one more?

And if everything that had been said about The Unattainable was true . . . If nothing else, it might prove an amusing dalliance.

He met Gideon's keen stare. "You're aware," he murmured, "that I rarely make a wager unless I stand to win."

"What a boast! And yet I think perhaps it will be *you* paying me. Remember, you've the rest of the horde to fend off." Gideon gestured to Brentwood and McElroy.

Justin pushed back his chair and got to his feet. "Some thing tells me," he drawled with a lazy smile, "that yc know where this beacon of beauty can be found."

Gideon's eyes gleamed. "I believe that would be Farthingale ball."

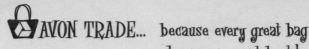